About the

K.D. Richards is a native of _____, area who now lives outside Toronto _____ husband and two sons. You can find her at kdrichardsbooks.com

New York Times and *USA Today* bestselling author **Heather Graham** has written more than a hundred novels. She's a winner of the RWA's Lifetime Achievement Award and the Thriller Writers' Silver Bullet. She is an active member of International Thriller Writers and Mystery Writers of America. For more information, check out her website, theoriginalheathergraham.com, or find Heather on Facebook and X @heathergraham

The Sinful Sleuths Club

A TRAP FOR TWO:

The Sinful Sleuths Club

K.D. RICHARDS

HEATHER GRAHAM

MILLS & BOON

First Published in Great Britain 2025
by Mills & Boon, an imprint of HarperCollins*Publishers* Ltd
1 London Bridge Street, London, SE1 9GF

www.harpercollins.co.uk

HarperCollins*Publishers*
Macken House, 39/40 Mayor Street Upper,
Dublin 1, D01 C9W8, Ireland

ISBN: 978-0-263-42105-7

MIX
Paper | Supporting
responsible forestry
FSC™ C007454

DARK WATER DISAPPEARANCE

K.D. RICHARDS

For Shara and Kendra.

Chapter One

Dominique "Nikki" King turned her Camry onto the familiar road leading to the house that had been her refuge for as long as she could remember. The limbs of the decades-old trees lining either side of the street swayed gently as if waving hello to an old friend. She made a right turn into the horseshoe driveway and got her first look at the modest farmhouse she hadn't seen in years.

Lakewood House. The house had been christened at some point years before her grandfather bought it. The name had stuck.

Her chest tightened. She pulled to a stop and let the car idle.

It was the first time she'd been back to her grandfather's house since he'd passed away a year earlier. It was her house now. Her grandfather had employed the services of a local handyman as a caretaker, and she had kept the man on retainer after she'd inherited the home. But it looked as if the monthly stipend had only extended to the basics. There'd never been much of a lawn. There was too much tree cover for any kind of grass to flourish, and since the house sat on nine acres of land, there weren't any neighbors within sight to complain about the curb appeal. The once bright white wooden siding was dirty, dingy, and several shingles were missing. The black shutters were faded and chipped. The windows themselves desperately needed a good scrubbing, and the pronounced dip in the two stairs leading up to the wraparound porch served as a warning to take care to anyone approaching the front door.

Tread carefully.

A warning she should have heeded more generally in life. Then she might not have found herself back in Carling Lake, New York, unemployed and a pariah among the political world she'd worked so hard to enter.

Just a temporary blip, she told herself for the thousandth time. It had almost become a mantra. She'd been putting off coming back to the house for too long, anyway. There were decisions that needed to be made. Whether to sell the house or keep it and rent it out. Carling Lake was a tourist town, so it wouldn't be too difficult to find renters on a regular basis. But the idea of strangers tromping through the house didn't sit well. Sleeping in her old bedroom. Making a mess of her grandfather's spotless kitchen. She wasn't sure she could stand it.

Well, there was plenty of time to figure all that out. Right now, she just wanted to get unpacked and settled in.

Without a job, she had no way to pay for her Washington, DC, apartment, so she'd broken the lease and put all of her furniture in storage. Two extra large suitcases of clothes, three boxes of knickknacks and miscellaneous items, and her laptop were pretty much all she had to her name at the moment. It was a precipitous fall for the girl voted most likely to become the first Black female president in her senior year of high school. For as long as she could remember, she'd been interested in politics, an interest she'd inherited from her grandfather, who had served on the Carling Lake town council for nearly twenty years.

After years of internships that didn't pay well, if at all, and various entry-level jobs, she'd climbed the ladder and finally landed a position as a policy aide to Thomas Manco, a member of New York's delegation to the House of Representatives. Her dream job working for a man she'd thought was an honest public servant with the sincere desire to help the people he represented.

Oh, how wrong she'd been on that one.

"Hey, you left DC to get away from all that," she said out loud, shaking thoughts of her ruined career from her head just as her phone chirped the receipt of a text message.

You there yet?

Carolyn Montgomery, Nikki's only work friend who hadn't stopped returning her calls and texts. Carolyn was the only person she'd told she was leaving DC for Carling Lake.

Just got here. Will call you tomorrow if I make it through the night. JK.

Nikki tossed the phone back into her purse, shut off the engine and exited the car.

She wheeled her suitcases to the porch stairs and tested that the tread would hold before hauling them, one at a time, to the front door. Last week, when she'd decided to temporarily relocate to Carling Lake, she'd contacted Pete Bonny, the man her grandfather had hired to act as caretaker of Lakewood House when he'd moved to Florida two years earlier. Pete had assured her the property, though a little worse for wear over the years, was perfectly habitable. She hoped he was right. Living in DC wasn't cheap, and what little money she'd managed to save would go quickly, even in Carling Lake, if she had to rent a place.

Luckily, her key turned easily in the lock, and the front door swung open into a living area that looked into the kitchen. The home's layout was unusual, but her grandfather had opened up as many walls as he could to make the home feel as spacious as possible. A small dining room sat adjacent to the kitchen, and tucked into the rear corner of the main floor was her grandfather's study, which was about the same size as the walk-in closet in her apartment back in DC.

The second floor was apportioned into three bed-rooms—a tiny guest room and two larger rooms that shared a Jack-and-Jill bath, the only bathroom in the house. A cozy, if oddly configured, space by anyone's standards, but it had been perfect for her and her grand-father.

She got busy pulling the dirty covers off the furni-ture and bringing in her belongings from the car. She'd just set the last box from her car on the living room sofa when the sound of an engine bloomed outside. She stepped to the open front door and watched as a me-tallic blue pickup bounced its way toward the house. Hitched to its rear was a boat Nikki recognized even without seeing the lettering on its side.

Annalise. Her grandfather had named the boat after his beloved late wife, Nikki's grandmother, who had died the year before she'd been born.

The truck pulled to a stop behind her red Camry, and Pete Bonny hopped out of the driver's side.

Pete was only ten years older than her thirty-two

years, but hard living had aged him. At just after three in the afternoon, his eyes were already bloodshot, and his thinning brown hair stood up in tufts over his head. His orange-beige skin looked rubbery, as if he'd spent too much time under a tanning light or, more likely, out on Carling Lake without using sunscreen. A sizable beer gut hung over the waistband of his jeans. Still, when he smiled, she could see a hint of the heartthrob the teenage girls in town had swooned over many years ago.

Pete climbed out of the truck. "Well, aren't you a sight for sore eyes."

Nikki grinned and bounded off the porch. "Hi, Pete."

He pulled her in for a quick hug before stepping back. "Your granddad always bragged about how smart and pretty you were, but I don't think he did you justice." Pete winked.

Her grandfather had been openly affectionate. He'd made sure she knew how proud he was of her. Still, her heart clenched at Pete's words—words she'd never hear directly from her grandfather again.

It had been more than a year since Bernard King had passed on peacefully in the Florida retirement home he'd moved to when the New York winters and the upkeep on his beloved Lakewood House had gotten to be too much for him. But she was still struggling to deal with the loss of the only real parent she'd ever had. Her mother and father had been more interested in calling themselves parents than in actually parenting once they were. High-powered careers as US diplomats had taken them all over the world, and caring for their only daughter hadn't been a priority. They'd stuck her in a boarding school when she'd turned six. It had been a point of contention between Grandpa Bernie and his son, her father, for years, but thankfully, she had still been allowed to visit her grandfather on breaks and during the summer. Then, not long after her tenth birthday, her parents had been killed in a car accident. Grandpa Bernie was granted guardianship, and he'd immediately taken her out of the boarding school and brought her to live with him in Carling Lake.

It had been a transition for both of them. Bernard King had spent his lifetime building up his trucking-and-shipping company, King's Trucking. As was tradition at the time, Grandma Annalise had raised their only son. But they were now all the family either of them had, and Grandpa Bernie had been determined to do things differently this time around. And he had, attending every dance recital, basketball game and piano concert that she'd been in. He'd bandaged scraped knees, set curfews and imposed punishments when called for. He'd been the father he hadn't been to his son. The father his son hadn't been in the ten years she'd known him.

She wasn't sure if she'd ever come to terms with never hearing his voice again or simply lounging beside him on the *Annalise* in the middle of Carling Lake again.

She pushed away the tears that threatened to come and focused on Pete.

"…so I figured you might like to have the boat."

"Thank you." She forced a smile. "You didn't have to go through all that trouble."

Pete waved away her words. "No trouble at all. It is your boat after all. Your grandfather allowed me to use it whenever I wanted, part of my compensation for looking after the house, so I primarily kept it at my place. But since you're back now, you should have it."

Pete didn't exactly sound thrilled about having to give up the boat, but he was right that it, as well as everything else her grandfather had owned, was now hers. Maybe she should have told Pete he could keep it, but what was the point of living lakeside if she didn't have a boat to take advantage of the lake.

Pete ducked his head and stepped back toward the truck. "Well, I'll get her docked for you."

Nikki took a step back toward the house. "Let me just put on my boots and I'll come help you."

Pete flashed a smile that didn't reach his eyes. "No, no need. I can handle this alone. You get yourself settled in."

Truth be told, as much as she was happy to have the boat, launching and docking it was the last thing she wanted to deal with at the moment. She was exhausted from the drive from DC, and she wanted to unpack and make a trip to the grocery store before it got dark.

She waved to Pete as he hopped back in the truck and started toward the lake at the back of the house.

Nikki walked through the space, memories rushing her as she did. In the kitchen, she ran a hand over the wooden countertops. A slip of paper on the floor caught her eye. A business card, homemade by the looks of it. There were no words or lettering on the card, only a symbol: a yellow fleur-de-lis. The only person who should have been in the house in the last year was Pete. It must belong to him.

She pocketed the card to ask Pete about it when he returned from launching the boat and focused on the more pressing task at hand.

By the time she'd lugged her two suitcases up to the second floor, she was breathing hard and wondering whether unpacking couldn't wait a little longer.

The first door to the right of the stairs opened into

the tiny bedroom she'd occupied when she was home from college for holidays.

Nikki rolled the suitcases past the room and toward her grandfather's bedroom. Her grandfather had taken anything of value with him when he'd moved to Florida, leaving his room a blank canvas. But that wasn't why she'd chosen this room. It was the bigger of the two rooms that opened into the bathroom, and unlike her tiny room, it had an unobstructed view of Carling Lake.

She might not have remembered the roads in Carling Lake, but she remembered how gorgeous the sun was rising over the water in the mornings.

It was too late to catch the sunrise, but Nikki glanced out of the window anyway. The lake was beautiful at any time of the day.

But it wasn't the lake that caught her attention now.

Pete jogged back toward the house. She was too far away to see the expression on his face, but from his body language, she could tell something was very, very wrong.

Nikki turned and dashed back down the stairs, throwing open the back door of the house as Pete bounded onto the back porch.

"What is it? Are you okay?" she asked, leading Pete to one of the old rocking chairs that lived out there.

"There's…a…body," Pete said between labored breaths.

Nikki turned and squinted toward the water. Her eyes scanned the lakeshore until they landed on something, she wasn't sure what. Red plaid maybe? Whatever it was, it was lying partially submerged in the lake.

She pulled her phone from her back pocket and dialed 911 before handing it to Pete. "When the dispatcher picks up, tell them what's going on. I'm going to take a look."

She ignored Pete's protests and stepped off the porch, walking fast toward the thing she'd seen.

As she got closer, it became clear that the object was a person. A female. And she looked young, late teens or early twenties, but it was hard to tell.

Nikki slowed. She was sure the police wouldn't want her to disturb the scene, but if the woman needed help, she didn't want to wait.

She lay in a prone position, her legs still in the water, dirty reddish-brown hair obscuring her face. Her body, the air around her even, was so motionless, it wasn't really necessary for Nikki to feel for a pulse. She did anyway, reaching for the woman's ashen wrist and pulling away, unsurprised when she didn't find any sign of life. Whoever the poor soul was, she'd been dead for quite some time.

Nikki stepped back, careful to plant her feet in the same soft ground she'd trodden moving forward, in an attempt to disturb the scene as little as possible. Now that the initial shock had worn off, she could see that the stranger was soaked from head to toe.

Maybe she'd fallen overboard and drowned, the currents of the lake washing her up on the property. Nikki said a quick prayer, then hurried back to the house to wait for the police with Pete.

It had been a long, trying day for her, but not nearly as bad a day as it had been for the poor woman lying lakeside.

Chapter Two

Terrence Sutton weaved his way through the streets of Carling Lake. He passed the turn leading to his aunt Charity's house, keeping his car pointed toward the sheriff's department. Good manners dictated his first stop in Carling Lake should be family, but this time, social niceties would have to take a back seat. He wasn't in town for a social visit.

He hadn't heard from his sister, Jill, in a week. While it wasn't unusual for his sister to let his calls and texts languish for a little while if she was caught up in a story, she had never been out of contact for so long. She knew he worried about the chances she took as an investigative reporter, digging up information many people would rather keep hidden. Over the years, they'd worked out a routine of sorts. When he called, she'd get back to him within twenty-four hours even if that response was only a quick text saying she was too busy to talk. And the same went when Jill called and left a message for him. His job as a detective with the Trenton, New Jersey, Police Department had its own set of dangers.

That's why he knew something was wrong. Jill wouldn't be out of touch for this long if there weren't. She wouldn't leave him to worry unnecessarily.

Terrence pulled his car into a parking space in the

small lot adjacent to the sheriff's station and checked his phone again. No messages or texts from Jill. His gut twisted a little tighter.

There had to be something here in Carling Lake that would lead him to his sister. He'd find it and Jill if it was the last thing he did.

First stop, make nice with the town sheriff. He was going to be running his own unofficial missing person investigation whether Sheriff Webb liked it or not, but it wouldn't hurt to grease the wheels if he could. Who knew what he'd find or whether he'd need local help. Best to play nice—at least at first.

Although he'd grown up in Carling Lake, he didn't make it back for visits very often. He recalled meeting Lance Webb some years back on a visit to see Aunt Charity, but he had no idea how the sheriff would react to having a Trenton cop running around town asking questions.

Terrence exited his Toyota Highlander and entered the sheriff's department.

A uniformed clerk sat behind a high desk. The clerk's eyes swept over Terrence, assessing him from head to toe as he approached. "May I help you?"

"I'm Detective Terrence Sutton with the Trenton PD. I'd like to speak with the sheriff, please."

The clerk's expression remained impassive. "Do you have an appointment?"

"I don't, but I'd appreciate it if he has a minute for me."

The clerk stared silently for a moment before raising the phone receiver and punching in four numbers. He turned his chair and lowered his voice so Terrence wasn't able to hear the conversation, but when he hung up the phone, he nodded toward the row of chairs in the lobby. "The sheriff will be out in a moment."

Terrence bypassed the seating area and moved to stand in front of a corkboard with a dozen or so flyers announcing everything from the upcoming Summer Festival to missing pets and a want ad for a babysitter. The board encapsulated Carling Lake—a town dependent upon its festivals and the recreational activities provided to tourists while at the same time being a permanent home to so many people.

From the age of eight until he'd gone away to college, he was one of the people who called Carling Lake home. He and Jill had been raised by Aunt Charity and Uncle Jarrod after their mother had dropped them off on her sister's doorstep one summer day when he was eight and Jill was five. Hope Sutton had begged her sister to watch the kids, saying she just needed a few days' break from being a single mother.

Even at eight years old, he'd known his mother wasn't like the other mothers. Hope couldn't have cared less if he and Jill made it to school on time, and she'd never once checked their homework or planned a nutritious meal. So when a week had turned into a month, he hadn't been all that surprised or concerned. It wasn't the first time his mother had disappeared on him and his sister. At least this time she'd left them with two responsible adults. His aunt always made them home-cooked meals, and Uncle Jarrod had taught him how to skip rocks on the lake. It was a little irritating that even though it was summer and school was out, Aunt Charity insisted they read for a half hour each day. Not being able to do whatever he wanted whenever he wanted had been an adjustment, but it had also felt kind of nice, like a weight he hadn't even realized he'd been carrying had been lifted.

As the weeks continued to tick by though, he'd begun to dread his mother's return. But the closer they got to the end of the summer, the harder it was for Aunt Charity to get her sister on the phone. When she finally did, she gave Hope an ultimatum—clean up her act and be the mother her kids deserved or sign over their guardianship to her and Uncle Jarrod. Five days after her call to her sister, Aunt Charity had the signed papers granting her legal guardianship of him and Jill in hand. His mother had paid extra to have the papers overnighted to her sister. In all his eight years, he'd never seen his mother pay extra for anything.

Hope Sutton had popped up from time to time in the ensuing years, mostly when she needed money. When she'd died from an unexpected aneurysm the year he'd turned twenty, it had fallen to him to make the decisions about her burial as her next of kin, even though the woman who'd given birth to him had never been his mother, not in any real sense of the word.

A loud buzzing noise pulled him out of his head.

A tall Black man wearing a dark brown uniform strode through the metal doors behind the clerk's desk. He and Sheriff Webb had a few notable characteristics in common—they were both Black men in law enforcement—but looks weren't one of them. The six-foot-three sheriff was taller by several inches, with a lithe frame as compared to Terrence's stockier, more muscled physique.

"Detective Sutton," the sheriff said, striding forward with his hand outstretched. "Good to see you again. What can I do for you?"

"Please, call me Terrence. Is there somewhere we can talk in private?"

"Let's go to my office. And you can call me Lance," the sheriff said before turning and leading him into the inner sanctum of the station.

Lance kicked off the conversation once they'd both settled in his office. "I take it you're not in Carling Lake just visiting Miss Charity."

"No. My aunt doesn't even know I'm in town yet."

One of Lance's eyebrows quirked up, along with the ends of his mouth. "You think so?"

The internet had nothing on Carling Lake's gossip network, so it was entirely possible his aunt already knew about his arrival in town.

"I'll rephrase. I haven't seen my aunt yet. But she is my next stop."

Lance leaned back in his chair, a curious expression on his face. "Well, whatever made you risk the wrath of Miss Charity and come here before you stopped by her place must be important."

"It is," he said. The anxiousness and fear currently lodged in his chest had become all too familiar in the last several days. "I'm here trying to track down my sister, Jill."

"As far as I know, Miss Charity doesn't have any visitors at the moment. What makes you think your sister is in Carling Lake?"

"I'm not sure Jill is in town to visit Aunt Charity. Or that she's here at all. I haven't been able to get in touch with her in a week. It's not like her to ignore me."

Lance's expression turned thoughtful. "A week is not that long."

"Maybe not for some people, but it is for Jill and me. Or rather it is a long time for her not to acknowledge my calls and texts at all. Since we are both single, live alone and have jobs that put us in the line of fire at times, we agreed that we'd respond to each other within twenty-four hours. I'll admit we usually don't actually engage in conversation more than once a month, if that, but we are in frequent contact via text."

"And Jill has ceased that contact." Lance's face finally took on a concerned expression.

He nodded. "No response to several calls and texts. It took me a little while to realize Jill hadn't responded to my last call within our agreed-upon twenty-four hours."

Terrence's stomach rolled as a wave of guilt hit. He should have noticed, but he'd been wrapped up in what was supposed to have been a major drug operation and had gotten distracted. All for naught, as it turned out. The bust had been a bust, and three days had gone by before he'd realized he hadn't heard from Jill. Three days when his career had rapidly gone into the toilet, and who knew what had happened to his sister?

"Okay," Lance said, the wheels almost visibly turning in his head. "I take it it's safe to assume you've called all her friends. You talked to her coworkers. Been by her place."

Terrence nodded. "Yes to all of that. Jill is an investigative journalist. I spoke to her editor at the newspaper she works for and several of her coworkers. They all said they hadn't heard from her. And her neighbors haven't seen her in days, although they all said that wasn't unusual. I also spoke to her best friend, but she hasn't spoken to Jill in a couple of weeks."

Lance tapped a pen on his desk blotter. "And her apartment?"

"She travels a lot for work, but she has a small place in DC. I drove there yesterday to check things out. Everything looked normal, except I found this." He pulled a plastic bag from his jacket pocket. Inside was a piece of paper with Carling Lake written on it and circled several times. Underneath was a drawing that looked like a fancy flower of some sort. "The handwriting is Jill's. I had a friend in the Philly PD dust it for fingerprints, but he only found Jill's prints on it."

"Okay, I mean, I get why you're concerned, but you don't have much to go on." Lance handed the plastic-encased paper back across the desk.

Frustration bubbled in Terrence's chest. "I know, but I can't shake the feeling that something is wrong."

"And she's your sister and you're not going to let it go until you know for sure she's okay. I get it. What can I do?"

Relief flooded through Terrence. He'd have gone it alone if he'd had to but having the sheriff on his side would be a big help if, as he feared, Jill had gotten herself in over her head.

"Right now, I'm not sure. I hadn't thought much past getting to Carling Lake and seeing if Jill was here or if she had been here."

Lance exhaled. "Well, as I said, I haven't heard she was in town, but I may have missed the latest news. Your aunt Charity though…nothing gets past that woman. If Jill is here or was here, she'd be the one to know."

The phone on the sheriff's desk buzzed before Terrence could respond. Lance picked up the receiver.

His face darkened as the person on the other end of the line spoke.

Terrence couldn't hear what was being said, but it was clearly not good.

Lance ended the call, rising as he did. "I've got to go. Someone's found a body."

Terrence rose as well. "In Carling Lake?" His heart thundered in his chest. *Jill*. "Have you got an ID on the body?"

Lance stopped his march toward the door. Silence hung thick in the room while he visibly contemplated whether to answer.

"I'm not trying to horn in on your case, Sheriff. It's just…" He couldn't bring himself to say what he was thinking. That the body could be his sister. But from the softening look on Lance's face, he didn't need to. Webb knew what was on his mind.

"Don't have an ID yet." Lance reached to open the office door.

"Do you know if the body is male or female?"

"It's female," Lance answered soberly.

Terrence's stomach churned, but he fell in step next to the sheriff. "I'm going with you."

Chapter Three

Nikki remembered Pete as a man of few words and was grateful that he hadn't seemed to have changed over the years. They'd moved to the front porch to wait for the police. Pete cradled a glass of water but still looked as if he might lose his lunch at any moment. The man was undeniably shaken and she couldn't blame him. She wasn't sure she'd ever get the sight of that poor woman out of her mind.

Pete cocked his head, and she heard the sound of an approaching vehicle. A black SUV with the Carling Lake sheriff's department logo on the side pulled to a stop alongside her Camry.

She'd met the previous sheriff briefly on one of her trips to Carling Lake before her grandfather moved to Florida. The man who hopped out of the driver's side of the SUV looked familiar, but she was sure she'd never been properly introduced to the new sheriff. He affixed his sheriff's cap on his head as he exited the car. The passenger door of the SUV swung open as Sheriff Webb rounded the hood.

All the breath rushed from her lungs when she saw the man who stepped from the car.

Terrence.

Her emotions boiled like water in a scalding hot pot. Anger. Elation. Remorse. Longing.

They'd once been inseparable, best friends on the edge of being much more. But all that had changed in what had seemed like an instant when they were seventeen.

Terrence gave no sign of having seen her or Pete on the porch. He leaped from the SUV, his face set in a determined expression.

The sheriff caught hold of Terrence's arm. "You need to stay here. This is a potential crime scene."

Terrence shook free of the sheriff's grasp. "I'm a cop."

"Not on my force." The two men stared at each other with dark expressions for a long moment before the sheriff added more softly, "It might not be something you want to see."

It was clear something was going on between Terrence and the sheriff. But at the moment, Nikki had a more pressing question. "Terrence."

He spun around. His hickory-brown eyes widened in shock when they landed on her. At least the feeling was mutual.

She strode down the porch steps and came to a stop in front of him.

"Nikki." The sound of her name in his deep baritone still sent a delicious chill down her spine. "What are you doing here?"

"Grandpa left the house to me, and as of today, I live here."

The expression on his face softened. "I heard he passed away. I'm sorry for your loss."

She was surprised to hear sincerity in his tone given

how he'd felt about her grandfather when he was alive. "Thank you. What are you doing here?"

Terrence's expression didn't change, and had she not known him so well, she would have missed his reaction. Surprise that quickly turned to displeasure. "I was with the sheriff when the call came in about a body. I'm in town looking for Jill…"

Her heart leaped into her throat. "Jill? What's wrong with Jill?"

Although her relationship with Terrence had been left in tatters as a result of the fraud between her grandfather and his uncle, she and Jill had managed to keep in touch and had become pretty good friends, since they'd both grown up in Carling Lake and lived in DC.

"No one has heard from her in more than a week, and I have reason to believe she might be in Carling Lake. I was in Sheriff Webb's office when the call came in that the body of a female had been found…" He swallowed hard.

His obvious torment at not knowing whether Jill was safe tempered some of her annoyance at his surprise appearance. She hadn't seen a lot of the body, but she'd seen enough to know it wasn't Jill.

"It's not Jill, Terrence."

"How can you…?"

Without thinking, Nikki reached out and took his hand. "I saw the body, checked for a pulse. And I had dinner with Jill three weeks ago when she was in DC for a story. It's not her down there."

He let out an audible breath.

The sheriff, who'd hung back, moved forward now. "I'm glad our victim isn't your sister, but she is somebody, and I need to get this investigation moving. It's my understanding that Pete Bonny made the call to the sheriff's office."

Nikki dropped Terrence's hand and stepped back, inclining her head toward the porch where Pete still sat. "He's a bit shaken up."

The sheriff nodded. "Understandable. I want to take a look at the scene. All three of you need to stay here."

The sheriff shot a look at Terrence that he ignored, if he noticed it at all. His gaze hadn't wavered from Nikki's face, but his expression had morphed into something unreadable once she had assured him Jill wasn't lying by the lake.

She couldn't see the body clearly from where she stood at the front of the house, but she watched the sheriff stride across the lawn and stop and bow his head before crouching.

"I thought you were working for some political muckety-muck in DC," Terrence said.

Nikki frowned, although she wasn't surprised by the contempt she heard in his voice. He'd always been the type of person who saw the world in black-and-white. Good or bad. Compromise and diplomacy weren't in his makeup.

She ignored his question and asked one of her own. "Why do you think Jill is in trouble?"

"I didn't say I thought she was in trouble."

"You didn't have to. You're in Carling Lake, a place you rarely visit. And you're here at Lakewood House, a place you swore you'd never set foot on again. That's more than enough to tell me how concerned you are about Jill."

Once upon a time, Grandpa Bernie and Terrence's uncle Jarrod had been best friends. Charity and Jarrod Jackson had been a source of support when Grandpa

Bernie had suddenly become the guardian of his griev-ing, sullen, more-than-a-little-angry ten-year-old or-phaned granddaughter.

The two nontraditional families had been close for many years. So close that Nikki thought of Charity as her aunt too growing up. But that had all changed when the automotive plant outside of town had closed and Jarrod lost his job. The Jacksons had fallen behind on their mortgage and were in danger of losing Lakewood House and everything they'd worked for. With Nikki set to leave for college the next year and Grandpa Ber-nie wanting to downsize from the five-bedroom colo-nial he owned on the other side of town, he'd offered to buy the Jacksons' property at market price, allowing them to pay off their mortgage and have a little extra money to start over.

It seemed as if the sale had been a win-win, but cracks in the friendship emerged soon after the papers had been signed. Jarrod Jackson came to resent Nik-ki's grandfather and began accusing Grandpa Bernie of tricking him into selling Lakewood House. Jarrod's hostility quickly trickled down to his nephew.

During their senior year of high school, Nikki had found herself looking at Terrence Sutton in a whole new way. For seven years, he'd just been her friend. The guy she swam in the lake with. Went fishing with. Kidded around with. But she suddenly noticed how his mus-cles rippled when he tossed Jill off the dock and into the lake. And how his brown eyes twinkled and how devastatingly handsome the dimple in his left cheek made him when he smiled. She'd seen that other girls were eyeing him anew as well. And she didn't like that one bit.

Fortunately for her, it seemed like whatever budding

feelings she was having for Terrence were reciprocated. Their long walks and moonlight chats by the lake had taken on a decidedly romantic tone. At the end of that summer, they'd promised to keep in frequent touch via email, and then Terrence had leaned over and kissed her softly. She'd nearly floated back to school.

By the time she'd returned to Carling Lake for Christmas break, Terrence's emails had turned terse, when he bothered to email at all. She'd thought—hoped—it was because he was focused on his college classes. They'd gotten into a huge argument on Nikki's first day back in town, with Terrence venting all his frustration about her grandfather having stolen his family's home and legacy. There had been no reasoning with him, and she'd soon lost her temper. They hadn't spoken for the rest of her visit. Nikki was grateful that Charity and Jill didn't seem to feel the same way as Jarrod and Terrence. But, like the elder men in their lives, their friendship had fractured right down the middle. Maybe irrevocably.

"You don't have to worry about my sister. I can handle whatever is going on with her myself."

"Oh, for goodness' sake." Nikki dragged her cell from her pocket and pulled up the contact for Jill Sutton.

"What are you doing?"

"Calling Jill."

"Told you she hasn't been answering her phone."

"Not when you've called her, and based on spending just five minutes with you, I can see why she might not want to."

Jill's phone rang then clicked over to voice mail. The message box was full. She slid her cell back into her pocket.

"I told you." Terrence scowled.

She planted a hand on her hip, worry clenched in her chest. Terrence wasn't her favorite person by far, but he adored his sister. If he was worried, that was enough for her to be worried as well. "What's your plan?"

"Look, I appreciate your concern…"

"No, you look. You and I may not care for each other, but Jill is my friend. If she's in trouble, I want to help her."

Terrence glared at her for a moment before holding up both hands in surrender. "Fine. If you want to help, tell me about your dinner with Jill. How did she seem? Was she worried or anxious about anything or anyone?"

Nikki shook her head. "The opposite actually. She was excited about a new story she'd just gotten a tip on."

Lines formed on Terrence's forehead. "A new story? What about?"

She shook her head again. "I have no idea. She wouldn't go into specifics. She just said that if her lead panned out, the article could be a career maker."

"I talked to her editor at the paper. He didn't mention any big story."

"Maybe she hadn't pitched it yet." She thought back on her dinner with Jill. "She did say that there was a lot of work to be done. That's why she didn't want to say too much right then."

"Did she say anything else? Give any hint who or what the story was about?"

"I'm sorry, Terrence. She didn't."

He fisted his hands at his sides, the frustration he was feeling evident on his face.

"I'm afraid I'm declaring this a suspicious death," the sheriff said. "An area of the property will be off-limits until further notice."

"How much of the property?" Nikki shot a look at

the house. She could probably get a room at the local bed-and-breakfast, but her bank account really didn't need the extra stress. Saving money, after all, was the primary reason she'd decided to return to Carling Lake and figure out her next step. The thought of going back to DC and bunking on a friend's sofa indefinitely was too humiliating to contemplate.

The sheriff appeared to pick up on her concern. "As long as it doesn't appear that the victim was ever inside the house, it should be all right for you to stay tonight. Would you consent to a search of the house and property?"

"Absolutely," Nikki agreed immediately. "I can tell you that the house was locked up tight when I arrived. It didn't look like anyone had been inside in weeks."

The sheriff turned to Pete, who still sat in a rocking chair on the porch. "What about it, Pete? When was the last time you were here to check on the property?"

Pete's face reddened. He was supposed to look in on the property at least once a week per the agreement with her grandfather. But from the guilt etched across his face at the moment, it appeared he hadn't been keeping up his end of the deal.

"Oh, well, I might not get out here as much as I used to. I'm not as spry as I once was."

From the looks on the sheriff's and Terrence's faces, they weren't buying what Pete was selling, and neither was Nikki. Pete hadn't batted an eye at launching the boat all by his lonesome.

"I guess I was out here a week and a half ago. Maybe a little more," Pete finally answered.

The sound of sirens cut through the air.

"That'll be my deputies and the forensics crew." Looking from Nikki to Pete, the sheriff said, "I'm going to have a deputy take your statements. Just sit tight and, please, have patience."

The sheriff strode away to the approaching cruisers.

Nikki snuck a glance at Terrence. His gaze trailed after the sheriff.

Have patience. Something told her that request was going to be easier said than done.

TERRENCE TRIED TO focus on taking in as much information as he could from the crime scene, but he couldn't stop his gaze from tracking to Lakewood House. It was the house that Aunt Charity and Uncle Jarrod had been living in when his mother dumped him and Jill off on them. And it was the house where he'd learned what it meant to really be part of a family. Until the fall of his freshman year of college, it had been the only home he'd ever known. And it should still be Aunt Charity's home, would still be if Bernie King, once his uncle's closest friend, hadn't swooped in and bought Lakewood House out from under his family when they'd hit a rough patch financially.

His uncle had learned the hard way that Bernie was no friend at all. Their friendship hadn't been the only casualty though. He and Nikki had begun dating during their senior year in high school, and despite going off to different colleges, they'd managed to keep their relationship fires burning those first few months away. Until the sale. Nikki just couldn't—or wouldn't—see how her grandfather's actions had been a betrayal. Then, during the spring semester of his freshman year, Uncle Jarrod had died of a sudden massive heart attack. He was convinced that the shame of losing his family home and having been stabbed in the back by his closest friend had led to Uncle Jarrod's death.

He studied the house now. After Lance had taken Nikki's statement, he'd searched the house and given the all clear. Nikki had disappeared inside without giving him a second glance. It was probably for the best. Their last conversation had taken place fourteen years ago, but it had left plenty of unpleasant memories. And he wasn't in Carling Lake to rehash the past.

Deputy Clarke Bridges had taken Terrence's official statement and was now taking video of the crime scene. A second deputy in waders searched the bank of the lake for evidence. Neither of them questioned Terrence's presence, and he tried to remain unassuming and unnoticed as he circled the body, the smell of decay wafting on the breeze.

The woman lay face down in the sand, her legs still floating in the water. Her dark hair was matted and tangled, and her light brown skin was mottled and gray from having been in the water. She wore black jeans and a short-sleeve shirt that exposed her arms. He couldn't see her features, but he suspected she was Hispanic or maybe Indigenous.

"I thought I told you to stay out front," Lance said, coming to a stop at his side.

Terrence ignored the question and pointed to the woman's wrist. "Did you notice this? It looks like a bruise."

Lance squatted next to the body. "There's one on the other wrist too. Looks like she might have been bound."

"Or handcuffed." He pointed higher on her arm this time. "And look at her upper arm here and here. More bruises."

"And a few burns." Lance looked at Terrence with anger in his eyes. "This woman was tortured."

Terrence wished he could disagree. "You'll probably find more bruises on other parts of her body."

Lance exhaled heavily. "I'll make sure the medical examiner documents them all and looks for signs of sexual assault."

They both fell silent for a long moment. The body bobbed with a ripple of the lake.

"I'm sure you've seen the bruising around her neck too."

Lance shot him a look. "Of course. But again, the medical examiner will have to tell us whether strangulation is the cause of death. Especially given the other bruising on her body, strangling her could have been part of the torture but not the cause of death."

His jaw tensed. "Someone put her through the wringer. It's possible she just drowned trying to get away from whoever did this to her."

Lance frowned. "Possible. But as far as I'm concerned, that still makes them responsible for her death."

Terrence couldn't agree more. He scanned the shore. Lakewood House was the only home in view. Privacy and seclusion were two of the perks of purchasing property in Carling Lake. Especially lakeside property. Most of the lots were several acres, and it was possible not to see a neighbor for days on end unless one made an effort to do so. "Any ideas where she could have gone into the water?"

"No idea. We'll do our best to figure it out, but it might not be possible. Especially if she went in off the side of a boat."

"Someone in Carling Lake must know her. It's a small town." He could feel his frustration level rising. First, Jill goes missing, and now a young woman turns up at the lakeshore dead. Things like this just didn't happen in Carling Lake. Certainly not without anyone knowing anything.

"I've got men canvassing now. We'll talk to everyone we can. If someone in this town knows her, we'll find out soon." Lance signaled for the deputy with the video camera to come closer. "Help me turn her over, will you?"

Terrence did as requested. They gripped the woman from opposite sides and gently pulled her onto dry land while the deputy documented their every move.

Lance patted the victim's back pockets. "No identification there."

The water had done extensive damage to the body, and it looked as if the animals in the water had also gotten to it.

"Do you recognize her?" Terrence asked.

Lance shook his head. "No. Never seen her."

"Any missing persons reports recently?"

Another headshake. "Not in Carling Lake or any of the surrounding towns. I'll put a call out of course, but it might take some time to track down an identity."

"Any idea how long she's been in the water?" He'd been on the police force for eleven years and a detective for almost five of those years, but he'd primarily worked in the narcotics division.

"The body is bloated, so at least a few days. The medical examiner will be able to be more exact." Lance's chin jutted in the direction of the white van that was coming up the driveway. The medical examiner had arrived.

Terrence straightened to his full height. "This woman is young. If she's been in the water for days, why hasn't anyone been looking for her? Parents. Friends. Someone. She must have been missed by now."

"I don't know, man," Lance said as they walked toward the medical examiner's van. "But I will get to the bottom of how she died. You just remember that you have no authority here. You're a private citizen in Carling Lake." Lance shot him another pointed look.

"I hear you, and I have more than enough on my plate trying to find my sister." He stopped walking. "I just…" He glanced at the house. He couldn't see Nikki through the window, but he knew she was inside. "Work fast, okay? It feels like something very dark might have slithered into town. And I don't think it will be safe for anyone until you get to the bottom of it."

Chapter Four

Terrence left soon after the medical examiner's arrival. He stopped by his aunt's house after leaving Lakewood House and discovered she already knew he was in town. He couldn't lie to her about Jill's disappearance, but he did his best not to show her how worried he truly was. She seemed to buy it, but he knew that wouldn't last if he didn't find Jill soon. He stayed for dinner, but Aunt Charity had moved into a tiny one-room cabin a few years earlier that wasn't conducive to guests.

He'd had the foresight to make a reservation at the Carling Lake Hotel, but they could only guarantee him one night. With the Spring Festival beginning, they were booked up for the week.

He'd checked in exhausted from the day's travel and the emotional toll, but he'd rallied enough to spend a few hours calling around to Jill's friends again, checking to see if anyone had heard from her, but to no avail. When he'd finally hit a wall and had lain down to get some sleep, he'd found it wouldn't come.

At half past six, he gave up. Showered and dressed, he went downstairs to the hotel's restaurant and, finding their breakfast menu wanting, headed for the one place in town that had never disappointed him. Lakeside Diner was a mainstay in the community, a place where Carling Lake residents and tourists congregated.

He wasn't surprised to find the diner nearly full when he entered just before seven. He caught the eye of Deputy Bridges, who sat with another man and a young boy at a table near the window. Sheriff's deputies had still been searching Lakewood House and combing the property for clues when he'd left there the previous evening, which explained why the large cup of coffee in the deputy's hand seemed to be doing little to chase away the exhaustion on the man's face.

Terrence nodded hello and took a seat at the counter on one of the few stools not already occupied.

Rosie Whitmer, the proprietor of Lakeside Diner, strode over. Her face broke out into a joyful grin when her eyes landed on him. "Well, will wonders never cease? Terrence Sutton, the long-lost son of Carling Lake, is back in town."

Terrence grinned at the woman who'd owned the diner for as long as he'd been alive. Since his trips to Carling Lake had mostly been limited to major holidays and only for a day or two at most, he hadn't had Rosie's food in years.

Rosie's tightly curled orange coif was now all gray, and her figure was fuller than he remembered, but her bright smile and gregarious personality appeared not to have changed at all.

"I don't know about 'long-lost,'" he replied, leaning forward over the counter to place a kiss on the cheek Rosie presented him. "How have you been, Rosie?"

"Fit as a fiddle and twice as spry. Your aunt Charity didn't mention you were coming to town."

"It was a spur-of-the-moment decision."

"Let's start with what I can get you to eat. Then you

can tell me what you've been up to since I've seen you last?" Rosie asked.

"Oh, I think you know exactly what I want." He grinned. "The breakfast platter with your world-famous blueberry pancakes, please. And I haven't been up to much except working longer than I care to admit. I'm afraid my life isn't interesting enough for the Carling Lake gossip circuit."

"We'll just see about that," she said, writing out his order then turning her back to put it on a spindle for the cook.

"Hey, Rosie, I'm just wondering, when was the last time you saw my sister?"

Rosie turned back to face him. "Jill? Huh, it must have been Christmastime. *She* came home to visit her aunt, like a good niece."

"I know, I know, I've heard it all from Aunt Charity. But if single guys like me didn't take the holiday shifts, the cops with families wouldn't be able to spend Christmas with their kids. You wouldn't want that, now would you?"

"Oh, you're really laying it on thick, you know." Rosie chuckled.

"I learned from the best."

The bell over the diner's door jangled and Rosie's face lit up again. Terrence glanced over his shoulder to see who'd garnered such a reaction and saw Nikki striding into the diner. Her eyes skimmed over him quickly, her smile dimming noticeably before she focused her gaze on Rosie.

"Now it really is like old times around here." Rosie came around the counter and enveloped Nikki in a bear hug that included a half minute of rocking from side to side. "I heard you were back in town and about that unfortunate business at Lakewood House. You doing okay, hon?"

It seemed like the town grapevine hadn't slowed any in the years since he'd moved away. Nor had Rosie's affection for Nikki dimmed. Maybe it was because Nikki lacked a mother figure, and Rosie had a naturally motherly personality, but she'd taken a young Nikki under her wing and had even given Nikki her first real job bussing tables the summer she'd turned fourteen. The two of them had a relationship nearly as close as mother and daughter, and it appeared that hadn't changed at all.

Nikki gently pulled free of the hug and beamed at Rosie. To anyone who didn't know her as well as he did, she looked to be taking the previous day's chaos in stride. But he saw the tiny lines creasing the skin under her eyes.

Nikki wasn't his concern. He was only in Carling Lake to track down Jill. His tumultuous relationship with Nikki was…something he didn't have time to ponder.

"It was a shock, finding that poor girl, but I'm fine. Sad for her family, but I'm sure the sheriff will identify her and get her body back to her family so they can lay her to rest."

"Sheriff Webb is the best there is. He'll get to the bottom of things, I have no doubt. Are you back in town to finally deal with Lakewood House?"

Nikki nodded. "It's time. I have to make some decisions about what I want to do with it. Sell it. Rent it… It was kind of a last-minute decision, so I figured I'd just show up and surprise you."

Rosie slid a sly look from Nikki to Terrence. "Last minute, huh? A lot of that is going around, or so I hear."

The bell over the diner door tinkled, drawing Rosie's attention.

Rosie groaned. "Oh, good grief."

Terrence turned toward the door.

It had been over a decade since he'd seen Melinda Hanes, but the woman hadn't changed much in the intervening years. She swept into the diner in an emerald green pantsuit and kitten heels. She'd drawn her auburn hair into a tight bun at the nape of her neck, and her makeup was impeccable. She made a beeline for the men sitting at the table nearest to the entrance, a beauty pageant smile fixed on her face.

"That woman is insufferable," Rosie said. "She comes in two or three mornings chatting up my guests and scouting for votes."

Terrence turned back to Rosie and Nikki. "Votes?"

"You know what happened with our last mayor?" Rosie's gaze tripped between him and Nikki.

Terrence nodded. His trips back to Carling Lake had been short and few in the last several years, but he did subscribe to the *Carling Lake Weekly* online, so he was well aware of the prior mayor's arrest for fraud, corruption and a host of other crimes.

"Well, Melinda apparently wants to step into her brother's shoes," Rosie said. "At least, with respect to running for mayor. And it seems like she has a pretty good shot."

Nikki tilted her head, her expression skeptical. "Really? It might not be entirely fair, but I'd think voters would be hesitant to vote for her given her brother's actions."

Rosie laughed dryly. "Oh, the voters of Carling Lake

are plenty hesitant, but as of right now, she's the only person who has indicated an interest in the position. I think that's why the town council has been dragging its feet about setting the date for the election, hoping someone else might step up, but they won't be able to hold off for much longer."

Terrence shot a glance over his shoulder. Melinda had moved on to another table, chatting with a man and a woman.

"You know, now that you're back in Carling Lake and with your degree, you'd make a terrific candidate for mayor."

Nikki laughed. "You're kidding, right? I've only been in town for a day."

"Nonsense." Rosie waved away Nikki's statement. "You're a hometown girl. You've got way more political experience than Melinda, and you actually care about the whole town. Melinda only cares about her family's business. And I guarantee some people will vote for you just because you're not Melinda. Tell her, Terrence. She'd be great, right?"

He had no doubt Nikki would be great at whatever she did. She always had been. But he doubted she wanted to hear that from him, so he said nothing.

Rosie frowned at his silence.

Nikki shook her head. "That's good to know, but I'm not your girl."

"Well, sit yourself down and let me get you something to eat." She slapped the stool next to Terrence with the rag from her shoulder.

Nikki quickly assessed the seating situation and chose to sit two stools away instead of next to him.

Rosie slid behind the counter. "Can I get you the special too, hon?"

"Sounds like heaven," Nikki answered.

"Coming right up." Rosie put the order in and grabbed the coffeepot. She flipped over the white mugs at his and Nikki's place settings and filled them nearly to the top. "I've got to make the rounds. Be right back."

The hum of the other diners' conversations and the clink of silverware against porcelain filled the silence between Terrence and Nikki. He snuck a glance at the woman who had once been his best friend and more.

Nikki had always been pretty, but in the years since he'd last seen her she had turned into a bona fide knock-out. Her short blondish-brown hair was cut in a bob that framed her face and accentuated a long, graceful neck. From the lines etched into the caramel-colored skin around her eyes, he guessed she'd gotten about as much sleep as he had. But her dark brown eyes were still sharp and lit with intelligence.

Terrence sipped black coffee while Nikki still dumped four creams into hers. Next came three spoonfuls of sugar. Some things never changed.

"Have you heard anything about Jill?" Nikki asked, pulling him from the past.

"No." His gut clenched with the answer. "I spent half the night calling anyone I could think of and reaching out to my law enforcement contacts."

"What about the DC police? Have they opened an investigation?"

"Not as such." The words came out as a growl.

Despite his best efforts, the DC police had refused to formally begin a search for Jill. Nothing was out of place at her apartment. The only things missing had been a small travel bag and some clothes, which supported the cops' belief that Jill had just gone off for work or maybe a vacation and had forgotten to tell friends and family. No amount of explaining that Jill would never do anything so careless would move the lieutenant he'd spoken to. Which was why he'd put in to use some of the considerable amount of leave he'd banked over the years and set out to find her himself.

As a cop, he understood on some level where the DC police were coming from. There was always more work than there were people, and every force had to prioritize. Most adults who were reported missing turned up unharmed at some point.

But he knew Jill. She would not disappear without a word.

"Well, I meant what I said yesterday. Jill is my friend, and our…relationship aside, anything I can do to help, just let me know."

"I've got it under control but thank you."

Silence landed between them again. Rosie was still circling the diner with a coffeepot, stopping at each table to top off cups and chat up the locals and tourists. A server set a plate of steaming blueberry pancakes in front of Terrence before hurrying off with his arms laden with plates of someone else's breakfast.

A small crowd had grown near the door, patrons lined up, waiting for an open table, but no one attempted to claim the empty seat between Nikki and Terrence. The server swept back through, sliding a plate overflowing with food in front of Nikki before gliding away again. She dug in.

"You never answered my question yesterday." Terrence swiveled so his body was angled toward her.

Nikki gave him a look that said she was searching her memory. "What question?"

"Why aren't you in DC?"

"I need to deal with Lakewood House."

"Curious timing. I happen to know that Congress is in session right now, which usually means aides are swamped."

Surprise spread across Nikki's face.

"What? I'm an informed citizen." He grabbed a fork and speared a clump of eggs from her plate, bringing them to his lips with a grin.

Her shoulders tensed. "I'm taking some time off." She put another bite of food in her mouth and avoided looking at him.

He didn't need to be an expert at reading body language to know there was something more to the "time off" excuse than she was saying. It wasn't his business, but he wasn't the type to let a mystery go unsolved, which was why he had the highest case closure rate of any detective in his precinct.

"I'm surprised you hung on to the house. I would have guessed you'd have sold it, considering you live in DC."

Nikki swallowed the bite she'd been chewing. "I thought about it. I'm still thinking about it. There are so many memories there."

He grunted derisively. "Yeah, I can see how it might suck to have someone else living in the house you loved."

She let her fork hit her plate with a clank and turned a heated gaze on him. "Come on, Terrence. Don't you think you're being more than a little immature at this point?"

He knew he was being a jerk. Whatever her grandfather had done, she'd had no hand in it, she'd been little more than a kid, just like him. But seeing her on property that should have been Aunt Charity's still hurt.

"Immature? You just won't ever get what that house

meant to my uncle, will you? What losing it did to him and my aunt."

"I get that it was hard for your family to sell the property—"

"Hard? That's an understatement if I ever heard one. Yes, it was hard for my uncle to face the fact that his best friend was buying his home out from under him. Making him look like a failure."

"No one bought Lakewood House out from under your aunt and uncle. It was a fair deal that your uncle agreed to."

"That's because he didn't realize—"

Rosie appeared in front of them, a deep frown creasing her face. "All right now. I love both of you, but y'all need to take this conversation out of my diner. You're disturbing my customers."

Terrence blinked and glanced around the diner. He hadn't realized how loud their argument had gotten. Every eye in the place was turned their way.

Nikki flushed pink. She dropped a twenty-dollar bill on the counter next to her nearly full plate before hopping off her stool and hurrying for the exit without another word.

The door closed behind her and the chatter picked up again.

Terrence turned back to his food and found Rosie scowling at him on the other side of the counter.

"You too." She picked up his plate, leaving him holding his fork midair. "Get on out of here."

"But I'm not finished yet."

"You're finished enough. And if you're not, well maybe you ought to think twice about coming into my place and making a spectacle of yourself."

"Look, I'm sorry."

"Out!" Rosie pointed to the door.

He'd seen that look on Rosie's face when they were younger. No amount of reasoning or begging and pleading would change her mind once she got it set.

He stood, grumbling some choice words about customer service, and laid down enough money to cover his bill.

Nikki's Camry was making a left turn onto Main Street through town when he pushed through the diner's doors into the parking lot.

He hadn't made much headway on finding Jill, but his gut told him Carling Lake had something to do with his sister's disappearance. He might be in town for a while. He couldn't permit his feelings about the past to interfere with locating Jill.

That meant clearing the air with Nikki. Whether she liked it or not.

Hopping into his Highlander, he drove the familiar roads to Lakewood House. Aunt Charity had always admonished him about his lead foot, but in this case, he was grateful. He pulled his car to a stop behind Nikki's Camry as she was getting out of the driver's side.

"Are you kidding me?" she said, stalking toward his car as he exited. "You followed me home?"

"It looks like both of us might be in town for a little while, and we can't keep making a scene. We need to clear the air."

"I don't have any air to clear. It's you who's been acting like an idiot for the past fourteen years, blaming my grandfather and me for slights that only exist in your head."

His jaw tightened. "You know full well that's not true. Your grandfather knew exactly—"

The rest of his statement was choked off by the sudden onslaught of shock and fear that bloomed in Nikki's eyes.

His right hand instinctively went for the gun on his hip before he remembered that he wasn't on duty. His weapon was locked in the glove compartment of the Highlander. Still, he angled his body so Nikki was behind him and turned to see what it was that had garnered her attention.

His heartbeat kicked up a notch when he saw the message that had been spray-painted on the detached two-car garage next to the house. It wasn't the most original, but it was still extremely effective.

LEAVE OR YOU'LL DISAPPEAR TOO.

Chapter Five

Nikki stood for a moment, breathing deeply, fighting to get control of her raging emotions. Shock. A small bubble of fear. Who would do something like this? The words were splashed across the faded black of the garage doors in white paint.

The vandalism itself wasn't that big a deal. A couple coats of primer and paint, and the doors would be like new. But the message—*Leave or you'll disappear too*—was obviously intended to scare her off. Why? And even more chilling, what did the vandal mean by "you'll disappear too"? Was that a reference to the body of the poor woman they'd found yesterday? Jill's sudden disappearance? Or was there someone else out there missing?

In a flash, the shock and fear she was feeling was joined by another emotion: rage.

Terrence wasn't the only one attached to the house. Despite its purchase having led to the loss of his friendship, Grandpa Bernie had fallen in love with Lakewood House. For that reason alone, Nikki was hesitant to sell. But she had her reasons as well. Years of fond memories of when the Suttons and Kings were close, and both families had gotten together for weekend picnics and holidays. She'd spent a lot of time playing with Terrence in this house when it had been owned by his aunt and uncle before her grandfather had purchased it.

She moved closer to Terrence. He pulled her toward his car and opened the passenger-side door, all but shoving her inside. "Give me your key to the house."

She already had it in her hand since it was on the same ring as her car key. She handed it over without question.

Popping the glove compartment open, Terrence pulled a holstered gun from inside. "Lock the door and call the sheriff." He snapped the holster onto his belt and unsheathed the weapon before slamming the door closed and heading for the house.

Part of her wanted to follow him. It was her house after all, but her rational mind said he was right. They didn't know if whoever had done this was still on the property, and she wasn't trained to confront criminals. The best thing she could do right now was to call Sheriff Webb and get Terrence backup in case he needed it.

She hit the button for the electronic locks and dialed the sheriff's office. She explained the situation, and the dispatcher assured her that someone was on their way and kept her on the line.

Carling Lake was a small town, but most of the homes, especially those on lakeside property, were spread quite a distance apart. Lakewood House was within walking distance of the downtown area, at least by Carling Lake standards, but it was still nearly a ten-minute drive from the sheriff's department.

Those minutes felt like an eternity. Terrence hadn't reappeared out of the house, and Nikki was just beginning to wonder if she should go inside and make sure he was okay when a sheriff's department SUV swung into the driveway with its siren off but its red-and-blue overhead lights flashing.

Seconds later, Terrence appeared from around the back of the house, his gun still in his hand but held low down by his thigh.

She watched in the rearview mirror as the sheriff pulled to a stop behind Terrence's car and stepped out, his gaze sweeping quickly over Lakewood House, his hand on his weapon.

"All clear," Terrence called out as he approached, holstering his gun.

Nikki let the dispatcher know that the sheriff had arrived and disconnected the emergency call before hopping out of the Highlander and joining the two men in front of the garage door.

"Looks like someone did a number on your garage," Sheriff Webb said.

She sighed. "Something like that."

They gave the sheriff a quick rundown on the events of the morning: having run into each other at Rosie's diner, getting into an argument and Rosie throwing them out, then returning to Lakewood House and finding the message scrawled on the garage door.

"This has to be connected to Jill's disappearance," Terrence said.

It was slight, but Nikki heard the tremor in his voice and knew that the graffiti had affected him as much as it had affected her. Maybe more so.

Sheriff Webb gave Terrence a sharp look. "We don't know that for sure." He circled Terrence and got an unobstructed look at the garage.

Terrence scowled. "What do you think 'leave or you'll disappear too' means then? As far as we know, Jill is the only person in Carling Lake who has disappeared."

The sheriff turned his back to the garage and faced Terrence. "We don't know if your sister was ever here in Carling Lake or if she was even ever headed here. The reference to disappearing could just as easily be related to the body of the woman we found on this property yesterday."

"Except she didn't disappear," Terrence growled.

The sheriff's eyes narrowed even further. "She likely disappeared from somewhere before her body washed up here. But more to the point, your jumping to conclusions is only going to hinder the investigation into where your sister is, as well as the investigation into this woman's death, and I don't need that."

Terrence took a step forward, into the sheriff's personal space. "You don't need—"

Sheriff Webb stiffened but held his ground.

The display of testosterone overload was simultaneously unhelpful and annoying. Nikki clapped her hands and pushed her way between the two men. "Alrighty then. This has been…something, but can we get back on track? The message is somewhat ambiguous but obviously meant to be threatening. I'm sure there's something you need to do to document it for the record, Sheriff?"

Sheriff Webb and Terrence glared at each other for several more seconds until Nikki sighed heavily.

The sheriff glanced at her, his face softening, which only seemed to make Terrence's glower harden.

"I'll get started," he said, stepping back from the male pissing contest with Terrence and heading for his SUV.

She pulled Terrence away from the garage so they could talk with some privacy. "What are you doing?"

Terrence jutted his chin in Sheriff Webb's direction. "He's not taking Jill's disappearance seriously."

"I don't get that at all. I think he's taking Jill's disappearance very seriously, but he's not her brother."

Terrence met her gaze, his eyes flashing in anger. "What is that supposed to mean?"

"It means he can be more objective than you can. Or even I can. He doesn't see everything that's happening in Carling Lake through the lens of a missing sister or friend. But that doesn't mean he isn't doing his best to locate Jill. And you need him. You have no jurisdiction here and having the sheriff's help is not something you want to just cast aside."

She watched him. He knew she was right, but he didn't like it. After a moment, the hard line of his jaw softened. She nodded and walked back to the detached garage where the sheriff was already taking photographs of the vandalized doors.

He lowered the camera, letting it hang from the strap around his neck as Nikki and Terrence approached.

"What's next?" she asked.

"Well, I know Terrence checked inside, but I want to do a quick walk-through with you, Ms. King, and make sure nothing was taken or disturbed in any way. I also think it's best for you to stay somewhere else, at least until we get a handle on what is happening out here."

She was already shaking her head. It wasn't just that she had to watch every penny now that she didn't have a job or any current prospects for one. Plain old pride and stubbornness wouldn't let her be run out of her grandfather's home. "I'll be fine."

Both men looked at her with displeasure now. At least she'd given them something to agree upon.

"Those locks are a joke," Terrence said. "Anyone who wants in is coming in."

"And I'm concerned that you weren't gone that long, right? You were at Rosie's for what? Forty minutes from the sound of it?"

"About that, give or take a few minutes," Nikki conceded.

"Yet someone managed to vandalize the property at the exact time you weren't home?"

Terrence took a protective step closer to her, and she wondered if he even realized he'd done so. "You think someone is watching Lakewood House?"

"Maybe." Sheriff Webb dipped his head. "Or, there's a lot of property here. Someone could be camping out. Living on the land. It's hard to say. That's why I think it's best that Ms. King stay somewhere else until we can sort it all out."

She shook her head firmly. Even if she'd had the money to pay for a hotel—which she didn't—she wouldn't go. "No. This is my property. I'm not letting anyone run me off. Come on, it's Carling Lake. It's not like the hotel and bed-and-breakfast here have top-of-the-line security."

Sheriff Webb tilted his head, his expression thoughtful. "Actually, I do know one place. A new B and B that just opened. With the Spring Festival so close, every available room is filling up fast, but—"

Nikki held up her hand to stop whatever was coming next. "It doesn't matter. I'm not leaving. I know how to protect myself if I need to."

The look Terrence gave her said he was dubious of her claim.

"I don't like guns, but Grandpa was concerned with me living in a big city. He bought me a pistol when I moved to DC, and he made sure I knew how to use it." She could tell that Terrence and the sheriff remained unconvinced, but she wasn't about to back down. "So, like I said, what's next?"

Sheriff Webb sighed. "I'll write up a report. You'll need it to make a claim to your insurance. You can pick it up later today. I'll also increase the frequency of patrols in this area."

"That's it?" Terrence said sharply.

"I'm open to hearing your suggestions," the sheriff shot back just as sharply. "That's what I thought," he said when Terrence remained silent. "You know how something like this goes. We'll keep an eye out, but it's not easy to catch vandals unless they keep vandalizing. Maybe this is just teens not wanting to lose their favorite hangout and hookup spot."

Nikki flinched at the idea that kids were hooking up in her grandfather's house.

The sheriff chuckled lightly. "Sorry for putting that image in your head, but empty house…small-town teenagers." He shrugged. "I'm sure you remember what it was like being that age."

She felt her cheeks heat because she could remember how she felt when they'd dated as teens, and Terrence and his family had lived at Lakewood House. Meeting him by the lake on warm starry nights. Or sneaking up to Terrence's room to make out for a few minutes before his aunt and uncle got home from work and bribing Jill not to tell. Or just sitting out on the back porch in the white Adirondack chairs that Terrence and Uncle Jarrod touched up every spring. Holding his hand on a warm summer evening.

Her gaze slid to Terrence's face, and she knew he

was recalling the same memories. She looked away quickly, focusing all her attention back on the sheriff.

"Okay. I'll come by later this afternoon," Nikki told the sheriff.

Terrence stayed at her side, and they watched the sheriff pack his gear away.

He turned to her as the sheriff's SUV backed out of the driveway. "I think you should listen to the sheriff and find somewhere else to stay."

She waved away the comment and started for the house. "You're not going to change my mind."

He scowled. "This is serious, Nik. We have no idea what's going on, but Lakewood House seems to have something to do with it. What if whoever did this isn't happy with you ignoring them and comes back?"

"I can take care of myself," she repeated, and continued walking.

He followed her, his scowl deepening. "I didn't say you couldn't." At the front door, they both stopped. He exhaled, running a hand over his short hair. "Will you just make sure all the doors and windows are locked? And be careful."

The look he turned on her stole her breath for a moment. "I will," she said once she was able to speak. "I have to go. I have a work conference call I can't miss."

That part was true at least. Carolyn had texted last night saying she thought she might have a line on a job. They'd agreed to sketch out a plan of attack. *Attack* because she was sure it was going to take a lot of convincing to get someone to hire her at the moment.

"Okay," Terrence said. "I'll wait for you to get inside."

She rolled her eyes, but a little part of her was comforted by the gesture. More than a little part of her. Despite how their romance had ended, she realized she still cared about Terrence, and she couldn't deny that it pleased her to see that he might still care about her.

Nikki went into the house, flipped the lock on the door and watched from the adjacent window as Terrence got in his car and pulled away.

Chapter Six

After leaving Nikki, Terrence focused on reaching out to anyone Jill might have been in contact with in Carling Lake. Several of her friends from high school still lived in or near town. Unfortunately, none of them had heard from or spoken to Jill recently. Frustration had him climbing the walls.

He stepped out of Lakeside Books, where a former classmate of Jill's now worked, and onto Main Street, the sign for Laureano's Hardware catching his eye. His investigation into Jill's whereabouts was at a standstill until he could think of a new avenue to pursue, but he knew one person in Carling Lake he could help, though she might not want it.

He crossed the street and entered the hardware store. Thirty minutes later, he hefted the gallon cans of primer and black paint into the back of his car and closed the rear door.

What was he doing?

Looking for a reason to go to Lakewood House and check in on her was what he was doing. Despite himself, he couldn't seem to stop worrying about Nikki being alone at Lakewood House. Which was why, even though she'd been clear that she didn't want his help, he'd just spent eighty bucks on paint and supplies for her garage.

You're a fool and a glutton, Uncle Jarrod's voice re-sounded in his head.

Maybe. He'd cared deeply for Nikki, and that hadn't stopped after her grandfather stole his family home as much as he'd tried to will it to. Even now, it seemed he couldn't stop himself from feeling…something for her.

Who was he kidding? He'd fallen in love with Domi-nique King at age fifteen, and she'd ruined him for all other women. No matter how hard he'd tried over the years, he'd always seemed to unconsciously compare every woman he'd dated to Nikki, and they'd always been found wanting. At some point, he'd realized how unfair he was being to these women, so now he kept all his relationships casual. It wasn't their fault he was stuck on a woman he could never have and shouldn't want. They didn't deserve to get hurt because of it.

But what did he deserve?

He pushed the question aside and turned the High-lander onto the Lakewood House driveway.

His head knew that Lakewood House belonged to Nikki now, but in his heart, it would always be Aunt Charity and Uncle Jarrod's place. He could almost see himself at various ages, like little ghost boys, running around the yard. Playing keep-away with Jill and Nikki. Uncle Jarrod teaching him to ride a bike on the then dirt driveway. Long summer afternoons down by the lake, swimming and lazing out under the sun. This place was part of his past. It had meant something to him once upon a time. It still did if he was honest with himself.

His and Jill's early childhood had been rough. Their mother, Hope Sutton, was unstable on her best day, chasing dreams of…he didn't know what, but they certainly weren't dreams of a stable home for her two children. Abandoning them with her sister and brother-in-law, ironically, was the most motherly thing Hope had ever done. They'd finally had a home and people who cared for them and allowed them to be children.

Until Bernard King snatched that safety and security away.

Then what are you doing here?

That was an excellent question but another one he pushed from his mind as he put the Highlander in Park and climbed out.

He was stacking the paint cans in front of the garage when the door to Lakewood House swung open and Nikki stepped out onto the porch.

"What are you doing?" She eyed him warily.

"Helping you clean up this mess."

"I told you I didn't need your help."

He fisted his hands on his hips and glared at her. "You want me to take it all back then?"

She drew in a deep breath and let it out slowly. "No. Sorry. Thank you."

It was a begrudging apology, but an apology nonetheless. He'd take it. "I'm going to get started unless you have any other objections."

In spite of himself, he couldn't help finding the slight scowl she shot at him cute, maybe even a little sexy. "No objections. Give me a minute to change and I'll help you."

Nikki disappeared back into the house.

The garage wasn't as old as the house itself, but it was old enough that it hadn't had automatic doors when he lived there. Bernard must have had an automatic lifting system installed because when he went to pull the handle to release the doors, he found that he couldn't raise them.

He walked around to the side and tried the side door.

When he'd lived at Lakewood House with his aunt and uncle, the door to the garage had been wonky. No matter what Uncle Jarrod did, the door never quite hung properly, which meant that it never locked properly either. If he jiggled the handle just right...yep, whatever the problem was, Bernard King had never fixed it.

He let himself in and grabbed an empty bucket, some all-purpose cleaner and a few rags to wash the doors down before painting.

He'd just finished filling the bucket when Nikki joined him outside. It was only early May, not quite summer yet technically, but you couldn't tell Mother Nature that. At two in the afternoon, the sun was high enough that its heat broke through the tree cover and warmed Carling Lake enough that Nikki had donned an old Carling Lake High T-shirt and a pair of ratty gray shorts. The T-shirt he recognized as one he'd given her oh-so-many years ago. Was wearing it now some sort of message? A reminder of what they'd once been to each other? Or maybe she was trying to tell him his gift meant so little to her now that she'd wear it to do grunt work, like painting.

Or it was simply the first shirt she'd found in her dresser, his rational mind chimed in.

It didn't matter, he thought, turning away from Nikki as she neared, but not before he caught the way her hips swayed as she walked. Carling Lake High and fifteen-year-old Nikki and Terrence were in the past, where they should stay. This wasn't about that. He was just helping someone who needed it.

He wiped down the doors while she stirred the primer using the long painter's stick he'd gotten from the hardware store. They each took a door and got started covering the message.

They worked in silence, but despite their earlier sniping, it was a comfortable, familiar silence.

Nikki had about a quarter of her door covered when she let out a chuckle. "This feels like déjà vu."

"Déjà vu?"

She looked at him with a smile that made his heart stutter. She was so beautiful. "You don't remember doing this once before? When we were fourteen?"

The memory burst into the forefront of his mind. He couldn't believe he'd forgotten it. "Oh yeah," he said with a groan.

She was laughing now. "I thought your uncle Jarrod was going to lose it for real."

"He did lose it." He grimaced, remembering how long and loudly his uncle had yelled.

"What in the world possessed you to take that car out?"

He bent to get more primer onto his roller. The answer to that question was complex. His uncle's prized silver Mustang GT had always been forbidden fruit. Uncle Jarrod rarely let him ride in the car, reserving that treat for special occasions, but drive it? No one, not even Aunt Charity, drove the 'Stang but Jarrod. That would have been enough to entice him to take the car for a spin, eventually. Moving in with his aunt and uncle had given him much-needed discipline and stability, but he'd inherited his mother's temper and propensity for risk-taking. But what had pushed him over the edge that particular day was Nikki. Or rather the desire to impress Nikki, the girl he'd recently realized he liked as more than just as a friend.

"Oh, you know. Fourteen-year-old boys who live in small towns with nothing at all going on tend to come up with very stupid ideas."

"It was a humdinger," she said, laughing. "You started out all right, though. Almost as if you knew what you were doing."

He smiled at the memory. "Yeah, I did not."

"Oh, I figured that out when you put the car in Reverse instead of Drive," she said, laughing harder now. "When you backed into the garage, I thought the whole thing was going to come down on your head."

"You could have tried to stop me," he said, giving her a wry look.

She shrugged, still laughing. "I guess I could have, but fourteen-year-old girls who live in small towns with nothing at all going on tend to rely on fourteen-year-old boys with stupid ideas for entertainment."

"How'd that work out for you?" He laughed now because they both knew how it had worked out.

She cringed. "Not great. We were relegated to doing grunt work for anyone in town who could scare up something for us to do that summer to pay for the new garage doors. That was not a fun summer."

They were both laughing now.

"Look on the bright side," he said, gesturing to the door, "we learned how to paint a garage door, a skill which has come in handy once again."

"That's a way to look at it." Nikki's phone beeped. His gaze followed her hand to where her cell peeked out of her back pocket. He pulled his eyes away when he realized he was staring at her ass, but not before she shot him a look that said she'd noticed.

He smiled boyishly before going back to painting the door.

She set her roller in the paint tray at her feet and looked at the phone, her smile falling away.

"Damn."

The word was little more than a whisper, but the look on her face had him setting his roller aside and stepping toward her.

"Everything okay?" He studied her face, not liking what he saw there. Not anger exactly. More disappointment.

"Everything is fine." She slid the phone back into her pocket. "Actually, it's not, but there's nothing anyone can do about it."

"You want to talk about it?"

She looked at him for a long moment, obviously considering it.

There was a time when they'd told each other everything. They'd been best friends. And even when their relationship had begun to veer into more-than-just-friends territory, their friendship hadn't suffered. If anything, it had grown deeper, like roots burrowing into the soil.

But now he wasn't sure if those roots still existed, and from the looks of it, neither was she.

Finally, she spoke. "I'm in Carling Lake because I was fired from my job."

He wasn't sure what he expected to hear, but it wasn't that. "You? Fired? What happened?"

He knew she worked as an aide for New York Representative Tom Manco. He wasn't much for politics, but he knew that a job like that was a great stepping-stone for someone who wanted to be in the political world like Nikki. She was politically savvy, diplomatic and legitimately one of the smartest people in any room she walked into, so he couldn't fathom her getting fired.

"Me. You know I believed in Tom. I mean, it's why I agreed to work on his campaign when he was a long shot." She paced a short line in front of him. "But going to Washington, DC, changed him. Or maybe it revealed who he really was. Isn't that what Michelle Obama said? Gaining power doesn't change you—it reveals who you are."

"Something like that," Terrence chimed in, but he wasn't sure Nikki heard him.

"Tom became all about keeping his seat. Fundraising. Hobnobbing with lobbyists. I mean, I'm not a neophyte. I get that that stuff has to be done if you want to have the space and network to get the really important legislation passed, but that's not why Tom was doing it, you know."

She looked at him for confirmation. He didn't know, but nodded.

"Anyway, I was disillusioned and thinking about moving on when I discovered discrepancies in the campaign's fundraising reports." She stopped pacing to look him in the eye. "I honestly thought they were just that, discrepancies. At least at first. I brought them to the chief of staff's attention, and she said she'd take care of it. Weeks passed, and no amendment was made, so I brought it up again. This time she told me to drop it, and I knew that it wasn't a mistake. Tom was misusing campaign funds. Paying his car note. Mortgage. Vacations." She looked down at the ground. "I reported it. Tom said it was a misunderstanding. Made the corrections. Put the money back into the accounts and fired me." She laughed, but it was without mirth. "Fired me and blackballed me. Nobody in DC will hire me."

Terrence stepped closer and used a finger to lift her chin. "I have never been more proud of you. You did the right thing. You hold your head up and own it."

A sizzle of electricity whipped through him, and he tried to read the look in her eyes. Every nerve in his body tingled.

The desire to kiss her at that moment was almost overpowering, and if he'd had to guess, he'd bet good money that she was feeling the same longing.

That's why he nearly cursed when the sound of a car's tire crunching over the gravel drive ruined the moment.

Nikki hesitated before taking three giant steps backward.

He sighed and turned toward the interloper. "Are you expecting someone?"

"No."

The man who stepped out of the car wasn't familiar. Short and stocky, he wore a well-cut brown suit despite the heat and had thinning blond hair that revealed the shiny white skin atop his head.

Terrence shifted so he stood between Nikki and the stranger.

"Good morning." The man's expression was polite, his smile open and practiced. Had it been a different decade, Terrence would have prepared for a spiel about encyclopedias or Tupperware. "Ms. King?" The man locked his gaze on Nikki.

"Yes. And you are?"

"Albert Chester, attorney-at-law."

Terrence glanced at Nikki to see if the name meant anything to her. She shrugged, indicating that it didn't.

"What can we do for you today, Mr. Chester?" Terrence said. Nikki would probably be unhappy with him for taking over the conversation, but given the recent events, he wasn't taking any chances with uninvited visitors.

Chester's smile dimmed a little. "I was hoping to speak to Ms. King about a very pressing matter I've taken on for a client. A private matter."

Nikki stepped from behind him, lightly hip-checking him out of the way. Yeah, she wasn't happy with him. What else was new?

"What kind of pressing, private matter?" she asked.

Chester's eyes darted between Nikki and Terrence, seemingly deciding whether to press the point.

There was no way he was leaving Nikki alone with a stranger.

Chester must have picked up on that. "My client has authorized me to make an offer on this property."

Nikki's brow rose in surprise. "Someone wants to buy Lakewood House?"

"That's right." Chester pulled a slim envelope from the inside pocket of his suit jacket and held it out to Nikki. "I think you'll find the offer more than generous."

Nikki didn't reach for the envelope. "Lakewood House is not for sale."

"I realize you haven't put the property on the market, but I think if you consider the offer my client is making—"

"Who is your client?" When Nikki still didn't make a move to take the envelope, Terrence took it from Chester's outstretched hand.

Chester frowned. "Well, that I can't share."

Terrence shot another glance at Nikki. "I guess it doesn't matter since, as I said, Lakewood House isn't for sale. I'd like for you to leave now, Mr. Chester."

"Now, Ms. King, I'm sure the house holds a lot of fond memories for you—"

Terrence cut him off. "The lady asked you to leave. You're officially trespassing now."

Chester's brow furrowed, and Terrence could almost see the thoughts rolling through the man's mind. Had

Chester really thought he'd come by and make a deal to purchase Lakewood House in what…a few minutes? Maybe because the house had been sitting empty for so long, he or his client had gotten the impression that Nikki didn't want the house.

But something about the whole thing stunk. Lakewood House had been empty for several years. Why was this offer to buy it coming up now? Had Nikki's return to Carling Lake set off some kind of chain reaction? Did Jill's disappearance fit in somewhere?

Something was going on, and Terrence didn't like not knowing what it was.

"Maybe after you take a look at the offer, you'll have a change of heart. My card is inside. Please call with any questions. Day or night." Chester shot them another car salesman–like smile before slinking back to his car.

"What was that about?" Nikki asked as they watched Chester's car retreat away from the house.

"I don't know. But I'm going to find out."

Chapter Seven

"You're going to find out?" Nikki asked. It was bad enough he'd interjected himself in the conversation with Albert Chester as if he owned the place or she needed protection. But now he was what? Launching his own investigation into the strange goings-on at Lakewood House?

Terrence frowned. "You can't think that everything that has happened here in the last couple of days is just coincidence."

"Of course not." She brought her hands to her hips. "But Lakewood House is my responsibility."

Terrence's frown deepened. "And Jill is my sister. All of this is connected. I feel it in my gut. If I figure out what's going on here, I think I'll find Jill."

She studied him for a moment. "Okay. Then we—" she emphasized the word by wagging her finger between the two of them "—will look into things together."

He shook his head. "No way. I have no idea what's going on. It could be dangerous. It probably is if Jill's disappearance is any indication."

She smiled what she knew was a cold smile. "It's cute how you think I was asking your permission." Not. Arrogant was more accurate. A pity he hadn't grown out of that unattractive character trait. "I wasn't. I'm in this whether you like it or not." She moved away from him, tossing the envelope from the lawyer onto the pavers leading to the house, picking up her paint roller and starting in on the garage door again.

Terrence trailed behind her but made no move to continue painting. "You're as stubborn as ever even though you have no training to deal with whatever this might turn out to be."

"That's why working together is the perfect solution. Your police training may come in handy, but you have absolutely no diplomatic skills whatsoever, if your tête-à-tête with the sheriff earlier was any indication. Together we're perfect." Heat flamed in her cheeks. "I mean we make the perfect team for finding Jill and getting to the bottom of whatever is going on here at Lakewood House."

She shot him a sidelong glance to see if he was at all affected by her saying they were perfect together; she'd been close to kissing him before Albert Chester had shown up. At least the lawyer's unbidden appearance had stopped her from making that mistake.

Terrence grabbed the roller from his paint tray, aggressively covering the last few spots of faded black paint.

He might not like what she'd said, but she suspected he knew she had a point. They'd always made a good team, his strengths and weaknesses complementing hers. But he always had to come around to seeing things her way in his own time. More importantly, there was nothing he could do to stop her from investigating, so they may as well do it together. If he *was* correct about the vandalism having a connection to Jill's disappearance—and she believed he was—she had just as much an interest in getting to the bottom of things as he did.

She shot him another sidelong glance. She didn't think it would take him long to see the wisdom in teaming up.

Five minutes later, he put the roller down again and faced her. "If we are going to work together, we have to trust each other. No running off without telling the other where we're going." Something in his eyes beseeched her. "I don't know what's going on here exactly, but I have a really bad feeling."

"Agreed." She held out her right hand. The warmth of his hand burned through her, and the scent of his woodsy cologne tickled her nose. "And for the record, I never stopped trusting you."

He held her gaze for one intense moment before the sound of yet another car turning onto the gravel drive had her snatching her hand away.

Terrence's brow rose. "Lakewood House is party central today."

"Sure seems that way," she mumbled.

Sheriff Webb pulled to a stop behind Terrence's car and got out.

Nikki took the opportunity to put some distance between her and Terrence and walked toward the sheriff. "I was headed to the station right after I grabbed a shower."

"I thought I'd save you a trip." Sheriff Webb thrust a brown envelope in her direction.

She took a peek inside and found the incident report for the vandalism on the garage. "Thanks. Any word on who the poor girl we found yesterday is? Was." She corrected herself.

The sheriff grimaced. "Not yet. The medical examiner was able to say that the cause of death was strangulation, which makes this a homicide. She puts the time of death at about twenty-four hours before you found her."

"She can't be any more specific?" Terrence said.

"She's working on it. The water makes things more difficult."

"We'd at least have somewhere to start if we could identify her, but I've searched through the county's missing person reports for the last two years, and nothing matches."

"She could be from anywhere," Terrence offered with a sad shake of his head.

"That is unfortunately true. Too many females disappear every year." Lance sighed heavily. "And it's why I'm concerned about you staying at Lakewood House alone, Nikki. This property is isolated and has direct access to the lake, which makes it easy for someone to sneak onto the property."

She sighed. "I've already been through this with Terrence."

"You should listen to him," Sheriff Webb said.

A pleased-as-punch smirk crawled across Terrence's face. Of course, the two cops would agree. But she wasn't a defenseless damsel in distress, and she wouldn't be acting like one.

"I've been turning something else over in my head since we found the threat painted on the garage doors," Terrence said after a moment. "The access to the lake doesn't just make it easy for someone to sneak onto the property. It's also ideal for anyone who wants to sneak off the property."

"Sneak off the property?" she asked, unsure what he was getting at.

Terrence nodded. "Say someone who's been using the lake access here for criminal activity, like transporting illegal contraband. Opioids and other drugs have been ravaging small rural towns like Carling Lake for years, even though the media and politicians seem to have just begun to take notice. I know you're the sheriff, but it would be foolish to think that Carling Lake has escaped these kinds of problems."

Sheriff Webb nodded sadly. "No, you're right. We have our fair share of drug-related crime and incidents. They've been increasing over the years, but it's hard for me to fathom that someone could have regularly been moving drugs through this town, and I haven't caught a whiff of it."

"Maybe it's not regular enough for you to have noticed yet. And maybe it's not drugs," Terrence said. "I'll tell you what though. If Jill heard about something like this—an organized criminal operation in the town where she grew up—she'd be all over it."

Nikki could see the idea had already taken root with him.

Sheriff Webb's expression darkened. "And if her nose is better than mine, she might have found herself in a world of trouble."

"That's why we have to find Jill soon."

"We're doing everything we can," the sheriff reiterated before changing the subject. "I didn't just come out here for Nikki. I was also looking for you."

"Well, you found me," Terrence said. "Although I'd like to know how you knew I'd be at Lakewood House."

The sheriff smirked. "It wasn't hard to deduce. I heard from Vincent Laureano that you'd been in his hardware store earlier buying paint and paint supplies."

Terrence's eyes rolled. "Of course. Too many years

of living in a city. I'd forgotten how much everyone is in everyone else's business in this town."

"Just part of our small-town charm," Sheriff Webb said with a grin. "Anyway, I wanted to let you know that I ran that symbol you showed me through the system, but it came up with nothing."

Nikki looked from one man to the other. "Symbol?"

"When Jill stopped answering my calls and texts, I searched her apartment for some indication of where she might have gone. I found this." Terrence pulled his phone from his pocket and called up a photo before passing it to Nikki. "A piece of paper with Carling Lake and some kind of symbol or flower on it."

"I've seen this before." Nikki used two fingers to make the part of the paper with the drawing bigger. "I found a business card on the kitchen floor the day I arrived at Lakewood House with this fleur-de-lis and nothing else on it."

Frown lines burrowed into the sheriff's forehead. "Fleur-de-lis?"

"It's what this is called. It's a symbol that's been used in politics, religion, architecture—you name it—for thousands of years and across cultures. It's fairly common, especially in places with French influences like New Orleans, where it's part of the official city flag."

"Okay, so why was Jill doodling it on this paper, and why has it shown up at Lakewood House?" Terrence said.

"All fine questions." Sheriff Webb stroked his chin. "Do you still have the card?"

"I think so." Nikki turned and jogged toward the house. Terrence and the sheriff followed at only a slightly slower pace.

Inside, she scanned the island counter where she'd

first seen the card, then the rest of the kitchen. Nothing. She closed her eyes for a moment, walking through what she'd done after she'd found the card the previous day. She remembered Pete had been there with her grandfather's boat. She'd taken her bags upstairs, then seen Pete running back toward the house after finding that poor girl's body.

What had she done with the card before all that?

She rewound through her memories. Coming into Lakewood House for the first time. Finding the card on the counter.

"I put it in my pocket." She spun toward the staircase and dashed upstairs.

The slacks she'd worn yesterday were in the middle of the pile of laundry growing in the corner of the room. She found the business card, a little worse for wear, in the pocket and brought it back downstairs. "This is it."

Sheriff Webb reached for it, but Terrence was closer. He took the card from her hand, handling it along its edges. "Not much to it. Just the fleur-de-lis symbol. No name, address, phone number."

He took a photo of it with his phone before holding it out to the sheriff.

"There's probably no point in looking for fingerprints, but I'll give it a shot," Sheriff Webb said, taking the card by the edges himself and sliding it into a plastic baggie he'd taken from his coat pocket. "I'm also going to widen the search beyond the county borders, but the results might take a little while to come in. Especially with the Spring Festival starting up in a few days. I won't have anyone to spare."

Terrence's hands clenched into fists. "This is more important than the festival. Jill could be in real trouble here."

"I understand that, and my department is doing everything it can to locate your sister," the sheriff reiterated through gritted teeth. "But it can't be our only focus, which is why I have a suggestion."

Nikki could read the thoughts passing through Terrence's mind on his face. Exactly where Sheriff Webb could shove his suggestion. "What do you suggest we do, Sheriff?" she interjected before Terrence could say what he was thinking.

The sheriff's gaze swung to her face, his brow rising at her use of the word *we*. "I think you should go talk to Carling Lake's newest resident, James West. He owns the art gallery on Main Street. Shares the building with the *Carling Lake Weekly* newspaper."

"Your suggestion is that I speak to an art dealer?" Terrence grumbled. "How is that going to help me find Jill?"

"James West is not your typical gallery owner," the sheriff said angrily. "Trust me. Go talk to him."

Terrence looked like his temper was about to blow. Nikki placed a hand on his arm and gave a minute shake of her head before turning back to Sheriff Webb. "Thanks for the suggestion. We'll go see him this afternoon."

The sheriff headed for the door, ignoring Terrence's grumbling about wasting time.

Truthfully, she couldn't see how an art dealer could help them, but if the sheriff was suggesting they talk to James West, there had to be a reason. And at this point, they had nothing else to go on and nothing to lose in finding out.

Chapter Eight

The stone-and-brick structure that housed the offices of the *Carling Lake Weekly* had endured. Over the years, the *Weekly* had shared the building with a host of other businesses, but Terrence was pretty sure this was the first art gallery. Carling Lake was getting a taste of the cosmopolitan.

The building sat on an entire Main Street block. He parked in a nearby lot, then he and Nikki rounded the building, passed the pair of large double glass doors of the newspaper and headed toward the more modest entry for the gallery at the other end of the block. A discreet sign announced this was the entry for The West Gallery in elegant gold lettering.

The space inside was a sweeping two-story expanse with support columns dotted throughout the open space and a set of curved stairs in the left rear corner. The lighting was subdued, but with the large picture windows along the front wall and the peaked skylight overhead, there was more than enough natural light flooding the space and accentuating the art lining the walls.

Nearly a dozen pieces hung on each side, with several more displayed on the temporary walls that had been erected in the open space.

From where he stood, Terrence could see that the

artwork had been done in various media—some ink drawings, some watercolors, other oils—but all done with a skill, talent and unique style that showed through in each canvas.

He and Nikki stopped in front of the piece near the entrance. A woman and young child beamed at them from the canvas so vivid and lifelike that had the small plaque next to it not stated it was an ink drawing, he'd have thought it was a photograph. What he didn't need to read to know was that whoever this woman and child were, they meant a great deal to the artist.

"This is…amazing," Nikki said, the awe in her voice palpable.

"Thank you." The Black man descending the circular staircase looked nothing like what Terrence had imagined of an artist. For one, he was large. Over six feet tall and wide with muscle tone that even his very well-cut slacks and tailored collared shirt couldn't disguise. He wore a pleasant enough smile, but his eyes reflected a worldliness and experience—not necessarily all good—that said he was a man not to be underestimated. Terrence didn't need to ask to know that this man had been in the military. Everything about the man screamed order, honor and sacrifice. "My wife and son."

Terrence and Nikki moved toward the man, meeting him roughly in the center of the gallery space.

Terrence extended his hand. "Detective Terrence Sutton. I don't know much about art, but even I can tell you are extremely talented."

The man shook his hand and gave a self-effacing smile. "James West. And thank you. That particular piece is one of my best, though not for sale, of course."

"Nikki King." She extended her hand now. "Your love for your family shines through in it."

"They are my everything." James gave her hand a quick shake before dropping it and turning back to Terrence. "Lance told me you might be stopping by."

Terrence couldn't stop the frown twisting his mouth downward. "Yes, well, I don't know how much he's told you about the reason I'm in Carling Lake. No disrespect, but I'm not sure how an artist can help me find my sister."

Nikki slapped his bicep lightly and gave him an exasperated look.

Yes, he was a bull in a china shop. It was a criticism he'd gotten a lot from his coworkers and several of the higher-ups on the force. And it was probably the reason he hadn't yet been promoted beyond the rank of detective. But it was also one of the reasons he had the best closure rate of all the detectives in the department. It might not look pretty, but he got answers.

James's smile grew. "I think Lance sent you to me because of my other business. Or rather, because of my family business. Why don't we go upstairs to my office? You can fill me in on all the particulars, and I can see if we can help."

He and Nikki followed James to a long narrow office. The side of the room with windows facing Main Street would have rivaled any top CEO's suite. A large executive desk and high back leather chair dominated the space. But that wasn't the most impressive thing about the office. On the other end of the space was a U-shaped table with three computer monitors, a laptop and several other electronics that Terrence wasn't familiar with.

"Whoa! This is quite the setup. Not what I'd expect in an artist's office," Terrence said.

"My studio is on the other side of the floor. It probably looks exactly how you'd imagine." James motioned them toward the comfortable-looking seating area that separated the two different parts of the office. Terrence settled in next to Nikki on one of the beige sofas while James took a seat on the matching sofa opposite them. "This is where I run the business side of the gallery and do a little bit of side work for my family's business, West Security and Investigations."

The name struck a chord. He hadn't immediately made a connection between James West and the elite security and private investigations firm. Lance's suggestion that he speak to the gallery owner made a lot more sense now. "West Investigations. I've heard of you guys."

"It's my brothers' business now, but I still dabble here and there. Mostly where it concerns the safety of my wife and son."

Terrence cocked his head to the side wondering why James West's wife needed the services of a security firm like West Investigations. But since it wasn't his concern, he refrained from asking.

James studied him as if he could read the thoughts rolling through Terrence's mind.

Nikki cleared her throat. "So, you are a private investigator?"

"Not me, no. It's why I dabble. Any work I do is under the supervision of one of my younger brothers. They just love that," James added wryly. "But Carling Lake is my home now and if, as Lance suggested, there's something nefarious going on, I want to know about it." His eyes went to slits. "And stop it."

Terrence had been around enough dangerous men to know one when he saw one, but for now, if James was willing to put the resources of West Investigations behind finding Jill, he was more than willing to accept that help.

He glanced at Nikki. She gave a slight, almost imperceptible nod, letting him know that she was on board.

Terrence slid to the edge of the sofa. "I'm looking for my sister, Jill." He told James about not hearing from Jill for days, going to her apartment and finding the scrap of paper with Carling Lake written on it and the fleur-de-lis doodle. Nikki picked up the story then, explaining the body of the woman they'd found on her property, the threatening message written on her garage doors and the business card with the same fleur-de-lis symbol.

With each passing minute, James's expression grew darker, the worry in his eyes deepening.

When he and Nikki finished speaking, the threesome sat in silence for several moments, turning over the sequence of events, trying to make the pieces fit into a logical, sensible scene.

James finally spoke. "There's definitely something unusual going on. Let's call my brothers." He stood. "See what they think our first steps should be."

And just like that, their ragtag investigation got some very real firepower behind it.

A minute later James initiated a video call on the largest of the three computer screens on his desk.

A man's face filled the screen when the call connected. He was younger than James but with enough similarities that no one would doubt that they were brothers. He too appeared to be sitting in an office surrounded by computer monitors similar to James's.

"Hey, bro." The younger man's smile reflected genuine happiness. "I've been trying to reach you."

"I know. Sorry about not calling back. I've been swamped with this gallery show coming up."

The younger man's smile grew even wider. "Nadia is so excited. Sean and Addy too. I'm sorry we can't get up there earlier to help you set up and all, but we will be there for your show."

James waved his brother off. "No worries. Erika's on the job, and there is nobody better at organizing an event than my wife. That's not why I'm calling though." He shot a glance at Terrence and Nikki and adjusted the computer monitor so they could be seen more fully by the wide lens camera projecting their images at the bottom of the screen. "Ryan, meet Nikki King and Detective Terrence Sutton. They need our help."

James quickly filled his brother in on the particulars of the situation. Just like James moments earlier, Ryan's expression darkened the longer James spoke. "How can we help?" he asked once James was done with his explanation.

"I've filed a missing person report with the DC police since Jill is officially a resident of DC, although she travels so much she's rarely at her apartment. They've gone above and beyond what they would do normally since I'm a fellow cop, but she's an adult and there are no signs of foul play—"

"But their hands are tied," Ryan chimed in.

"Right," Terrence said. "So they can't pull her phone records or try to find her using the GPS."

Ryan typed on the keyboard in front of him. "It's not exactly legal on our end either, but I'll see what I can do."

"Thanks." Terrence rattled off his sister's cell phone number and the name of her carrier.

"I might be able to help with that too, now that you

mention the carrier's name," Nikki said, biting her lower lip as if she wasn't quite sure about the truth of her statement. "I know someone who works there. Their policies about giving out information are pretty strict, but you can talk to him."

All three men looked at her with a question in their eyes. "My boss—my former boss—was on the Communications and Technology subcommittee. I met a lot of corporate bureaucrats and lobbyists in the field."

"I'll take whatever contacts I can get," Ryan said.

Nikki drew her phone from her purse and rattled off the number of her contact for Ryan.

"There's one more thing," Terrence began to say as Nikki put her phone away. "The fleur-de-lis symbol. Its appearance in Carling Lake and in Jill's apartment can't be a coincidence. The sheriff ran it through his system and got no hits. I'm guessing you may be able to do a wider search. Maybe it's a calling card of some sort. If so, it would at least point us in the direction of where to start."

"It could."

Based on Ryan's tone, Terrence could tell he wasn't convinced. "Jill is an investigative reporter. She digs into powerful people's secrets and deceptions. Her last big piece broke up a large opioid ring and took down a handful of county council members in West Virginia who, at the very least, were looking the other way while these drugs ravaged their residents. She has a habit of getting under the skin of the wrong people. Lance is good at his job, but anyone doing something criminal in this town is going to take pains to keep it from him. But someone has to know about it."

"I'll put out feelers, but something like that could take some time," Ryan said.

"I'll also see what I can dig up," James offered. "People might be more willing to talk to a local, not that you two aren't from Carling Lake, but it's been a while since you've lived here according to the town scuttlebutt."

Ryan smirked. "You haven't lived in Carling Lake for a whole year yet. Have you so thoroughly charmed everyone that they already think of you as a hometown boy?"

James beamed at his brother. "What can I say? I'm a charming guy."

A smile played at Nikki's mouth. "We'll take all the help we can get. Thank you."

Ryan focused his attention back on Terrence, all business again. "I'm sure you don't plan to sit around and wait. What's your next step?"

Terrence nodded. "You're right. My gut is telling me Jill can't afford for us to take a wait-and-see posture. It's been a week." He left the rest of what he was thinking unsaid. That it could already be too late. He wouldn't let himself think that way. He couldn't. "I'm sure that whatever Jill was working on brought her here to Carling Lake. I've checked in with my aunt, who hasn't seen her, and Jill's friends, so I'm going to start scouring the rest of the town. Someone has to have seen her. Talked to her. Something. I'll go door-to-door if I have to."

Resolve flooded his body. He'd talk to everyone in this town and search every house if that's what it took.

Nikki placed a hand on his. "Half the town knows you're here looking for Jill, and the other half will know by the end of the day. Anyone who knew anything about Jill's whereabouts and wanted to help would have come to you."

Surprised, he turned to look at Nikki. "What are you saying? You don't think Jill made it to Carling Lake?"

If she didn't believe they'd find Jill, why had she insisted on helping him?

She shook her head. "That's not what I'm saying."

James spoke softly. "I think what Nikki is getting at is that whoever your sister came to see in Carling Lake doesn't want you to know she was here. If you find that person, you'll be a lot closer to finding your sister."

Chapter Nine

"Well, that wasn't at all what I expected," Nikki said as she and Terrence stepped out onto the sidewalk. She hadn't known what to think when Sheriff Webb sent them to an art gallery, but it definitely hadn't been the former sniper/security specialist/artist that was James West.

Terrence donned a faux shocked expression. "What? You mean to tell me the gallery owners in DC don't look like they could bench-press a minivan and have connections to elite private security firms?"

Nikki laughed. "I don't know any gallery owners in DC, but I'm going to go out on a limb and say no." The city was full of culture and art, but her job had left her precious little time to take advantage of any of it.

"Yeah." He let himself smile. "That's probably a good assumption. I have a feeling James West is one of a kind, but I'm glad he's on our side."

They turned toward the parking lot where Terrence had parked the Highlander.

"Where to next?" Nikki asked, walking slightly faster than usual to keep up with his long stride.

"I want to speak to Lakewood House's caretaker, Pete Bonny. Maybe he's noticed something out of the ordinary going on at or around Lakewood House."

"That sounds like a good idea. I need to talk to him about getting Grandpa's boat to the house. Sheriff Webb wouldn't let him dock it the other day because of the crime scene, but now that I've got the all clear, I really would like to take the *Annalise* out on the lake again."

They approached the Highlander. Terrence reached for the passenger door and held it open for her to slide inside.

"We had some good times on that boat. Do you remember the time my uncle and your grandfather took us fishing and we caught that huge bass?"

She shot him an incredulous look. "Um…we? If I recall correctly, *I* was the one who snagged that beauty."

He leaned forward into the space created by the open door. "And if I recall correctly, you would have never gotten it on the boat if I hadn't helped you reel it in." His brown eyes sparkled in amusement.

"I think your memory is faulty. You should have that checked out."

Memories of a time when it had been so easy for them to be in each other's presence—when that was all either of them needed to be happy and content—flooded through her. At the moment, with Terrence standing so close, it was hard to remember how or why it had all gone so wrong. How they'd let it go so wrong. Maybe they could fix it? Get back what they'd lost. His uncle and her grandfather were gone. Maybe she and Terrence could find a way back to each other.

She guessed that some of what she was thinking had been reflected on her face. He had always been able to read her so easily.

The amusement that had been in his eyes moments before was gone, replaced now by unmistakable desire.

She leaned toward him, the urge to be closer, both physically and emotionally, too strong to resist.

Terrence stepped back, the charge in the air dissipating. "We should get going." He shut the door.

She took several deep breaths in an attempt to slow her racing heart and stem the embarrassment of his rejection. He'd felt the frisson of attraction between them, she was sure of it. And his reaction made it clear he had no intention of giving in to it. Fine. She wasn't about to throw herself at any man.

She'd recovered a modicum of dignity by the time he rounded the car and got into the driver's seat. She pulled her phone from her purse while he started the engine and put the Highlander in Drive. "I'm going to give Pete a call and let him know we're coming."

"No problem, but don't mention the plan to question him. Just let him think our visit is all about the boat. I have a tow hitch, so I can haul the *Annalise* back to Lakewood House and help you launch it."

"Okay."

He continued to outline his plan, seemingly unaffected by the intensity of the prior moment. "And maybe you can ask for a glass of water or to use the restroom? Some excuse to get inside the house and poke around?"

She shot a skeptical look across the car. "Pete's kind of curmudgeonly."

"It's worth a try. All he can say is no. I'd do it, but I think he'd be more likely to let you inside."

"You don't really think Pete has anything to do with Jill's disappearance or that girl's death, do you?"

Terrence looked thoughtful. "I don't know. But he had access to Lakewood, which puts him on the suspect list as far as I'm concerned."

She wasn't comfortable invading Pete's privacy, but

if he'd been using her grandfather's home for criminal activity or—God forbid—to commit murder, she'd make sure he paid for it.

"Okay. I'll try."

Terrence shot a smile across the car. "Great. And while you do that, I'll try to find out if he's seen anything suspicious at Lakewood House or anywhere else in Carling Lake lately."

She felt her forehead crease with frown lines. "Like I said, Pete might not take too well to being ambushed with questions."

Terrence frowned but kept his focus on the road as he turned out of the parking lot. "Don't worry. I've dealt with my fair share of curmudgeons."

She made the call. Pete hadn't sounded happy to be getting visitors but said he'd have the boat ready for them when they got there.

The Bonny family had owned several hundred acres of land high up in the Carling Lake Mountains for longer than most current residents could remember. Despite being longtime residents, the Bonny family, or what was left of them, were peripheral members of the community at best. She didn't recall them having ever participated in Carling Lake social events, and they were unlike other residents who made a point of shopping as much as possible in town. She knew from her grandfather's updates that Pete preferred to drive thirty miles west and patronize the big-box stores. The more generous-minded folks in town noted that taking care of Lakewood House and a few of the other seasonal cabins in the area was Pete's only source of income and that maybe he could only afford to buy in bulk. Those with a more begrudging attitude toward the man took umbrage at his failure to shop at local businesses.

Pete Bonny probably wouldn't have been her choice to watch after Lakewood House, but Grandpa Bernie had always felt strongly about supporting everyone in the Carling Lake community, so Nikki wasn't surprised when he'd told her he'd enlisted Pete's help with the family home.

They turned off the highway and onto a narrow back road that wound its way into the densely wooded area. A few miles later, Terrence took a right turn onto an unpaved road, the Highlander's tires kicking up a cloud of dirt that followed them to their destination.

Terrence pulled his car to a stop between Pete's pickup and a large maple tree with No Trespassing and Keep Out signs nailed to its trunk. The trees cast shadows over the dilapidated state of the small prefabricated home that had enough junk strewed around the surrounding yard that the property could have been mistaken for a scrapyard. Amongst the detritus, still on its trailer, was Grandpa Bernie's boat.

Nikki hopped out of the car, wariness flowing through her.

Pete stepped out of the house onto the small front porch as Terrence rounded his car and stopped beside her.

"You okay?" he asked.

She nodded. "Yes. Fine." She didn't know what it was about Pete, but he'd always made her uncomfortable. She'd only been to Pete's property once when she was younger, and she'd been with her grandfather then, who'd always made her feel safe no matter what the situation.

Nikki glanced at Terrence. Grandpa Bernie hadn't been the only person who'd made her feel safe when she was younger.

"Got the boat all ready for ya." Pete's voice broke into her thoughts.

"Great. Thanks so much, Pete. Um…sorry to impose upon you, but could I possibly use your restroom?"

The wrinkles on Pete's face deepened with his frown. "Yeah, I guess so," he answered after a moment.

The interior of the home was grim, sparse and impersonal. A small eat-in kitchen opened onto a living area where a worn and faded gray sofa faced a television set. Pete had formed a makeshift end table out of two milk crates and a piece of cardboard. A dirty bread plate and an empty beer bottle sat on top.

Nikki's eyes roamed the space, looking for any sign of Jill—a scrap of clothing, her phone, anything that might indicate she'd been in the house—but found nothing.

Off to one side was a short hallway. She walked past the kitchen and to the first door. A bathroom with no sign that anyone but Pete had used it in a while.

She headed for the second door in the hall but hesitated. Taking note of what was out in plain view after being allowed inside the house was one thing, but going into his room would most definitely cross a line into snooping. She wasn't as convinced as Terrence that Pete knew anything about Jill's disappearance, the poor girl they'd found or why anyone would want her to leave Lakewood House. But if she was wrong and there was a clue to Jill's whereabouts in this house?

It was enough to have her pushing the door to the room open. The decor was just as sparse in this room as it was in the main living area of the home. A bed and a dresser were the only pieces of furniture. She searched under the bed and in each of the drawers, careful not to disturb anything, and again found nothing.

Terrence might not be happy to hear it, but as far as she could tell, nothing in this house indicated that Jill had ever been inside.

She rejoined Terrence and Pete outside. Terrence had moved his car, backing it up to the trailer so it could be hitched.

"Nothing at all unusual?" Terrence's voice carried across the yard as Nikki approached the men. Terrence crouched on one side of the boat, attaching the safety chains and brake line.

Pete stood on the other side, glaring. "I already told you, I ain't seen nothing funny. I just do the job I was hired to do."

"And I really do appreciate everything you've done," Nikki said, coming to a stop beside Terrence. He looked up at her expectantly.

She gave a little shake of her head to indicate that she hadn't found anything useful inside the house. Terrence donned a frown to match the one on Pete's face.

Pete turned his glare on her. "I guess you won't be needing me anymore since you're moving into the place?"

She hadn't thought about it before now, but he was right. She didn't need him to keep an eye on the house, but she suspected he needed the stipend he'd been getting for caretaking at Lakewood House.

"Well, I don't need a caretaker per se, but Lakewood House is old, and it hasn't been occupied for a while. I'm sure there's a bunch of stuff that I'll need to take care of. Why don't you give me a little bit of time to settle in, and then I'll call you?"

Pete didn't exactly look happy about the offer, but he gave a gruff nod of acceptance.

Terrence straightened. "We're all done here."

"You ain't done till you check the brake lights work and walk around the entire rig, son. I've seen more'n one person lose their boat on the highway 'cause they failed to do a simple walk around."

Terrence's shoulders stiffened at the admonishment. "You're right. It's been a while since I trailered a boat."

Pete jerked his head at Nikki. "Hop in the cab and tap the brakes, will ya?"

She did as requested while Terrence and Pete walked around the boat, their paths crossing at the back of the rig and each ending on the opposite side from where they'd begun.

She hopped out of the car and joined Pete now at the rear driver's side of the Highlander. "Looks good?"

Pete patted the bow of the boat, his face softening. "Looks good."

"You know if you ever want to take her out, just let me know," Nikki said.

Pete gave her a small smile. "I just might."

Terrence joined them. "Look, I know you said you hadn't seen anything odd at Lakewood House, but what about this." He held out his phone. The photo of the business card with the fleur-de-lis was on-screen.

Pete leaned toward the phone, his eyes squinted. For a moment, Nikki thought she saw recognition in his eyes, but a second later, they were back to a flat emptiness. "What is it?"

"It's a business card I found in the kitchen at Lakewood House," Nikki offered. "Have you ever seen it before?"

"Can't say that I have. Kinda funny for a business card. What kinda business is it for?"

"We don't know." Terrence swiped the screen, and the photo of Jill's note came up. "But I found this piece of paper at my sister's apartment—Jill. You might remember her."

Pete shrugged, which Nikki interpreted as a no.

"She's a reporter, and she's gone missing," Terrence said. "I think she came here to Carling Lake, maybe following a story that has something to do with this fleur-de-lis symbol."

"Fleur-de-what?" Confusion clouded Pete's expression, but Nikki couldn't tell if it was genuine or faked.

"Fleur-de-lis. That's what it's called," Terrence said, frustration tingeing his words. "Look again. Are you sure you've never seen a card like this or the symbol before?"

Pete didn't glance down at the phone's screen this time. "I told ya. I ain't ever seen nothing like this floor-de-liz before." He took several steps toward the house. "You got your boat hitched up. It's time for y'all to get on now. I got things to do."

Pete stalked back to the house. The front door closed with a slam.

She and Terrence got into the Highlander.

"He recognized the fleur-de-lis," Terrence said.

"I thought so, but it's hard to tell for sure given Pete's sour attitude."

He put his car in Drive and began easing it forward slowly. The Highlander could handle the rough dirt path without a problem, but the boat and trailer might not. "I think he recognized it," he confirmed without taking his eyes off the road in front of him. "Whether he knows what it means, if anything, is another question."

She studied his face, finding determination and something else she couldn't quite name there. "You didn't push him on it though?"

"No, I didn't."

His voice had fallen to just above a whisper. The expression she hadn't been able to name before came to her then. He looked haunted.

"Why not?"

He remained silent for so long she assumed he wasn't going to answer.

"There was a missing eight-year-old boy a couple of years ago. I was the lead on the case. We got lucky, got a description of the kidnapper early and found a guy who matched it living in the boy's neighborhood. He had a record of domestic abuse against his wife and child. An arrest for assault against a prior girlfriend that had gone nowhere when she refused to testify. Another for lewd behavior. My gut told me he was our guy. I questioned him for hours, but this guy knew the system. I didn't have enough to hold him, so we let him go. We assigned a man to watch him, but wires got crossed somewhere. By the time we figured it out, he was running. He didn't get far. Patrol pulled him over before he got out of state. The boy was in the trunk, but it was too late."

A heaviness fell over the interior of the car, weighing on Nikki's chest. She reached across the space between them and put a hand on his arm. "I am so sorry."

"Maybe if I hadn't pushed. What did you say earlier? I lacked diplomacy? Maybe if I had been more diplomatic, taken a softer approach—"

"This guy sounds like he was a psychopath. Nothing you did or didn't do could have stopped him from doing what he did. He's the one responsible—the only one responsible—for that child's death." She squeezed his arm.

Terrence gave his head a shake as if he were freeing himself from the horror of his memories. "Yeah, well, I'm not taking any chances with Jill's life. We need more information. If Pete recognized the fleur-de-lis, someone else in Carling Lake would too. We just have to find them."

Chapter Ten

Terrence had no idea why he'd told Nikki about Brian Malroy's kidnapping case. It had been nearly three years now, and he still thought about the eight-year-old every single day. His captain had forced him to see the department psychologist when it had become obvious that his way of dealing with the loss of the little boy was to fall into a bottle of rum every night. His shrink said it was normal to feel guilty but that he needed to forgive himself if he wanted to be of use to all the other people who needed his help. That had been enough to get him to lay off the booze, but forgiving himself? He hadn't yet figured out how to do that.

He shot a glance across the car at Nikki. They'd been riding in silence for the past several minutes. He wondered if his confession had brought back memories of all the times they'd commiserated with each other as teenagers. Worrying over failed tests, tough teachers and college admissions woes seemed outright ludicrous in the face of the adult problems they both faced now.

And yet, despite the odds, here they were some fifteen years later, still leaning on each other for support. Not to mention the moment they'd shared after leaving The West Gallery. He had no idea where that had come from. No, that wasn't true. He'd felt it the moment he'd laid eyes on Nikki at Lakewood House. The attraction between them was still there and as strong as ever. Maybe stronger. But that didn't mean they had to give in to it. None of the things that had pushed them apart fourteen years ago had changed. They'd only called a temporary truce in order to help Jill. Nothing could change the fact that Bernie King had stolen his aunt and uncle's home right out from under them—and that he'd never forgive the man for having done so.

But should the granddaughter be held responsible for the sins of her grandfather? The thought pressed down on him.

He pushed it away as he turned onto the Lakewood House property. He had bigger fish to fry right now, like figuring out the next step in the search for Jill.

Nikki jumped out of the car and guided him as he turned it around carefully in the driveway and backed the boat up slowly toward the lake. Just as he was beginning to worry that he was getting too close to the water, she called out for him to stop.

He put the car in Park, set the emergency brake and got out.

She'd already released the straps and was reaching for the boat crank.

"I can do that," he said.

"It's not a problem. I've done it thousands of times when Grandpa and I used to take the boat out on the water."

"You sure? That was a long time ago."

She shot him a look. "You do a lot of boating in Trenton?"

He didn't try to stop the smile that spread across his face. "Touché."

Her return smile made his heart stutter.

The boat slid into the water, making a small wave.

"If you want to help," Nikki said while keeping hold of the line at the front of the bow, "you can release the hook for me."

He did and wound it back up while she tethered the boat. "I guess DC hasn't knocked all of Carling Lake out of you."

"Ha ha." She hip-checked him and, for a moment, it felt like they were fifteen again.

The smile on his face fell away as something over Nikki's shoulder caught his attention.

Smoke. Coming from a window in Lakewood House.

His sudden change in demeanor registered with Nikki. "What?" She turned and followed his line of sight. "Oh no!"

She took off in a sprint toward the house.

"Nikki, wait!"

She didn't slow down. "We've got to try to stop it," she called over her shoulder.

He cursed under his breath and picked up his pace, running after her.

Carling Lake's fire department was all volunteer. It would take time to get everyone mobilized. Time Lakewood House might not have. Whatever their differences, they both loved Lakewood House. He was no more willing to let the home burn down than she was.

He caught up to Nikki just as she was about to push through the back door. "Wait a minute." He grabbed her wrist, pulling her to a stop.

If looks could kill, he'd be on his way six feet under.

"You have to test the handle and make sure it's not hot. And we need to stand off to the side when we open the door. The oxygen from the outside could fuel the fire if we're not careful."

"Okay, let's do it then."

His phone was still in the Highlander. "Do you have your phone?"

"No, it's in my purse in the car."

"You should get it and call 911." And it would get her out of the line of fire, literally.

He knew the answer before she spoke though. "No way. I know where the fire extinguisher is. You need my help."

He thought about pointing out that she could just tell him where to find it but arguing with her now only wasted time.

He placed his hand on the doorknob. It was cool. That was a good sign. The smoke seemed to be coming from a window on the side of the house near the front. The space Bernie King had used as an office if memory served. If the fire was contained to that room, it was probably okay to enter.

He gestured for Nikki to stand back from the door, then opened it.

A haze of smoke filled the home. He pulled his jacket collar to cover as much of his face as he could and stepped into the home.

Nikki did the same, veering off toward the kitchen. "Grandpa kept a fire extinguisher under the sink."

Terrence turned toward the front of the house. He was right that the origin of the fire appeared to be in the small office. The smoke was thicker there, although thankfully, he didn't see any flames. He walked toward the room carefully.

The door to the office was open. It took a moment for his eyes to adjust, but when they did, he could see that the fire seemed to have been started in a wastepaper basket and was now climbing the nearby curtains.

He shrugged out of his jacket and beat at the flames shooting out of the trash can. The fire caught the hem of his coat and raced upward, catching his sleeve. He dropped the jacket and stepped back, pain searing his skin.

Nikki rushed into the room, pushing him aside. "Move."

She pulled the pin, pointed the extinguisher at the fire and squeezed the handle, sending a stream of white foam shooting out at the base of the inferno. She worked her way up the window until all the flames were snuffed out.

They stumbled from the office, still thick with smoke, and out onto the porch. The burn radiated pain throughout his arm.

Nikki's eyes filled with concern. "Oh my God, you're hurt." She crossed the porch to him.

"I'm okay," he said through gritted teeth.

"No, you're not. That burn looks serious. Stay here." She hopped off the porch and ran around the side of the house. She returned less than a minute later, her cell phone to her ear.

"Yes, Lakewood House. The fire is out, but we need an ambulance."

"It's not that bad."

The look she shot at him was quelling. "And the sheriff. I don't think this was an accident."

He heard the dispatcher's promise that help was on the way before Nikki ended the call.

"I don't need an ambulance." The second after he'd spoken, a lightning bolt of pain zinged up his arm, making him cringe and putting a lie to the statement.

"Yeah, I can see that." Soot marked Nikki's face, and they both smelled like smoke. Their clothing was probably a lost cause. "I'm pretty sure you'll need to go to the hospital to have this cleaned and bandaged. Don't argue." She cut off his protest before he got started. "You need to be in one piece if you're going to help Jill."

The sound of sirens cut off any further protests.

His evening had just taken a noticeably downward turn. Nikki's statement to the 911 dispatcher played through his head as he watched the ambulance shriek toward them, followed closely by the sheriff's SUV.

"You told the dispatcher that you didn't think the fire was accidental."

She pulled her gaze from the emergency vehicles to look at him. "You do?"

"No, I agree with you. This wasn't an accident." He'd known that the moment he'd seen the flames shooting out of the trash can. He doubted very much Nikki would have thrown a lit match or another incendiary device away carelessly. But he almost wished he could believe she had. Because if this wasn't an accident… "Somebody wants you out of Lakewood House, and it looks like they are willing to go to the extreme to make it happen."

And that scared him more than he wanted to admit.

Chapter Eleven

The EMTs insisted on transporting Terrence to the hospital. As a silent nod to just how much the burns to his arm must have hurt, he hadn't put up a fight. Nikki followed in her car, arriving just behind the ambulance to a relatively quiet clinic. There was only one other patient in the waiting room, and he appeared to be struggling with a spring flu.

Terrence was whisked into an exam room immediately. Nikki followed, shooting a look that turned the nurse who attempted to stop her's march past the admissions desk to stone.

As the doctor examined Terrence, she worked to chase away the tremor of fear that hadn't stopped running through her since she'd noticed Terrence's injury. She'd felt a level of terror she'd never felt before and hoped to never feel again when she'd run into the office and spotted fire crawling up the sleeve of Terrence's shirt.

She drew in a shuddering breath and pushed the images away. He was going to be fine.

As if reading her thoughts, the doctor spoke. "You were very lucky. These burns aren't nearly as bad as they could have been. I'm going to clean the wound and dress it with a bandage. You'll have to repeat the process at home while it heals, but I'll leave you with a sheet of instructions. I'll also write you a script for a pain reliever."

"I'll be fine with a couple of aspirin," Terrence replied.

The doctor, an older man who had gone mostly gray and had eyes that looked as if they'd seen it all, raised his eyes from the burn on Terrence's arm. "Burns can be tricky injuries, Mr. Sutton. Follow my instructions and yours should heal without any permanent damage." The tone of the doctor's voice made apparent what he'd left unsaid—don't follow my instructions at your own risk.

Terrence nodded. "Don't worry, doc. I'll do what you tell me. I have no desire to see you again. No offense."

The doctor smiled. "None taken. I wish more of my patients would follow your lead." He tucked the tablet he'd been tapping notes into under his arm. "Give me a couple of minutes to get everything I'll need together, and I'll be right back to take care of that wound for you."

The doctor started for the door, stopped to greet Sheriff Webb and stood aside to let him into the room before disappearing into the hall.

"How are you doing?" the sheriff asked, coming to stand next to the bed. From the swing of his gaze from her to Terrence, then back to her, she knew the question was directed at both of them. Her emotions swirled and twisted inside of her to the point that she wasn't sure how to answer his question, so she let Terrence answer first.

"The doc says the burns aren't that bad. He's going to bandage them up, and I should be out of here any minute."

"That's good to hear." The sheriff's eyes swung to Nikki's face.

"I'm fine. Not a scratch on me." She tried for a reassuring smile, but from the look on Sheriff Webb's face, she was pretty sure she'd failed.

"You should get checked out while you're here," he said.

"That's not a bad idea," Terrence seconded. His concern for her was also written all over his face.

She doubted there was anything the doctor could do for her, and she no longer had medical insurance to cover a hospital stay anyway. Physically, she wasn't hurt, but mentally and emotionally, she felt like she was treading on thin ice.

She shrugged in answer.

After a moment, the sheriff moved the conversation in a different direction. "The fire marshal has declared the fire arson, but I doubt that comes as any surprise."

"The flames leaping from the trash can kind of gave it away," Nikki deadpanned.

Sheriff Webb held up his hands in a don't-shoot-the-messenger motion. "We got a print off the wastepaper basket. Maybe we'll get a hit. The good news is, thanks to your quick action, the damage was confined to the office. You'll need to have some work done in there, but the remainder of the house is sound. As much as it pains me to say this, there's no structural reason you can't stay there. That said, I think you should consider finding another place to stay until we get to the bottom of whatever is going on."

"Not happening." If anything, the attack on the house had increased her resolve to stay. She needed to be there if Lakewood House was attacked again to protect it and, hopefully, to get a glimpse of whoever was targeting her home.

Sheriff Webb sighed heavily and shook his head, a

look of resignation on his face. "The medical examiner also finished the autopsy and got back toxicology results. It looks like our Jane Doe was a heroin user, but it had no hand in her death, according to the medical examiner. Doc sticks by the strangulation call and puts her age at nineteen or thereabouts. I've got an officer searching the missing person reports in the area again with a revised age range."

"That poor girl," Nikki said, thinking about the tragic loss of such a young life. A look at the anger on Terrence's face told her he was thinking the same thing.

"We met James West and spoke with his brother Ryan. They've agreed to see if they can find out more about the fleur-de-lis symbol and see if it connects to anyone or anything in or around Carling Lake."

Sheriff Webb grinned. "I'm glad you listened to me."

Terrence pushed himself up straighter in the hospital bed. "You could have told us why you wanted us to speak to him. I've heard of West Investigations, but the name didn't click for me when you sent us his way."

"They are good people to have on your side."

"True." Terrence nodded. "And hopefully they turn up something for us."

"We also showed Pete the fleur-de-lis and asked him if he knew anything about it." Terrence shot her a look she ignored. "We thought he recognized it, but he pretended that he didn't."

"I'm not surprised," the sheriff said. "Pete's picture is right there next to *ornery* in the dictionary. The man can be downright mean when he gets a few drinks in him, although nowhere near as nasty a piece of work as his nephew."

Nikki searched her memories. "I don't remember Pete having a nephew."

"Dana," Terrence offered the name. "He was a few years younger than us. In Jill's class, or maybe a year behind her. Pete's older brother's boy, I think."

"His parents named him Dana Bonny?"

"Yeah, he got a lot of ribbing for it too until the other kids realized, as Lance said, he was a nasty piece of work. The teasing stopped right fast after that. He was basically your typical bully. Picked on the younger, weaker kids. Lied. Cheated. Stole. Got away with a lot of it because his father was an even nastier piece of work, and no one wanted to confront him about his son."

Nikki tried again to pull up an image of Dana in her mind and failed. "I don't remember him at all."

"You're the better for it. I caught Dana hassling Jill once. Put the fear of God in him. Like most bullies, he's a coward at heart, but I wouldn't turn my back on him." Terrence shifted his attention to the sheriff. "Do you know where he is now?"

Sheriff Webb gave him a questioning look. "No. When he's not in my jail cell, I never know exactly what Dana is up to, but I can guess it's probably not good. Why?"

"I want to talk to him. Maybe he'll tell us what Pete wouldn't."

Sheriff Webb shook his head slowly. "You said it yourself. Dana Bonny is a man you want to steer clear of."

Terrence's eyes narrowed. "I wasn't afraid of Dana when we were kids, and I'm not afraid of him now. And if he knows something that could help me find Jill, he's going to tell me."

A commotion in the hall grabbed all their attention, forestalling any response from the sheriff.

Charity Jackson burst into the room, a mini tornado

of a woman, the scent of White Diamonds by Elizabeth Taylor swirling in her wake. "Oh my goodness. Terrence, are you okay? I came as soon as I heard you'd been hurt. What did the doctor say? You better have a darn good reason for not calling me, boy." She threw her arms around him even as she shot questions at him faster than he could have possibly responded.

"I'm fine, Aunt Charity. It's just a minor burn. I didn't call because I didn't want to worry you."

She took a step back and slapped him lightly on the arm that wasn't injured. "I worried because you didn't call." She slapped his arm again.

"Maybe you shouldn't assault the patient," Sheriff Webb interjected.

Nikki remembered it being difficult to raise Charity's ire, but once she was worked up, it was best to stand back and let her temper run its course. This was apparently something the sheriff hadn't yet learned.

Charity shot him a look over her shoulder that had him taking two steps back. "And why didn't you call me? Isn't it standard police procedure to notify the next of kin?"

"I'm not dead, Aunt Charity," Terrence said, exasperated. "Here, sit." He motioned toward the rolling stool in the corner where Nikki stood out of the way of Charity's wrath.

She grabbed the stool and rolled it over to where Charity waited next to Terrence's bed.

"Thank you, sweetheart," she said. "It's good to see you even if it is under trying circumstances."

"It's good to see you too, Charity," Nikki responded.

Charity turned back to her nephew, wringing her hands. "First Jill, now you. Have you heard from your sister at all since we last spoke?"

"Not yet."

"I know you don't want me to worry, but I am beginning to. Jill has always been unpredictable, but she's never out of touch this long. And it's obvious you think something is wrong." The hand wringing sped up.

"Aunt Charity, now don't you worry. I'm looking for Jill and so is the sheriff." Terrence nodded toward him. "I'm sure we'll find her, and she'll tell us we are all overprotective and overreacted." He paused. "I hope you didn't drive in the state you're in."

"I drove her."

All eyes in the room turned toward the door. A young, slim Black woman stood in the threshold. Nikki mentally ran through the girls she'd known in Carling Lake who this could have been but came up short.

"Yes, Talia came by the house to drop off your bags from the hotel and offered her well wishes for your speedy recovery. Imagine my surprise."

"Sorry." Talia looked as if she'd rather be anywhere in the world except in this exam room. "Miss Melinda packed up your things from your room and sent me to deliver them to your aunt's house since we'd heard about the fire and you getting injured and all. She says she's sorry she can't extend your stay, but the hotel is booked."

Nikki assumed that the Miss Melinda Talia referred to was Melinda Hanes, and that Talia worked for her.

"Nothing to be sorry for," Terrence said, smiling over his aunt's head at the woman hovering in the doorway. "I'm sorry you had to go out of your way."

"That was very nice of you," Sheriff Webb said. Talia blushed.

"I'll just leave your things." She dropped the bag near the closet by the door and backed out of the room.

"Thank you," Terrence called after the fleeing woman.

The sheriff headed for the door. "It's dark outside, and I'm just going to make sure she gets to her car safely."

Charity tsked. "If that man doesn't ask her out soon, I just might do it for him. Those two have been circling each other for months now."

Terrence shook his head. "Lance is a grown man. I'm sure he can get his own dates."

Aunt Charity rolled her eyes. "Yeah, he seems to be just about as good at getting and keeping a woman by his side as you are." Her gaze landed pointedly on Nikki, sending heat crawling up the back of her neck.

"Aunt Charity," Terrence snapped, then stopped, taking in a deep breath and letting it out slowly. "Listen, could I stay with you? As you heard, the hotel could only give me the one night."

"I'm sorry, Terrence." Charity shook her head, but she didn't look sorry. "You know how small my place is. It's why you and Jill stay at the hotel or the B and B when you come to visit."

"Yeah, of course, you're right," Terrence said, frustration tingeing his words. "Don't worry about it. I'll figure something out."

"You should stay at Lakewood House." Nikki thought she saw a hint of a smile on Charity's face.

"I'm not sure that's a good idea." Terrence shot a questioning glance at Nikki.

Sure, she and Terrence had only called a temporary truce, which was delicate at best. But if she was brutally honest with herself, the message on the garage and the fire had scared her. She didn't want to let whoever was behind these attacks run her out of Lakewood House, but she wasn't totally comfortable staying there alone anymore. Letting Terrence have the guest room could solve both their problems. Of course, given the feelings he'd awakened in her, it might also create a host of new issues, but it was something she was prepared to risk at this point.

"I think it's a good idea," she said before she could change her mind.

Charity and Terrence looked at her with surprise written across their faces. "I've got the spare room at Lakewood House, and if the hotel is full, the B and Bs in town are probably full as well. There isn't another option."

"See, it's perfect." Charity smiled.

"I appreciate the offer, but…" Terrence stared at her for a long moment.

"Oh, come on, Terrence. It isn't safe for Nikki to stay at Lakewood House alone, not with a vandal and arsonist on the loose. This way, you can make sure Nikki is safe."

"Well, I can take care of myself," Nikki interjected before Charity turned her into a damsel in distress, "but we do have to figure out a game plan for finding and talking to Dana. This way we can strategize, and I can make sure you get some rest."

"Are you talking about Dana Bonny?" Charity asked.

Terrence turned back to his aunt. "Yes. You know him?"

"Everybody knows him. There's no mystery about where he'll be. He inherited his father's place just outside of town, but at least three to four nights a week, you can find him saddled up to the bar at Whistler's over in Stunnersville."

Stunnersville was about fifteen miles west of Carling Lake. Whistler's was a dive bar sometimes populated by the bikers in the area and always a place that attracted people looking for trouble. Which were apparently Dana's kind of people.

If Charity knew that Dana frequented Whistler's, it was a sure bet that the sheriff knew as well. Maybe he'd thought it best not to encourage them to seek Dana out, especially not at Whistler's, but his keeping this information from them rankled Nikki. From the look on Terrence's face, he'd come to the same conclusion and felt the same way.

"I'll head over there as soon as the doctor lets me out of this place." Terrence swung his legs so they hung over the side of the bed.

"Not today, you won't." Charity pressed her palm firmly against Terrence's chest, holding him down.

"Aunt Charity, I know you're worried about me, but I'm fine. I promise. We don't know what's going on with Jill, and I don't want to lose any more time."

"I am worried about you, but even if I wasn't, Dana won't be at Whistler's tonight, for sure. Whistler's is closed on Mondays."

Terrence let out a curse.

Charity shot him the same look she'd given to them as teens when one of them cursed in front of her.

"Sorry," he said, looking very much like a chastened teenager under his aunt's glare.

"Tonight you'll rest at Lakewood House. If Jill hasn't turned up by tomorrow, you can track down Dana and ask your questions." Charity patted Terrence's thigh as if everything had been settled.

"Really, I'm fine with you staying in the guest room." It cut against Nikki's grain to admit weakness, but after the events of the day, she didn't want to stay at Lakewood House alone. "I'd really appreciate it if you did."

He gave Nikki a searching look. "Okay. Thank you for the offer."

"Of course."

She let out a breath of relief. It was settled. Tomorrow night, they'd face whatever potential dangers lurked at Whistler's.

And tonight at Lakewood House, they'd face a wholly different kind of threat—sleeping under the same roof.

Chapter Twelve

The white cotton bandage covering most of his forearm struck Terrence as a bit much, but he kept his thoughts to himself. Anything to get out of this hospital.

"Okay. I'm all done here. I'll be back in a moment with your prescription and discharge orders." The doctor pulled the blue nitrile gloves off his hands and tossed them in the trash before striding from the room.

"Are you really okay? Maybe the doctor should keep you here overnight for observation?" Aunt Charity pressed the back of her hand to his forehead, just like she'd done when he was sick as a little boy.

"I'm fine, Aunt Charity." He reached for his aunt's hand and squeezed. "The burns aren't that bad, and the doctor said there should be no permanent damage."

Nikki patted his aunt's shoulder as a ringtone sounded. "I'll make sure he rests tonight." She fished her phone out of her purse and frowned at its screen. "I'm sorry, I have to take this." She walked from the room.

"Promise me you'll take it easy," Aunt Charity said, pulling Terrence's attention from Nikki as she retreated to the hallway to take her call.

He hesitated. His gut was telling him that time was

of the essence if he was going to find Jill unharmed. "I'll take it easy tonight."

She pulled a sour face. "I guess I'll have to be content with that. I'm sure Nikki will take good care of you."

"I wish you hadn't pushed her into offering to let me stay at Lakewood House. I'm not sure that it's a good idea."

"Of course it's a good idea. I think you're reading the situation all wrong, dear. That girl is terrified. Having someone else in the house will be a comfort."

Was his aunt right? There was a time when he'd known Nikki's moods better than she had. But no more.

"Aunt Charity, you have to understand. Nikki and I have agreed to work together to find Jill, but I wouldn't call us friends."

"Of course you are friends. You've been friends since you were both knee-high to a grasshopper. And a little more than friends for a while there if this old memory serves."

"Whatever we were fifteen years ago, we certainly aren't now." A frown twisted his lips. "Too much has happened. Too much has been lost."

His aunt sighed heavily, her shoulders slumping. "I've let this go on for far too long, but you and your uncle are so much alike. Stubborn and pigheaded."

"Aunt Charity, what are you talking about?" He felt the frown lines deepen around his mouth.

"I'm talking about the anger Jarrod and you have toward Bernie King and, by extension, Nikki."

"Uncle Jarrod had a right to be angry. So do I. Bernard King stole our family home."

"No. No, he didn't."

"What are you saying, Aunt Charity? I was there. Bernie King was supposed to be your and Uncle Jarrod's friend, but when he saw the opportunity to grab Lakewood House out from under you, he took it."

"You were there, but you don't know everything."

"I don't understand."

"Bernie bought Lakewood House from your uncle and me because we asked him to."

His aunt's words stunned him. "You what?"

"Your uncle loved that house and the surrounding land. His grandfather built it and his mother inherited it from him. It was Jarrod's dream to pass it down to you and Jill when the time came. But the upkeep on the house and the land was so costly. It was always a struggle. Several times we considered selling part of the land off, but Jarrod was adamantly opposed, and somehow we always found a way. Until your uncle lost his job at the auto manufacturing plant."

"I remember. That's when Uncle Jarrod started working for King's Trucking."

"Bernie gave your uncle a job when we were at our lowest, but it wasn't enough. Your uncle had been a manager at the auto plant, and trucking just didn't pay the same. And we'd taken a second mortgage out on the house and property a few years earlier to cover Jarrod's mother's hospice care. The bank was threatening to foreclose. We *asked* Bernie to purchase the house so at least it wouldn't fall into the hands of developers. He'd always admired the property, and your uncle and I figured, at least if Lakewood House couldn't be ours, it would go to someone who'd love it and was a friend."

As his aunt spoke, he mentally pictured a puzzle scrambling and reforming to create a totally different picture than what it had looked like moments before. "So Bernie bought Lakewood House to help you?"

A lock of hair fell from the messy bun Aunt Charity had thrown atop her head as she nodded. "He did, and paid enough for it that we paid off the second mortgage and had a bit of money to get you off to college."

"I really don't understand then. Why was Uncle Jarrod so angry that Bernie bought Lakewood House?"

His aunt patted his hand gingerly. "Your uncle was a proud, proud man. He took losing the family home hard, even though he'd agreed it was best to sell it. Harder than either of us could have anticipated. I think it just became easier for him to blame Bernie than it was to blame himself."

"Well, Bernie could have still let us live at Lakewood House. Pay rent."

Aunt Charity snort laughed. "Paying rent for the house he'd owned a year earlier. Your uncle never would have agreed to it. No. We did the right thing by selling, and I think your uncle knew that even if he didn't want to face it."

Terrence felt like he was coming out of a fog. "Why didn't Bernie ever say anything? Tell the world that Uncle Jarrod's version of things wasn't what actually happened."

"Because he was Jarrod's friend, even if Jarrod couldn't see that."

"So, all this time I've been angry at Bernie King? And at Nikki for defending her grandfather's actions—"

Aunt Charity looked at him with sad eyes. "Neither of them deserved it."

"But why didn't Nikki ever tell me the truth?"

"My guess? I don't think she knew the truth. For the same reason, Bernie didn't tell anyone else what had really happened. He didn't want it to get out and cause Jarrod any more pain."

It felt like a chunk of lead had taken root in his stomach. All this time, Nikki had been right. "Nikki always defended her grandfather."

"Maybe that was enough for him."

"I owe Nikki an apology." He hoped she accepted it, although he wouldn't blame her if she didn't.

"You do and so do I. And I owe you an apology. I should have stopped your uncle from infecting you with his anger and told you the truth about all this a long time ago. Maybe then you and Nikki would have remained friends or even—"

"None of this is your fault, Aunt Charity."

"No, I bear some responsibility. Your uncle, well, he was who he was, but I should have intervened with you. I thought the whole thing would eventually blow over, but it didn't. And then Jarrod left us so suddenly. It just got harder and harder to tell you the truth. You and Nikki had both left Carling Lake and were getting on with your lives. It just seemed best to leave well enough alone. But now with the two of you back in Carling Lake, I can see that I was wrong not to have said something sooner."

Part of him was angry with his aunt, but another part understood she'd done what she thought was best at the time. His uncle Jarrod had been so angry, and he'd adopted that anger as his own. That was no one's fault but his.

"It's okay, Aunt Charity. I understand." He leaned over and wrapped his arms around his aunt. Over her shoulder, he could see Nikki pacing outside the door of the exam room, still on her call, her facial expression serious.

How would she react when he told her the truth about the sale of Lakewood House? After years of accusing her grandfather of stealing his family's home, would she be able to find it in her heart to forgive him?

"You know. Despite everything, I've always held out hope that Lakewood House might one day be back in the family."

His gaze moved back to his aunt. "I wouldn't hold my breath if I were you. Nikki loves that place and frankly, I can't see Jill or I ever being able to afford to buy it back."

She made a half turn, looking from him to Nikki and back. "We shall see. It doesn't hurt for an old lady to hold out hope."

"I TALKED TO my friend working on Lyon's campaign," Carolyn said.

Nikki skirted out of the way of a nurse as she waited for the punch line from Carolyn. "And?"

"He didn't say no."

She let out a sigh of disappointment. "Great." She turned to start the loop she'd been pacing again. Charity stepped out of Terrence's room, followed by Terrence carrying his overnight bag. Charity kissed his cheek and headed down the hall in the opposite direction from the exit.

"We knew it might not be easy to find you a new job with Manco bad-mouthing you behind the scenes. My friend said to send him your résumé. That's good, because no one has credentials like you. Since Lyon is running as an outsider with the knowledge and courage to fight corruption and the big donors, I decided not to shy away from the fact that you stood up to Manco and did the right thing at great cost to your career. I think he liked that, so don't give up hope."

"Right, and if this job doesn't work out, I can always run for mayor," Nikki said, bitterness tingeing her voice.

"Come again?"

She exhaled, rubbing at the headache growing behind her left temple. "Nothing. It's just something a friend here said to me. That the election for mayor is coming up and I should run."

There was a beat of silence on the other side of the phone line. "Maybe you should."

"Come on, Carolyn. Get serious."

"What? Why not? That's the goal, right? Elected office."

It was no secret to her colleagues that she had plans to run for elected office at some point, but she'd envisioned taking that step years from now. "Yes, of course, in, like, ten, fifteen years."

"Why wait? The opportunity is presenting itself now. And plenty of big-name politicians have started their careers as small-town mayors. Michael Bloomberg. Pete Buttigieg. Grover Cleveland."

Nikki chuckled. "Grover Cleveland?"

"Hey, he was the mayor of my hometown of Buffalo before winning the New York governor's office and then the presidency, so don't knock old Grover."

She turned to see Terrence headed for her. "Yes, here I go. Literally. I have to get off the phone. Hey, Carolyn—thank you. I can't tell you how much I appreciate all your help."

"Don't sweat it. We have to watch each other's backs. I'm emailing you my friend's contact info. Don't forget to send him your résumé ASAP."

"Everything okay?" Terrence said as she ended the call.

"Great." The last thing she wanted to do right now

was get into a conversation about the sad state of her career. She scanned the hall beyond his shoulder. "Where's Charity? I figured we'd drop her off at her place before heading to Lakewood House."

"Sy Martin from Aunt Charity's church came in to the ER a little while ago. The doctor thinks she's just got a touch of indigestion, but Aunt Charity wants to stay with her until they get the all clear. She'll catch a ride home from Sy when she's released."

"Okay then. We should get going." Nikki reached out and took his duffel bag from his hand and hooked it over her shoulder, ignoring the irritated look Terrence shot her as she did. "It's been an awful day, and I still have to see the damage at the house."

"Lance gave the okay for you to occupy Lakewood House still, so it probably looks worse than it is," he said as they headed for the exit.

"I hope you're right."

The automatic doors at the front of the clinic slid open on their approach, and they stepped out into the cool night air.

The clinic shared a single-level commercial building with a dollar store and a bakery, both of which had long since closed.

She led Terrence to the second row of the parking lot, where she'd haphazardly parked her car earlier. Thankfully, there were more than enough empty spaces so that her atrocious parking shouldn't have been too much of an inconvenience to anyone.

"I don't have the money for remodeling or redecorating, and at this point, even the insurance deductible might be out of reach." She used her key fob to unlock the car and opened the passenger door, holding it for Terrence to slip into the seat.

He smiled wryly, sliding his bag off her shoulder. "You know I'm fine. Perfectly capable of opening my own door and carrying my own bag."

"I promised your aunt I'd make sure you rest, and I keep my promises, so get in the car."

"Yes, ma'am." He gave a mock salute. She didn't want to encourage him, but she couldn't hold back the smile that turned up the corners of her mouth. His levity was a welcome respite from the stresses of the day at the moment.

She closed the door and hustled around to the driver's side of the Camry.

Twenty minutes later, they arrived at Lakewood House.

Nikki hit the light switch on the wall next to the door, illuminating the space. The door to the office was closed. The only sign of the fire visible from outside the room was soot marks around the door and frame.

"It looks different than I remember it." His eyes roamed over the living room, dining area and kitchen.

"Grandpa Bernie had most of the walls taken down on this floor and had the kitchen updated."

"It's different but nice."

"Well, you already know where everything is." She sat his duffel bag down by the stairs, then headed for the kitchen and opened the door to the fridge. "I still haven't been to the market, but I have the fixings for a bacon, lettuce and tomato sandwich if you're hungry."

He leaned against the newel post at the bottom of the staircase. Exhaustion appeared to be catching up with him.

"I'm not hungry. As much as I hate to admit it, what I'd like most right now is to climb into bed and sleep for eight hours straight."

Nikki closed the fridge and crossed back to the stairs. She squinted her eyes at him when he scooped his bag from the floor before she could get to it. "Come on. I'll show you to the guest room." It also happened to be his old bedroom when his family had lived at Lakewood House, which led to another feeling of déjà vu. She wondered if he felt it too, but if he did, he showed no signs.

She led him up the stairs and to the bedroom on the other side of the Jack-and-Jill bathroom.

"Let me just put some clean linens on the bed."

"You don't have to put yourself out. I'm okay on the couch if that's easier."

But she had already stepped into the bathroom and grabbed clean sheets from the linen closet.

She worked quickly, changing the bed linens while Terrence moved to the window overlooking the lake.

"This used to be my room," Terrence said quietly.

Nikki looked up from smoothing the sheets. "I know. I always slept in the small room across the hall when I came to visit because I always thought of this one as yours, even after Grandpa Bernie moved in."

"You remember when we used to climb out of this window and sit on the roof of the back porch in the summer?"

The memory brought a smile to her face. "Of course. We used to think we were so cool. Hanging out on the roof." They'd had their first kiss on that roof.

After making the bed, she came to stand next to him at the window. The night sky was clear enough to see all the way across the lake to Carling Island.

"I remember sneaking out of the house and rowing over to the island."

"Yeah, I do too." That was something a lot of the teenagers used to do. To make out and…more. It was thinking about the *more* part with Terrence that was making her body tingle at the moment.

She wasn't sure which of them moved first, but she was very aware of the moment his lips covered hers. Red-hot desire coursed through her, banishing all rational thought beyond one. She wanted Terrence. She opened to him, deepening the kiss and steering them closer to completely losing control.

It felt as if someone had doused her with ice-cold water when Terrence broke off the kiss and stepped back abruptly. "I have to tell you something."

"What is it?" Her heart beat wildly, both from the heat of the kiss they'd just shared and from the feeling of foreboding that had sprung into her chest.

Terrence took another step back, putting more distance between them. "While we were at the clinic earlier, Aunt Charity told me that she and Uncle Jarrod *asked* your grandfather to buy Lakewood House from them."

Nikki shook her head, trying to clear it. "I don't understand. Your uncle loved this place."

"He did, but apparently, the upkeep of the house got to be too much for them and the bank was going to foreclose. My aunt and uncle didn't want the property falling into the hands of a developer so they asked your grandfather to buy it."

"But your uncle was so angry at Grandpa Bernie?"

"I know. Apparently, Uncle Jarrod took the loss of Lakewood House harder than he thought he would. Losing the family home, everything he and his parents and grandparents had worked for, it was too much of a slap to his pride. At least, that's what Aunt Charity thinks. He needed someone to blame, and your grandfather became that someone."

"Why didn't your aunt say something? Why didn't Grandpa Bernie?" She felt as if she were riding an emotional seesaw. A moment ago, she'd been high on the need to be with Terrence. But now? She wasn't sure what she was feeling beyond shock and confusion. Nothing he was saying made sense, except that it did. Wasn't he just saying what she'd always believed to be true? That her grandfather was the man she'd known him to be all along.

"Aunt Charity says she thinks your grandfather saw that my uncle was hurting and embarrassed, and he didn't want to add to that. She thought my uncle Jarrod would eventually come to his senses, but there wasn't time for him to come around."

Jarrod Jackson had passed away from a heart attack six months after selling Lakewood House. It was an immense loss for Terrence's family, as well as the town. It had also been the death knell for any chance of reviving her and Terrence's relationship. Terrence had wanted nothing to do with the man whose actions he felt had contributed to his uncle's death. Or his granddaughter.

She stared at Terrence, trying to take in everything he'd said. His words felt like a kick to the gut. For years, he'd believed the worst about her grandfather and destroyed their friendship and budding romance as a result. Even when she'd called and texted, tried to reason with him, he'd ignored her, going so far as to block her on his phone and on his social media.

"Look, I know I've been an idiot and I'm so sorry."

"Sorry just isn't going to cut it." She fought back angry tears. "You blamed my grandfather for years for something he didn't do. You wouldn't even listen to me when I tried to tell you that Grandpa Bernie would never steal Lakewood House from your aunt and uncle."

"I know. I was stupid. So stupid. But Uncle Jarrod was so angry, and if I'm honest, I was pretty angry about having to leave the first place that felt like a real home."

She felt sick. Her guts twisted with regret and remorse. Grandpa Bernie had died knowing that Terrence, someone he'd once cared for like a son, hated him for something he hadn't done. She didn't know if she could ever forgive Terrence for that.

"I don't know what to say. I need time to think." She started for the door.

"I can't say enough how sorry I am for what I did to us. For hurting you. I just hope you can find it in yourself to forgive me."

Nikki paused at the door and looked at him over her shoulder. "Honestly, I'm not sure if I can."

Chapter Thirteen

The sun had just begun to top the mountains when Nikki rose for the day. Sleep had been elusive, so it hadn't been difficult to rise before Terrence stirred. She'd done as she'd promised Carolyn and submitted her résumé for the position with the Lyon campaign after leaving Terrence's room the night before. Either Carolyn's friend owed her a big favor or the campaign was desperate, because less than five hours later, she already had an email asking to set up a time for a phone interview. It might not go anywhere, but the glimmer of hope was enough for now.

With everything that had happened since she'd returned to Carling Lake, she hadn't found the time for grocery shopping. She headed for the diner. Despite the early hour, there were already patrons seated in the diner.

The frown on Rosie's face as Nikki approached made it clear that Rosie had neither forgotten nor forgiven the scene that Nikki and Terrence made the last time they were at the diner.

"I'm sorry," Nikki said, sliding onto a stool at the counter. "My behavior was way out of line."

Rosie's frown stayed fixed on her face. "You two put on quite the show."

Guilt shot through her. "I know and I am truly sorry, and it will never happen again. I promise."

Rosie sighed. "I remember a time when the two of you were inseparable. Best friends."

"That was a long time ago." And somehow the last several hours had made it feel even longer.

"Not that long. Don't you think it's time to let this feud between your grandpa and Jarrod go?"

It was sage advice and for a while, she'd thought that's exactly where she and Terrence were headed. But now? She wasn't sure if that would ever be in the cards. She wasn't about to discuss it with Rosie, at least not until she worked out what she wanted to do about Terrence's revelation.

"Can I get two of the breakfast specials?" It wasn't a subtle change of subject.

Rosie sighed again. "Coming up." She called the order through the cutout in the wall separating the dining area from the kitchen before focusing on Nikki again. "You must be awfully hungry this morning."

"It's not just for me." Nikki cleared her throat awkwardly. "I'm sure you heard about the fire at Lakewood House."

Rosie nodded. "Yes, of course. I'm so glad you're okay, and I heard there wasn't too much damage."

"No, there wasn't, thankfully. But Terrence was hurt."

Alarm flashed in Rosie's eyes.

"Not badly. Minor burns, but he needed a place to stay, and he had been hurt helping me, so he stayed in the guest room at Lakewood House last night."

Rosie quirked an eyebrow, a small smile starting. "Is that so?"

"Rosie, don't go thinking—"

The bell over the diner door tinkled, drawing Rosie's attention before Nikki could set the record straight.

Melinda swept into the diner. "Good morning, Rosie. Could I get a coffee, please? Nikki!" Melinda leaned forward and placed an air kiss on each of Nikki's cheeks. "I didn't get to chat with you the last time you were here at the diner. It's so lovely to have you back in town."

"Thanks, Melinda. It's nice to see you again as well. How are you?"

"I'm great." Melinda flipped her hair, which flowed in gentle waves today, over her shoulder. "You probably heard I'm thinking about throwing my hat into the ring and running for mayor."

Nikki smiled tightly. "I have heard. Good luck."

"Oh, well, thank you so much, but I don't think I'll be needing luck. I hope I can count on your vote, if you're planning on staying in town, that is."

"I don't really know what my plan is at—"

Melinda cut her off, dropping her voice to a whisper. "I heard about your little professional setback. I'm sure you'll find something. You know, if you're up for it, my campaign will be looking for volunteers soon." Her words dripped with condescension.

"Actually, I'm thinking about running for mayor myself." The words popped out of her mouth, surprising her and Melinda from the stunned look on the other woman's face.

"You're running for mayor?"

The rational part of her brain screamed no, but pride wouldn't let her back down in front of Melinda. "Maybe. I'm considering it."

"You can't possibly believe you'd win."

"Of course she could win," Rosie said, sliding a to-go

cup at Melinda. "She grew up here, and she has political experience."

Melinda frowned. "She hasn't lived here for what? A decade? Come on, Nikki. You don't know the town, the community, like I do."

"I think I know the community very well. And I care about the people in it."

Melinda pulled a few dollar bills from her purse and set them on the counter. "That's all well and good, but do you even meet the qualifications? You have to be a resident of Carling Lake."

"I've moved back into Lakewood House, so that shouldn't be a problem if I choose to run."

Melinda grabbed her coffee, her face scrunched as if she'd smelled something foul. "Well, may the best woman win." She didn't wait for a response before flouncing out of the diner.

"Looks like you may have just made an enemy there, Madam Mayor." Rosie laughed her way into the kitchen.

TERRENCE WASN'T SURE when he'd fallen asleep after having spent most of the night trying to work out if there had been a better way to tell Nikki the truth about their families' feud. Not kissing her before dropping the bomb that he'd blown up their friendship and beginning relationship based on a lie would have probably been a good start. But an inexplicably primal urge had come over him at that moment. He hadn't been able to stop himself. And based on the hurt in her eyes when she'd left his room the night before, that may just be the last time he ever did. His gut clenched at the thought.

He showered and dressed before descending the stairs and padding into the kitchen. Nikki stood in front of the coffee maker, spooning sugar into a steaming coffee mug.

"Good morning."

Her shoulders stiffened. "Morning." She scooped one more spoonful of sugar into the mug and stirred vigorously. "I haven't had a chance to go grocery shopping, so I went by the diner and picked up breakfast."

She pointed to the cardboard carton in the middle of the island, then sat at the other side in front of her own breakfast. It didn't go unnoticed that she'd put as much distance as possible between the two of them while staying in the kitchen.

"Thanks." He grabbed a mug from an overhead cabinet and poured himself a cup, ignoring the sugar and cream Nikki had set out. She'd gotten him pancakes and home fries with a side of bacon and toast. A more decadent and fattening breakfast than the coffee and bagel he was used to, but his stomach was already growling, so he dug in.

A labored silence fell between them as she ardently avoided looking at or speaking to him.

He sighed. "Thanks for letting me stay the night, but I think it's best if I find another place."

Nikki set her coffee cup down on the counter so hard he was amazed it didn't shatter. "So you're going to bail on me again."

"I'm not bailing on you. You're obviously upset with me, and with good reason. I just wanted to give you space."

"I didn't ask for space. Not now. Not then."

"What do you want?"

"I want you to keep your part of our agreement. We work to find Jill and to figure out who is targeting Lakewood House together."

He studied her. Her body language screamed that she was still angry with him, which was bound to be problematic. But the desire to be near her, to prove to her that he really was sorry, was overriding his concerns. That and he wasn't at all sure she was safe on her own. "Okay."

"Okay."

They both returned to sipping their coffee silently for a moment.

"After you left my room last night, I had trouble falling asleep, and I remembered that there were a couple of structures out on Carling Island. Do you remember them?"

Lines formed between her eyebrows. "I think so. A house and a smaller shed or something."

"Yeah, well, I think we should go out there and take a look. Jill could have gone to the island for some reason, and if she hurt herself out there, she'd have no way of calling for help. I do remember there was no cell phone reception on the island."

He could tell before she spoke that he hadn't convinced her. "Last I heard, even the local teens don't go out to that island anymore. And Jill would have needed to borrow or rent a boat to get out there. Even if she drove over by herself, whoever she got the boat from would have raised a red flag when she didn't bring it back."

"Maybe," he answered, annoyed by her pushing back on his plan. Everything she was saying made sense, but he wasn't about to leave any stone unturned when it came to finding his sister. "But maybe she rowed out. Aunt Charity still had the old canoe in her garage the last time I visited."

"We should ask her if it's still there."

"I will, but either way, I want to check out the island. We can't go to Whistler's to track down Dana until later tonight, and I haven't gotten anything from the guys at West Investigations yet, so boots-on-the-ground investigation is all we have left."

"It's a good thing we got the boat from Pete yesterday. We can use it to get to the island."

"Just give me twenty minutes, and I'll be ready to go."

Twenty minutes later, he'd laced up his sturdiest boots and holstered his gun at his hip. He didn't expect trouble on a deserted island, but with the strange goings-on recently, he wanted to be ready for it if it appeared.

He found Nikki on the dock behind Lakewood House. She was already on the boat and had donned a life jacket. "There's a vest for you." She pointed to the bright orange preserver resting against a seat. "I've already done the safety checks, so we're ready to go when you are."

He fastened himself into the vest while Nikki started the boat's engine. She slowly navigated them away from the dock and out onto Carling Lake.

The journey from Lakewood House to Carling Island took nearly a half hour when traveling by canoe, which was how they'd made their way to the island as teens. The *Annalise* got them there in a fraction of the time.

Nikki brought the boat close to the island's dock. It was older than either of them, but surprisingly, it looked to still be in pretty good shape.

He tied the boat off and glanced over at Nikki when she came to stand next to him as he studied the island for the first time in nearly fifteen years. It was still early enough in the morning for a light fog. Carling Island was a big rock in the middle of the lake with a small pebble-strewn shoreline. At the top of a hill at the center of the island stood a time-and storm-ravaged old house. The house had stood unoccupied at least since he and Nikki were kids. Back then, the rumor had been that the house was owned by a New York City banker who'd loved the place almost as much as he'd loved the mistress who he kept hidden away in it. When his wife had found out about the affair and the house, she'd made sure she'd gotten it in the divorce and had let it rot away out of spite. To this day, he had no idea if the story was true or not, but whoever owned the home certainly didn't care about it much.

"There's no other boat docked here," Nikki said. "Not even a canoe."

He'd noticed. Even though he'd known finding Jill on the island was a long shot, he couldn't help but hope that the answer to her disappearance was something as simple as she'd made her way out here and gotten stuck somehow.

"There's another dock on the other side. Maybe her boat is there." It was possible but unlikely that Jill would have had to circle the island to dock there, which wouldn't have made much sense.

From the look on Nikki's face, she was thinking the same thing, but she said nothing.

"Well, we're here now, so let's have a look." He hopped onto the dock, then extended a hand to help Nikki off the boat. She ignored it, making her way without his assistance.

He bit back a curse and fell in step beside her. The breeze followed them up the hill to the house.

All the windows had been covered with plywood

boarding, and they found a new-looking lock on the front door.

"Huh," Nikki said, eyeing the lock. "It seems like someone is keeping up with the property after all."

He inspected the plywood covering the nearest window. It had been through a few storms, but no way had it been there more than a few months. "Yeah, I've been wondering about that since we pulled up to the dock. Someone has clearly been taking care of it, although it could still use some work. It's serviceable though, which would be unlikely if no one had been coming to the island for years."

Lines creased Nikki's forehead. "That is a little weird."

Terrence stepped off the small front porch and headed around the side of the house.

"Where are you going?" Nikki asked, following.

"I want to see if there's another way in."

"Don't you think you might be getting a little bit obsessed with this? I mean, it's pretty obvious Jill isn't here."

He stopped and turned. "You can go wait on the boat. Actually, that might be a good idea. I don't like the feel of this place."

Nikki's expression darkened. "I'm not going to wait for you on the boat. And that feeling you have might just be your internal alarm warning you away from breaking and entering."

"Look, I'm going into this house. You can do whatever you want." He turned and stormed toward the back of the house.

This alliance of theirs was breaking down fast. He knew he was mostly to blame for that, but regardless of responsibility, if they were going to continue working together, they'd have to hash out the past and come to some understanding going forward. He'd wait until they got back to Lakewood House before bringing it up, but they'd have to deal with this. Soon.

The dock at the back of the house was in better shape than the one at the front, increasing the number of concerns and questions he had regarding exactly what was happening on this island. Unfortunately, the rear dock was also noticeably empty of any vessels.

A new lock had also been installed on the rear door of the house. However, whoever had installed the plywood over the windows hadn't done as good of a job back here. One of the pieces of wood had come loose from a rear window and now lay forlorn in the yard near the house. Luckily, the window it had come from was on the first floor. He grabbed the window sash and, with a bit of effort, got it open far enough that he and Nikki could both slide through.

The interior was dark and empty except for animal droppings and copious amounts of trash that appeared to span several decades.

Once they were both inside, he eased the window closed, then jumped as something scurried over his foot.

"We're disturbing the rats," Nikki said, turning on the flashlight on her phone.

He did the same and led the way through the first floor, spying nothing of interest.

"We could split up. One of us searches upstairs while the other searches downstairs. It will make things go faster," he said.

Nikki looked at him as if he'd grown two heads. "Um, I don't even want to be in this creepy house. I'm definitely not going exploring on my own."

"We stick together then."

They headed toward the front of the house. The large two-story entryway opened onto a circular staircase leading to the second floor. He climbed the stairs, taking each step gingerly. Four doors branched off the hallway. They checked each of the rooms, finding more trash covered in a thick layer of dirt and grime.

They crept back down the stairs. Off the foyer was a single door. He opened it and found that it led to a set of stairs to the basement. They headed down with their cell phones, providing only a small circle of light around their immediate area. The basement was so dark it was difficult to make out anything. They could have been walking into a trap or a completely empty space. It was impossible to know.

The staircase ended at a dirt floor. He held the phone out, moving it in a slow circular motion, illuminating the space in front of him.

The basement was utterly empty. Even the decades-old detritus and animal droppings they'd found upstairs were absent from the space, which immediately put him on alert. Someone had cleaned up down here, that much was obvious. But why clean the basement and not the main floor?

"What is that?" Nikki took several steps forward, shining the light from her phone toward one corner of the room.

He grabbed her arm and pulled her back. "Hang on. Let me go first." He wasn't sure what he was looking at, but he wasn't going to take any chances. He held the phone out in one hand and hovered his other hand at the gun on his hip.

He stepped forward slowly, conscious that Nikki was at his back, letting his brain process what he was seeing.

Handcuffs. No, that wasn't accurate. Shackles. Four

metal cuffs attached to chains attached to metal loops bolted to the concrete wall in what he estimated to be six-feet intervals.

"Dear God," Nikki whispered from behind him. "It's like a prison."

More like a dungeon. His mind flashed onto a picture of the young girl they'd found at Lakewood House. He had a strong suspicion who had been held here. They needed to get out of this house now.

He turned to face Nikki and relay that urgent message, but before he could get it out, a sharp creak sounded above them, followed by footsteps.

Someone else was in the house.

They were trapped.

Chapter Fourteen

Nikki's heart pounded frantically. Terrence raised a finger to his lips and shut off the light on his phone. She did the same with her own phone. There was no way out of the house without going back upstairs, and she doubted very much whoever was up there now was friendly. She glanced at the shackles on the ground and shuddered. Definitely not friendly.

"We have to get out of here," Terrence whispered. "Follow me, and on my signal, run for the boat as fast as you can. I'll be right behind you." He paused before speaking again. "But if I'm not, don't wait for me. Go. Get to Lance."

She shook her head. "I'm not leaving you. We came to this island together and we're leaving together."

She held his gaze until he finally gave a short nod.

He took her hand, and they started up the stairs slowly, making their footsteps as soft and quiet as possible. They stopped at the top of the stairs. The door was still firmly closed, but the voices on the other side of it were loud enough to hear most of what was being said.

"What are we going to do?" The voice was deep and male.

A different male, one with a higher voice, responded, "…moved the goods…okay for now but…it's only temporary." Nikki hadn't caught the entire response, but the part she had made it clear whatever the men were doing in this house, it wasn't on the right side of legal.

It did appear as if she and Terrence had gotten lucky on one front, however. The voices sounded as if they were coming from the rear of the house, where the men must have docked their boat. That would explain why they hadn't seen the *Annalise* and why they appeared to be oblivious to the presence of anyone else on the island with them—at least so far. That could change in an instant if either of the men came downstairs or went outside to the front of the house.

"What do we do about our other problem?"

"Why are you asking me so many questions? I don't know. I'll figure it out. I just need some time, okay." Footsteps pounded on the old wood floors.

Terrence brought his mouth to her ear. "I think they're at the back of the house. As quickly but as quietly as you can, head for the front door and the boat."

She nodded her agreement and held her breath as Terrence pushed the basement door open. She followed him into the small hall, then eased by him toward the front door. There was no sign of the men. They'd either stopped talking or moved into a room where they couldn't be heard from the hall.

Nikki did as Terrence had instructed and moved as quickly and quietly to the front door as she could. The door squeaked when she pulled it open. She didn't stop to see if the men had heard. As soon as her foot hit the front porch, she began to run.

The hill hadn't seemed steep or treacherous when she and Terrence had climbed up to the house, but running at top speed had her concerned about falling and possibly breaking a bone. Or her neck. Fear of falling kept her from glancing over her shoulder to see if Terrence was behind her as he'd promised. She said a quick prayer he was and kept moving.

She made it to the dock, adrenaline giving her an extra boost as she leaped onto the boat. She went straight for the rope tied to the dock.

Her heart went into her throat when the boat rocked and she felt the presence of another person on board. She was relieved to see Terrence scrambling for the steering wheel.

The relief was short-lived.

The men from the house had spotted them. They ran down the hill toward the dock, guns raised.

The noise from the engine starting almost covered the sound of gunshots. Almost. Bullets pelted the water on either side of the boat as Terrence pulled away from the dock at a speed much faster than was safe.

"Get down," he yelled, ducking as much as he could himself.

She did as he said and felt the boat lurch forward as he pushed the *Annalise* to go even faster.

The men were running on the dock, still firing. But the boat was too far away now for the bullets from their handguns to have a chance.

Nikki raised her head above the side of the boat to get a look at their pursuers. Both were white men who appeared to be in their late twenties or early thirties. One was stocky, and though it was hard to gauge how tall he was, given the distance between them now, he was taller than the second man by a couple of inches. Both were dressed in work boots, jeans and dark windbreakers. The stocky man had dark hair while the shorter guy had a lighter, though not quite blond, mane. The boat careened around a corner, and she lost sight of them.

She rose and went to Terrence's side.

"I'm not taking us back to Lakewood House," he said without looking at her. "Just in case."

Her heart was still beating a mile a minute, and the grave expression on Terrence's face did nothing to slow it. "Just in case of what?"

His expression grew darker, and he didn't respond.

Her thoughts whirled with possibilities until one pushed its way to the forefront of her mind. "Oh, God. Do you think they are headed for the house?"

"The public access is closer to the sheriff's station. I'll dock us there. Lance needs to know about this as soon as possible, and I won't be able to get cell service this far out on the water."

"You didn't answer my question."

He shot her a glance but remained quiet for the rest of the short ride to the dock.

At the dock, she tied up the boat. Terrence had his phone out and was calling the sheriff before they'd stepped off the boat.

Nikki's phone vibrated as they headed for the sheriff's office. Ryan West had sent an email with the information he'd promised and copied Sheriff Webb and Terrence.

Minutes later, they were in a small conference room with the sheriff sitting across from them, taking notes as they recounted their ordeal. He'd already sent two deputies out to Carling Island with a promise to follow up as soon as he got the details from Nikki and Terrence.

"Shackles?" Sheriff Webb's brows went up to his hairline.

"Bolted to the wall. Four of them side by side." Nikki shuddered at the memory. "It was like some medieval prison."

"Not *like* a prison. It *was* a prison for someone—multiple someones," Terrence said gravely.

The sheriff tapped his pen against his notepad. "You have a theory?"

"Unfortunately, I do."

Dread twisted into a knot in Nikki's stomach. Instinctively, she knew whatever Terrence's theory was, she wasn't going to like it. Though she supposed a basement full of shackles was never going to lead to anything good.

"I think the men who shot at us are part of a human trafficking ring. The dead woman we found was probably one of their victims," Terrence said.

"Human trafficking in Carling Lake?" The disbelief in Sheriff Webb's voice was palpable.

Terrence frowned. "No one thinks it could happen in their town, but trafficking is far more widespread than people know or want to admit."

"I know all that but…" the sheriff started.

"Listen, those shackles were in that house for a reason. And you can't deny the extensive abuse that woman we found suffered. Carling Lake has easy access to the interstate, and if those guys have been hiding women on the island, who would know?"

Nikki could see Sheriff Webb gearing up to defend his hometown, and while she understood the sentiment, she'd been raised in Carling Lake, and she still thought of it as her home. Terrence had made good points, but there were holes in his logic.

She held up her hand. "Terrence's theory has some merit, but I don't see how anyone could transport people back and forth to the island without someone noticing. I mean, on any given day, there are fishermen, day cruises and any number of other people out on the lake."

"Carling Lake might just be a pass through on the way to wherever the final destination is," Terrence said. "One of many, probably. That's most likely, actually. It's a tourist town, so locals will be used to seeing unfamiliar faces. Traffickers generally have several different routes mapped out for moving their victims around the country. Even out of the country. They switch up their routes to better avoid detection. These guys might only bring their victims through Carling Lake once a month or once every couple of months. And if they are working under the cover of night, it's more than possible no one has noticed. Or someone has noticed but didn't know what they were seeing or didn't think anything of it."

Nikki sat beside Terrence at the table, but she turned to face him head-on now. "How does Lakewood House figure into your theory?" Because she knew it did somehow. The vandalism. The fire. Finding the woman's body on the property. His refusal to take them back to Lakewood House after those guys shot at them.

Terrence looked her in the eye. "If you're a bad guy and you need access to the private lake, what better place than an empty house with a dock?"

Nikki swallowed hard. Somewhere inside, she knew that he'd hit the nail on the head, but she wasn't ready to accept it. "You're saying you think human traffickers have been using Lakewood House to smuggle women?"

Terrence nodded.

Nikki lurched forward, putting her head between her legs in an attempt to stop the bile rising in her throat.

Sheriff Webb pushed to his feet and went to the small fridge in the corner of his office. "Take it easy. This is only a theory."

Terrence rubbed her back in small circles. "Breathe.

That's it. Look, even if I'm right, there's nothing you could have done to stop this. You aren't responsible."

She accepted the cold bottle of water from the sheriff without lifting her head. "How can I not be responsible? I own Lakewood House. I should have known what was going on there. I should have installed a security system, video cameras, an alarm, something."

Terrence stopped rubbing her back. "You hired Pete Bonny to be the caretaker."

She sensed more than saw the look that passed between the two men. She straightened. "You think Pete has something to do with human…this?" She couldn't bring herself to say the words in relation to the man she knew. Pete was a difficult person, but preying on vulnerable women? He'd have to be a monster.

Sheriff Webb's jaw twitched. "I'm definitely going to have a talk with him. If he's not involved, he might have seen something."

Terrence stood. "Maybe I should go—"

The sheriff held out a hand. "Absolutely not." Terrence shot him a death glare. "You know how these investigations go. There is a protocol. You have no jurisdiction here."

Terrence glanced at Sheriff Webb. "I think Jill stumbled on this human trafficking ring, and she came up here to investigate. If Pete or somebody else involved realized she knew about what they were doing and grabbed her…" Emotion filled Terrence's voice.

Nikki took his hand in her own. "We don't know that's what happened."

He looked at her. "When those guys were talking back at the house, they said they'd 'moved the goods.' I think they were talking about moving their victims to another place where they'd be less likely to be found.

One also asked what they should do about 'their other problem.' I think they were talking about Jill. What else could 'the other problem' be?"

The sheriff put a hand on Terrence's shoulder. "A lot of things. Don't let your imagination run away with you, man. It won't help. Work with what you know. Good, solid investigative work is what's going to help us find your sister."

"Sheriff Webb is right. West Investigations sent us what they found on the fleur-de-lis." She'd recalled seeing the email while Terrence spoke to the sheriff after they'd docked the boat. "Let's comb through that and see if we can find any connections that will help us find Jill while the sheriff pursues this."

She could tell he wasn't happy about it, but Terrence finally nodded. "Okay."

Some of the tension in Sheriff Webb's shoulders eased. "I'll have a deputy accompany you back to Lakewood House. Those guys are probably on their way out of town as we speak, but I'm not taking any chances. My deputies have taken the department boat out to Carling Island. Nikki, would you mind if I borrowed your boat?"

"Of course not."

The sheriff looked between Nikki and Terrence. "This situation just got infinitely more serious. I think both of you may be in more danger than you realize. My advice? Get as far away from Carling Lake as you can."

Chapter Fifteen

Terrence had no intention of taking Lance's advice, and although he did wish Nikki would, he knew it would be a waste of time to broach the topic with her. Lance had Deputy Bridges drive them back to Lakewood House with instructions that the deputy should stay and keep watch over the house until Lance returned with Nikki's boat.

They rode in silence until Deputy Bridges said, "So, Nikki, I heard you're running for mayor."

Terrence's eyebrows rose. "You are? You've been back for what, a day? Two?"

Nikki frowned. "I know this town as well as anyone. I grew up here, and unlike you, I came home regularly."

"I didn't say you didn't. I'm just surprised you'd want to take on such a big responsibility so soon after moving back."

"I didn't say I was running for mayor, just that I was considering it, and I only said that much because I let Melinda Hanes get under my skin."

"Ah, well, you're not alone in that. That woman could rub the pope the wrong way," Deputy Bridges said with a wry smile.

"I think you'd make a great mayor," Terrence said. And he did. She'd always cared about people. And she had more integrity than any person he'd ever met.

Nikki shot him a look from the other side of the car. "Two seconds ago, you sounded mortified by the idea."

"I was surprised, but the more I think about it, the better it sounds. You love this town. You love politics, obviously, and you're a great leader."

She studied him like she wasn't quite sure what to make of his compliment for a moment. "Well, then thank you. But like I said, I don't know if I'm really running. I've got a line on a job back in DC, and if that pans out, it makes a lot more sense than running for mayor."

"I'm sure you'll make the right decision for you," Terrence said as Bridges turned the cruiser onto Lakewood House's driveway.

The deputy remained idling in the driveway when Terrence and Nikki got out of the car and went into the house.

Terrence pulled out his phone as he headed up the stairs to his room.

"What are you doing now?" Nikki asked.

He turned back halfway up the stairs. "I need to call Jill's editor. If Jill was onto a trafficking ring here in Carling Lake, he would know. I talked to him when I couldn't get a hold of Jill, but he blew me off. Told me not to worry, Jill would turn up, and he wouldn't tell me anything about what she was working on."

"And you think you can get him to tell you now?"

Terrence's eyes lit with fire. "Oh, I know he will."

Colby Marquez's gravelly voice came over the line after the second ring. "Marquez."

"Mr. Marquez, this is Terrence Sutton. Jill Sutton's brother."

"Oh, Mr. Sutton. How are you? Has Jill been in touch?"

"She has not, and I'm more concerned than ever."

"Well, as I told you before, I can't share anything about what your sister was working on."

"Law enforcement talks. What do you think your sources on the DC force would think about an editor who's unwilling to help an officer find his missing sister?"

"You're blackmailing me?"

"No. But I will if that's what it takes to find my sister. When I'm done, no cop in the tristate area will talk to your reporters. Is that what you want?"

"Come on, Jill is a professional. She can handle herself."

"I have reason to believe Jill learned of a human trafficking ring operating in our hometown of Carling Lake. I can't prove it yet, but I think she came here and either asked someone the wrong question or saw something she shouldn't have. Now she's disappeared. If anything happens to her because you didn't tell me everything you know, losing sources will be the least of your troubles. I'll make sure of it."

"Hang on." Marquez's voice rose.

"No, you hang on. There's no way Jill would have chased a story this big without talking to you about it first."

A loud sigh came from the other side of the line. "Okay, okay. Jill did bring me a story about a possible human trafficking ring. But her sources were spurious at best. A woman contacted her saying that her sister, who'd run away several years earlier, had been in touch asking for help. The woman wouldn't give her name or any details at all, but she said that she'd been able to track the call through her cell phone provider as having come from Carling Lake."

"Did the woman say anything else?"

"Not that Jill mentioned."

"Nothing about a fleur-de-lis?"

"A fleur...no. I told you everything that Jill told me. And I told her it wasn't enough to warrant pursuing, considering her other assignments."

"Is there anything else at all you can tell me that might help me find Jill?"

"No, nothing. Do you... Do you really think she is onto a human trafficking ring?"

Terrence ignored the question. "Is there anyone else Jill would have spoken to about this?"

"You know Jill. She keeps her cards close to her vest. She barely tells me anything." Marquez paused. "So you really think Jill is in trouble?"

"I really do." Terrence let out a breath. "Call me if you or anyone at the paper hears from her, okay?"

He ended the call and glanced out the window, looking onto the front yard at Lakewood House. The sheriff's department cruiser was still parked in the driveway. The call to Jill's editor had all but confirmed his suspicions about why Jill had come to Carling Lake. And it had sent the fear he felt for his sister into the stratosphere.

Despite the persuasiveness of Lance and Nikki's argument for why he should let Lance handle the investigation, he couldn't help but feel he should also be out on the island, looking for any clues that might lead them to Jill's whereabouts. Or better yet, tracking down Pete Bonny. He was sure now that Pete had recognized the fleur-de-lis and was kicking himself for not pressing the issue with the man. Lance had promised to send a deputy to question Pete, but whether he had already done so and what had come of it, Terrence didn't yet know. There was no point in calling Lance either. He said he'd bring the *Annalise* back to Lakewood House when he finished his investigation, and there was no cell service on the island.

He'd have to wait, not his strong suit in the best of circumstances, and this certainly wasn't the best of circumstances.

Terrence retrieved his laptop and headed back downstairs as Nikki emerged from the fire-ravaged office with a .22 and an ankle holster in her hand.

"You sure it's safe to be in there?" he asked.

"Safe enough." She placed the gun next to her laptop on the coffee table in front of the couch, then sat, lifting her leg and strapping on the ankle holster.

"I thought you didn't like guns." He sat down next to her.

"I don't. But we're talking about potential human traffickers here who have already shot at us." She snapped the gun into the holster and covered it with the cuff of her pant leg. "So, how should we do this? Split up the information West sent us?" She pulled her laptop onto her lap.

"That's probably the fastest way. There are only a few files. Why don't you take the last three attachments, and I'll work through the first three? Then we can summarize them for each other or point out anything we think the other should read for themselves."

"Sounds like a plan."

The first of the three files he was supposed to read was a Word document. A report that looked to have been prepared by West that combined a variety of source information about a criminal enterprise being run out of the southwest states. What had once been a loose partnership between various gangs with territory along the border in Texas, New Mexico and Arizona had in recent years gotten more organized. Based on the information he was reading, these guys were a nasty bunch of creeps known to be involved in drugs, gunrunning, identity theft and smuggling people over the border for exorbitant sums. Just the kind of people who wouldn't think twice about branching out into human trafficking. The truly interesting part, though, was that members of the gang each had a tattoo of a symbol that resembled a fleur-de-lis, the same fleur-de-lis that Nikki had found on the business card at Lakewood.

Ding ding ding! They had a winner. These had to be the guys they were looking for.

"I think I've got something." He shifted closer to Nikki on the sofa. The scent of her lilac perfume tickled his nose, reminding him of their kiss the previous night. He shook off the memory and forced himself to focus. "This report is about a gang out of the southwest that uses the fleur-de-lis symbol to self-identify."

Nikki's eyes scanned his screen. "Not a very scary symbol for guys involved in all this." She pointed to the computer.

"No, but if you're trying to fly under the radar, it's less suspicious than a skull and crossbones. Most importantly, if they are already involved in smuggling desperate people across the border, they have the means and opportunity to make the leap into trafficking."

Nikki looked away from the screen and out the window. "You know, as much as I don't want to believe something so vile could be taking place in Carling Lake, it seems more and more likely that you're right about what's been going on here."

"I don't want to believe it either, but—"

The rest of his sentence was cut off by the sound of an approaching car outside.

He went to the window and immediately recognized the lawyer's car from yesterday.

"That lawyer, Chester, is back."

"Why is it some people can't take no for an answer?"

"Do you want me to deal with him?" He opened the door.

Nikki grabbed his wrist, stopping him. "No, I got this."

She moved past him and out onto the porch. He followed her outside.

The deputy was already approaching the car.

"It's okay, Deputy. I know this man." Nikki walked from the porch toward the car.

Terrence wouldn't have gone that far. They didn't know anything about Chester, but he planned to remedy that as soon as possible. He'd all but forgotten about the lawyer's offer to buy Lakewood House, but now he couldn't help but wonder whether the offer on Lakewood House wasn't a coincidence.

"Ms. King," Chester said, eyeing the deputy as he retreated back to his cruiser. "I was hoping you had time to give some thought to my client's offer."

"I'm sorry if I didn't make myself clear when you visited the first time, but I'm not selling."

"Now let's not be hasty. My client understands it can be emotional to part with a home. We are willing to increase our offer by a substantial amount to ease your transition from the home."

He recognized the suspicion in Nikki's eyes. "A substantial amount?"

Chester's smile was cocksure. "Fifty thousand dollars. But my client is very anxious to close this deal and take possession of the house, so we'd need an answer in forty-eight hours."

"Well, I've already given you my answer. Lakewood House is not now, nor will it ever be, for sale."

Chester's smile fell.

"I do have a question for you though. Why is your client so interested in purchasing Lakewood House?"

"I'm afraid I can't share that with you," he said with irritation in his voice.

"Then I don't think we have anything else to talk about. I'd like you off my property."

Chester glared. "Ms. King—"

Terrence took a small step forward. "The lady asked you to leave."

The two men scowled at each other for a moment before Chester shifted his markedly chillier gaze back to Nikki. "My client is willing to wait another forty-eight hours. I suggest you use that time to seriously consider their offer. I assure you, it's in your best interest to do so."

"Did that sound like a threat to you?" Nikki asked as they watched Chester back out of the driveway.

There was no doubt in Terrence's mind it was a threat. And Chester and his client were about to discover he didn't take kindly to his friends being threatened.

Chapter Sixteen

Deputy Bridges resumed his watch, and Terrence followed Nikki back inside the house.

"I'm going to take this upstairs to my room. I'll let you know if I find anything." Nikki grabbed her laptop and hurried up the stairs.

He didn't try to stop her. He needed to make a call that he didn't want her to overhear, anyway. Moments later, he was on the line with Ryan West.

"I have a favor to ask," Terrence said once they'd gotten through the initial pleasantries.

"Shoot."

He gave Ryan the truncated version of the events that had taken place in the last couple of days, as well as his theory about the possibility that the gang Ryan had sent them information on had ventured into human trafficking.

"That's some pretty heavy stuff, but that crew is nasty enough to be involved."

"And if they are, they're more dangerous than I imagined. Nikki's home is isolated and without any security at all. I'm wondering if you can't help me out with a recommendation for a system. Something I can get locally and fast."

"Of course. I'll look into it today and get back to you ASAP."

"Thanks."

Terrence spent the next two hours calling his law enforcement contacts in the southwest to dig up the information that never made it into the official reports or news articles. Anything at all on suspected gang members or crimes that the cops were sure the gang pulled but couldn't prove. The unofficial files all cops kept in their heads or in old notebooks. Theories, gut feelings, rumors that couldn't be used in a court of law or even to bring a person in for questioning.

Lance returned Nikki's boat in the late afternoon. He'd found the dungeon basement and copious amounts of trash, but not much else. He had been able to pull several fingerprints from the shackles and was hopeful something would pop there. He left with Deputy Bridges as dusk began to fall.

When Terrence finally stopped for dinner—spaghetti marinara Nikki prepared while he'd been on the calls—he was surprised to find that she had done some calling of her own.

She slid handwritten notes across the table toward him. "Cops aren't the only ones with sources. I called a couple of reporters I know in Texas and Arizona. That's what they know about the gang."

It was the most she'd said to him since they'd gotten back from the sheriff's office. Despite their harrowing experience earlier in the day, it was clear she was still angry with him. He still thought they needed to sit down and hash things out so they could move forward as friends, or maybe more. Being shot at by a couple of thugs had put one thing in perspective, and that was that he still cared about Nikki. He'd regret for the rest of his life having let his pride come between them. And if he could make it right? Get them back on the track they'd been on before he'd blown up their burgeoning relationship? He was open to it if she was.

But now was not the time for that discussion. Especially when there was another, more pressing discussion they needed to have.

He'd finished his dinner in record time, hungrier than he'd realized. He set his fork across the now empty plate and spoke. "I want to head over to Whistler's at nine. It's a little early for that crowd, but I want to make sure I don't miss Dana if he shows up tonight."

Nikki wiped her mouth with a napkin. "Okay, I can be ready to go at nine."

"About that."

She held up a hand and glared across the table at him. "I'm going."

"Whistler's is no place for a lady. Hell, it's no place for a man. The people who frequent that place are volatile when they aren't drunk. I think it would be best if you stay here and let me go alone."

"You've been telling me for days that staying at Lakewood House alone wasn't safe for me. Now it is?"

He gritted his teeth. "You know that's different. I can call Lance and have him send another deputy."

"That won't be necessary. If it's safe enough for you to go, it's safe enough for me to go." She rose and carried her plate to the sink before striding from the kitchen.

He sighed, resigned. "I guess we're both going then."

Nikki was waiting for him by the front door at nine. They made the twenty-minute drive to Whistler's in silence. The bar was housed in a one-story building with a gravel parking lot and glitchy pink-and-yellow neon Open sign over the door.

The lot was already half-full when they pulled in. A couple of motorcycles, two or three muscle cars and a handful of pickups ranging in newness were parked in haphazard rows.

Terrence backed the Highlander into a spot at the very end of the lot nearest to the exit. He'd have preferred parking closer to the door in case they needed to beat a hasty retreat, but this was the only area of the gravel lot where he couldn't be blocked in by another vehicle. It would have to do. Hopefully, Dana would be inside and be willing to answer a few questions. Even though he had the thought, he couldn't bring himself to believe it.

Two men loitered outside the door. Given that it wasn't the kind of bar that strictly enforced the laws about smoking inside, Terrence could only imagine what sort of business had necessitated the men stepping outside.

He shut off the engine and turned to Nikki. "Are you sure you want to do this?"

She rolled her eyes at him and reached for the door handle. "Yes. Now come on. Let's go."

He got out and walked around to her side of the Highlander. The men at the door eyed them suspiciously but moved farther away from the entrance, disappearing around the side of the building as they approached.

He took a steadying breath, then held the door open for Nikki to enter. Only half the heads in the bar turned toward them when they entered. Although this was his first time inside, Whistler's had been around since he and Nikki were kids, and its reputation hadn't changed much over the years. If anything, it had gotten worse. It was the kind of place that attracted people who didn't want to know your name. Or anything else about anybody who frequented Whistler's.

A couple of really rough-looking guys sat at a table at the rear of the bar, their heads huddled together. A table in the middle of the space hosted four men clad in leather. Two of them had scantily clad women, also in leather, sitting on their laps. At a booth near the door, a man who looked like he'd seen better days nursed a beer and stared sightlessly at the television over the bar, although there was no way he could have possibly heard it over the music blaring from the overhead speaker and the chatter of the other patrons.

They grabbed two empty stools on the far side of the bar. Terrence took the stool next to the wall and turned so his back was to it. He wasn't about to put his back to anyone in this place.

He scanned the people in the bar. They'd all gone back to whatever they'd been doing before he and Nikki walked in. None of the men in the bar looked remotely familiar.

He held up two fingers when the bartender sidled over, and said, "Jack on the rocks." One of Nikki's brows went up when the bartender turned his back. "Trust me, you would not want to sample the wine selection in a place like this."

The corners of her mouth crept up and his stomach did a flip-flop.

Terrence had his phone out when the bartender returned with their drinks. "Have you seen this woman? She's my sister and she's been missing for a few days." He thrust the phone at the bartender before the man had the chance to walk away, hoping to tug at his heartstrings a bit. The bartender was an older man, slightly stooped over and balding, who looked to be in his seventies, although Terrence suspected he was quite a bit younger and hard living had just taken its toll.

Nikki looked at him with a question in her eyes. They were at Whistler's to find Dana, but it wouldn't hurt to ask about Jill as well.

The bartender gave Jill's photo a long look. "Can't say that I have. Sorry."

Terrence bit back a curse. He'd been hoping to find some concrete evidence that he was on the right track with the theory that Jill had found out about the trafficking ring and begun her own investigation.

The bartender's eyes slid over to Nikki. She gave him a smile, and after shooting a quick, wary gaze at Terrence, he turned back to her with a tentative one of his own.

Jealousy tangled a knot in his stomach. He narrowed hard eyes on the bartender.

"How about this symbol?" Nikki elbowed him lightly and motioned to his phone. He swiped to the photo of the fleur-de-lis, then turned the screen so the bartender could see it.

He didn't look as long this time. "Nope. Sorry."

It was a long shot, but Terrence was still disappointed.

Two strikes. If Dana didn't show up, the night would be a complete bust.

"Thanks anyway." Nikki's smile for the bartender grew brighter.

"Your next drink is on the house." He winked.

Terrence tossed back his whiskey and tried to reason with the green-eyed monster clawing at his insides. If a bit of flirting got the information, it was more than worth it for him to play the silent sidekick.

"That's kind of you." Nikki shifted on her stool and leaned closer to the bar. "You know, I grew up in Carling Lake. An old friend of mine actually recommended this place. Said he comes in here a lot. I was kinda hoping to see him tonight. Dana Bonny."

"Yeah, Dana. He's over there at his regular table." The bartender jerked his head toward the table with the tough-looking guys, and Terrence saw what he hadn't when they'd first walked in. Another smaller table in the dark corner behind them with a single man hunched over a glass. "He showed up early tonight, already three sheets to the wind."

Nikki turned in the direction the bartender indicated. Her eyes went wide, and she grabbed his arm, squeezing tightly enough to make him wince. "Terrence, that's one of the guys who shot at us earlier today."

He shifted a bit, trying to get a better look at the man in the corner. He'd been too busy getting them away from Carling Island to get a good look at the men who'd shot at them, and although the man in the corner did fit the description of the shorter man Nikki described to Lance, he looked nothing like the Dana of fifteen years ago.

"Stay here," Terrence said in a voice that brooked no disagreement.

He pushed away from the bar, and once again became the focus of several of the patrons.

Dana looked up.

Terrence may not have recognized Dana, but Dana seemed to have no trouble recognizing him. He was out of his seat in an instant, launching the half-full glass that had been on the table in front of him a moment earlier through the air.

Unfortunately, Dana had the aim of a drunk. The

glass went wide, hitting a very large man with a scar trisecting his cheek in the back of his head.

The mood in the bar shifted in a flash.

Terrence held up his hands in a surrender pose as Scarface turned in his direction. "Hey, my friend is drunk. He's sorry, man." He didn't dare take his eyes off Scarface to see where Dana had gone.

The apology had no effect. Scarface stepped forward and threw a punch that landed on Terrence's face.

His head snapped back, but he recovered quickly and came up swinging. Scarface was big but slow and untrained. Terrence threw another punch and sent him flying backward over a table.

Another man from the table charged. The next several minutes was chaos, with patrons of the bar either throwing punches, dodging blows or scrambling to get out of the bar. He mentally kicked himself for having brought Nikki along and hoped she'd taken cover.

He glanced at the bar where she'd been sitting, but a hard right hook kept him from determining whether she was still there. He drove a fist into the stomach of the man who'd just hit him, then threw an elbow at another man who'd jumped into the fray.

The sheriff would no doubt have already gotten a call about the melee and was on the way, so he could expect to have a black eye and get an earful all in one night.

And all for nothing, since he hadn't gotten to question Dana, who'd somehow managed to disappear in the mayhem.

He pushed through the bodies toward the bar. Nikki was crouched between the two seats they'd been sitting in before the fighting started. He grabbed her and pulled her toward the swinging door that led to the kitchen. He stayed close behind as they fled out of the door leading from the kitchen outside, apparently not being the first to take this route since the door stood wide open.

They rounded the building and ran toward the Highlander. He pulled out of the parking lot and pointed them toward Carling Lake just as the first sirens sounded behind them.

Nikki turned in the passenger seat. He glanced at the rearview mirror. Three sheriff's cruisers turned into the parking lot behind them.

Nikki faced forward. "I guess Dana didn't want to talk."

"No, I guess he didn't."

Dana may have gotten away, but now that he was sure Pete's nephew was involved in whatever was going on in Carling Lake, he wouldn't let Dana slip away so easily the next time.

Chapter Seventeen

Despite the chilly night, Nikki put the car window down and let the breeze wash over her. Adrenaline raced, still pumped through her veins. She'd never been in a bar fight before, but if she ever was again, she wanted Terrence by her side. He was amazing.

"You okay?" Terrence asked.

She was still shaking, but she didn't think he could see that in the dark interior of the car. She took a deep breath and let it out. "Yeah, I'm… I'm fine." At least she hoped she would be by the time they got back to Lakewood House.

The look on his face said he didn't believe her.

She peered at him. "I should be the one asking you if you're okay. You got it worse than I did." She reached across the car and touched the cut above his right eye.

He winced and she drew her hand back. "I'll be okay. A few bumps and bruises. They'll heal in a couple of days."

Nikki was glad she wasn't driving. She couldn't have recounted the route they took to get home, but suddenly they were pulling to a stop in front of the house.

They entered the house, and Nikki switched on the lights.

Terrence's eyes narrowed, and he swore. "You're

bleeding." He ran the pad of his thumb lightly over her cheek.

She hadn't felt a thing, but when she turned to look at herself in the mirror next to the door, there was a bright red slash along her right cheek. As if acknowledging the injury had somehow made it real, she could suddenly feel the throbbing pain in her cheek.

"Come on." Terrence led her upstairs, easing her down to sit on his bed, then marched into the bathroom connecting their rooms.

He returned with a handful of cotton balls and a bottle of hydrogen peroxide. "I should have never let you go into that bar. I'm so sorry I put you in danger." He sat next to her and soaked a cotton ball in peroxide.

"It's just a scratch," she said, flinching as he gently swabbed the cotton ball over her cheek. "And I wanted to go with you. I wanted to help you."

"I'm not sure I deserve your help." Terrence didn't look at her as he spoke, focusing on wetting another cotton ball.

She took the cotton from his hand and drew it over the cut over his eye.

He flinched but didn't look up. She placed a finger under his chin and lifted his face until his gaze met hers. "You deserve it and you have it."

His mouth was inches from hers. She wasn't sure who leaned in, but in a moment her lips were on his, the time and emotional distance that had been between them forgotten in a wave of blinding arousal. She felt his hands on her face, a gentle feathery touch that slid down her arms and to her waist. He pulled her onto his lap, taking their kiss from soft and tentative to hungry. She met his desire with her own fiery need.

His lips moved from her mouth to her throat while

his hands roamed beneath her cotton top. "Are you sure about this?"

She was sure she wanted this. Wanted him. But warning bells were going off in her brain. She knew she should heed them, but she also knew she wouldn't. Tonight was tonight. It didn't have to be anything more than that. One night. And tomorrow? To paraphrase Scarlett O'Hara, tomorrow was another day. She'd deal with whatever the fallout was then. Based on the way Terrence's hands felt roaming over her back, cupping her backside and pulling her even closer to him, it was a night that would be well worth it.

She arched her back, pressing her core into his throbbing erection. "I'm sure."

Terrence groaned, then shifted so that seconds later, she was on her back on the bed. Terrence eased his body over hers.

Need crackled between them. He found her mouth again, and they kissed, molding their bodies, one to fit the other, even as their clothes became an increasingly intolerable barrier.

Her fingers went to the waistband of his jeans. He shed his clothing quickly, then stripped her.

His hands and lips traveled over her with abandon. She loved the feeling of him. The hard curves of his body. The smell of his aftershave. The softness of his lips.

Their kisses became more tender even as their urgency to couple grew exponentially. She loved what his touch was doing to her, his hot kisses on her most intimate places eliciting sensations in her that she'd never felt before. There'd been other men, but none of them had ever made her feel the way Terrence was making her feel at this moment.

Her body throbbed for him. "Terrence, please."

He pulled away long enough to grab a condom and sheath himself.

Her eyes were trained on his face as he slid inside her. Raw emotion, emotion she saw reflected in Terrence's eyes, ricocheted through her. They moved together, spiraling ever closer to ecstasy. The magnitude of the sensations swirling deep inside her made her shudder. She ran her fingers over his broad chest and shifted to bring him in deeper.

"You feel so good." He dropped his head to her breast, almost as if in prayer. When he lifted his head again, his eyes were hazy with desire. He kissed her hard, a kiss she greedily returned.

Sparks shot through her, heat permeating her entire being. She wanted more, needed more, even as each shock of pleasure had her wondering if she could stand more. Energy pulsed between them, tethering her to Terrence in a way she'd never felt before.

A way she was sure in that moment she could never feel with anyone else.

When she finally tumbled over, Terrence was right there with her.

Afterward, neither of them moved or even spoke. Nikki rested her head against Terrence's chest and listened to his heartbeat, content to lie entwined for however long this lasted.

She wasn't sure what had passed between them, but it was real and powerful.

And it had the potential to break her heart all over again.

NIKKI STARED AT the man sleeping beside her. They'd been little more than kids when they'd dated back in high school and college. He'd been her first lover, and for a time, she'd thought he would be her only lover. Although they'd never explicitly discussed a long-term future, it's where she'd thought their relationship was headed back then. It wasn't meant to be, but she'd never forgotten how making love with Terrence had felt. As if she were safe. Adored. Home. The way it felt last night. And maybe that was why she felt a little ill at the thought that sleeping with him couldn't happen again.

Terrence opened his eyes, a smile spreading across his lips. "Good morning."

"Good morning."

"What time is it?"

"Quarter to nine."

He yawned. "It's early." He reached for her. "Especially given our late night."

Nikki slid from his grip, grabbing Terrence's shirt from the floor and shrugging into it. She turned back to face Terrence, who'd pushed up into a sitting position. "We need to talk."

"Words a man never likes to hear the morning after."

She released a deep breath. "Last night was incredible, but I don't think it should happen again."

"Last night was incredible, and that's exactly why I think it should happen again. I'd be thrilled if it happened again right now."

Despite her attempt not to, her eyes fell to his lap. He wasn't exaggerating. He was more than ready for a repeat of last night's exploits. Her sex began to throb in response. She dragged her focus back to his face before she gave in to the desire that was building inside her.

"I'm serious, Terrence."

He gave her a lascivious smile. "I've never been more serious in my life."

"Terrence."

"Nikki, come back to bed." He patted the spot next to him that she'd vacated.

"Last night was great, but it doesn't change anything that's happened between us. There's still years of hurt and anger that I'm not sure we can get past."

"And I think we can. We were friends once. More than friends. And we can be again."

"That was a long time ago."

"Not that long." He leaned forward, and the sheet around his waist slid dangerously low. He didn't seem to notice, or if he did, he ignored it. "I am so sorry for not listening to you. For blindly following in my uncle's anger. If I could go back and do it again, I'd do it all differently."

"But we can't go back."

"No, but we can start again. Right here. Now."

The sound of a car approaching the house interrupted their conversation.

Terrence grabbed his pants from the floor and got out of the bed. He pulled them on and strode to the window. "It's James West."

"I'll go get dressed."

"Nikki. I hear what you're saying. But just so we're clear, I'm going to do my best to prove to you that we have something special. Something worth fighting for."

Nikki turned and hurried to her room.

With guests literally on her doorstep, she didn't have time to consider how she felt about Terrence's declaration.

She took the fastest, coldest shower ever and dressed in jeans and a sweater.

Terrence had made coffee and was pouring cups for

James and the pretty woman who sat next to him at the kitchen table.

"You remember James," Terrence said. "And this is his wife, Erika."

"Nice to meet you, Erika. Good to see you again, James."

Erika tilted her head and smiled, a twinkle in her eye.

"Sorry about bursting in on you so early, but I knew Terrence was anxious to get some sort of security set up for the house. I got a recommendation from Ryan, and he had a system couriered overnight."

She shot an annoyed glare at Terrence. He hadn't mentioned getting a security system for her house.

"You got a home security system for Lakewood House."

"I did."

His calmness spiked her ire. She knew her irritation wasn't all about the security system. Her feelings for Terrence were in turmoil, the lines between them more blurred than ever, and she didn't like it one bit. "Without discussing it with me. I can't afford a security system."

"Don't worry about the cost. I'll take care of it."

"I am worried about the cost, and you won't take care of it. Lakewood House is my responsibility."

"It may be your responsibility, but I care about it too. And you. You need a security system."

"Listen," James said. "The system was a gift."

"I can't accept a gift from you."

"Come on, Nikki." Terrence ran a hand over his head. "It's just a couple of cameras and an alarm."

"It's not just a couple of cameras and an alarm. It's you making decisions without consulting me."

He held his hands up in surrender. "Look, I'm sorry.

I should have asked you first. But this is about your safety. Please."

"Okay," she said, annoyed, "but a couple of cameras and an alarm. That's all."

"That's all." Terrence grabbed his jacket from the back of the sofa and faced James. "Let me show you around the exterior of the property."

"I'm sorry if we caused a problem between you two," Erika said. "I told James we should call before we came over. But if it makes up for bursting in on you two, I made scones." She held up a plastic Tupperware container.

"It more than makes up for it. And I'm the one who should be apologizing for arguing in front of company." Nikki grabbed a serving plate from the cabinet. "Things between Terrence and I have been tense lately. Well, more than just lately. More like for the last fourteen years."

Erika whistled. "That's a long time to be tense."

Nikki laughed. "You're telling me." She opened the Tupperware container and transferred the scones onto the serving plate. "Terrence and I were friends for a long time. And then we weren't friends for a long time and now… I don't know what we are. He's been holding a grudge against my family and me for years for something I told him my grandfather didn't do."

"And I take it he didn't believe you." Erika moved to the sink and rinsed the now empty Tupperware container.

"He did not." Nikki slid onto a bar stool. She gave Erika a quick summary of her history with Terrence, the feud between her grandfather and his uncle, and how it had killed their relationship. "And I realize I did the same thing, letting this thing between him and Jarrod drive a wedge between Terrence and me. He sided with his uncle, and I sided with my grandfather, but neither of us knew the truth."

"But you're still angry at him."

"I know it doesn't make any sense, and I don't know why I'm dumping all this on you. You probably think I'm crazy."

"Not crazy. I think you need someone to talk to. Someone to listen. I'm happy to be that person."

Nikki smiled. "Thank you."

"You're welcome." Erika returned the smile. "Can I offer you one piece of advice though?"

Nikki extended a hand. "Please."

"Life is too short to hold grudges and nurture feuds. You and Terrence clearly still care about each other. If there is any way for you two to get back your friendship, don't waste time with anger."

Was that what she was doing? Wasting time? She still couldn't deny she cared about Terrence. Maybe even more than that. In a little more than a year, she'd lost her grandfather and her job, which had taught her that life was unpredictable and not to take anything for granted.

The sound of tires on the gravel driveway put an end to their conversation.

Erika looked out of the kitchen window. "The sheriff is here."

A minute later, all three men strode into the house.

"Sorry to barge in on you when you're entertaining," Sheriff Webb said.

"No worries. Erika and James dropped by to welcome me to the neighborhood with scones and a home security system."

The sheriff smiled warily. "Not a bad welcome."

"Would you like a scone?" Nikki motioned to the platter. "I can make more coffee."

"No, no thanks. I've been subsisting on coffee since yesterday. An early morning call from Terrence telling me that you'd been able to identify Dana Bonny as one of the men that shot at you didn't help me get any beauty sleep."

Nikki turned to Terrence, surprised. "You called Lance?"

"While you were asleep. I wanted to let him know about Dana."

"Are you still contending you don't know anything about the brawl at Whistler's last night?" Lance's gaze moved between Terrence and Nikki.

"Not a thing," Terrence said straight-faced.

"Well, it looks like your face might have been there unless Nikki did that to your eye," the sheriff said.

Terrence smiled. "I tripped."

"Yeah, right. I'll go with that for now." Sheriff Webb shot a look at Nikki.

She gave a tight-lipped smile. The sheriff obviously knew they'd been at Whistler's last night, but if he and Terrence were going to pretend he didn't, she was happy to go along with them.

James's and Erika's expressions said they weren't buying the excuse either.

"We were finally able to identify the woman we found on your property," Lance said. "Her name is Anna Fernandez Alcalá. She disappeared from a women's shelter in McAllen, Texas, last year."

"And no one was concerned?" Nikki said.

There were thousands of vulnerable women out there, but it was hard to believe that in this day and age, anyone could disappear without notice.

"A counselor at the shelter filed the missing person report, but it wasn't unusual for women to move out of the shelter without notifying the staff."

She shook her head in disgust. "Just the kind of vulnerable young woman monsters prey upon."

"Unfortunately, yes," the sheriff said.

"Texas. That tracks with the information on the gang that West sent us."

"I noticed that as well," the sheriff said.

James's face had darkened as the conversation went on. Now he looked ready to spit nails. "I think I speak for my brothers when I say anything West can do to assist your investigation, Sheriff, you just let us know."

"I appreciate that. Right now, we're trying to track Ms. Alcalá's movements after she ran away from the homeless shelter. I expect it will be slow going. She was nineteen but didn't have a driver's license, bank account or credit cards. No cell phone that we know of. We can't use any of our usual means to trace her."

"So, what's the next step?" Terrence asked.

Sheriff Webb sighed. "Based on your identification of Dana as one of the men who shot at you, we were able to get a warrant for his arrest, but we haven't found him yet."

"What about Pete?" Terrence asked.

Lance shook his head. "We don't have probable cause for a warrant or to formally bring him in, or any evidence he's committed a crime."

"Pete definitely wasn't the second guy shooting at us," Nikki offered.

"I've sent a deputy to his place to see if he'd voluntarily come to the station for questioning, but it appears as if he's disappeared," the sheriff said.

Now it was Terrence who looked ready to spit nails. He let out a curse.

Nikki shared in his frustrations. It seemed that for every step forward, they took two steps back. "The Bonny family used to own a pretty large swath of land. Even though they sold most of it off years ago, Pete and probably Dana know these mountains better than anyone. If they want to get lost, it's going to take time to find them."

"What about the other guy who shot at us?" Terrence asked.

"Still working on an ID."

"So you're nowhere." Terrence's frustration filled the room.

Sheriff Webb slapped his palm against his thigh. "Investigations take—"

"Time. Yes, I know," Terrence spat.

"Look, we're doing everything we can." The sheriff moved to the front door, and they all followed.

Sheriff Webb opened the door and stepped out onto the front porch before turning back. "Just sit tight. Why don't you take another look at that information that West Investigations sent you? Maybe something will pop out at you that didn't before."

Nikki and Terrence watched through the open front door as their visitors got into their cars and drove away. "You're not going to listen to him, are you?"

"Wasn't planning on it," Terrence said, turning to look at her. "Why?"

"Because I have an idea."

Chapter Eighteen

The drive to Albert Chester's office took a little over an hour. Terrence hadn't protested when Nikki explained that she wanted to talk to the lawyer, which convinced her that he suspected the attorney might be connected to everything that had happened in the last several days, just like she was. She couldn't picture the mild-mannered lawyer involved with human trafficking, but anything was possible. At the very least, he knew who his client was, and that person might be involved. She wanted that name and she thought she knew how to get it.

The law firm occupied a multifloor cookie-cutter building and stood amongst other multifloor cookie-cutter buildings. The receptionist, a young brunette woman, greeted them when they entered the law firm's lobby.

"May I help you?" The woman gave a tight smile.

"My name is Dominique King. I'd like to see Mr. Chester, please?"

"Do you have an appointment?"

"I do not, but I'm sure he will find the time to meet with me."

The woman's smile tightened, and she picked up the phone on her desk.

"You still haven't said how you plan to make Chester tell you who his client is," Terrence said, keeping his voice low.

"I'm going to use the thing he wants against him."

"You're in luck," the receptionist said, replacing the phone's receiver on its chassis. "Mr. Chester has some time now. He'll be right out."

The lawyer appeared behind the glass doors separating the reception area from the offices less than a minute later. He pushed through the doors with a flourish, a bright smile on his face.

"Ms. King, what a lovely surprise. Can I take this unexpected meeting to mean you come bearing good news?"

"I have been thinking about your offer a great deal." Not a lie exactly. She had been thinking about the offer on Lakewood House. Who was behind it and why? If a little manipulation was what it took to get the information she wanted, she was okay with that.

"Well, all right then. Let's go to my office and discuss this further."

She and Terrence followed Chester, and she ignored the wary look Terrence shot at her.

Once they were seated in Chester's large corner office, the attorney got right to business. "So, as I mentioned, my client would like to move quickly to close the deal but is willing to pay a substantial bonus to compensate you for the inconvenience."

"Before we get to that, I want to know who I'd be selling to." Nikki crossed her legs and leaned back in the silk upholstered chair.

Chester's smile dimmed. "As I've explained, I don't have the authority to do that."

"Then we have no deal." Nikki stood and Terrence followed suit.

Chester pushed to his feet. "Hang on there. Are you saying that if I give you the buyer's name, you'll sell?"

"I'm telling you that the only way I'll sell is if you tell me your client's name."

He hesitated for a long moment. "Let me make a call. If you would wait outside, it will just take a moment."

Nikki and Terrence stepped out of the office together.

"He's calling his client," Terrence said.

"I hope so." She could see Chester on the phone through the long vertical glass window next to his office door.

Terrence looked at her with shrewd eyes. "But you have no intention of selling Lakewood House, right?"

She pulled Terrence farther away from Chester's office. She couldn't hear him inside with the door closed, but she wasn't taking any chances. "Of course not. But I've been thinking about it, and what if the person offering to buy Lakewood House is also involved in the trafficking ring? It would make sense. Now that I'm back in Carling Lake, they'd lose access to the private dock. But if they bought Lakewood House, their problem would be solved. The vandalism and arson could all just be a way to push me toward selling."

"I don't know." Terrence seemed unconvinced. "It makes some sense, and while I don't hold lawyers in great esteem, Chester works for what passes for a reputable law firm. I don't know if they'd be involved with traffickers and arsonists."

"What lawyer knows everything their client is up to?"

"Good point."

Chester's office door opened. "Thank you for waiting. Please, come in and have a seat." His expression was solemn. "My client wasn't happy about your condition, but she did give me permission to reveal who she was."

"She?" Nikki couldn't help the punch of surprise she felt. It was probably sexist, but she hadn't even considered a woman could be behind all this.

"Melinda Hanes is the buyer on behalf of her family corporation, Hanes Hospitality Services."

"Melinda Hanes," Nikki repeated.

"Yes. I believe being from Carling Lake, you're familiar with the Hanes family hotel and B and B."

Of course she was. But that didn't explain Melinda's offer.

"Why would Melinda Hanes want to buy Lakewood House?"

Chester sighed. "As Carling Lake becomes more of a tourist destination, the need for guest accommodations has increased. Several new B and Bs have cropped up in the area and the Haneses want to make sure they retain their market share. Lakewood House is uniquely situated."

"You mean the property Lakewood House is on is uniquely situated. Lakewood House itself is far too small to convert into a B and B."

"Well, that is true." Chester shifted in his chair and looked uncomfortable. "Of course, the offer is for the entire property, and once you sell, Ms. Hanes is free to do with it as she chooses. But the property is perfect for her plans."

Which was to tear down Lakewood House. If Nikki had been inclined to sell before, she definitely wouldn't have been now that she knew Melinda's plans for the property. Lakewood House meant too much to too many people for her to ever let anyone tear it down.

Nikki stood again. "Thank you for your time, Mr. Chester."

"Where are you going? You said—"

"I said I would consider selling if I knew who the buyer was. I have considered it and my answer is a resounding no."

Chester rounded his desk and stalked toward Nikki. "Now wait just a darn minute."

Terrence stood, putting his body between her and Chester. "The lady gave you her answer."

The attorney's glare was venomous. "The lady lied about her intentions."

Nikki shrugged. "You win some, you lose some. Tell your client I won't ever sell to her or anyone else who plans to knock down Lakewood House."

She strode from the office with Terrence at her side. She was pretty sure that Melinda's offer hadn't been motivated solely by business, at least not once Nikki had mentioned the possibility of running for mayor. Melinda had probably figured she could kill two birds with one stone by buying Lakewood House—getting rid of a potential rival for the mayorship and picking up a coveted property for her family's business. Well, she couldn't say she was sorry to disappoint the conniving businesswoman turned wannabe politician.

"You might have just made an enemy."

"I've been doing that a lot lately," Nikki said, thinking about her former boss. "Melinda Hanes will have to just get in line."

Chapter Nineteen

"Well, I guess that was a waste of time." Nikki sounded despondent.

"Not necessarily." Terrence changed lanes and merged onto the interstate.

Nikki glanced over at him. "What do you mean?"

"Now we know the person trying to buy Lakewood House doesn't have anything to do with the trafficking ring." He changed lanes again and pushed the Highlander to go faster. He was relieved at least to have an answer to one mystery, but it didn't help him at all when it came to finding Jill.

Nikki made a sour face. "Melinda could still be behind the vandalism and arson."

His gut said no. "I don't think so. Surreptitiously trying to buy Lakewood House is one thing, but arson?" He shook his head in disbelief. "It's not really the Haneses' style."

"You know Ellis Hanes is in jail."

"For fraud. That's a lot different than arson."

"Maybe."

They rode in silence for several miles. He was sure Melinda was nothing more than an opportunist. Dana Bonny, however, was a key player in whatever was going on.

"Are you up for a detour?"

"Depends. Where to?"

"Dana Bonny's place. We still need to talk to him, and maybe we'll have better luck if we find him at home."

"You know where he lives?"

He merged onto the exit off the highway that led back to Carling Lake. "Aunt Charity said he inherited his father's place. Thaddeus Bonny had a farm off old Route 20."

"Okay. Let's see if Dana is more willing to talk today."

Dana wasn't the only person he wanted to talk to. "Speaking of talking. We never finished discussing what happened last night between us."

Nikki stared out of the front window. "I think I was pretty clear earlier. Last night was great, but it can't happen again."

"Why not?" He turned off the interstate and onto Route 20. Once a main thoroughfare, it was primarily used by the handful of homeowners who lived off the road now.

"Why? Until a few days ago, we hadn't spoken in over fourteen years."

"Exactly. We've already wasted so much time. Let's not waste any more."

Nikki looked across the car now. "We can't just move from not speaking for years to—what? I don't even know what it is you want. Do you?"

He knew what he wanted. He looked over at Nikki. "You. I want you." He held her gaze for a moment longer before shifting his eyes back to the road.

She let out a shaky breath but otherwise didn't respond to his declaration.

Her silence stung, but he reminded himself that he had several years of hurt to make up for. It made sense that she didn't believe him when he said he wanted to pick up where they'd left off. Well, not where they left off exactly. They were adults now, and he was ready for a committed adult relationship. And if he had to work to prove that to her, he was up for the challenge.

He turned the Highlander off the main road onto a long driveway that ended in front of a rundown two-story home. Several junker cars in various states of disrepair littered what should have been the front yard. Once a working farm, the expansive plot of land lay fallow and desolate now. An unpainted barn with a rusted metal door sat twenty yards behind the house, the only other structure in sight for miles.

Terrence and Nikki got out of the car and went to the door. No one answered their knock. He peered through the front windows. They were unadorned by blinds or curtains, but the grime and dirt made it difficult to tell if there was anyone inside.

"Maybe he's in the barn?" Nikki said, pointing beyond the house.

They trooped through the tall grass toward the barn. He waved to Nikki to stand aside as they approached. He tried the door. It was heavy. He pushed harder. It squeezed and groaned but began to move.

He finally got it open enough to see inside. Then froze.

"What is it?" Nikki moved to his side.

The red Prius was parked in the middle of the barn, a thin veneer of dust and dirt covering it.

"Jill's car."

LANCE PULLED TERRENCE aside while Deputy Bridges took Nikki's statement. "What do you think you're doing?"

"I think I'm searching for my sister. And finding her

car on Dana Bonny's property gives you all the probable cause you need to search his house."

"I'm surprised you didn't take it upon yourself to search the house," Lance said, exasperated.

"Come on! I did what I had to do, and now we've got a solid lead connecting Bonny to Jill's disappearance."

A deep-seated chill had settled into his bones the moment he'd recognized Jill's car in Dana's barn. He hadn't been able to bring himself to open the trunk of the car, the fear of what he might find inside overriding all of his police training. But when Lance had informed him that the car was empty, except for a suitcase, he'd nearly fallen to his knees with relief. Jill wasn't inside.

"And if he gets a halfway decent lawyer, he could get whatever case we make against him thrown out of court—"

"I don't care about the court," Terrence yelled. "I care about finding my sister."

Lance held out both hands. "Okay, okay. But you dragged Nikki out here without knowing what or who you might find. It was reckless, and either one of you could have been hurt."

"I'd never do anything to hurt Nikki."

"No? You two have already been shot at by Bonny. Now you bring her here. Look, I don't know either of you that well, and I understand your desire to find your sister. I do. But you're a cop. You know how to handle yourself. Nikki isn't. I know there's nothing I can do to stop you from rushing headlong into danger, but, man, if you care about this woman, don't drag her along with you."

Lance stalked away without giving him a chance to respond.

When Lance finally let them go, Nikki had insisted

on driving them back to Lakewood House, not trusting him to drive.

He stayed silent the entire way.

"Are you okay?" Nikki asked once they were back at the house.

He fell onto the sofa, emotionally exhausted. "Okay? I don't know. When I saw that car, I thought…" Tears threatened to spill from his eyes. "Nikki, I don't know what I'm going to do if…"

She wrapped her arms around him. "Hey, there is still hope."

"Is there?" he said, his face tucked into her shoulder. "The longer a person is missing, the less likely it becomes that they'll be found. I don't even know exactly when Jill disappeared."

Nikki cupped his cheek and leaned back until she could look into his deep brown eyes. "We'll find her." She pulled him closer, placing a kiss on one corner of his mouth. "We'll find her." She kissed the other corner.

He pulled away just enough to look at her face. Desire shimmered in her eyes. The same desire he felt bubbling inside. He wanted her. Needed her now.

He leaned forward slowly, giving her the chance to back away.

Ever so lightly, she caressed his jaw with her thumb, and met his heated kiss with matching fervor. Her hands slid around his neck, her lips curling into a smile even as they continued their kiss.

He deepened their kiss, and she shifted, swinging one leg across him so that she straddled him. He groaned. It was all he could do not to throw her down and ravage her like some caveman. There was nothing in the world he wanted more than to make love to her again. To make love to her every day for the rest of his life, of that he was sure, although he knew it was too early to share that thought with her. But she'd been adamant that sleeping together had been a mistake. He didn't want her to do anything she'd regret. Damned conscience.

He broke off the kiss, panting. "Wait."

She shook her head and lowered her lips to his neck. "No. No more waiting."

He groaned again, his head becoming fuzzy as the blood rushed to other parts of his body. "I don't want you to regret…"

She leaned back so her gaze locked with his. "The only thing I'd regret is not being with you. Not having you inside me right now. I want this. I want you to stop thinking and start doing."

He couldn't control the erotic shiver that raced through him at her words.

Nikki tugged his head down so that his lips met hers again.

He wrapped an arm around her waist and surged upward, holding her against him. She wrapped her legs around him. His erection pressed into her center. God help him. He wasn't sure they'd make it to the bed.

Mine. Mine. Mine. The word was part chant, part prayer marching across his brain as he carried Nikki up the stairs and sat her gently on the bed.

He lowered himself down beside her and claimed her mouth again. As much as he burned to be inside of her, the sizzle that flowed through him when their lips met was addictive. She hummed against him, shifting so he was between her legs.

Piece by piece, they shed their clothes, their kisses moving from fiery to sweet and back again.

"You're beautiful," he whispered reverently, staring at her naked form.

She gave him a lust-filled smile, reaching both her arms up to him. "Come here and show me how beautiful you think I am." She arched her hips and the last of his control broke.

He sheathed himself quickly, then found his place at her entrance. Balancing his weight on his elbows, he stared into Nikki's eyes as he entered her slowly.

She felt…perfect. Absolutely perfect.

Fully seated at her core, he shuddered.

Nikki gripped his shoulders and rolled her hips. "More."

He complied, moving slowly and steadily, then faster, driving her close to the edge but careful not to push her over. He entwined their fingers and raised her hands above her head and slowed the tempo, wanting to make this last for as long as possible.

Eyes closed, Nikki chanted his name, nearly overwhelming him. He wouldn't last much longer. He increased his tempo, feeling his orgasm building.

Nikki's legs tightened around him, her eyes flying open and locking on his. "Terrence." She moaned.

He let go of her hands and gripped her hips, tilting her so he could seat himself deeper inside her, and drove them faster, harder, any tenderness lost in the driving need for release.

Eyes closed, she convulsed around him, screaming his name as she came. His head fell back as his own orgasm took him.

He dropped down on the bed next to Nikki, still shuddering. He pulled Nikki in close to his side, and she rested her head against his bare chest. The cut above his eye throbbed, but it was a pain well worth it if it meant sharing Nikki's bed.

He drew small circles on her back as his pulse slowly returned to normal. "How do you feel?"

Nikki chuckled softly and pressed a kiss to his shoulder. "Don't you know how I feel?"

"That's not…not what I meant." He felt heat climb the back of his neck.

Nikki propped herself up on an elbow. "I know what you meant. And I told you, I wanted you to make love to me. I'm fine."

He was happy to hear her refer to what they'd done as making love, as opposed to a cruder term, but it wasn't enough. He wanted more from her, and he needed her to know that.

"I know I hurt you, and I understand that it will take time before you fully trust me again, but I want that. I want you to trust me. I want us to try to make a relationship work."

She slid away from him. "It's not just about the past and our families' feud. We don't really know each other anymore."

"You know that's not true. You know me better than anyone else on this earth and you would, even if we spent the next fifty years apart."

She shook her head. "You live in Trenton, and I live… I don't even know where I live. I don't even have a job."

"Those are just details. We can work all that out." He took her hand in his and drew in a deep breath. "What I'm asking is that we try? Fourteen years ago, we were on our way to something incredible, and I think we can still get there. I think we can get to something even better, because now I understand what's really important—you. Us. We can't change the past, but we can move forward. Together. If you want to."

He held his breath. Time slowed to a near stop. He'd never wanted anything more than to hear Nikki say she wanted to be with him. To try to make a life with him.

"I need time to think."

It wasn't what he wanted to hear, but it wasn't a no. He'd hold on to that for now.

"Take all the time you need. I'm not going anywhere."

Chapter Twenty

Terrence awoke before dawn. Nikki slept curled up next to him. He brushed his fingertips over the soft skin of her shoulder. The burst of sheer satisfaction at the sight of her face, so peaceful in sleep, on the pillow was everything he'd ever wanted even though he hadn't realized it. Or rather, hadn't let himself think about it.

Nikki was the woman he wanted, and Lance was right. He had to do whatever it took to keep her safe.

He started to rise, attempting to slip from the bed without waking her.

Nikki's arm tightened around his waist. "Where do you think you're going?"

He didn't want to start their renewed relationship out with a lie, so he tried deflection. "Shh." He dropped a kiss on her forehead. "I just want to check something out."

Nikki's eyes opened. "Check what out?"

"It's nothing for you to worry about. You should go back to sleep. It's still early."

Nikki sat up and fixed him with a stare. "No keeping secrets. No shutting each other out or pushing each other away. I want to try to get back what we had. Something deeper and truer even, but we can only get there if we're completely honest with each other. Completely, Terrence."

He sighed. "I'm going back to Pete Bonny's place. I'm hoping to catch him at home. He might have some idea where his nephew could be hiding."

"You don't think Sheriff Webb has asked him about that?"

"If he's found him, I'm sure he has, but Lance isn't likely to share that information with me, especially not after yesterday. And now, more than ever, I want to know what Pete didn't tell us when we picked up the boat the other day."

Nikki swung her feet over the side of the bed and started for the bathroom. "Okay, give me a minute to get dressed."

"No."

She turned back around to look at him. "What?"

"I can't let you go with me."

She scowled. "This again?"

He crossed the room and took her hands in his. "It's not like before. We're dealing with some very dangerous and potentially desperate people who have shot at us. And then finding Jill's car. I may already be too late to save her—"

Nikki squeezed his hands. "You can't think that way."

"Not thinking it doesn't make it any less true. I may have to face the worst. But I couldn't take it if my actions got you hurt. I just got you back. I can't risk losing you."

Nikki slipped her arms around his neck and drew him close. "You aren't going to lose me. And you're crazy if you think I'm going to let you investigate without me."

"Nikki—"

"No, you listen to me now. If we're going to do this, we're going to be full partners. You've got my back and I've got yours. Always." Her words were impassioned. Her eyes were full of sincerity and full-hearted. He had no doubt that she meant every word.

"Always."

While she showered, Terrence got coffee started. There was still little in the house to eat, so he made them both egg sandwiches and ate his while Nikki got dressed. Then he took a quick shower, and they were off as dawn began to crest. As far as he knew, Lance and his deputies still hadn't yet caught up with Pete to talk. But Terrence figured he might have better luck if he approached the man early.

"Are you sure this is a good idea?" Nikki asked as he drove them toward Pete Bonny's property.

The cop in him mentally answered with a resounding no. It wasn't clear whether Pete knew or had a hand in the criminal activity of his nephew, but the fact that Lance hadn't been able to track him down wasn't a good sign. "It's better than sitting at Lakewood House waiting for something to happen."

He pulled to a stop in front of Pete's home. They'd only taken a few steps toward the door when he saw that it was cracked open. "The door is open. Stay behind me."

They crept toward the door together. It didn't look as if the door had been forced. Maybe Pete had simply gone out and forgotten to close it all the way. Since the deputy Lance had sent out to speak with Pete would have certainly noticed the open door, he could assume Pete had been home in the last twenty-four hours. Was he here now?

"Pete?" No response. "It's Terrence Sutton and Nikki King. Are you in there?" He stepped to the door with Nikki at his side. "Pete? Hello? Your door is wide open."

There was nothing but silence from within the house.

The hairs on the back of his neck stood up. Something was wrong.

He peered around the open door. "Pete, are you in there?"

He crossed the threshold, Nikki behind him.

A plate sat on the kitchen table, the uneaten crusts of a sandwich and crumbs still on it. One cabinet door was open, and a chair had been overturned on its side. He and Nikki crept through the house to the bedroom. Three of the four dresser drawers were open, their contents strewn on the bed and the floor. The fourth and lowest drawer had been pulled completely free. It rested next to the dresser, the shirts inside seemingly undisturbed. The closet door stood open with several empty hangers askew.

"There's no one here," he said.

"I don't know if that's a good thing or a bad thing. This place looks like it's been ransacked," Nikki said.

He turned and led her from the bedroom back into the living area. "Yeah, the question is, who did it?"

She looked at him with curiosity in her eyes. "What do you mean?"

"I don't think the place has been ransacked as much as someone decided to leave in a hurry."

Her gaze swept around the room again. "Really? How can you tell?"

"Take the kitchen, for instance. There's only a single cabinet door open, which suggests that someone was looking for something specific and expected to find it in that cabinet. The chair is overturned, but that could have been done in the rush. Clothing is thrown about in the bedroom, but the bed is undisturbed, as were the nightstands. I'd say someone packed in a hurry rather than searched the place."

"Someone. You mean Pete. You think he's running," she said.

Terrence turned in a slow circle, taking in every inch of the space. "I think it's possible. Maybe even likely."

Nikki shook her head, a look of disbelief on her face. "I can't believe Pete would have anything to do with a human trafficking ring."

He'd seen enough as a detective that people rarely surprised him anymore. Soccer moms who ran hundred-thousand-dollar-a-year drug operations. Little old ladies who regularly stole for sport. Kids not old enough to vote leading organized gangs. People had a seemingly infinite capacity for crime, especially when it was profitable.

Something caught his eye. A piece of paper stuck out from under the sofa. He crossed the living space and bent to pick it up. "He might not have, at least not directly."

"What is that?" Nikki looked over his shoulder.

"It looks like the list of homes Pete has been hired as caretaker for and his schedule for checking up on them. He's got three places he takes care of in addition to Lakewood House."

"This is the address for the old Pierce place." Nikki pointed to the first address on the list. "And this one here is Ricky Tanner's place." She pointed at the last address. "But I don't recognize this one here."

It was familiar to him. He didn't know who owned the house, but the address wasn't that far from Aunt Charity's cabin. "I think it's that new all-glass modern place some financier or hedge fund person is building not far from Aunt Charity's place. She drove me past the property the last time I was in town to visit." A thought struck him. "I can't believe I didn't realize this earlier." Terrence shook his head, mentally flogging himself.

Nikki cocked her head to one side. "Realize what?"

"Pete has access to at least four homes that he knows will be empty at any given time." He shook the paper in his hand. "These three houses and Lakewood House. If you wanted to move women through town without anyone noticing, they'd be the perfect hiding places."

Nikki reached into her purse. "We should call the sheriff."

He shook his head. "All we have is conjecture. There's not a judge in the state who would give Lance a warrant to search any of the three houses based on what we have."

"But I'm guessing you have a plan."

"I'm going to go check them out myself. As Lance said, I have no jurisdiction in Carling Lake, so I don't need a warrant."

"I don't think that was what Lance meant by pointing out you had no jurisdiction. You can be arrested for trespassing and breaking and entering."

He was already moving toward the door. She followed him. "It's a chance I'm willing to take. Pete and Dana could be holding Jill in one of these places. And other women." He stopped and gave her a long look. "But I understand if it's not a chance you want to take."

"I said we were in this together, and I meant it."

He shot her a smile as they got into the car. And he plugged the first address into his GPS. "I think we should leave the second address for last. It's closest to town and also mostly glass, both of which make it less desirable for hiding someone."

"Okay, so that means the Tanner place is first, then," Nikki said, reading the address he'd punched into the GPS.

He started the engine and pointed them in the direction the GPS directed. "It's the most isolated."

They made it to the house in record time.

His memory had served him well. The house had a rustic feel with a stone and log fronting, but it was large and looked to have been well taken care of in the owner's absence. It also appeared to be vacant. The driveway was empty. There wasn't a hint of movement from inside the house as the car approached.

He got out of the Highlander and met Nikki at the hood. Nikki already had her gun in her hand, and he pulled his.

They tried the front door and found it locked. They rounded the house to the back door and discovered that it, too, was locked. The shades on all the windows were pulled down, so there was no way to see in from the outside.

He was contemplating whether it was worth it to break in and check out the house thoroughly or whether he should just move on to the second house on Pete's list when Nikki grabbed his arm.

"Wait. Do you hear that? It sounds like metal clanging."

He stilled, closed his eyes and listened. After a few seconds, he heard it. It sounded like someone was banging metal on metal. "It's coming from inside." That answered his question about whether it was worth it to go inside. "Stand back."

Nikki moved off to the side of the back door.

He kicked the lock once. Twice. On the third try, the door splintered but held. He gave it one more fierce kick, and the door swung open.

The daylight streaming in from the broken door cast shadows over the spaces. The main level of the house was really just one very large room with pillars setting off designated areas—living room, dining room, kitchen.

He moved into the house with Nikki at his back, her gun as steady as a pro. He tried the light switches on the wall next to the door he'd kicked in. Nothing happened. The electricity appeared to have been shut off.

Nikki laid a hand on his shoulder. "Listen."

They both stilled. The banging had grown louder. It was definitely coming from inside.

"Downstairs." He swept his gaze across the space until it fell on a door under the staircase. He headed that way, opening the door slowly and peering down the stairs. It was too dark to see anything, but using the flashlight from his phone could potentially alert whoever was down there to their presence if kicking in the back door hadn't.

The clanging stopped.

"Help." The word was low and scratchy, as if the person uttering it hadn't had water in a long time. Still, he'd have known that voice anywhere.

Jill.

Forgetting every bit of police training he'd ever had, he rushed down the stairs. "Jill? Jill, it's Terrence. Where are you?"

A whimper came from the far corner of the basement. He pulled his phone from his pocket and engaged the flashlight.

Jill was huddled on the floor. Her hair was matted

with dirt, and her usually glowing medium brown skin was filthy. An empty food tray sat on the ground at her side and a ratty wool blanket covered her legs. A metal chain, much like the ones they'd found at the house on Carling Island, ran from a hook in the wall and was attached to the cuff around Jill's wrist. Even in the dim light, he could see where it had cut into her skin, leaving bloody bruises.

More rage than he'd have thought possible flared inside him. And it didn't fade at all when he noticed that Jill wasn't alone.

Pete Bonny lay on his side next to her. He'd been shackled to the wall at his ankle, and his hair was matted with dirt and blood at the temple. He was deathly still.

Terrence's gaze swung back to Jill. She shrunk farther into the corner. Then slowly, her face seemed to register that he wasn't there to hurt her. To register who he was. "Terrence."

He holstered his gun and was by her side in two steps, followed closely by Nikki. He reached for the chain connecting his sister to the wall and spoke to Nikki. "Check on Pete, would you?"

Nikki moved to Pete's side, pressing two fingers to his neck while she slid her gun into her ankle holster. "There's a pulse, but it's faint. Really faint."

He tapped his phone, bringing up the keypad and dialing 911. "Just hang on, sweetheart. We're going to get you out of here."

"Nine-one-one. What's your emergency?" the operator said on the other end of the phone line.

Before he could answer, a different, closer voice spoke. "Hang up that phone. Now." Terrence whirled, dropping the phone and reaching for his gun at the same time.

"I would not do that if I were you." Dana Bonny stood by the stairs, holding a gun on them. The tall man who'd been with him on Carling Island stood beside him with his own gun aimed in their direction.

"Throw your gun and the phone over here. Now!" Dana yelled.

Terrence hesitated for a moment, but with Dana holding a gun on them, he had no choice. He slid his gun and the phone across the floor.

"Is everything okay? What is your emerg—"

Dana stomped on the phone, cutting off the voice on the line. They could only hope that the operator was able to get a location for the call and would dispatch law enforcement to check it out.

Jill whimpered.

"Now stand up. Get your hands in the air."

Again, he and Nikki did as told. There wasn't much choice. He couldn't take the chance that they'd start shooting.

Dana smiled an oily gapped-tooth smile. He jerked a nod at his companion. "Well, isn't this a nice parting gift? We only came back here to clean up loose ends." Dana motioned toward Jill and Pete. "But you two—" Dana's expression hardened. "You're the reason why we have to shut down operations in Carling Lake and find a new transport hub. You disrupted my business and cost me money. I'm going to take a lot of pleasure in killing you both."

Chapter Twenty-One

Nikki fought to hide the panic swelling in her chest. "You won't get away with this. The sheriff knows you shot at us on Carling Island and all about the trafficking."

"Oh, does he now? Well, there's a difference between what the sheriff knows and what he can prove," Dana sneered. "And once I get rid of you lot, there will be a lot less so-called proof." He raised the gun in his hand a little higher.

Nikki felt Terrence's body tighten like a coil next to her. She knew him well enough to know he was preparing to do something. Something heroic and incredibly stupid given the two guns trained on them. He'd tossed his gun about two feet away and to the side. Her gun was in its holster hidden beneath her pant leg, but she couldn't get to it without alerting Dana and his minion.

"I don't understand," she blurted. "Why did you attack Pete? Isn't he part of your trafficking ring?"

Dana laughed. "Uncle Pete? He doesn't have guts. I used him to find out when the owners of the homes he took care of wouldn't be there. They were perfect."

"Pete needs medical attention."

"Uncle Pete should have stayed out of my business. There's nothing I can do to help him now."

The man beside Dana scowled. "Let's just get this over with."

"Wait. If you're going to kill us, I think we at least deserve to know exactly why."

"You think you deserve—" Dana laughed derisively.

Nikki ignored his tone. "Yes. I remember you when you were a kid." A lie, but she'd do whatever she had to in order to get Dana to see them as human and not obstacles to him getting away with his crimes. "You were always a risk-taker, but you were never an evil person. How did you get involved in this?"

"What can I say? Small-time risks that led to bigger, more profitable ventures. Isn't that how upward mobility, promotion within an organization, works? Nobody thinks twice about it when it's college-educated criminals climbing the corporate ladder. But I was never going to be a nine-to-five job kind of guy. The opportunity arose, and the money was too good to pass up."

"You kidnap and exploit women," Terrence snapped. "It's not a job. It's a crime."

"You sound just like your sister over there," Dana snarled. "I knew the moment I found out she was snooping around she was going to be trouble."

"So you kidnapped her?" Nikki asked.

"She's too old to make her a part of my business. I needed time to figure out what to do about her, but then you came to town." Dana glared.

"What about the dead girl I found at Lakewood House? Did you kill her?" Nikki asked. As scared as she was, she still wanted to know the whole sordid story.

"My associate here got a little too aggressive when the girl tried to run away. An unfortunate mistake."

Nikki looked at the man beside Dana. He stared back at her with flat, emotionless eyes. He hadn't so much as flinched at having been labeled a murderer. "Who is he?"

Dana slid a sidelong glance at his companion. "A representative of the man in charge."

"The man in charge," Terrence said. "Who would that be?"

"That's none of your concern, especially since you'll never meet him. Or anyone else, for that matter."

"Enough talk," the man beside Dana growled. "What do you want to do with them?"

Terrence slid closer.

"I figure take 'em deep into the woods, put a bullet in them and let the animals feast," Dana said.

"What about the old guy?"

"We'll have to take care of him when we come back to clean up the house so no one ever knows we were here. You heard what she said anyway." Dana jerked his head at Nikki. "He's in bad shape after the beating you gave him. You've got to learn to control yourself." Dana gave his partner a disgruntled look. "We can bury him in the woods and get the hell out of here."

Anger at the callousness with which Dana was talking about his own uncle soared inside her, along with fear of what he had planned for them.

Dana took a key from his pocket and tossed it at Terrence, who caught it. "Unlock your sister and help her up. If you try anything funny, I'll put a bullet in your girlfriend."

Terrence went to Jill, unlocking her wrist from the cuff and lifting her to her feet.

"Now, we're going up those stairs and outside."

Dana and his partner shifted to either side of the stairwell, leaving a large swath of space for them to pass up the stairs.

Terrence helped Jill upstairs and Nikki followed behind them.

At the top of the stairs, Nikki scanned the main floor for a weapon. Dana's partner grabbed her arm and pulled her against him. "Don't get any ideas, huh?"

The two men pushed them out the front door and across the lawn toward the dense trees lining the property. Despite there still being plenty of daylight left, the density of the trees surrounding them left them shrouded in semidarkness. That alone would have made the little hike they were on terrifying enough, but with two stone-cold criminals pointing guns at their backs, it was as if they were caught in a horror movie. One that did not promise a happy ending.

They marched through the woods for nearly a half hour before Dana told them to stop.

"Turn around," Dana commanded.

They did so, Jill still leaning heavily against Terrence. She looked over at Terrence, but his eyes were glued to Dana and the other man with the gun.

They were out of time. If they were going to get out of this, they'd have to do something now.

Dana raised his gun with a smirk. "Any last words?"

THERE WAS NO way Terrence was going to let Dana Bonny and his henchman kill Jill or Nikki. Hiking through the woods half carrying his injured sister wasn't exactly conducive to planning the takedown of two armed human traffickers, but it's the situation he had to work with. He'd managed to whisper to follow his lead as they walked. He was about to find out if Nikki would do the same.

"Any last words?"

"Now!" Terrence screamed, letting go of Jill.

She crumpled to the ground with a dramatic flourish, drawing Dana's gaze her way.

He seized upon Dana's momentary distraction and launched himself at the man. He caught movement out of the corner of his eye and hoped that it was Nikki taking the opportunity to run from the gunmen. There was no time to be sure though.

He grabbed Dana's arm, attempting to twist the gun away from him and toward the ground. Dana was stronger than he looked, but this was a fight not only for his life but for Nikki's and Jill's lives as well. That gave him an extra boost of strength that Dana could never match. Dana swung his free hand, his fist connecting with Terrence's face. The punch sent him reeling back, but he didn't let go of Dana or the gun. The momentum pulled Dana off balance. The two men toppled to the ground, still locked in a battle for the weapon.

Terrence kicked out his legs, throwing Dana off him. As he did, the gun flew from Dana's hand. He dived toward it, but Dana tackled him before he could reach it. A well-placed punch to the nose had him seeing stars. Precious time lost.

Dana crawled toward the gun, his hand wrapping around it just as Jill stumbled into the fray armed with a thick tree branch. The branch came down on Dana's arm with a sickening crunch.

Dana's howl was cut off by another swing of the branch, this one connecting with the side of his head. Dana fell to his stomach in the dirt, stunned but not knocked out. He'd recover in a moment and be madder than ever.

Terrence pushed to his feet. Ten feet from him, Dana's friend had seemingly lost his gun too, but he held

Nikki around the waist in a death grip, attempting to drag her away into the woods.

As the man lifted Nikki's feet from the ground, she bent forward, sinking her teeth into his wrist. He screamed and dropped her.

Next to him, Dana shifted, recovering quickly from Jill's blow to his head. Jill, however, had not recovered as fast. Having used what limited energy she had stored up, she squatted in the dirt next to a nearby tree, still clutching the branch but obviously spent.

If Dana got his gun back, they were all dead.

Terrence scanned the ground, his eyes landing on the gun at the same time as Dana's did. They scrambled toward the weapon, but before either reached it, a gunshot thundered, echoing off the trees.

For a moment, it seemed as if everything froze—from the breeze to the small forest animals scurrying away from the ruckus they were causing. Time stood still.

Then Dana's partner stumbled backward away from Nikki. Both of his hands were pressed against his chest. He took two more steps backward, then fell to his knees before rolling onto his back.

Nikki's eyes were wide and wild. She pointed the gun from her ankle holster at the man.

Terrence took advantage of everyone's momentary shock to scoop Dana's gun from the ground and level it at the man. "Don't move."

Dana glared. "You don't have the guts."

His voice little more than a growl, Terrence said, "One wrong move. Just give me a reason."

The sound of engines broke through the trees.

Terrence tensed, hoping that the sounds were that of the cavalry coming and not Dana's boss.

Moments later, three sheriff's department ATVs cut a path through the brush.

Sheriff Webb jumped off his ATV and pulled his gun, Deputy Bridges and another one close behind. "Terrence, Nikki, are you both okay? We got an emergency call from your cell phone number, and I was able to triangulate your GPS with help from James. What's going on here?"

Terrence filled him in quickly and held Dana at gunpoint while the deputies cuffed him and the other man. Then he passed Dana's gun off to the sheriff and ran to Jill's side.

"I'm okay," she said in a weak voice.

Since it was clear that she was not okay, he called out, "We need EMTs ASAP."

Sheriff Webb and Nikki joined him at Jill's side, and the sheriff radioed for EMTs and more backup while Nikki did her best to help him make Jill as comfortable as possible.

Jill rested her head against his shoulder, exhausted from her ordeal.

Terrence looked across at the woman he was falling in love with again. "Good job back there."

She smiled at him, then shifted her attention to Jill, brushing a strand of matted hair from her face. "We always did make a good team."

He smiled now too. "Yes, yes, we always have."

Chapter Twenty-Two

Jill sat up in the hospital bed, chatting happily with the nurse taking her blood pressure. She had been dehydrated and had several bumps and bruises but was otherwise fine. She'd even felt well enough to argue with the doctor when he'd told her he was keeping her overnight for observation. Terrence had finally done the unthinkable and brought in the big guns to convince her to listen. Aunt Charity had worked her magic and promised that she wouldn't leave Jill's side before she was discharged.

Lance and his men had searched the other properties Pete acted as caretaker for, but so far, they hadn't found any other girls. The FBI was being called in, but with the way trafficking rings operated, one hand often didn't know what the other did in order to make it harder for the authorities to take down the entire operation. The knowledge that other victims were out there was like a gut punch in the midst of his happiness over having found Jill alive.

Nikki stopped next to Terrence outside the hospital room door, wrapping her arms around his waist.

"How'd your call go?" he said.

"Great." Nikki shifted so she could look him in the eye. "I withdrew from consideration for the job."

"You what? Why?"

"This town meant a lot to Grandpa Bernie. And it means a lot to me. I've always known I wanted to run for elected office and do what I could to make life better for people. It's a little sooner than I planned, but I think I'm ready. I'm going to throw my hat in the ring for Carling Lake mayor."

Terrence pulled her into a hug. "Congratulations. This town is lucky to have you."

"I haven't won yet."

"You will." He dropped a kiss on her head.

She looked into his eyes. "I made another decision. I want us. I want to be with you."

A smile bloomed on his face and he crushed his mouth against hers. After a long moment, she pulled back from the kiss.

"Of course, running for mayor means I'll be moving into Lakewood House permanently and staying in Carling Lake."

"We'll figure it out. Trenton isn't that far away, and the most important thing to me is making our relationship work this time."

Nikki pressed a kiss to his mouth. "Me too." She snuggled in closer to his side and glanced into the hospital room. "How's Jill?"

"The doctor says she's fine. He's keeping her overnight but expects she'll be able to go home tomorrow, as long as she promises to rest for a few days."

"That's great." Nikki gave his waist a squeeze. "Of course, she's welcome to stay at Lakewood House if she's not ready to go back to DC just yet." Her voice sounded tentative, as if she weren't sure how he'd feel about the offer.

He gazed down into her dark brown eyes. "Thank you."

"Of course. Jill is my friend."

"I think she's going to need friends and family around her for a while. The doctor feels good about her physical recovery, but he warned Jill that her mental and emotional recovery will probably be much harder. He suggested a psychiatrist, but Jill didn't seem too open to it."

"Give her time. She might change her mind in a few days."

"I hope so. She says that Dana didn't hurt her, but I don't know…"

"Hey. Let's take one step at a time. Jill knows we're here for her, and we will do whatever it takes to help her get through this."

He pulled her closer. "I don't know what I'd do without you."

Nikki pulled back just enough so she could look at him. "It's a good thing you don't need to worry about that then." She hesitated a moment. "You know, talking to someone isn't a bad idea for you either."

He arched his eyebrows.

"You've been through a lot too. Jill going missing, wondering where she was or if she was hurt. Just… think about it."

He nodded.

"Hey, guys. How is Jill doing?"

Terrence turned with Nikki still in his arms. Lance stood behind them. "She's going to be okay."

"Excellent. I'm glad to hear that even if I'm not happy about you two seeking out Dana Bonny on your own." Lance narrowed his gaze at them. "But we can discuss that later."

Terrence was pretty sure that by "discuss," Lance meant telling them off for jumping into a dangerous situation without calling him first. So be it. If that was the price he had to pay for saving his sister, he was more than happy to pay it. "Have you got a name from Dana's partner yet?"

"Yeah, William Weigel. Career criminal."

"Have either of them made a statement?"

Lance shook his head. "Not a word beyond 'I want a lawyer.' But they'll break. Guys like them always do. They're just the foot soldiers though. They might not know that much about the overall operation."

"What about Pete?" Nikki asked.

"He's in bad shape, but he'll survive. Cracked ribs. A couple of broken teeth. He regained consciousness enough to tell me that he'd confronted his nephew after news of you two being shot at made it around town. He denies knowing about the trafficking ring, but he says he knew that Dana sometimes used the houses he acted as caretaker for to party."

"Very professional," Terrence deadpanned.

"You get what you pay for," Lance shot back. "No offense, Nikki."

"None taken." She gave a small smile.

"Do you believe Pete's telling the truth when he says he didn't know about the trafficking?"

Lance threw up his hands. "Who knows? People have an extraordinary capacity for ignoring what they don't want to see."

Terrence couldn't argue with that.

"Do you think your sister is up for making a statement? If I can get some details, I might be able to use them to get those guys to talk."

He and Nikki had already given Lance their statements, but the EMTs had whisked Jill away.

The three of them stepped into Jill's hospital room. Aunt Charity sat beside the bed, holding Jill's hand.

The nurse finished typing on the tablet she held and looked up. "Only three visitors at a time."

Aunt Charity stood. "I'll go grab coffee. Anyone want anything?"

They all declined, and Aunt Charity left with the nurse.

"Ms. Sutton, I'm Sheriff Lance Webb. First, let me just say how relieved I am that you're going to be okay."

"Not more relieved than I am, Sheriff." Jill smiled.

Lance returned her smile. "I'm sure I'm not." He flipped his small notebook open to a clean page. "If you're up for it, I'd like to ask you a few questions."

"I'm up for it. Ask away."

"Okay, well, let's start at the beginning. What brought you to Carling Lake?"

Jill took a deep breath and let it out slowly. "I got a call about a week ago from a woman who said she'd escaped from a trafficking ring but that her friend was still being held captive."

Lance scribbled on the notepad. "Did you get this woman's name?"

Jill shook her head. "She wouldn't give me her name, and the call came from a blocked number."

"Okay. What else did the woman say?"

"She didn't want to tell me too much. She was terrified, as you can imagine. She told me that she'd been promised a job as a live-in nanny for a rich family upstate by a man she'd met in a bar. He was supposed to drive her to her new job, but instead he took her to a warehouse where there were three other women. They were beaten and assaulted, then transported somewhere else. The woman wasn't sure where because she was in and out of consciousness. But she did hear the men talking about Carling Lake. And she remembered they both had the same very distinctive tattoo on their biceps."

Jill paused and took several deep breaths. It was clear that telling the woman's story was taking an emotional toll on her.

"We can take a break if you need one," Lance offered.

"No. No, I'm okay. She said she managed to get away when one of the clients—that's what she said the men who kidnapped her called them, 'clients'—" disgust permeated Jill's tone "—passed out. She grabbed the cash from his wallet and a card with the same symbol the men had tattooed on their arms and ran. She gave me the card when we met up."

"How did she find you?" Nikki asked.

"I have no idea. She said she didn't know what to do or who she could trust. I'm not sure how she decided to trust me, but I'm glad she did."

"So you came to Carling Lake to investigate a possible human trafficking ring on your own," Terrence growled.

Lance shot him a quelling look.

"Yes, Terrence. I came to Carling Lake to investigate on my own because that's what I do. I'm an investigative reporter, or did you forget, big brother?" His sister pinned him with a scowl.

"I haven't forgotten, but—"

Nikki grabbed his arm and squeezed. "Maybe we should just let Jill tell her story for now."

"That would be ideal," Lance said. "What happened when you arrived in Carling Lake, Ms. Sutton?"

"You can call me Jill. I knew I'd need to keep a low profile, so I decided to stay at Lakewood House rather than with Aunt Charity. I knew it was just sitting there empty, and I didn't think you'd mind, Nikki."

"Of course not." Nikki reached for Jill's hand. "I wish you'd told me though."

"I know I should have. I'm sorry. Anyway, the night I arrived, I was exhausted. I dropped my suitcase in your living room and fell asleep in your guest bedroom. I didn't even bother with making the bed up, I was so wiped out. At some point in the night, I woke up, and these two guys were in the room with me. They grabbed me, and I've been locked in the basement of that house ever since. They'd bring me water and a little food once a day."

Terrence's chest burned with fury. Dana Bonny had better thank his lucky stars he was locked away in a prison cell. Instead of imagining ways to seriously hurt him, Terrence pulled his phone from his pocket and scrolled to the photograph of the business card Nikki found in the kitchen at Lakewood House. "Is this the card?"

"Yes. How?"

"You must have dropped it. Nikki found it at Lakewood House."

"And Dana and Weigel both have fleur-de-lis tattoos," Lance said. "Given the interstate nature of this crime, the Feds will probably take over, but it's a good start for connecting them to the trafficking ring.

"That's enough for now." Lance closed his notebook. "I may have to speak to you again, but for now, rest."

Lance headed for the door.

"I'm going to go check on your aunt. Give you and Jill a moment alone together." Nikki raised her lips to his for a kiss before following Lance out of the room.

Terrence sat on the edge of Jill's hospital bed and

took her hand in his. "You gave me the scare of my life, kid."

"I'm sorry about that. I am. But—" Jill's eyes twinkled "—it looks like some good came of all this. You and Nikki?" She wiggled her eyebrows suggestively.

"I'm glad to see your ordeal hasn't dulled your investigative prowess."

"I'm just happy you and Nikki have finally come to your senses. You two belong together."

Terrence smiled at his sister. "You know what? For once, I'm not going to argue with you."

Chapter Twenty-Three

Nikki eyed the pile of clothes on her bed. "I have nothing to wear to this gallery opening. I really don't think I can go."

"Are you kidding me?" Jill reclined on the bed next to the pile. She wore a black jumpsuit with gold chunky jewelry. A butterfly hairpin adorned her short afro. She looked very bohemian chic. "You have more clothes on this bed than I've owned in my entire life. Not to mention the dresses Erika brought over for you to try on."

In the week since Nikki and Terrence had found her in that basement, Jill had regained most of her strength and energy. She'd talked to her editor and started on the first article in what she was planning to be a multiarticle news spread about her investigation into the trafficking ring. Jill had uttered the word *Pulitzer* in an excitedly hushed tone more than once.

"And you should feel free to wear any of them. I have more than enough." Erika pinned a lock of Nikki's hair up. She'd been working on creating an effortless-looking updo for the past half hour. Nikki had to admit, between the makeup that Jill had applied and the hair, she looked pretty great.

"I think you're just all in a tizzy because you and my brother are going on your first date." Jill grinned.

Nikki rolled her eyes at her friend. "It's hardly our first date."

"It's your first date as adults. The first one that really matters."

Even though he and Jill had been staying with her at Lakewood House for the last several days while Jill recuperated, Terrence had made a point of calling her and asking her to attend the gallery opening as his date, very gentlemanly. It had made her feel a little giddy.

"Okay, I'm making an executive decision," Jill said, lifting herself off the bed. "You should wear the red dress."

"No. No way." Nikki stepped away from the mirror.

"Definitely." Erika clapped her hands. "You looked amazing in that dress. Terrence is going to lose his mind when he sees you in it."

"No. It's way too—"

"Sexy," Jill said.

"Alluring," Erika purred.

"Revealing," Nikki responded.

"That's what makes it perfect." Jill giggled.

Nikki gave in and slipped into the dress. The neckline plunged, revealing more cleavage than she usually did, but she loved the vibrant red color and the loose, flowy skirt that fanned out when she twirled. She was a knockout in this dress. There was no doubt about that. While Nikki put the finishing touches on her outfit, Erika transferred her keys, money and identification from her everyday purse to the little red clutch she had brought over with the dress.

Jill came to stand behind Nikki as she looked at herself in the mirror. "Terrence is going to have a stroke when he sees you."

"Let's hope not," Nikki said wryly.

"I've got to get to the gallery." Erika started for the bedroom door. "I'll come by tomorrow and pick up the other dresses, if that's okay."

"Of course." Nikki grabbed the clutch and walked her new friend to the front door of the house, Jill trailing behind.

"I'm going to catch a ride with Erika, so I'm leaving as well." Jill grabbed her coat from the closet next to the front door.

"You don't have to do that. You can ride with Terrence and me."

Now it was Jill who rolled her eyes. "I'm not going to be the third wheel on your date." Jill put a hand on each of Nikki's shoulders. "Don't worry. You and Terrence are perfect together." She bussed Nikki on her cheek and followed Erika out of the house.

Nikki watched her friends drive away. Dusk had begun to fall, and the trees surrounding the house made it even darker than it actually was.

She closed the door and checked out her image in the mirror once again. She did look pretty amazing. And this was Terrence. She'd known him her entire life. Loved him most of it.

All the air whooshed out of her lungs.

She loved him. Despite the years and the petty feud and whatever else, she loved him. And now she knew she always would.

The doorbell rang and she jumped.

Letting out a breath, she did the best she could to still her racing pulse, to no avail.

"Here we go." She pulled open the door.

Terrence stood on the porch holding a dozen red roses and wearing a perfectly cut black suit. He was pretty alluring himself. She let her eyes roam over him from head to toe, appreciating the view.

"You look amazing," he said, stepping into the house and pressing a kiss to her cheek. He'd gone to James's place to get ready, insisting that they'd do this date right with him picking her up at her door.

"So do you."

She took the roses from him and put them into water.

"Should we go?" She grabbed the clutch from the side table under the mirror.

"Not just yet. I have something I want to show you." Terrence took her hand and led her to the door.

"We're going to be late if we don't leave soon."

"Don't worry. These things never get started on time. Anyway, James will understand if we're late. He helped me set this up for you."

"Set what up?"

"You'll see." He led her onto the porch and around the side of the house.

Her boat had been decorated with white twinkle lights. As they drew closer, she could see that a bistro table had been set up on deck, two flutes and a silver bucket at its center with champagne chilling inside.

"What is all this?"

"We'll get to the gallery opening, but I wanted to make sure this date was special. That we got some time together, just the two of us."

"How did you possibly set all this up without me knowing? I've been inside all day."

"It took some planning but having my sister and Erika on my side, distracting you, helped a lot."

Nikki laughed. "They did their job. I didn't suspect a thing."

"Good." Terrence grabbed the open champagne bottle and poured them both a glass. "To us."

Nikki didn't take her eyes off his as she sipped. She set her glass aside, and he did the same as she stepped into his arms.

She sank into their kiss, filling it with all the things she felt for him. When she pulled back, she slid a sidelong glance at the padded bench seats. "I think we're about to be very late to this opening."

A slow, seductive smile slid across Terrence's face. "Honey, there's nowhere else I'd rather be."

* * * * *

TANGLED THREAT

HEATHER GRAHAM

For Roberta Young Peacock, a true Florida girl,
with lots of love and best wishes.

Prologue

The History Tree

"They see her…the beautiful Gyselle, when the moon is high in the sky. She walks these oak-lined trails and sometimes pauses to touch the soft moss that drips from the great branches, as if she reaches out for them to touch what is real. In life she was kind and generous. She was beloved by so many. And yet, when brought so cruelly to her brutal and unjust death at the infamous History Tree, she cast a curse on those around her. Those involved would die bitter deaths as well, choking on their own blood, breath stolen from them as it had been from her," Maura Antrim said dramatically.

The campfire in the pit burned bright yellow and gold, snapping and crackling softly. All around them, great oaks and pines rose, moss swaying in the light breeze. The moon overhead was full and bright that night, but cloud cover drifted past now and then, creating eerie shadows everywhere.

It was a perfect summer night, and perfect for storytelling. She was glad to be there, glad to be the storyteller and glad of the response from her audience.

Maura's group from the resort—teenagers and adults alike—looked at her, wide-eyed.

She refused to smile—she wanted to remain grave—though she was delighted by the fascination of the guests assembled around her. She had been grateful and pleased to be upgraded to her position of storyteller for the Frampton Ranch and Resort, an enterprise in North Central Florida that was becoming more renowned daily as a destination. The property had been bought about five years back by billionaire hotelier Donald Glass, and he had wisely left the firepit and the old riding trails as they were, the History Tree right where it grew, the ruins of the old plantation just as they lay—and amped up the history first, and then the legends that went along with the area.

Maura wasn't supposed to be on tonight—she shared the position with Francine Renault, a longtime employee of Donald Glass's hotel corporation, probably second in command only to the main resort manager, Fred Bentley. The two of them were known to argue— but Francine stayed right where she was, doing what she wanted. Despite any arguments, Donald Glass refused to fire either Francine or Fred, who, despite his stocky bulk, moved around the resort like a bat out of hell, always getting things done.

Fred Bentley had watched Maura at the start of the evening; she thought that he was smiling benignly— that he approved of her abilities as a social hostess and storyteller.

It was hard to blame him for fighting with Francine. She was…a difficult personality type at best.

And sharing any job with Francine wasn't easy; the woman had an air of superiority about her and a way of treating those she considered to be "lesser" employees very badly. Francine was in her midthirties—and was a beauty, really, a platinum blonde, dark-eyed piece of perfection—and while Maura had turned eighteen, Francine considered all of Donald Glass's summer help annoying, ignorant children.

The young adults—or "camper" summer help— were fond of gossiping. It was rumored that Francine once had an affair with Donald Glass, and that was how she held on to her position—and her superiority.

Glass was married. Maybe Francine was blackmailing him, telling him that if she wasn't given a certain power, she'd tell his wife, Marie, and Marie—or so rumor had it—could be jealous and very threatening when she chose to be. Hard to believe—in public Marie was always the model of decorum, slim and regal, slightly younger than Donald but certainly older than Francine.

Teens and young adults loved to speculate. At Maura's age, the thought of any of the older staff together—all seeming so much older than she was at the time—was simply gross.

Tonight, by not being there, Francine had put herself in a bad position.

She hadn't shown up for work. A no-show without a call was grounds for dismissal, though Maura seriously doubted that Francine would be fired.

Maura looked around, gravely and silently survey-
ing her group before beginning again.

She didn't get a chance—someone spoke up. A
young teenager.

"They should call it the Torture Tree or the Hang-
man's Tree...or something besides the History Tree,"
he said.

The boy's name was Mark Hartford, Maura thought.
She'd supervised a game at the pool one day when
he had been playing. He was a nice kid, curious and,
maybe because he was an adolescent boy, boisterous.
He also had an older brother, Nils—in college already.
Mark's brother wasn't quite as nice; he knew that many
of the workers were his own age or younger, and he
liked to lord his status as a guest over them. He was
bearable, however.

"The Torture Tree! Oh, lord, you little...heathen!"

Nils had a girlfriend. Rachel Lawrence. She was
nicer than Nils, unless Nils was around. Then she behaved with a great deal of superiority, as well. But,
Maura realized, Nils and Rachel *were* at the campfire
that night—they had just joined quietly.

Quietly—which was amazing in itself. Nils liked to
make an entrance most of the time, making sure that
everyone saw him.

Rachel had her hands set upon Mark's shoulders—
even as she called him a heathen. She looked scared,
or nervous maybe, Maura thought. Maybe it was for
effect; Nils set his arm around her shoulders, as a good,
protective boyfriend should. They made a cute family

picture, a young adult male with his chosen mate and a young one under their wings.

Maura was surprised they were on the tour. Nils had said something the other day about the fact that they were too mature for campfire ghost stories.

"Torture Tree—yes, that would be better!" Mark said. He wasn't arguing with Rachel, he was determined that he was right. "Poor Gyselle—she was really tortured there, right?"

Mark and the other young teens were wide-eyed. Teenagers that age liked the sensational—and they liked it grisly.

"She was dragged there and hanged, so yes, I'm sure it was torture," Maura said. "But it was the History Tree long before a plantation was built here, years and years ago," Maura said. "That was the Native American name for it—the Timucua were here years before the Spanish came. They called it the History Tree, because even back then, the old oak had grown together with a palm, and it's been that way since. Anyway, we'll be seeing the History Tree soon enough," she said softly. "The tree that first welcomed terror when the beautiful Gyselle was tormented and hanged from the tree until dead. And where, so they say, the hauntings and horrors of the History Tree began."

Maura saw more than one of her audience members glance back over the area of sweeping, manicured lawn and toward the ranch, as if assuring themselves that more than the night and the spooky, draped trees existed, that there was light and safety not far away.

The new buildings Donald Glass had erected were

elegant and beautiful. With St. Augustine just an hour
and a half in one direction and Disney and Univer-
sal and other theme parks just an hour and half to the
south—not to mention a nice proximity to the beaches
and racetrack at Daytona and the wonder of Cape Ken-
nedy being an hour or so away, as well—Frampton
Ranch and Resort was becoming a must-see location.

Still, the ranch had become renowned for offering
Campfire Ghost Histories. Not stories, but histories—
everything said was history and fact…to a point.

The listeners could hear what people claimed to
have happened, and they could believe—or not. And
then they'd walk the trails where history had occurred.

"You see, Gyselle had been a lovely lost waif, raised
by the Seminole tribe after they found her wandering
near the battlefield at the end of the Second Seminole War. She was 'rescued' by Spanish missionaries
at the beginning of the Third Seminole War, though,
at that point, she probably didn't want or need rescu-
ing, having been with a Seminole family for years. But
'saved' and then set adrift, she found work at the old
Frampton plantation, and there she caught the eye of
the heir, and despite his arranged marriage to socialite
Julie LeBlanc, the young Richard Frampton fell head
over heels in love with Gyselle. They were known to
escape into the woods where they both professed their
love, despite all the odds against them—and Richard's
wife, Julie. Knowing of her husband's infidelity, Julie
LeBlanc arranged to poison her father-in-law—and let
the blame fall on Gyselle. Gyselle was hunted down as
a murderous witch, supposedly practicing a shaman's

magic or a form of voodoo—it was easy to blame it on traditions the plantation workers didn't really understand—and she was hanged there, from what was once a lover's tree where she had met with Richard, her love, who had promised to protect her..."

She let her voice trail. Then she finished.

"Here, in these woods, Gyselle loved, not wisely, but deeply. And here she died. And so they say, when the moon has risen high and full in the night sky—as it is now—those who walk the trails by night can hear her singing softly 'The Last Rose of Summer' with a lovely Irish lilt to her voice."

"What about the curse?" a boy cried out.

"Yeah, the curse! That she spoke before she died—swearing that her tormenters would choke on their own blood! You just said that she cursed everyone, and there are more stories, right?" Mark—never one to be silent long—asked eagerly.

Maura felt—rather than saw—Brock McGovern at her side. He was amused. Barely eighteen, he'd nevertheless been given the position of stage manager for events such as the campfire history tour. He'd been standing to one side just behind her as she told her tale with just the right dramatic emphasis—or so she believed.

He stepped forward, just a shade closer, nearly touching her.

"Choking on their own blood? Kind of a standard curse, huh?" he teased softly and for her ears alone.

Maura ignored him, trying not to smile, and still,

even here, now, felt the rush she always did when Brock was around.

Brock was always ready to tease—but also to encourage and support whatever she was doing. He had that ability and the amazing tendency to exude an easy confidence that stretched far beyond his years. But he was that sure of himself. He was about to leave for the service, and when he returned, he planned to go to college to study criminology. Barely an adult, he knew what he wanted in life. She was sure he was going to work hard during basic training; he'd work hard through the college or university of his choice. And then he'd make up his mind just where he wanted to serve—FBI, US Marshals, perhaps even Homeland Security or the Secret Service.

He shook his head, smiling at her with his unusual eyes—a shade so dark that they didn't appear brown at times, but rather black. His shaggy hair—soon to become a buzz cut—was as dark as his eyes, and it framed a face that was, in Maura's mind, pure enchantment. He had already had a fine, steady chin—the kind most often seen on more mature men. His cheekbones were broad, and his skin was continually bronzed. He was, in her mind, beautiful.

He'd often told the tales himself, and he did so very well. He had a deep, rich voice that could rise and fall at just the right moments—a voice that, on its own, could awaken every sense in Maura's body. They had known each other for three years now, laughed and joked together, ridden old trails, worked together... always flirting, nearly touching at first, but always aware that, when summer ended, he would head back down to Key West and she would return to West Palm Beach—about 233 miles apart, just a little too far for a high school romance.

But this summer…

Things had changed.

She had liked him from the time she had met him; she had compared any other young man she met to him, and in her mind, all others fell short. He'd been given a management job that summer, probably because he was always willing to pitch in himself, whether it came to working in the restaurant when tables needed bussing or hauling in boxes when deliveries arrived. He'd gained a lean and muscular physique from hard work as much as from time in the gym, and he had a quick mind and a quicker wit, cared for people, was generous with his time, and was just…

Perfect. She'd never find anyone so perfect in life again, Maura was certain, even though she knew that her mother and father smiled indulgently when she talked about him in glowing terms—she was, after all, just eighteen, with college days and so much more ahead of her.

This summer they'd become a true couple. In every way.

A very passionate couple.

They'd had sex, in her mind, the most amazing sex ever, more meaningful than any sex had ever been before.

Just the thought brought a rush of blood to her face.

But…she believed that they would go on even

through their separation, no matter the distance, no matter what. People would think, of course, that she was just a teenager, that she couldn't be as madly in love as she believed she was. So she was determined that no one would really realize just how insanely fully she did love him.

She turned to Brock. He was smiling at her. Something of a secret smile, charming, sexy…a smile that seemed to hint that they always shared something unique, something special.

She grinned in return.

Yep. He had become her world.

"Take it away," she told him.

"The curse!" he said, stepping in with a tremor in his voice. "It's true that while being dragged to the tree—which you'll see soon on our walk—the poor woman cried out that she was innocent of any cruel deed, innocent of murder. And she said that those who so viciously killed her would die in agony and despair. The very woods here would be haunted for eternity, and the evil they perpetrated on her would live forever. They had brought the devil into the woods, and there he would abide."

He smiled, innately charming when he spoke to a group, and continued, "I think that storytellers have added in the choking-on-blood part. Very dramatic and compelling, but…there are records of the occasion of the poor woman's demise available at the resort library." He set his flashlight beneath his chin, creating an eerie look.

"And," Maura said, "what is also documented is that

bad things continued to happen on the ranch—under the same tree, the condemned killer, Marston Riggs, tortured and killed his victims in the early 1900s, and as late as 1970, the man known as the Red Tie Killer made use of the tree as well, killing five men and women at the History Tree and leaving their bones to fall to the ground. But, of course, we don't believe in curses. The History Tree and the ranch are perfectly safe nowadays…" She looked at Brock. "Shall we?" she asked.

"Indeed, we shall," he said, and the sound of his voice and the look that he gave her made her long for it to be later, when they had completed the nighttime forest tour—and were alone together.

They walked by the grove, where there was a charming little pond rumored to invigorate life—a handsomely written plaque commemorating the Spaniard Reynaldo Montenegro and his exploration of Florida.

Brock said to the tour group, "Here we are at the famous grove where Reynaldo Montenegro claimed to have found the Pond of Eternal Youth."

It was as great tour; even the adolescents continued to ask questions as they walked.

"I'm happy to have been the tour guide tonight," Maura murmured to Brock. "But I can't believe that Francine just didn't show up."

"If I know Francine, she'll make a grand entrance somewhere along the line, with a perfect reason for not being on time. She'll have some mammoth surprise for everyone—something way more important than speaking to the guests. Hey, what do you want to bet that we see her somewhere before this tour is over? Here, folks," Brock announced, "you'll see the plaque—an inquisition did come to the New World!"

The copse, illuminated only by the sparkling lights that lit the trail, offered a sadder message—that of tortures carried out by an invading society on the native population it encountered.

They passed the ruins of an old Spanish farm and then they neared the tree.

The infamous History Tree.

The tree—or trees—older than anyone could remember, stood dead center in the small clearing, as if nothing else would dare to grow near. Gnarled and twisted together, palm and oak suggested a mess of human limbs, coiled together in agony.

Maura stopped dead, hearing a long, terrified scream, then realizing that she'd made the sound herself.

From one large oaken branch, a body was hanging, swaying just slightly in the night breeze.

She didn't need to wonder why Francine Renault had been derelict in her duty.

She was there…part of the tour, just not as she should have been.

Head askew, neck broken. She was hanging there, in the place where others had been hanged through the years, again and again, where they had decayed, where their bones had dotted the earth beneath them.

Brock had been right.

Francine Renault had indeed shown up before the tour was over.

THE POLICE FLOODED the ranch with personnel, the medical examiner and crime scene technicians.

The rich forest of pines and oaks and ferns and earth became alive with artificial light, and still, where the moss sagged low, the bright beams just made the night and the macabre situation eerier.

Detective Michael Flannery had been put in charge of the case. Employees and guests had been separated and then separated again, and eventually, Maura sat at the edge of the parking lot, shivering although it wasn't cold, waiting for the officer who would speak with her.

When he got there, he wanted to know the last time she had seen Francine. She told him it had been the night before.

Where she had been all day? In the office, in the yard with the older teen boys and at the campfire.

Had she heard anyone threaten Francine?

At least half of the resort's employees. In aggravation or jest.

The night seemed to wear on forever.

When she was released at last, she was sent back to her own room and ordered to stay there until morning.

When morning came, her parents were there, ready to take her home.

She desperately wanted to see Brock.

Her parents were quiet and then they looked at each other. Her father shook his head slightly, and her mother said softly, "Maura, you can't see Brock."

"What?" she demanded. "Why not? Mom, Dad— I'm about to leave home. Go to college, really be on

my own. I love you. I'm going to come home. But…
I'm almost eighteen. I won't go without seeing Brock."

Her father, a gentle giant with broad shoulders and
a mane of white hair, spoke to her softly. "Sweetheart,
we didn't say that we wouldn't let you see Brock. We're
saying that you *can't* see Brock." He hesitated, looking
over at her mother, and then he continued with, "I'm so
sorry. Brock was arrested last night. He was charged
with the murder of Francine Renault."

And with those words, it seemed that her world fell
apart, that what she had known, that what she had believed in, all just exploded into a sea of red and then
disappeared into smoke and fog.

Chapter One

"I'm assigned to go back to Florida. To stay at the Frampton Ranch and Resort—and investigate what we believe to be three kidnappings and a murder. And the kidnappings may have nothing to do with the resort, nor may the murder?" Brock McGovern asked, a small note of incredulity slipping into his voice, which was surprising to him—he was always careful to keep an even tone.

FBI Assistant Director Richard Egan had brought him into his office, and Brock had known he was going on assignment—he just hadn't expected this.

"Yes, not what you'd want, but, hey, maybe it'll be good for you—and perhaps necessary now, when time is of the essence and there is no one out there who could know the place or the circumstances with the same scope and experience you have," Egan told him. "Three young women have disappeared from the area. Two of them were guests of the Frampton Ranch and Resort shortly before their disappearances—the third had left St. Augustine and was on her way there. The Florida Department of Law Enforcement has naturally been there already. They asked for federal help on this. Shades of the past haunt them—they don't want any more unsolved murders—and everyone is hoping against hope that Lily Sylvester, Amy Bonham and Lydia Merkel might be found."

"These are Florida missing persons cases," Brock said. "And it's sad but true that young people go to Florida and get caught up in the beach life and the club scene. And regrettable but true once again—there's a drug and alcohol culture that does exist and people get caught up in it. Not just in Florida, of course, but... everywhere." He smiled grimly. "I go where I'm told, but I'm curious—how is this an FBI affair? And forgive me, but FBI out of New York?"

"Not out of New York. FDLE asked for you. Specifically."

"I see."

Egan didn't often dwell on the emotional or psychological, but the assistant director hesitated and then said, "You could put your past to rest."

Brock shrugged. "You know, one of the cooks committed suicide not long after the murder. Peter Moore. He stabbed himself with a butcher knife. He'd had a lot of fights with Francine Renault—the victim found at the tree. They suspected he might have killed himself out of remorse."

Egan offered him a dry grimace. "I know about the cook, of course. You know me—I knew everything about you on paper before I took you into this unit. I'm not sure anyone would have made a case against him in court. That's all beside the point—the past may well be the past. But there's the now, as well. They're afraid of a serial killer, Brock," Egan said. And he continued with, "The badly decomposed remains—mostly bones—of another young woman who went missing several months ago were recently found in a bizarre way—they were dumped in with sheets from several hotels and resorts at an industrial laundry that accepted linens from dozens of places—Frampton Ranch and Resort being one of them."

"I see," Brock said.

He didn't really see.

That didn't matter; Egan would be thorough.

"Yes, this may be a bit hard on you, but you're the one in the know. To come close to a knowledge of the area and people that you already have might take someone else hours or days that may cost a life… You're the best man for this. Especially because you were once falsely accused. And, I believe, you may just solve something of the mystery of the past. And quit hating your own home."

"I don't hate my own home. Ah, come on, sir, I don't want to play any cure-me psychological games with this," Brock said.

Egan shook his head and leaned forward, his eyes narrowed—indicating a rise in his temper, something always kept in check. "If I thought you needed to be cured, you wouldn't be in my unit. Women are missing. They might be dead already," he said curtly. "And then again, they might have a chance. You're the agent with a real sense for the place, the people and the surrounding landscape. And you're a good agent, period. I trust in your ability to get this sorted."

Brock greatly admired Egan. He had a nose for sending the right agent or agents in for a job. Usually.

But Brock was sitting across from Egan in Egan's office—in New York City. He, Brock, was an NYC agent.

And while Brock really didn't dislike where he came from—he still loved Florida, especially his family home in the Keys—he had opted to apply to the New York office of the Bureau specifically because it was far, far away from the state of his birth.

The New York City office didn't usually handle events in Florida, unless a criminal had traveled from New York down to the southern state. Florida had several field offices—including a multimillion-dollar state-of-the-art facility in Broward County. That was south—but Orlando had an exceptional office, close enough to the Frampton place. And there were more offices, as well.

Even if the Frampton Ranch and Resort was in a relatively isolated part of the state, a problem there would generally be handled by a more local office.

"Frampton Ranch and Resort," he heard himself say. And this time, years of training and experience kicked in—his voice was perfectly level and emotionless.

It was true: he sure as hell knew it and the area. The resort was just a bit off from—or maybe part of—what people considered to be the northern Ocala region, where prime acreage was still available at reasonable prices, where horse ranches were common upon the ever-so-slightly rolling hills and life tended to be slow and easy.

There were vast tracts of grazing ground and great live-oak forests and trails laden with pines where the sun seemed to drip down through great strands of weeping moss that hung from many a branch. It could be considered horse country, farm country and ranch county. There were marshes and forests, sinkholes and all manner of places where a body might just disappear.

The Frampton ranch was north of Ocala, east of Gainesville and about forty-five minutes south of Olustee, Florida, where every year, a battle reenactment took place, drawing tourists and historians from near and far. The Battle of Olustee, won by forces in the state; the war had been heading toward its final inevitable conclusion, and then time proved that victory had been necessary for human rights and the strength and growth of the fledgling nation, however purposeless the sad loss of lives always seemed.

Reenactors and historians arrived in good numbers, and those who loved bringing history to life also loved bringing in crowds and many came for the campgrounds. The reenactment took place in February, when temperatures in the state tended to be beautiful and mosquito repellent wasn't as much a requirement as usual. During the winter season—often spring break for other regions—the area was exceptionally popular.

The area was beautiful.

And the large areas of isolation, which included the Frampton property, could conceal any number of dark deeds.

He'd just never thought he'd go back to it.

Certainly, time—and the path he had chosen to take in life—had helped erase the horror of the night they had come upon the body of Francine Renault hanging from the History Tree and his own subsequent arrest. He'd been so young then, so assured that truth spoke for itself. In the end, his parents—bless them—had leaped to the fore, flying into action, and their attorney had made quick work of getting him out of jail after only one night and seeing that his record was returned to spotless. It was ludicrous that they had arrested him; he'd been able to prove that it would have been impossible for him to have carried out the deed. Dozens of witnesses had attested to the fact that he couldn't have been the killer, he'd been seen by so many people during the hours in which the murder must have taken place. He could remember, though, sitting in the cell—cold, stark, barren—and wondering why in God's name they had arrested *him*.

He discovered that there had been an anonymous call to the station—someone stating that they had seen him dragging Francine Renault into the woods. The tipster had sworn that he would appear at a trial as a witness for the prosecution, but the witness had not come to the station. Others had signed formal protests, and the McGoverns' attorney had taken over.

So many people had come forward, indignant, furious over his arrest.

But not Maura. She had been gone. Just gone. He couldn't think of the Frampton Ranch and Resort without a twinge of pain. He had never been sure which had broken him more at the time—the arrest or the fact that Maura had disappeared as cleanly from his life as any hint of daylight once night had fallen.

They had been so young. It had been natural that her parents whisked her away, and maybe even natural that neither had since tried to reach the other.

But there were times when he could still close his eyes and see her smile and be certain that he breathed in the subtle scent of her. Twelve years had gone by; he wasn't even the same person.

Egan was unaware of his reflections.

"Detective Michael Flannery is lead investigator now. He was on the case when you were arrested for the crime, but he wasn't lead."

"I know Flannery. We've communicated through the years, believe it or not. I almost feel bad—he suffered a lot of guilt about jumping the gun with me."

"He's with the Florida Department of Law Enforcement now, with some seniority and juice, so it seems," Egan informed him. "Years ago, when the murder took place, the federal government wasn't involved. Flannery doesn't want this crime going unsolved. He knows you're in this office now. His commander told me that he keeps in touch with you." Egan paused. "It doesn't sound as if you have a problem with him—you don't, right?"

"No, sir, I do not."

Even as a stunned kid—what he had been back then—Brock had never hated Detective Flannery for being one of the men who had come and arrested him.

Flannery had been just as quick to listen to the arguments that eventually cleared Brock completely of any wrongdoing. While Brock knew that Flannery was furious that he had been taken and certain that there had been an underlying and devious conspiracy to lead him and his superiors so thoroughly in the wrong direction, he had to agree that, at the time, Brock had appeared to be a ready suspect.

He'd had a fight with Francine that day, and it had been witnessed by many people. He hadn't gotten physical in any way, but his poor opinion of her, and his anger with her, had probably been more than evident—enough for him to be brought in for questioning and to be held for twenty-four hours at any rate.

"I'm curious how something that happened so long ago can relate to the cases happening now," Brock said.

"It may not. The remains of the dead girl found in the laundry might have been the work of one crazed individual or an acquaintance seeking vengeance, acting out of jealousy—a solitary motive. It might be coincidence the way she was found—or maybe a killer was trying to throw suspicion upon a particular place or person. But…a lot of the same individuals are still there now who were there when Francine Renault was killed."

"Donald Glass—he's around a lot, though he does spend time at his other properties. Fred Bentley—I imagine he's still running the works. Who else is still there?" Brock asked.

Egan handed him a pile of folders. "All this is coming to your email, as well. There you have those who are in residence—and dossiers on the victims. Yes,

Glass and Bentley are still on the property. There are other staff members who never left—Millie Cranston, head of Housekeeping. Vinnie Marshall, upgraded to chef—after Peter Moore's death, I might add. And then…" He paused, tapping the folders. "You have some old guests who are now employees."

"Who?"

"Mark and Nils Hartford," Egan told him. "Both of them report directly to Fred Bentley. Mark has taken over as the social director. Nils is managing the restaurants—the sit-down Ranch Roost and the Java Bar."

Brock hadn't known that the Hartford brothers—who'd seemed so above the working class when they'd been guests—were now employed at the very place where they had once loved to make hell for others.

"Flannery said this is something he hadn't mentioned to you. One of your old friends—or acquaintances—Rachel Lawrence is now with FDLE. She's been working the murder and the disappearances with him."

"Rachel? Became…a cop?" Brock shook his head, not sure if he was angry or amused. Rachel had never wanted to break a nail. She'd been pretty and delicate and… She'd also been a constant accessory of Nils Hartford.

"I guess your old friend Flannery was afraid to tell you."

"I don't know why he would be. I'm just a little surprised—she seemed more likely to be on one of those shows about rich housewives in a big city, but I never had a problem with her. That the Hartford brothers both became employees—that's also a surprise. They made me think of *Dirty Dancing*. They were the rich kids—we were the menial labor. But the world changes. People change."

"Flannery's point, so it appears, is that a number of the same players are in the area—may mean something and may not. There have been, give or take, approximately a thousand murders in the state per year in the last years. But that's only about four percent per the population. Still, anything could have happened. Violent crime may have to do with many factors—often family related, gang related, drug related, well…you know all the drills. But if we do have a serial situation down there—relating to or not relating to the past—everyone needs to move quickly. Not only do you know the area and the terrain, you know people and you know the ropes of getting around many of the people and places who might be integral to the situation."

"Yes. And any agent would want to put a halt to this—put an end to a serial killer. Or find the girls—alive, one can pray—or stop future abductions and killings."

Egan nodded grimly and tossed a small pile of photos down before him. Brock could see three young, hopeful faces looking back at him. All three were attractive, and more grippingly, all three seemed to smile with life and all that lay before someone at that tender age.

"The missing," Egan said. He had big hands and long fingers. He used them to slide the first three photographs over.

The last was a divided sheet. On one side was the likeness of a beautiful young woman, probably in her early twenties. Her hair had been thick and dark and curly; her eyes had been sky blue. Her smile had been engaging.

"Maureen Rodriguez," Egan said. He added softly, "Then and now."

On the other side of the divided sheet was a crime scene photo—an image of bones, scattered in dirt in a pile of sheets. In the center of the broken and fragmented bones was a skull.

The skull retained bits of flesh.

"According to the investigation, she was on her way to Frampton Ranch and Resort," Egan said.

Brock nodded slowly and rose. "As am I," he said. "When do I leave?"

"Your plane is in two hours—down to Jacksonville. You've a rental car in your name when you arrive. I'm sure you know the way to the property. Detective Flannery will be waiting to hear from you. He'll go over all the particulars."

Brock was surprised to see that Egan was still studying him. "You are good, right?" he asked Brock.

"Hey, everyone wants to head to Florida for the winter, don't they?" he asked. "I'm good," he said seriously. "Maybe you're right. Maybe we can put the past to rest after all."

"I LOVE IT—just love it, love it, love it! Love it all!" Angie Parsons said enthusiastically. She offered Maura one of her biggest, happiest smiles.

She was staring at the History Tree, her smile brilliant and her enthusiasm for her project showing in the brightness of her eyes and her every movement. "I mean, people say Florida has no history—just because it's not New England and there were no pilgrims. But, hey, St. Augustine is—what?—the oldest settlement continually…settled…by Europeans in the country, right? I mean, way back, the Spaniards were here. No, no, the state wasn't one of the original thirteen colonies. No, no Puritans here. But! There's so much! And this tree… No one knows how old the frigging oak is or when the palm tree grew in it or through it or with it or whatever."

Angie Parsons was cute, friendly, bright and sometimes, but just sometimes, too much. At five feet two inches, she exuded enough energy for a giant. She had just turned thirty—and done brilliantly for her years. She had written one of the one most successful nonfiction book series on the market. And all because she got as excited as she did about objects and places and things—such as the History Tree.

The main tree was a black oak; no one knew quite how old it was, but several hundred years at least. That type of oak was known to live over five hundred years.

A palm tree had—at some time—managed to grow at the same place, through the outstretched roots of the oak and twirling up around the trunk and through the branches. It was bizarre, beautiful, and so unusual that it naturally inspired all manner of legends, some of those legends based on truth.

And, of course, the History Tree held just the kind of legend that made Angie as successful as she was.

Angie's being incredibly successful didn't hurt Maura any.

But being here… Yes, it hurt. At least…it was incredibly uncomfortable. On the one hand it was wonderful seeing people she had worked with once upon a time in another life.

On the other hand it was bizarre. Like visiting a mirror dimension made up of things she remembered. The Hartford brothers were working there now. Nils was managing the restaurants—he'd arrived at the table she and Angie had shared last night to welcome them and pick up their dinner check. Of course, Nils had become management. No lowly posts for him. He seemed to have an excellent working relationship with Fred Bentley, who was still the manager of the resort. Bentley had come down when they'd checked in— he'd greeted Maura with a serious hug. She was tall, granted, and in heels, and he was on the short side for a man—about five-ten—but it still seemed that his hug allowed for him to rest his head against her breasts a moment too long.

But still, he'd apparently been delighted to see her.

And Mark Hartford had come to see her, too, grown-up, cute and charming now—and just as happy as his brother to see her. It was thanks to her, he had told her, and her ability to tell the campfire histories, that had made him long to someday do the same.

The past didn't seem like any kind of a boulder

around his neck. Certainly he remembered the night that Francine had been murdered.

The night that had turned *her* life upside down had been over twelve years ago.

Like all else in the past, it was now history.

Time had marched on, apparently, for them—and her.

She'd just turned eighteen the last time she had been here. When that autumn had come around, she'd done what she'd been meant to do, headed to the University of Central Florida, an amazing place to study performance of any kind and directing and film—with so many aspects thrown into the complete education.

She'd spent every waking minute in classes—taking elective upon elective to stay busy. She was now CEO of her own company, providing short videos to promote writers, artists, musicians and anyone wanting video content, including attorneys and accountants.

Not quite thirty, she could be proud of her professional accomplishments—she had garnered a great reputation.

She enjoyed working with Angie. The writer was fun, and there was good reason for her success. She loved the bizarre and spooky that drew human curiosity. Even those who claimed they didn't believe in anything even remotely paranormal seemed to love Angie's books.

Most of the time, yes, Maura *did* truly enjoy working with Angie, and since Angie had tried doing her own videos without much success, she was equally happy to be working with Maura. They'd done great bits down in Key West at the cemetery there—where Maura's favorite tomb was engraved with the words *I told you I was sick!*—and at the East Martello Museum with Robert the Doll. They had filmed on the west coast at the old summer estates that had belonged to Henry Ford and Thomas Edison. And they'd worked together in St. Augustine, where they'd created twenty little video bits for social media that had pleased Angie to no end—and garnered hundreds of thousands of hits.

Last night, even Marie Glass—Donald's reserved and elegant wife—had come by their dinner table to welcome them and tell them just how much she enjoyed all the videos that Maura had done for and with Angie, telling great legends and wild tales that were bizarrely wonderful—and true.

Maybe naturally, since they were working in Florida, Angie had determined that they had to stay at Frampton Ranch and Resort and film at the History Tree.

Maura had suggested other places that would make great content for a book on the bizarre: sinkholes, a road where cars slid uphill instead of downhill—hell, she would have done her best to make a giant ball of twine sound fascinating. There were lots of other places in the state with strange stories—lord! They could go back to Key West and film a piece on Carl Tanzler, who had slept with the corpse of his beloved, Elena de Hoyos, for seven years.

But Angie was dead set on seeing the History Tree, and when they'd gotten to the clearing she had started spinning around like a delighted child.

She stopped suddenly, staring at Maura.

"You really are uncomfortable here, aren't you? Scared? You know, I've told you—you can hire an assistant. Maybe a strapping fellow, tall, dark and handsome—or blond and handsome—and muscle-bound. Someone to protect us if the bogeyman is around at any of our strange sites." Angie paused, grinning. She liked men and didn't apologize for it. In her own words, if you didn't kiss a bunch of frogs, you were never going to find a prince.

"Angie, I like doing my own work—and editing it and assuring that I like what I've done. I promise you, if we turn something into any kind of a feature film, we'll hire dozens of people."

Angie sighed. "Well, so much for tall, dark—or blond—and handsome. Your loss, my dear friend. Anyway. You do amazing work for me. You're a one-woman godsend."

"Thanks," Maura told her. She inhaled a deep breath.

"Could you try not to look quite so miserable?"

"Oh, Angie. I'm sorry. It's just…"

"The legend. The legend about the tree—oh, yes. And the murder victims found here. I'm sorry, Maura, but… I mean, I film these places because they have legends attached to them." Angie seemed to be perplexed. She sighed. "Of course, the one murder was just twelve years ago. Does that bother you?" Staring at Maura, she gasped suddenly. "You're close to this somehow, right? Oh, my God! Were you one of the kids working here *that* summer? I mean, I'd have had no idea…

You're from West Palm Beach. There's so much stuff down there. Ah!" It seemed that Angie didn't really need answers. "You wound up going to the University of Central Florida. You were near here…"

"Yes, I was here working that summer," Maura said flatly.

"Your name was never in the paper?"

"That's right. The police were careful to keep the employees away from the media. And since we are so isolated on the ranch, news reporters didn't get wind of anything until the next day. My parents had me out of here by then, and Donald Glass was emphatic about the press leaving his young staff alone."

"But a kid was *arrested*—"

"And released. And honestly, Angie, I am a little worried. Even if it has nothing to do with the past, there's something not good going on now. Haven't you watched the news? They found the remains of a young woman not far from here."

"Not far from here, but not *here*," Angie said. "Hey," she said again, frowning with concern. "That can't have anything to do with anything—the Frampton ranch killer committed suicide, I thought."

"One of the cooks killed himself," Maura said. "Yes, but… I mean, he never had his day in court. Most people believed he killed Francine—he hated her. But a lot of people disliked her."

"But he killed himself."

"Yes. I wasn't here then. I did hear about it, of course."

Angie was pensive for a moment, and then she

asked, "Maura, you don't think that the tree is…evil, do you?"

"*Trees*—a palm laced in with an oak. And no. I'm quite accustomed to the spooky and creepy, and we both know that places don't become evil, nor do things. But people can be wicked as hell—and they can feed off legends. I don't like being out here—not alone. There will be a campfire tonight with the history and ghost stories and the walk—we'll join that. I have waivers for whoever attends tonight."

"What if someone doesn't want to be filmed?" Angie asked anxiously. "You tell the story just as well as anyone else, right? And the camera loves you—a perfect, slinky blonde beauty with those enormous gray eyes of yours. Come on, you've told a few of the stories before. You can—"

"I cannot do a good video for you as a selfie," Maura said patiently.

"Right. I can film you telling the story," Angie said. "Just that part. And I can do it now—I think you said that the stories were told by the campfire, and then the historic walk began. I'll get you—right here and now—doing the story part of it. Oh, and you can include… Oh, God!" Angie said, her eyes widening. "You weren't just here—you saw the dead woman! The murdered woman… I mean, from this century. Francine Renault. And they arrested a kid, Brock McGovern, but he was innocent, and it was proved almost immediately, but then… Well, then, if the cook didn't do it, they never caught the killer!"

Maura kept her face impassive. Angie always wrote

about old crimes that were unsolved—and why a place was naturally haunted after ghastly deeds had occurred there.

She did her homework, however. Angie probably knew more than Maura remembered.

She had loved the sad legend of the beautiful Gyselle, who had died so tragically for love. But, of course, she would have delved as deeply as possible into every event that had occurred at the ranch.

"Do they—do they tell that story at the campfire?" Angie asked.

Maura sighed. "Angie, I haven't been here since the night it happened. I was still young. My parents dragged me home immediately."

She was here now—and she could remember that night all too clearly. Coming to the tree, then realizing while denying it that a real body was hanging from it. That it was Francine Renault. That she had been hanged from a heavy branch, hanged by the neck, and that she dangled far above the ground, tongue bulging, face grotesque.

She remembered screaming…

And she remembered the police and how they had taken Brock away, frowning and massively confused, still tall and straight and almost regally dignified.

And she could remember that there were still those who speculated on his guilt or innocence—until dozens of people had spoken out, having seen him through the time when Francine might have been taken and killed. His arrest had really been ludicrous—a detective's desperate bid to silence the horror and outrage that was beginning to spread.

Brock's life had changed, and thus her life had changed.

Everything had changed.

Except for this spot.

She could even imagine that she was a kid again, that she could see Francine Renault, so macabre in death, barely believable, yet so real and tragic and terrifying as she dangled from the thick limb.

"Oh," Angie groaned, the one word drawn out long enough to be a sentence. "Now I know why you were against doing a video here!"

Angie had wanted the History Tree. And when she had started to grow curious regarding Maura's reluctance to head to the Frampton Ranch and Resort—especially since the resort was supposedly great and the expense of rooms went on Angie's bill—Maura had decided it was time to cave.

She hadn't wanted to give any explanations.

"Angie, it's in your book, and you sell great and your video channel is doing great, as well. It's fine. Really. But because they did recently find what seems to be the remains of a murder victim near here, I do think we need to be careful. As in, stay out of these woods after dark."

"There is a big bad wolf. Was a big bad wolf... But seriously, I'm not a criminologist of any kind, but I'd say the killer back then was making a point. Maybe the bones they found belonged to someone who died of natural causes."

Angie wasn't stupid, but Maura was sure that the look she gave her tiny friend at that moment implied that she thought she was.

"Maybe," Angie said defensively.

"Angie, you don't rot in the dirt on purpose and then wind up with your bones in a cache of hotel laundry," Maura said.

"No, but, hey—there could be another explanation. Like a car accident. And whoever hit her was terrified and ran—and then, sadly, she just rotted."

"And wound up in hotel sheets?"

Maura asked incredulously. Angie couldn't be serious.

"Okay, so that's a bit far-fetched."

"Angie, it's been reported that the remains were found of a murder victim. Last I saw, they were still seeking her identity, but they said that she was killed."

"Well, they found bones, from what I understand. Anyway," Angie said, dusting her hands on her skirt and speaking softly and with dignity and compassion, "I wish you would have just said that you were here when it happened. Let's get out of here. I'm sorry I made you do this."

"You didn't make me do it. If I had been determined not to come back here, I wouldn't have done so. But it's going to get dark soon. Let me shoot a bit of you doing your speech by the tree while I still have good light."

Maura lifted her camera, looked at the tree and then up at the sky.

They wouldn't have the light much longer.

"Angie, come on—let's film you."

"Please—you know the stories so well. Let me film you this time."

"They're your books."

"But you'll give me a great authenticity. I'll interview you—and you were here when the last crime occurred. I'm surprised they haven't hacked this sucker to the ground, really," Angie said, looking at the tree. "Or at the very least, they should have video surveillance out here."

"Now, that would be the right idea. They have video surveillance in the lobby, the elevators—and other areas. But for now, please?"

They were never going to be able to leave.

"All right, all right!" Maura said. She adjusted the camera on its lightweight tripod and looked at the image on the camera's viewing screen. "I've got it lined up already. I'll go right there. You need to get it rolling. The mic is on already, and you can see what you're filming."

"Hey, I've used it before—not a lot, but I kind of know what I'm doing," Angie reminded her.

Maura stepped away from the camera and headed over to the tree. Angie had paid attention to her. She lifted her fingers and said, "In three…" and then went silent, counting down the rest by hand.

Maura was amazed at how quickly it all came back to her. She told the tale of the beautiful Gyselle and then went into the later crimes.

Ending, of course, with the murder of Francine Renault.

"A false lead caused the arrest of an innocent young

man. But this is America, and we all know that any man is innocent until proved guilty, and this young man was quickly proved innocent. He was only under arrest for a night, because eyewitness reports confirmed he was with several other people—busy at work—when the crime took place. Still, it was a travesty, shattering a great deal of the promise of the young man's life. He was, however, as I said, quickly released—and until this day, the crime goes unsolved."

She finished speaking and saw that Angie was still running the camera, looking past her, appearing perplexed—and pleased—by something that she saw.

"Hello there! Are you with Frampton Ranch and Resort? You aren't, by any chance, the host for the campfire stories tonight, are you?"

Angie was smiling sweetly—having shifted into her flirtatious mode.

Curious, Maura turned around and started toward the path.

If a jaw could actually drop, hers did.

She quickly closed her mouth, but perhaps her eyes were bulging, as well. It seemed almost as if someone had physically knocked the breath from her.

Brock McGovern was standing there.

Different.

The same.

A bit taller than he'd been at eighteen; his shoulders had filled out and he appeared to have acquired a great deal more solid muscle. He filled out a dark blue suit and tailored shirt exceptionally well.

His face was the same…

Different.

There was something hard about him now that hadn't been there before. His features were leaner, his eyes...

Still deep brown. But they were harder now, too, or appeared to be harder, as if there was a shield of glass on them. He'd always walked and moved with purpose, confident in what he wanted and where he was going.

Now, just standing still, he was an imposing presence.

And though Angie had spoken, he was looking at Maura.

"Wow," Angie said softly. "Did I dream up the perfect assistant for you—tall, dark and to die for? Who the hell... The storyteller guy is wickedly cute, but this guy..."

He couldn't have heard her words; he wasn't close enough.

And he wasn't looking at her. He was staring at Maura.

"That was great," he said smoothly. "However, I don't consider my life to have been *shattered*. I mean—I hope I have fulfilled a few of the promises I made to myself."

Maura wanted to speak. Her mouth wouldn't work.

Angie, however, had no problem.

"Oh, my God!" Angie cried.

Every once in a while, her Valley girl came out.

"You—you're Brock McGovern?" she asked.

"I am," he said, but he still wasn't looking at Angie.

He was locked on Maura. Then he smiled. A rueful smile, dry and maybe even a little bitter.

"Here—in Florida," Angie said. "I mean—at the History Tree."

He turned at last to face Angie. "I'm here for an investigation now. I'm going to suggest that you two head back to the resort and don't wander off alone. A woman's remains were found at a laundry facility not far from here, and there are three young women who have gone missing recently. Best to stay in the main areas—with plenty of people around."

"Oh!" Angie went into damsel-in-distress mode then. "Is it really dangerous, do you think? I'm so glad that you're here, if there is danger. I mean, we've seen the news…heard things, but seriously, bad things aren't necessarily happening here, right? It's just a tree. Florida is far from crime-free, but… Anyway, thank God that you're here. We didn't really think we needed to be afraid, but now you're here…and thank God! Right, Maura?"

Maura didn't reply. She'd heard Angie speaking as if she'd been far, far away. Then she found her voice. Or, at least, a whisper of it.

"Brock," she murmured.

"Maura," he returned casually. "Good to see you. Well, surprised to see you—but good to see you."

"Investigation," she said, grasping for something to say. She seemed to be able to manage one word at a time.

"I just told you—they found a woman's remains, and three young women who have been reported missing had a connection to the Frampton Ranch and Resort. The FDLE has asked for Bureau help," he explained politely.

"Yes, we were just talking about the young woman's remains—and the missing girls. I, uh, I think I'd heard that you did go into the FBI," she said. "And they sent you…here." There. She had spoken in complete sentences. More or less. She'd been almost comprehensible.

"Yes, pretty much followed my original plans. Navy, college, the academy—FBI. And yes, I'm back here. Nothing like sending in an agent who knows the terrain," he said. "Shall we head back? I am serious. You shouldn't be in the woods alone when…well, when no one has any idea of what is really going on. We're not trying to incite fear. We're just trying to get a grip on what is happening, but I do suggest caution. Shall we head back?"

He was the same.

He was different.

And she was afraid to come too close to him. Afraid that the emotions of a teenager would erupt within her again, as if the years meant nothing…

If she got too close, she would either want to beat upon him, slamming her fists against his chest, demanding to know why he had never called, never tried to reach her and how it had been so easy to forget her.

Either that, or she would throw herself into his arms and sob and do anything just to touch him again.

Chapter Two

"The soil—clay based, some sand—like that covers most of the north of the state," Rachel Lawrence said.

She was seated across from Brock with Michael Flannery in the Java Bar on the Frampton property.

Rachel had changed. Her nails were cut short, clean of any color. Her hair was shorter, too. She still wore bangs, but her dark tresses were attractively trimmed to slide in angles along her face.

Everything about her appearance was serviceable. The girl who had once cried over a broken nail or scuffed sneakers had made an about-face.

She had greeted Brock politely and gravely, and seemed—like Flannery—to be anxious to have him working on the case with them.

"There's the beginning of a task force rumbling around," she'd told him when they'd first met in the coffee bar. "I'm lucky to be working with Michael Flannery—very lucky. But at this moment, while our superiors are listening, and they were willing to accept FBI involvement, they don't necessarily all believe that we are looking at a serial killer and this situation is about to blow up and get out of hand. It's great to have another officer who knows the lay of the land, so to speak."

"Yes, I do know it. And I've got to say, Rachel, I'm happy to see that you are working for the FDLE—and that you're so pleased to be where you are."

She made a face. "Oh, well, there was a time when I thought I wanted to be rich and elite, own a teacup Yorkie in a designer handbag and be supported in fine fashion. But I do love what I do. Oh—I actually do have a teacup Yorkie. Love the little guy!"

It had been far easier to meet back up with Rachel—and even Nils and Mark Hartford—than Brock had expected.

Time.

It healed all wounds, right?

Wrong. Why not? He believed he was, as far as any normal psychology went, long over what had happened regarding his arrest for murder at such a young age—he'd barely been in jail before his parents arrived with their attorney, his dad so indignant that the icy chill in his eyes might have gotten Brock released before the attorney even opened his mouth.

Truly, he had seen and heard far worse in the navy. And, God knew, some of the cases he'd handled as an agent in a criminal investigation unit had certainly been enough to chill the blood.

Still…the haunting memories regarding the forest and the History Tree clung to him like the moss that dripped from the old oaks.

"A Yorkie, huh?" he asked Rachel, remembering that she was there.

They both grinned, and he assured her that he liked dogs, all dogs, and didn't have one himself only because it wouldn't be fair to the animal—he was always working.

Rachel went on with the information—or lack of it—that she had worked to obtain.

"Some of our elegant hotels have special bedding, but…lots don't. The sheets around the remains might have come from five different chain hotels that cover North Florida, Central Florida and the Panhandle, all of which have twenty to forty local franchises. That means that Maureen Rodriguez might have been murdered anywhere in all that area—buried first nearby or somewhere different within the boundaries—and then dug up and wrapped in sheets."

"You checked with the truck drivers making deliveries that day, naturally?" Brock asked her.

She gave him a look that was both amused and withering. "I did go to college—and I majored in criminology. I'm not just a piece of fluff, you know."

Detective Michael Flannery grunted. "She's tailing me—I'm teaching her everything I know. And," he added, "how not to make the same mistakes."

Brock nodded his appreciation for the comment and asked, "Were you able to narrow it down by the drivers and their deliveries?"

"The way it works is that they pick up when they drop off," Rachel said. "So it's not as if they're kept separately. It's almost like recycling receptacles—the hotels have these massive canvas bags. The sheets are all the same, so they drop off dirty and pick up clean replacements. The laundry is also responsible for getting rid of sheets that are too worn, too stained, too whatever. But the driver drop-offs do narrow it down to hotels from St. Augustine to Gainesville and down to northern Ocala. I have a list of them, which I've emailed and…" She paused, reaching into her bag for a small folder that she presented to Brock. "Here—hard copy."

He looked at the list. There were at least thirty hotels with their addresses listed.

"All right, thank you," he told her. "I'd like to start by talking to Katie Simmons—the woman who reported Lydia Merkel missing. And then the last person to see each of the missing young women."

"Cops have interviewed all of them. I saw Katie Simmons myself," Flannery told him. "I'm not sure what else you can get from her."

"Humor me. And this list—I'd like you to get state officers out with images of all the women. Let's see what they get—they'll tell us if they find anyone who has seen any of them or thinks they might have seen someone like them. We need the images plastered everywhere—a Good Samaritan could call in and let us know if they saw one of the women walking on the street, buying gas…at a bar or a restaurant."

"The images have been broadcast," Flannery said. "I asked for you, but come on. We're not a bunch of dumb hicks down here, you know."

Brock grinned. "I'm a Fed, remember?"

Flannery shrugged. "You're a conch," he reminded Brock, referring to the moniker given to Key West natives.

"I get you, but I'm not referring to local news. I mean, we need likenesses of the young women—all four of them—out everywhere. We need to draw on media across the state and beyond. And we need to get them up in all the colleges—there are several of them in the area. All four of the women were college age— they might have friends just about anywhere. They might have met up with someone at a party."

"I'll get officers on the hotels and take the colleges with Rachel. She and I can head in opposite directions and cover more ground." Flannery hesitated. "I've arranged for us to see the ME first thing, so we'll start all else after that—I assumed you wanted to see the remains of Maureen Rodriguez."

"Yes, and thank you," Brock told him. "Do I meet you at the morgue?"

"No, we'll head out together—if that's all right with you. I have a room here and so does Rachel. I'm setting mine up as a headquarters," Flannery said. "I'll start a whiteboard—that way, we can keep up with any information any of us acquires and have it in plain sight, as we'd be doing if we were running the investigation out of one of our offices."

"A good plan," Brock said. "But tomorrow I would like to get started over in St. Augustine as quickly as possible."

"All right, then. We will take two cars tomorrow morning. Compare notes back here, say, late afternoon.

Get in touch sooner if we have something that seems of real significance. It's good that you decided to be based here. Easier than trying to come and go."

Flannery hesitated, looking at Brock. Then he shrugged. "Mr. Glass actually came to me." He lowered his voice, even though there was no one near them. "On the hush-hush. Said his wife didn't even know. Seems he's afraid himself that someone is using this place or the legends that go with it."

Brock drained his cup of coffee. "Can you set me up with Katie Simmons for some time tomorrow?" he asked Rachel.

"Yes, sir, I can and will," she assured him. "She's in St. Augustine."

Brock stood.

They looked up at him.

"And now?" Flannery asked.

"You wanted me here because I know the place," Brock said. "I'm going to watch a couple of the people that I knew when I worked here. See what's changed—and who has changed and how. I'm not leaving the property tonight. If there's anything, call me. And I'll check in later."

"You're going to the campfire tales and ghost walk?" Flannery asked.

"Not exactly—but kind of," Brock said. He nodded to the two of them and headed out, glancing at his watch.

He did know the place, that was certain. Almost nothing on the grounds had changed.

His father had heard about the place—that it was a

great venue for young people to work for the summer during high school. There was basic housing for them, a section of rooms for girls and one for boys. They weren't allowed off the grounds unless they had turned eighteen or they were supervised; any dereliction of the rules called for immediate dismissal. The positions were highly prized—if anyone broke the rules, they were damned careful not to be caught.

Of course, fraternizing—as in sex—had not been in the rules.

Kids were kids.

But with him and Maura…

It had felt like something more than kids being kids.

He still believed it. He wondered if, just somewhere in her mind, she believed it, too.

MARK HARTFORD PROVED to be excellent at telling the stories—despite the fact that he'd told Maura that he was afraid that night. Well, not afraid but nervous.

"You were so good!" he had said to Maura when he saw that she and Angie were going to be in his audience. "So good!"

He'd been just about fourteen when she knew him years before; he had to be about twenty-five or twenty-six now. He'd grown up, of course, and he still charmed with a boyish energy and enthusiasm that was contagious. His eyes were bright blue and his hair—just slightly shaggy—was a tawny blond. He'd grown several inches since Maura had seen him, and he evidently made use of the resort's gym.

Angie was entranced by Mark. But she'd always

been unabashed about her appreciation of men in general—especially when they were attractive. Maura didn't consider herself to be particularly suspicious of the world in general, but she did find that she often felt much older and wiser when she was with Angie—warning her that it wasn't always good to be quite so friendly with every good-looking man that she met.

"I'm sure you're just as good a storyteller," Angie had told Mark.

"I try—I have a lot to live up to," he'd said in return, answering Angie, smiling from one of them to the other.

Maura was somewhat pleased by the distraction. Angie had been talking incessantly about Brock and she'd finally stopped—long enough to do a new assessment of Mark Hartford.

She had decided that she liked young Mark Hartford very much, as well.

They'd already seen Nils in the restaurant. Mark and Nils were easily identifiable as brothers, but Mark's evident curiosity and sincere interest in everyone and everything around him made him the more naturally charming of the two.

"Ooh, I do like both brothers. But the other guy…the FBI guy… Hey, he was the one they arrested—and he turned out to be FBI! Cool. I appreciate them all, but that Brock guy…sexier—way sexier," Angie had said.

Actually, Maura found Angie's honesty one of the nicest things about her. She said what she was thinking or feeling pretty much all the time.

Now the tales were underway. Mark was telling them well. Maura allowed herself to survey his audience.

There were—as there had always been, so it seemed—a group of young teens, some together, some with their parents. There were couples, wives or girl-friends hanging on to their men, and sometimes a great guy admittedly frightened by the dark and tales and hanging on to his girlfriend or wife or boyfriend or husband, as well. There were young men and women, older men and women—a group of about twenty-five or thirty in all.

She couldn't help but remember how her group had been about the same size that night twelve years ago—and how they had all reacted when they reached the History Tree.

She had screamed—so had several people.

Some had laughed—certain that the swinging body was a prop and perhaps part of a gag set up by the establishment to throw a bit of real scare into the evening.

And then had come the frantic 911 calls, the horror as everyone realized that the dead woman was real and Brock trying to herd people away and, even then, trying to see that the scene wasn't trampled, that as a crime scene it wasn't disturbed…

Only to be arrested himself.

Tonight, Maura had her camera; she also had waivers signed by everyone in the group. She'd been lucky that night—everyone had been happy to meet her and Angie—and they all wanted their fifteen minutes of fame. They were fine with being on camera with Angie Parsons.

They were still by the campfire.

She was thinking about Brock.

Determining how much she was going to video after Mark's speech, she looked across the campfire to the place where the trees edged around the fire and the storyteller and his audience.

Brock was leaning against a tree, arms crossed over his chest, listening.

He was no longer wearing a suit; he was in jeans and a plaid flannel shirt—he could pass himself off as a logger or such. Her heart seemed to do a little leap and she was angry at herself, angry that she could still find him so compellingly attractive.

Twelve years between them. Not a word. They weren't even friends on social media.

He must have sensed her looking at him. She realized that his gaze had changed direction; he was looking at her across the distance.

He nodded slightly and then frowned, shaking his head.

He didn't want to be on camera; she nodded.

She turned away, dismissing him.

She tried to focus on the words that Mark Hartford was saying.

The stories were the same. Until they came to the History Tree.

There, a new story had been added in. Mark talked about the tour that had come upon Francine Renault.

He wasn't overly dramatic; he told the facts, and admitted that, yes, he had been among those who had found her.

The story ended with the death of the cook, Peter Moore, who had stabbed himself and been found in the freezer, his favorite knife protruding from his chest.

A fight had gone too far, or so the authorities believed, and Moore had killed Francine. And then later, in remorse or fear that prison would be worse than death, he had committed suicide.

On that tragic note, the story of the History Tree ended. As did the nightly tour.

Mark then told his group that they needed to head back—there had been some trouble in the area lately and the management would appreciate it if guests refrained from being in the forest at night and suggested that no one wander the woods alone.

As they began to filter back, Maura saw that Brock didn't go with the others.

She might have been the only one to note his presence; he had apparently followed silently at a bit of a distance, always staying back within the trees.

She turned when the group left. As they headed back along the trail, Brock stepped from his silent watching spot in the darkness of the surrounding foliage. He walked to the History Tree.

He stood silently, staring up at it, as if seeking some answer there.

Mark was asking if the tourists wanted coffee or tea or a drink before they called it a night.

Angie had already said yes.

Maura turned away from Brock purposefully and followed Angie and Mark. Once they reached the lodge, she would beg off.

All she wanted to do that night was crawl into a hole somewhere and black out.

Her room and her bed would have to do—even if she didn't black out and lay awake for hours, ever more furious with herself that she was allowing herself to feel...

Anything about him. Anything at all.

"I've seen some strange things in my day," Rita Morgan, the medical examiner, said. She was a tall, lean woman, looked to be about forty-five and certainly the no-nonsense type.

"Many a strange thing, and some not so strange. Too many bodies out of the ocean and the rivers, a few in barrels, some sunk with cement." She pursed her lips, shaking her head. "This one? Strange and sad. As long as I've done this, been an ME, it still never ceases to amaze me—man's inhumanity to fellow man." She looked up at Brock and Flannery and shook her head again. "Thing that saves me is when I see a young person get up and help the disabled or the elderly—then I get to know that there's as much good out there as bad—more, hopefully. Yeah, yeah, that doesn't help you any. I just... Well, I can show you the remains. I can't tell you too much about them. No stomach content—no stomach. I had disarticulated bones with small amounts of flesh still attached—and a skull."

She stepped back to display the gurney that held the remains of a young woman's life, tragically—and brutally—cut short.

"It looks as if she was killed a long time ago—

but from my brief, she was only missing about three months," Brock said, looking from Flannery to the medical examiner.

And then to the table.

Bits of hair and scalp still adhered to the skull.

"Decomposition is one of those things that can vary incredibly. I believe she was killed approximately two months ago. Particular to situations like this, the internal organs began to deteriorate twenty-four to seventy-two hours after death. The number of bacteria and insects in the area have an effect on the outer body and soft tissue. Three to five days—you have bloating. Within ten days, insects, the elements and bacteria have been busy and you have massive accumulations of gas. Within a few weeks, nails and teeth begin to go. After a month, the body becomes fluid."

"The skull retains a mouthful of teeth," Brock noted.

"Yes, which is why I believe decomp had the best possible circumstances. Lots of earth—and water. Rain, maybe. Even flooding in the area where the body was first left. As I said, there's no way to pinpoint an exact time of death. It's approximately two months' time. I also believe, per decomp, that she was left out in the elements—maybe a bit of dirt and some leaves were shoveled over her. It's been a warm winter, and the soil here can be rich—and as we all know, this is Florida. We have plenty of insects.

"The question is, after all that decomp in the wild, how in the world did she come to be in sheets at an industrial laundry? But that's your problem. Mine is cause of death. Not much to go on, as you can see, but enough." She pointed with a gloved hand. "That rib bone. You can see. The scraping there wasn't any insect—that was caused by a sharp blade. There's a second such mark on that rib—would have been the other side of the rear rib cage. In my educated estimation, she was stabbed to death. Without more tissue or organs I can't tell you how many wounds she sustained—exactly how many times she was stabbed—but I do imagine the attack would have been brutal, and that she probably suffered mortal damage to many of her organs. There's no damage to the skull."

"Were there any defensive wounds you were able to find on the arm bones?" Brock asked.

Flannery was standing back, letting Brock ask his own questions, since the detective had already seen the remains and spoken with the ME earlier.

"No, there were no defensive wounds, Special Agent McGovern," Dr. Morgan said. "She was stabbed from behind. She might never have seen her killer. Or she might have trusted him—or her. It was violent assault, I can tell you that. But—I am assuming that she didn't want to be stabbed to death—she had to have been taken by surprise. She never had a chance to fight back at all. Some of what I've been saying I'm assuming, but I am making assumptions based on education and experience. I'm the ME—you guys are the detectives. Can't help having an opinion."

"Of course, that's fine, and thank you," Brock said. "The sheets are at the lab? Still being tested?"

"Yes. They can't pinpoint the sheets to a certain hotel because too many of them buy from the same supplier."

She covered the remains.

She looked at Brock curiously, studying him. Then she smiled broadly. "You came out all right, it seems." She glanced over at Flannery. "Despite what you did to him."

"Hey, I acted on the best info I had at the time," Flannery said.

"Rash—hey, he was a newbie at the time. Didn't know his—oh, never mind. But good to see you—as a law enforcement officer, Agent McGovern."

"Well, thank you. I'm sorry, did we meet before?" he asked her.

She shook her head. "I was new in this office. But I assisted at the autopsies for both Francine Renault and the cook, Peter Moore..." She left off, shrugging. "I knew that they'd brought you in—one of the summer kids. Because you were seen in some kind of major verbal altercation with her. And arrested, from what I understand, on a *tip*."

She didn't exactly sniff, but she did look at Detective Flannery with a bit of disdain.

"I say again, I acted on the best info I had at the time. And yeah—I guess he came out all right," Flannery said with something that sounded a bit like a growl in his voice. He eyed Brock, as if not entirely sure about him yet.

"I spent only one night in jail. Trust me, I spent many a worse night in the service," he assured Dr. Morgan and Flannery.

Flannery looked away, uncomfortable. Dr. Morgan smiled.

"Thank you," he told her. "If there's anything else that comes to mind that might be of any assistance whatsoever…"

"I'll be quicker than a rabbit in heat," she vowed solemnly.

He arched his brows slightly but managed a smile and another thank-you.

Brock and Flannery left the county morgue together. They'd come in Flannery's official vehicle; it would allow them to bypass heavy traffic if needed, Flannery had said.

Brock preferred to drive himself, but that day, while Flannery drove, it gave him a chance to look through his notes on the victim.

"She stayed at the Frampton Ranch and Resort three months ago," he murmured out loud. "Her home was St. Pete. She wasn't reported missing right away because she was over eighteen and had been living alone in St. Augustine, working as a cocktail waitress—but hadn't shown up for work in over a week. Says here none of her coworkers really knew her—she had just started."

"The perfect victim," Flannery said. He glanced sideways at Brock. "The other missing girls… You have the information on them, too, right?"

"Yeah, I have it online and on paper. I have to hand it to Egan. He believes in hard copy and there are times it proves to be especially beneficial."

"And saves on eyestrain," Flannery muttered. He glanced Brock's way again. "You know, I asked for you specifically. Hope you don't mind too much. Can't help it. Still think there's something with that damned resort, even if I can't pin it. Well, I mean, back then, of course, it had to do with the ranch. Francine Renault worked there—and died there. But...that tree has seen a lot of death."

He said it oddly, almost as if he was in awe of the tree. Brock frowned, looking over at him. Flannery didn't glance his way, but apparently knew he was being studied.

"Well, bad stuff happens there," Flannery said.

"Right—because bad people like the aspect that bad things happened there."

"You think it should be chopped down."

"It might dissuade future killers."

"Or just cause them to leave their victims somewhere else," Flannery said. "Or create a new History Tree or haunted bog or...just a damnable stretch of roadway."

"True," Brock agreed.

"What drives me crazy is the why—I mean, we all study this stuff. Some killers are simply goal driven—they want or need someone out of the way. Some killings have to do with passion and anger and jealousy. Some have to do with money. Some people are psychotic and kill for the thrill or the sexual release it gives them. Years ago, it was just Francine. Now, that Francine—I didn't find a single soul who actually said they liked her, but it never seemed she'd done anything bad enough to make someone want to kill her. She seemed to be more of an annoyance—like a fly buzzing around your ear."

"Maybe she was a really, really annoying fly—buzzing at the wrong person," Brock said. Then he reminded the detective, "Peter Moore committed suicide. There was no note—but maybe he did do it, because he was afraid of being apprehended, or felt overwhelming remorse or was dealing with an untreated mental illness that led him down a very dark path. Seems to me that everyone accepted the fact that he must have done it—though he sure as hell didn't get his day in court."

Flannery glanced his way at last. "But you don't think that Peter Moore killed Francine any more than I do."

Brock hesitated and then said flatly, "No. And I knew Peter Moore. He hated Francine, but he held his own with her—he didn't really have to answer to her. He was directly under Fred Bentley. I don't think he killed Francine. I don't even think that Peter Moore killed himself."

Flannery nodded. "There you go—see? There was a reason I needed you down here. Damn, though, if it doesn't seem like homecoming somehow."

"What do you mean?"

"I mean, I can't just buy the theory that Peter Moore did it, either. In my mind, the killer might have helped him into that so-called suicide. No prints but Peter's on the knife in his gut, but hell, the kitchen is filled with gloves."

"So it is."

"That beauty is back, as well," Flannery said, glancing his way once again.

Brock didn't ask who Flannery meant. That was dead obvious. Maura.

"Did you ask her up here?" Brock asked him.

"Me?" Flannery was truly surprised. "I barely met her back in the day, and she was fairly rattled when I did... Well, you were there. You didn't ask for her to be here? I'd have thought, at least, that the two of you would still be friends. You were hot and heavy back then, so I heard—the beautiful young ones!"

"I hadn't seen her since that night until I saw her again late yesterday afternoon—out by the tree."

"Ah, yes, she's with that web queen or writer—or whatever that little woman calls herself," Flannery said. He looked over at Brock. "Is that what they call serendipity?"

Brock didn't reply. He was looking at his portfolios on the missing women. He'd already read through them on the plane, but talking things out could reveal new angles.

"All right," Brock said. "Maureen Rodriguez was out of the house and just starting a new life. So she wasn't noted as missing right away. But Lily Sylvester was supposed to check in with her boyfriend. She'd come to the Frampton ranch because she wanted to see it. She stayed at a little hotel on the outskirts of St. Augustine one night after her visit, and then she was supposed to meet with a girlfriend at a posh bed-and-breakfast in the old section of the city. She never showed that day and her friend called the cops right away."

He flipped through his folders.

"Friends and family were insistent about Lily," Flannery told him. "She was as dependable as they come. Is," he added. "We shouldn't assume the worst."

But it was natural that they did.

"All right, moving on to Amy Bonham. She stayed at the Frampton ranch. She told one of the waitresses that she was excited about a surprise job opportunity the next day. She was supposed to be heading in the other direction—toward Orlando and the theme parks. She also stayed at a chain motel the night right after she was at the Frampton ranch and disappeared the next day. I know you certainly looked into her 'job opportunity.'"

Flannery nodded. "We've had officers interviewing people across more than half the state."

"But no one knew anything about it."

"No. But the waitress at the Frampton ranch—Dorothy Masterson—swears that Amy was super excited. Dorothy believed that she was looking for work at one of the theme parks."

"And you checked with all the parks."

"Of course. Big and small."

Brock went on to his third folder. "Lydia Merkel."

Flannery nodded; he'd already committed to memory most of what Brock was still studying.

"Lydia. Cute as a button."

"You met her? You knew her?" Brock asked, frowning.

"I met her briefly—I was in St. Augustine. The wife had her nephews down and I was taking them on one of the ghost tours. Lydia was on our tour. All wide eyes and happiness. Can't tell you how stunned I was when the powers that be called me in and told me that we had another missing woman—and that I recognized her." He glanced quickly at Brock. "You know how it goes with missing persons reports. Half of the time someone is just off on a lark. There's been a fight—a person has taken off because they want to disappear. But I just don't think that's the case." He was silent. "Especially since we found the remains of Maureen Rodriguez."

"And you can't help but think that Frampton Ranch and Resort is somehow involved."

Flannery nodded grimly.

"Lydia had told a young woman she was working with—Katie Simmons—that she wanted to take her first days off to drive over and see the History Tree. We're not just working this alone. I have all kinds of help on this. We do have officers from the Florida Department of Law Enforcement out all over—not to mention the help we've gotten from our local police departments. I keep feeling like I'm looking at some kind of puzzle with pieces missing—except that the frame is there. Because there was only one thing the girls—or young women—had in common."

"They had left or were coming to the Frampton Ranch and Resort," Brock said.

He felt a sudden pang deep in his heart or maybe his soul—someplace that really hurt at any rate.

He glanced over at Flannery. "The four of them are between the ages of twenty-two and twenty-nine," he said.

"Lydia Merkel was—is—twenty-nine. She was at

the ranch with friends for her birthday. On the tour, she talked about loving ghost stories—and how excited she was going to be to see the infamous History Tree."

Seriously—the tree should have been bulldozed.

Not fair—the tree wasn't guilty. Men and women could be guilty; the tree was just a tree—two trees.

"Funny, isn't it?" Flannery asked. "I mean, not ha ha funny, just…strange. Maybe ironic. The History Tree is two trees. Entwined. And you're here—because I asked for you particularly because I knew you were FBI, criminal section—and I'm here. And Miss Maura Antrim is here. We're all kinds of entwined. And I can't help but think that we still know the killer—even if twelve years have gone by."

"Yep. We're all tangled together somehow, like that damned tree. And so help me God, this time I really want to have the answers…and to stop the killing," Brock said quietly.

"You don't disagree with me?" Flannery asked him.

Brock shrugged grimly.

"But you don't disagree—you don't think I'm being far-fetched or anything?" Flannery pressed.

"No, I just wonder what this person—if it is the same killer—has been doing for twelve years," Brock said. And then added, "Although…maybe he hasn't been lying dormant. It's a big state filled with just about everything in one area or another. Forests, marshes, caverns, sinkholes, the Everglades—a river of grass—and, of course…"

"That great big old Atlantic Ocean," Flannery said. "So, there you go. My puzzle. Are there pieces missing? Did the three young ladies who disappeared just run off? Or…"

"Has someone been killing young women and disposing of corpses over the last twelve years?" Brock finished. He took a deep breath. "All right, I guess I'm going to do a lot of traveling. There will be dozens of people to question again. But I think I'll start at the library at Frampton ranch."

ANGIE WAS A late sleeper, something Maura deeply appreciated the next morning. She wanted some on-her-own time.

She had gotten a lot of great footage for Angie's internet channel on the tour the night before.

Martin had ended up loving being on camera—and it had loved him. They were going to do the campfire again that night, get more video and put together all the best parts.

She'd behaved perfectly normally, even though she was ready to crawl out of her own skin. While on the tour, she'd expected to see Brock materialize again.

It hadn't been until the very end that she'd realized he'd been there all along—watching from the shadows, from the background.

But he'd never approached her. She'd seen him later in the lounge, briefly, when she and Angie walked in after the trek through the woods. He'd been deep in conversation with a slightly older man in a suit—she'd seen him earlier and remembered him vaguely. He was a cop of some kind; he'd been there the night that Francine Renault was killed. She had seen him earlier in the day as well, walking around the ranch with a woman. Maura hadn't seen the woman's face, just the cut of her suit, and for some bizarre reason she had noticed the woman's shoes. Flat, serviceable.

And she'd thought that perhaps the woman was a cop or in some form of law enforcement, too.

Angie hadn't seemed interested in talking to any of them—Maura had been glad. She'd left Angie in the lounge, waiting for her appointed drink with Mark, and Maura had slipped quickly upstairs, wanting nothing more than to be in her room, alone.

Once there, she'd lain awake for hours, wondering why something that had happened ages ago still had such an effect on her life—on her.

Why... Brock McGovern could suddenly walk back into her life and become all that she thought about once again. So easily. Or why she could close her eyes and see the man he had become and know that he was still somehow flawed and perfect, the man to whom she had subconsciously—or even consciously—compared to everyone else she ever met.

He hadn't so much as touched her.

And he hadn't looked at her as if he particularly liked her. He'd simply wanted her—and Angie—to be safe. Nothing more. Stay with people. He was a law enforcement officer, a Fed. He worked to find those who had turned living, breathing bodies into murdered, decaying bodies—and he tried to keep all men and women from being victims. His job. What he did.

A job he always knew he wanted.

She had to stop thinking about him, and that meant

she needed to immerse herself in some other activity—research. Books, knowledge, seeking…

She had always loved the library and archives at the Frampton ranch. One thing Donald Glass did with every property he bought was build and maintain a library with any books and info he had on that property. It was fascinating—much of it had been put on computer through the years, but every little event that had to do with the property was available.

The hotel manager—solid, ruddy little Fred Bentley—had never shown any interest in the contents of the library.

Nor, when she'd been alive, had Francine Renault. But the libraries were sacred. No matter what else the very, very rich Donald Glass might be, he loved his history and his libraries, and anyone working for him learned not to mess with them.

For this, she greatly admired Glass. Not that she knew the man well—he'd left the hands-on management to Francine and Fred when Maura had been working there. And back then, she and Brock had both spent hours in the library—often together—each trying to one-up the other by finding some obscure and curious fact or happening. It was fun to work the weird trivia into their presentations.

That had been twelve years ago.

But Brock was suddenly back in her life.

No, he wasn't in her life. He just happened to be here at the same time.

Because a woman had been murdered—and others had disappeared.

Concentrate... There was a wealth of information before her. Bits and pieces that might offer up something especially unusual for Angie Parsons.

The library room was comfortable and inviting, filled with leather sofas and chairs, desks, computers—and shelves upon shelves of files and books.

Donald Glass had acquired an extensive collection; he had books on the indigenous population of the area, starting back somewhere between twelve and twenty thousand years ago. Settlers had arrived before the end of the Pleistocene megafauna era. The Wacissa River—not far away in Jefferson County near the little town of Wacissa—had offered up several animal fossils of the time, and other areas of the state—including Silver Springs, Vero, Melbourne and Devil's Den—had also offered up proof of man's earliest time in the area.

Way back that many thousands of years, there had been a greater landmass and less water, causing animals—and thus hunters—to congregate at pools. Artifacts proving the existence of these hunter-gatherers could be found in countless rivers—and even out into the Gulf of Mexico.

Mammoths had even roamed the state.

By 700 AD, farming had come to the north of Florida. There were many Native American tribes, and many of those were called Creek by the Europeans and spoke the Muskogee language. But by the time the first Frampton put down roots to create this great ranching and farming estate, Florida Indians of many varieties—though mostly Creek—were being lumped together as Seminoles, largely divided into two groups: the Muskogee-speaking and the Hitchiti-speaking.

There were wonderful illustrated books describing fossils and tools found, creating images of the people and the way they lived.

According to the one she pulled from the shelf there had been a colony of Seminole living in the area when Frampton first chose his site.

They had held rites out at what was already a giant clearing in the forest. It was the Native Americans who had first called it the History Tree. The Timucua had first named it so; the Seminoles in the area had respected the holiness of the tree.

Maura—like the writer of the book—didn't believe that the Native American tribes had practiced human sacrifice at the tree. But as war loomed with the Seminole tribe, the European populace had liked to portray the native people as barbarians—it made it easier to justify killing them.

So the tree had gotten its reputation very early on.

Gyselle—who became known as Gyselle Frampton, since no one knew her real surname—had arrived at the plantation soon after it was built in the late 1830s. Spanish missionaries had "rescued" her from the Seminole, but she was fifteen at the time and had been kidnapped at the age of ten—or that was the best that could be figured. Oliver Frampton—creator of the first great mansion to rest on the property—had been a kind man. He'd taken her in, clothed her, educated her and had still, of course, given her chores to do.

She was a servant and not of the elite. She was not, in any way, wife material for his son.

That hadn't stopped Richard Frampton from falling in love with his father's beautiful servant/ward.

But Richard had underestimated his wife. Back then, a wife was supposed to be a lovely figurehead, wealthy to match her husband and eye candy on the arm of her man. Unless she was very, very, very rich—and then it wouldn't matter if she was eye candy or not.

But Julie LeBlanc Frampton had been no fool and not someone to be taken lightly.

She discovered the affair—and knew that her husband loved Gyselle deeply. Perhaps she was angry with her father-in-law for not only condoning the affair but perhaps finding it to be fine and natural. Wives weren't supposed to get in the way of these things after all.

Or maybe the situation was just convenient for her plan.

She hid the taste of the deadly fruit of the manchineel tree in a drink—one that Gyselle usually made up for the senior Mr. Frampton right before he went to bed made up of whiskey, tea and sugar.

The old man died in horrible pain. Julie immediately pointed the finger at Gyselle.

She created such an outcry and hysteria that the other servants immediately went for poor Gyselle. The master had been well loved. And without trial or even much questioning, they had dragged Gyselle out to the History Tree—thought to surely be haunted at that time and also a place where the devil might well be found.

Gyselle died swearing that she was innocent—and cursing Julie, those around her and even the tree.

After she was hanged, she was allowed to remain there until she rotted, until her bones fell to the ground.

Three years later, Julie Frampton died. At the time no one knew what her ailment was—tuberculosis, it sounded like to Maura.

But in the end, the true poisoner did die choking on her own blood—and confessing to the entire room that she had murdered her father-in-law.

"Maura!"

She had become so involved in what she was reading that the sound of her name made her jump.

She'd been very comfortable in one of the plush leather chairs, feet curled beneath her, the book—*Truth and Legends of Central Florida*—in her arms.

Luckily, she didn't drop it or throw it as she was startled. It was an original book, printed and bound in 1880.

"Mr. Glass!" she exclaimed, truly started to see the resort's owner. He usually kept to himself; Fred Bentley was his mouthpiece.

She quickly closed the book and stood, accepting the hand he offered to her.

Donald Glass, in his early sixties now, Maura thought, was still an attractive man. He kept himself lean and fit—and had maintained a full head of salt-and-pepper hair. His posture was straight; his manners tended to be impeccable. He'd never personally fired anyone that she knew of, in any of his enterprises. He left managers—like Fred Bentley—to do such deeds.

He was customarily well liked and treated kindly by magazines when he was included in an article.

Donald Glass used his money to make more money, granted. That was the American way. But he did it all in one of the best possible manners—preserving history and donating to worthy causes all the while.

Whether he was into the causes or simply into tax breaks, no one really looked too closely.

But he tended to do good things and do them well.

"Miss Antrim, how lovely to have you here again," he said, smiling. "And I'm delighted that you've brought Angie Parsons with her incredible ability to show the world interesting places—and provide wonderful publicity for those places!"

"I'd love to take the credit, Mr. Glass," Maura told him. "Angie heard the story about the History Tree. She couldn't wait to come."

"Well, however you came to be here, I'm most delighted. Still sorry—and I will be sorry all my life—about Francine. She was…"

He paused. Maura wondered what he'd been about to say. That Francine Renault had been a good woman? But she really hadn't been kind or generous in any way.

"No one deserved to die that way," he said. "Anyway… I did consider having the tree torn out of the ground. But I thought on it a long time and decided that it was the *History Tree*. They didn't burn down the building when a famous woman died in a room at the Hard Rock in Hollywood, Florida, and…" Again, he paused. "I decided that the tree—or trees—should stay. Not to mention the fact that the environmentalists and preservationists would create a real uproar if we were to cut it down. It's hundreds of years old, you know. And yes—as you learned last night, we do tell the story at the campfire and continue the walk by the tree."

"Trees aren't evil," Maura said.

She wondered if she was trying to reassure him—or if it was something she said but doubted somewhere in a primal section of her heart or mind.

"No, of course not. A tree is a tree. Or trees are trees," he said and smiled weakly. "Anyway, I'm delighted to see you. And thankful for the work you're doing here with Miss Parsons."

"I'm not sure you need us. You've always had a full house here."

He didn't argue.

"I'm sure Marie will be delighted to see you, too."

"A pleasure to see her," Maura murmured.

Marie was perhaps ten years younger than her husband; they had been together for thirty years or so. Like her husband she kept herself fit, and she was an attractive and cordial woman. Her public manner was pristine—every once in a while, Maura had wondered what she was *really* thinking.

Glass lifted a hand in farewell and said, "Enjoy your stay." He started to walk away and then turned back. "I don't mean to be an alarmist, but…be careful. I'm sure you heard. Remains were found nearby. And several young women have disappeared, as well. Whether they ran away or…met with bad things… I know you're smart, but…be wary."

"Yes, I've heard. And I'll be careful," Maura said.

She watched him for a moment as he headed out of the room and then she opened the book again. Words swam before her as she tried to remember where she'd left off.

She heard Glass speaking again and she looked toward the door, thinking that he had something else to say.

But he wasn't speaking to her.

Brock was at the doorway, his tone deep and quiet as he replied to whatever Glass had said.

The length of Maura's body gripped with tension, which angered her to no end.

She hadn't seen or heard from him in twelve years.

He and Glass parted politely.

Brock headed straight for her. He smiled, but it seemed that his smile was grave.

His face seemed harder than the image of him she'd held in her mind. Naturally. Years did that to anyone.

And he'd always wanted to be law enforcement. But that job had to take a toll.

"I thought I'd find you here," he said softly.

"Yes, well, I… I'm here," she said.

She didn't invite him to sit. He did anyway. She wondered if he was going to talk about the years between them, ask what she'd been doing, maybe even explain why he'd just disappeared after the charges against him had been dismissed.

Elbows on his knees, hands folded idly, he was close—too close, she thought. Or not really close at all. Just close because she could feel a strange rush inside, as if she knew everything about him, or everything that mattered. She knew his scent—his scent, not soap or aftershave or cologne, but that which lurked beneath it, particular to him, something that drew her to him, that called up a natural reaction within her. She knew that there was a small scar on the lower side of his abdomen—stitches from a deep cut received when he'd fallen on a haphazardly discarded tin can during a track event when he'd been in high school. She knew there was a spattering of freckles on his shoulders, knew…

"You really shouldn't be here—you need to pack up and go," he said. His tone was harsh, as if she were committing a grave sin by being there.

She couldn't have been more surprised if he'd slapped her.

"I beg your pardon?" she demanded, a sudden fury taking over.

"You need to get the hell out—out of this part of the state and sure as hell off the Frampton Ranch and Resort."

Why did it hurt so badly, the way he spoke to her, the way he wanted to be rid of her?

"I'm sorry. I have every right to be here. It's a public facility and a free country, last I heard."

"No, you don't—"

She stood, aware she badly needed to leave the room.

"Excuse me, Special Agent—or whatever your title may be. You don't control me. I have a life—and things to do. Things that need to be done—here. Right here. Have a nice day."

She stood—with quiet dignity, she hoped—and headed quickly for the door.

How the hell could he still have such an effect upon her?

And why the hell did he have to be here now?

Another body. Another life cut tragically short. His job.

Brock was right; she was the one who shouldn't be here.

Chapter Three

To say that he'd handled his conversation with Maura badly would be a gross understatement.

But he couldn't start over. She was angry and not about to listen to him—certainly not now. Maybe later.

The library seemed oddly cold without her, empty of human life.

Brock needed to get going, but he found himself standing up, studying some of the posters and framed newspaper pages on the walls.

There was a rendering of the beautiful Gyselle, running through the woods, hair flowing, gown caught in a cascade.

Donald Glass didn't shirk off the truth or try to hide it; there were multiple newspaper articles and reports on the murders that had taken place in the 1970s.

And there was information on Francine Renault to be found, including a picture of her that was something of a memorial, commemorating her birth, acknowledging the tragedy of her death—and revealing that, while it was assumed she had been murdered by a disgruntled employee, the case remained unsolved.

Going through the library, Brock couldn't help but remember how shocked he had been to find himself under arrest. He'd been young—and nothing in his life had prepared him for the concept that he could be unjustly accused of a crime. He'd known where he wanted to go in life—but his very idealism had made it impossible for him to believe that such a thing as his being wrongly arrested could happen.

The world just wasn't as clean and cut-and-dried as he had once believed.

Of course, he had been quickly released—and that had been another lesson.

Truth was sometimes a fight.

And now, years later, he could understand Flannery's actions. There had been an urgency about the night; people had been tense. The police had been under terrible pressure.

Brock had usually controlled his temper—despite the fact that Francine had been very difficult to work with. But the day she had been killed, his anger had gotten the best of him. He hadn't gotten physical in the least—unless walking toward her and standing about five feet away with his fists clenched counted as physical. Perhaps that had appeared to be the suggestion of underlying malice. Many of his coworkers had known that he was always frustrated with Francine—she demanded so much and never accepted solid explanations as to why her way wouldn't work, or why something had to be as it was.

Like almost everyone else, he had considered Francine Renault to be a fire-breathing dragon. Quite simply, a total bitch.

She had been a thorn in all their sides. He had just happened to pick that day to explode.

After his blowup, he'd feared being fired—not arrested for murder.

He didn't tend to have problems with those he worked with or for—but he had disliked Francine. In retrospect, he felt bad about it. But she had enjoyed flaunting her authority and used it unfairly. Brock had complained about her to Fred Bentley many times, disgusted with the way she treated the summer help. Her own lack of punctuality—or when she simply didn't show up—was always forgiven, of course, because she was above them all. That night, Brock had been quick to put Maura Antrim on the schedule—as if he had known that Francine wouldn't be there.

Until she was—dangling from the tree.

As the police might see it, after they'd been pointed straight at Brock by the mysterious anonymous tipster, he'd been certain to be on the tour when Francine's body had been discovered, a ready way to explain any type of physical evidence that might have been found at the History Tree or around it.

At the time, Brock had wanted nothing to do with Detective Flannery. He'd been hurt and bitter. He was sure that only his size had kept him from being beaten to a pulp during his night in the county jail, and once he'd been freed, he found that his friends had gone.

Including, he now thought dryly, the woman he had assumed to be the love of his life.

Maura had vanished. Gone back home, into the arms of her loving parents, the same people who had once claimed to care about Brock, to be impressed with his maturity, admiring of his determination to do a stint in the service first and then spend his time in college.

Calls, emails, texts, snail mail—all had gone unanswered. It hurt too much that Maura never replied, never reached out, and so he stopped trying. He had joined the navy, done his stint and gone on to college in New York.

And yet, oddly, through the years, he'd kept up with Michael Flannery. Now and then, Flannery would write him with a new theory on the case and apologize again for arresting Brock so quickly. Flannery wasn't satisfied; he needed an explanation he believed in. He explored all kinds of possibilities—from the familiar to the absurd.

Francine had been killed by an interstate killer, a trucker—a man caught crossing the Georgia state line with a teenage victim in his cab.

She had been killed by Donald Glass himself.

By college students out of Gainesville or Tallahassee, a group that had taken hazing to a new level.

She had even been killed, a beyond-frustrated Flannery had once written, by the devils or the evil that lived in the forest by the History Tree.

Frustration. Something that continued to plague them. But then, Brock had been told that every cop, marshal and agent out there had a case that haunted them, that they couldn't solve—or had been considered closed, but the closure just didn't seem right, and it stuck in his or her gut.

Standing in the library wasn't helping any; Francine Renault had been a dead a long time, and regardless of her personality, she hadn't deserved her fate.

The truth still needed to be discovered.

More than ever now, as it was possible that her murderer had returned to kill again.

Brock left the library.

Before he left for his interviews in St. Augustine that day, he had to try one more time with Maura. He had to find her. He hadn't explained himself very well.

In fact, he had made matters worse.

He had known Maura so well at one time. And if anything, his faltering way of trying to get her far, far from this place, where someone was killing people had probably made her stubbornly more determined to stay.

He'd admit he was afraid.

Beautiful young women were disappearing, and with or without his feelings, Maura was certainly an incredibly beautiful woman.

And there was more working against her.

She was familiar with the Frampton ranch and many of the players in this very strange game of life and death.

"MAYBE WE SHOULD move on," Maura said. She and Angie were sitting in the restaurant—Angie had actually wakened early enough for them to catch the tail end of the breakfast buffet, a spread that contained just about every imaginable morning delight.

The place was renowned for cheese grits; savoring a bite, Maura decided that they did remain among the best tasting she'd ever had. There were eggs cooked in many ways as well, plus pancakes, fruit, yogurt, nuts and grains and everything to cater to tastes from around the country.

Angie, too, it seemed, especially enjoyed the grits. Her eyes were closed as she took a forkful and then smiled.

"Delicious."

"Did you hear me?"

"What?"

"I was thinking we should move on."

Angie appeared to be completely shocked. "I… Yes, I mean, I know now about you—I mean, when you were a kid—but I thought we were fine. This is the perfect place to be home base for this trip. We can reach St. Augustine easily, areas on the coast—some of those amazing cemeteries up in Gainesville. I…"

She quit speaking. Nils Hartford, handsome in a pin-striped suit, was coming their way, smiling.

They were at a table for four and he glanced at them, brows arched and a hesitant smile on his face, silently asking if he could join them.

Angie leaped right to it.

"Nils! Hey, you're joining us?"

"Just for a minute. My people here are great—we have the best and nicest waitstaff, but I still like to oversee the change from breakfast to lunch," he said, sliding into the chair next to Maura. "You're enjoying yourself?" he asked Angie.

"I love it!" she said enthusiastically. "And last night—your brother was amazing. I mean, of course, I know that Maura had his job at one time, and I know Maura, and I know she was fantastic, but I just adored your brother. Keep him on!"

Nils laughed. "Oddly enough, that would have nothing to do with me. My brother reports directly to Fred Bentley, as do I. Couldn't get him hired or fired. But he's loved that kind of thing since we were kids. I was more into the cranking of the gears, the way things run and so forth." He turned toward Maura and asked anxiously, "And you—you okay being back here?"

"I'm fine," Maura said.

"Well, thank you both for what you're doing." He lowered his voice, even though there was no one near. "Even Donald is shaken up by the way we keep hearing that young women have been heading here or leaving here—and disappearing. Seriously, I mean, a tree can't make people do things, but... I guess people do see things as symbols, but—we're keeping a good eye on it these days. We never had arranged for any video surveillance because it's so far out in the woods—and nothing recent has had anything to do with the tree, but...anyway, we're going to get some security out there.

"Donald has a company coming out to make suggestions tomorrow. We have cameras now in the lobby, elevators, public areas...that kind of thing. But dealing with security and privacy laws—it's complicated. I mean, the tree is on Donald's property and it's perfectly legal to have cameras at the tree. And with today's tech—improving all the time, but way above what we had twelve years ago—the tree can easily be watched. Anyway, it's great that you're helping to keep us famous."

"A true pleasure," Angie told him.

He smiled at Angie and then turned back to Maura, appearing a little anxious again. "I just—well, I know you thought I was a jerk—and I was, back then. I did feel superior to the kids who had to work." He laughed softly and only a little bitterly. "Then the stock market crashed and I received a really good comeuppance. Odd, though. It's like 'hail, hail, the gang's all here.' Me, Mark, Donald, of course, Fred Bentley, other staff…and now you and Brock and Rachel."

"Rachel?" Maura echoed, surprised.

"Oh, you didn't know? Rachel is with the Florida Department of Law Enforcement now—she's working with Detective Mike Flannery. They've stationed themselves here—good central spot—for investigating this rash of disappearances. I think it's a rash. Well, everyone is worried because of the remains of the poor girl that were found at the laundry."

"Oh! Are you and Rachel still…a twosome?" she asked.

"No, no, no—friends, though. I have a lot of love for Rach, though I was a jerk to her when we were teens. I'm grateful to have her as a friend. And can you imagine—she's like a down and dirty cop. Not that cops can't be feminine. But she made a bit of a change. Well, I mean, she has nice nails still—she just keeps them clipped and short. Short hair, too. Good cut. She's still

cute. But I hear she's hell on wheels, having taken all
kinds of martial arts—and a crack shot. Great kid, still.
Well, adult. We're all adults—I forget that sometimes.
And hey, what about you and Brock? I was jealous as
hell of you guys back then, you know."

She certainly hadn't known.

"Of the two of us?" she asked. "And no—I hadn't
seen him since that summer. I'm afraid that we aren't
even social media friends."

"I'm sorry to hear that. But I guess that… Well, it
was bad time, what happened back then." He bright-
ened. "But you're here now. And that's great! I believe
you recorded a tour? And more, so far? I'd like to think
that you could spend days here—"

"We *are* spending days here," Angie assured him.
"I guess we're like the cops—or agents or officers or
whatever. We're in a central location. We'll head to St.
Augustine and come back here, maybe over Gainesville's way. It's just such a great location."

"Well, I'm glad. That's wonderful. If I can do anything for either of you…"

His voice trailed oddly. He was looking toward the
restaurant entrance. Maura saw that Marie Glass had
arrived and seemed to be looking for someone.

"Excuse me," he said, making a slight grimace. "Our
queen has arrived. Oh, I don't mean that in a bad way,"
he added quickly. "Marie never meddles with the staff
and she's always charming. I mean *queen* in the best
way possible, always so engaging and cordial with the
guests and all of us." He made a face. "She's even nice
when she knows an employee is in trouble, never fal-

ters. Just as sweet as she can be—while still aloof and elegant. Regal, you know?"

"Yes, very regal," Maura agreed.

Marie was looking for Nils, Maura thought, and as she noted their table and graced them with one of her smiles, Nils stood politely, awaiting whatever word she might have for him.

But she wasn't coming to speak with Nils. As she approached them, she headed for the one chair that wasn't occupied and asked politely, "May I join you? I'll just take a few seconds of your time, I promise."

"Of course, Mrs. Glass, please." Maura said.

Marie Glass sat delicately. "My dear Maura, you are hardly a child anymore, and though I do appreciate the respect, please, call me Marie."

Maura inclined her head. It was true. She was hardly a child. Marie simply had an interesting way of putting her thoughts.

"I know my husband and the staff here have tried to let you know how we appreciate the publicity your work here will bring us—and free publicity these days is certainly wonderful," Marie Glass began. "But we'd also be willing to compensate you if you want to show more of the resort—if you had time and if you didn't mind." She paused, flashing a smile Maura's way. "We love your reputations—and would love to make use of you in all possible ways. I am, of course, at your disposal, should you need help."

"Oh, that's a lovely idea," Angie said. "I'd have to switch up the format a little—as you know, I bring to light the unusual and frankly, the *creepy*, so—"

"Oh, bring on the creepy," Marie Glass said. She grinned again, broadly. "We do embrace the creepy, and honestly, so many people visit because of the History Tree. But we thought that allowing people to see how lovely the rest of the resort is... Well, it would make them think they should stay here and perhaps not just sign up for the campfire histories and the ghost walk into the forest. If it's a bit more comprehensive, we could use your videos on our website and in other promotional materials."

"I'm happy to get on it right away. Well, almost right away," Angie said cheerfully. "We did have plans to wander out a bit today, but we'll start on a script tonight. Maura's a genius at these things."

Maura glanced over at Angie, not about to show her surprise. So far, she hadn't known they were wandering out that day, and she wasn't sure that she was going to come up with anything "genius" after they got back.

From wherever it was that they were apparently going.

"Thank you ever so much," Marie said, standing. Her fingers rested lightly on the table as she turned to Maura. "We always knew our Maura was clever— we'd hoped to have her on through college and beyond, but, well...very sad circumstances do happen in life. Ladies, I will leave you to your day." She inclined her head to Nils. "Mr. Hartford, would you come to the office with me?"

As soon as they were out of earshot, Maura leaned forward. "Where is it that we're wandering off to today?"

"Well, it was your idea—originally, I'm certain," Angie said.

"Where?"

"St. Augustine, of course. You said it wasn't much of a drive and that we could easily get there and back in a day. I want to head to the Castillo de San Marcos—did you know that it's the oldest masonry fort in the continental United States? And I'm not sure how to say this, but St. Augustine is the oldest city in the country *continually* inhabited by European settlers. Think that's right. I mean, the Spanish started with missions and then stayed and... I have it all in my notes. Though I know you—you may know more than my notes!"

Maura glanced at her watch. It wasn't late—just about ten. If they left soon, they could certainly spend the afternoon in the old city, have dinner at one of the many great restaurants to be found—perhaps even hear a bit of music somewhere—and be back for the night.

"Okay," she said. "I had thought you wanted to finish up around here today—maybe even leave here and stay in St. Augustine or perhaps head out to the old Rivero-Marin Cemetery just north of Orlando. I just had no idea—"

"I thought you loved St. Augustine."

"I do."

"So it's fine."

"Sure. But we don't have permits, and while people film with their phones all the time now, what you're doing is for commercial purposes and—"

"We'll film out in front of places where I might need a permit to film inside. And if you don't mind, when we get to the square, I'll have you tell that tale about the condemned Spaniard who kept having the garrote break on him so that they finally let him go. Now, that's a great real story."

"The square is called the Plaza de la Constitución."

"Right. Yeah, but it's still a square," Angie said, grinning. "It is a square, right?"

"The shape is actually oblong."

"Okay, technicalities are important. But the story is great. About the man."

"His name was Andrew Ranson and he wasn't a Spaniard. He was a Brit and he had been working on an English ship and was accused of piracy. He absolutely declared that he was innocent but met his executioner with a rosary clutched in his hands. While he was being garroted, the rope broke, and the Catholic Church declared that his survival was a miracle. He recuperated, but when the governor asked that he be returned to be executed, the Church refused to give him back. He was eventually pardoned."

"And it's real—proving my desire to show all these stories. We're back to truth being far stranger than any fiction. And there's so much more. It is okay to go today, right?"

"Yes, it is, sure—let's sign this tab and get going right away."

Maura asked for the bill, but as she did so, her old boss came striding over to their table, a massive smile on his face.

Fred Bentley was powerfully built, stocky, not fat,

but to Maura, it had always seemed that a barge was coming toward her when he strode in her direction.

He still had a head full of dark hair—dyed? She didn't know, but he had to be over fifty now, and it was certainly possible. He kept a good tan going on his skin, adding to his appearance of being fit, an outdoor man who loved the sun and activity.

He hadn't been a bad man to work for—he had certainly been better than Francine, who had changed her mind on a dime and blamed anyone else for any mistake.

Maura lowered her eyes for a moment, feeling guilty. Francine had not been nice. That didn't make what had happened to her any less horrible. Maura had to shake the image of Francine's lifeless body hanging from the tree. It haunted her almost daily.

"Maura, Angie," Fred said cheerfully. "Please, not a bill to be signed," he assured them. "What you're doing—in the midst of all this—is just wonderful. We're so grateful, honestly. Anything, anything at all that we can do, please just say so."

Maura smiled, uncomfortable. Angie answered him enthusiastically, telling him how she loved the grounds, the beauty of the pool and the elegance of the rooms, and, of course, most of all, the extra and unusual aspect of the campfire tales and the history walk. She was delighted to tout such a wonderful place.

To her surprise, Maura stood and listened and smiled, and yet, inside, she found that she was suddenly wondering about Fred.

Where was he when Francine Renault had been hanged from the great branches of the History Tree?

St. Augustine was, in Brock's opinion, one of the state's true gems. Founded in 1565 by Pedro Menéndez de Avilés, the city offered wonders such as the fort, the old square, dozens of charming bed-and-breakfast inns, historic hotels, museums, the original Ripley's Believe It or Not! Museum, ghost tours, pub tours and all manner of musical entertainment.

The city also offered beautiful beaches.

But that day, he hadn't come to enjoy any of the many wonderful venues offered here.

As asked, Detective Rachel Lawrence had set up a meeting with Katie Simmons, the coworker who had reported the disappearance of one of the missing women, Lydia Merkel. She was possibly the last one to see Lydia alive.

They were meeting at La Pointe, a new restaurant near the Castillo—Katie hadn't wanted to talk where she worked, though Brock intended to go by after their meeting, just to see if anyone else remembered anything that they might have missed when speaking with officers before.

The restaurant was casual, as were many that faced the old fort and the water beyond, with wooden tables, a spiral of paper towels right on the table and a menu geared to good but reasonable food for tourists.

Katie Simmons was there when he arrived; if he hadn't seen a picture of her in his files, he would have recognized her anyway. She was so nervous. She saw him as he entered through the rustic doorway, and her straw slipped from her mouth. She quickly brought her fingers to her lips as iced tea dribbled from them. She was a pretty young woman with soft brown hair and an athletic build, evident when she leaped to her feet, sat and stood once again.

She must have realized who he was by the way he had scanned the restaurant when he had entered. Maybe it was his suit—not all that common in Florida, even for many a business meeting.

She waited for him to come to the table.

He smiled, offering her his hand, hoping to put her at ease quickly.

"Katie, right?" he said.

"Special Agent McGovern?"

"Call me Brock, please," he said as he joined her at the table. "And please sit, and I hope you can relax. I can't tell you how grateful I am that you've agreed to speak with me. I know you've already told the police about Lydia, but as you know, we're hoping that we can find her."

Katie sat and plucked at the straw in her tea, still nervous. It looked as if tears were starting to form in her eyes.

"Time keeps going by… It's been weeks now. I don't know how she could still be alive."

A waiter in a flowered shirt was quickly at their table. Brock ordered coffee and he and Katie both requested the daily special, a seafood dish.

"I don't want to lie to you, but I also don't think you

should give up," Brock told her when the waiter had gone. "People do just disappear—"

Katie broke in immediately. "Not Lydia! Oh, you had to know her. She was so excited to have moved here. She loved the city, loved working here—and there was more, of course. Lydia is a wonderful musician. She's magic with her guitar. She has the coolest voice—not like an angel, more like… I don't know, unique. She can be soft, she can belt it out… I love listening to her! She was going around getting gigs—and our boss is a great guy. He does schedules every week and talks to us before he sets them up. That allowed Lydia to set up her first few gigs."

"She was performing before she left here?" he asked.

"Oh, she only had two performances. One was for a private party out on a boat—but good money. They just wanted a solo acoustic player. And then another was at a place called Saint, which is a historic house that just became a restaurant—or kind of a nightclub. Can you be both? Or maybe you could say the same of a lot of places here—restaurant by day, club, kind of, by night with some kind of musical entertainment."

"Thanks. Do you know who hired her for the boat?"

"Sure. An association of local tourist businesses—it's called SAMM," she said and paused to grin. "St. Augustine Makes Money. That's really the name. Only you don't have to be in the city to belong—people belong from all kinds of nearby locations. In fact, half of the members, from what I understand, are really up in Jacksonville. We're the cute historic place, you know—Jacksonville is the big city. And where most people come in, as far as an airport goes." She grew somber again. "But she wasn't working the night before she disappeared. We were out together that night. She was leaving in the morning. She was so excited. Her career—her musical career—wasn't skyrocketing, but it was taking off."

"And according to what I've learned, she did leave in her own car."

"Yes, and she loved her car. It was old, but she kept it up—she kept great care of it. Oh, and that's why she chose her apartment. She could park there for free. Right in this area—well, out a bit—but still in what we consider the old section. I mean, you could walk to her place if you had to."

"Her car was never found," Brock noted. He'd read everything he could about Lydia before coming here today. And, of course, one of the reasons it was easy for law enforcement to consider the fact that she might have disappeared on purpose had to do with the fact that her car had never been found.

Katie was instantly indignant. "I know that—and I'm so sorry, but it made me wonder if the cops are stupid. The state is surrounded by water—oh, yeah, not to mention swamps and bogs and sinkholes and the damned frigging Everglades! Someone got rid of her car. I'm telling you—there is no way in hell that Lydia left here willingly—that she just drove away. Okay, I mean, she did drive away that morning, but... I didn't worry until I didn't hear from her. I know she would have called and texted me pics of the History Tree. When she didn't... I swear, I didn't panic right away, but when I didn't hear from her by that night, I knew something was wrong. I called the ranch, and they told me that she'd never checked in. That's when I called the police. And they all told me she might have just taken a detour. I told them that her phone was going straight to voice mail, and they still tried to placate me. I had to wait the appropriate time to even report her as a missing person with people really working on the case. Then I found out that two other young women had disappeared, and then…"

She broke off.

Brock continued for her, "And then they found the remains of Maureen Rodriguez. Katie, as I said, I don't want to give you false hope. But don't give up completely. People are working very hard on this now, I promise you." He hesitated—an agent should never make a promise he couldn't guarantee he could keep, but…

"Katie, I promise you, I won't stop until we know what happened to her."

She smiled with tears welling in her eyes.

"I believe you," she said.

Their lunches arrived. As they ate, Brock allowed her to go on about her friend. They hadn't known each other that long; they had just hit it off. She loved old music and Lydia loved old music. They had loved going to plays together, too, and were willing to travel a few hours for a show, and they both loved improv and ghost tours and so on…

He thanked her sincerely when the meal was over; she had taken his business card, but also put his direct line into her phone. He promised to call her when he knew something—good or bad—and they parted ways.

He decided to stop by the offices of SAMM next, wanting a list of those involved in the boat event during which Lydia Merkel had played, and then he'd be on to the restaurant where she'd entertained at her one gig on the mainland.

Someone, somewhere, had to know something.

Her car hadn't been found.

She'd only had one credit card; it hadn't been used outside the city. No one disappeared without a trace. There was always a trace.

He just had to find it.

Chapter Four

"I am standing here on Avenida Menendez in historic St. Augustine in front of a home that was originally built in 1763. While it was in 1512 that Juan Ponce de Léon first came ashore just north of here, and 1564 when French vessels were well received by the Native population, it was in 1565 that Pedro Menéndez came and settlement began.

"It was while the Spanish ruled in 1760—nearly two centuries later—that Yolanda Ferrer's father first built the house that stands behind me. In 1762, Spain ceded Florida to the British in exchange for Cuba, and Yolanda and her young husband, Antonio, left for Havana. But in 1783, Florida was ceded back to the Spanish in exchange for the Bahama Islands. Yolanda came back to claim the home her father had built, and the governor granted the home and property to her. At that time, she was a young and beautiful bride, and she thought that she and her husband would live happily ever after—but it wasn't to be.

"Yolanda, deceived by her husband, argued and pleaded with him not to leave her—and then either fell to her death or was, perhaps, pushed to her death, in the courtyard behind the house, where, today, diners arrive from all over the world to enjoy the fusion cooking of one of St. Augustine's premier chefs, Armand Morena.

"Through the years, the house has changed. It stood for a while as an icehouse and as a mortuary. For the last fifty years, however, it has changed hands only once, being a restaurant for those fifty years. But it wasn't just as a restaurant that the building was haunted by images of the beautiful, young Yolanda, sometimes weeping as she hurries along the halls, sometimes appearing in the courtyard and sometimes in what was once her bedroom and is now the manager's office. Yolanda is known to neither hurt nor frighten those who see her. Rather, witnesses to her apparition claim that they long to reach out and touch her and let her know that her story is known and that, even today, we are touched by her tragedy."

Maura finished her speech and waited for Angie to cut the take on the camera. Angie did so but awkwardly, and Maura thought briefly about the editing she was going to have to do. She much preferred it when Angie did the talking, but Angie had already spoken in front of the Castillo and Ripley's, and at the Huguenot Cemetery, the Old Jail, the Spanish Military Hospital Museum and several other places. She had begged Maura to let her do the filming on this one and Maura had acquiesced.

The sun was just about gone. And Maura was tired. As much as she loved St. Augustine, she was wearying of seeing it as if she was reliving that old vacation movie with Chevy Chase.

"Ready for dinner?" she asked Angie.

"Oh, you bet. We're going to have to come back. I loved what I called the square—the Plaza de la Constitución. I mean, that's the whole thing, isn't it? Executions took place there once, and now it's all beautiful, and there is a farmer's market, and people come for musical events and more. I love the streets surrounding it, the beautiful churches and all. I'm so glad we came."

"I've always loved this city," Maura agreed. "But I'm tired and starving. Have you picked out a place you'd like to go?"

There were plenty of choices.

Angie hesitated. She winced. "If I picked a particular restaurant, would you think that I was being ghoulish?"

Maura arched a brow warily. "Ghoulish? I don't know of any new horrific restaurant murders in St. Augustine."

"The restaurant is quite safe—no blood and guts in the kitchen or elsewhere, as far as I know," Angie assured her. "But…" she said and hesitated again. "It is the last place one of the missing girls had a music gig—I think I saw some video—because Lydia Merkel was playing her guitar and singing there not long before she disappeared. It's called Saint."

"Oh," Maura murmured. "Really, I'm not—"

"You wouldn't have even known, I don't think, if I hadn't told you."

Maura had read news reports; she had seen videos

of the young women, including Lydia Merkel, who had worked here in St. Augustine, before her mysterious disappearance.

She hadn't remembered the name of the restaurant where the girl had played, nor even the name of the restaurant where she had worked.

"Please? I can't help but want to see it," Angie said.

Of course, Angie wanted to see it. If the poor woman's body was found and her murder was never solved, she would become another Florida legend.

She didn't have the energy to fight Angie, and besides, she doubted that the restaurant itself had been any cause of what had happened.

"Okay. Is it close? I'm sure you know. Are we walking? I don't think it existed the last time I was up here. I'll google it," she told Angie.

"Two blocks to the east and then one to the south," Angie said.

"We'll leave the car and walk."

Saint was like many restaurants in the historic district—once upon a time, it had been someone's grand home. Maura thought that it might have been built in the 1800s during the Victorian era; a plaque on the front assured her she was right: 1855. Originally the home of Delores and Captain Evan Siegfried.

Abandoned after the Civil War, it had become an institution for the mentally ill in the 1880s, a girls' school in 1910, a flower shop in the 1920s, a home again briefly in the 1950s before it was eventually abandoned—then recently restored by the owners of Saint.

The restaurant's original incarnation as a home was

evident as they entered; there was a stairway to the second floor on the right, and on the left was what had once been a parlor—it now held a long bar and a few tables.

They were led around to what had probably been a family room; there, to the far rear, was a small stage, cordoned off now, but offering a sign that told them that Timmy Margulies, Mr. One-Man Band, would be arriving at 8:00 p.m.

As the hostess led them to their table, Maura stopped dead—causing a server behind her to crash into her with his tray and send a plate of gourmet french fries and something brown and wet and covered with gravy to go flying to the floor.

Maura was instantly apologetic, beyond humiliated, and—what was worse—she had stopped in surprise.

Brock McGovern was seated at a table near the door, deep in conversation with a woman who was wearing a polo shirt with the restaurant's logo but not the tunic worn by the waitstaff.

Of course, now he—like the rest of those in the place—was staring at her.

She truly wanted to crawl beneath the floor.

Apparently he admitted to the woman that he knew Maura; he was standing, about to head her way.

She winced and ignored him, trying to help the waiter whose tray she had upturned, stooping down to help.

"It's fine, it's fine—really!" the young waiter told her, smiling as he met her eyes, collecting fallen plates.

"Oh, dear," Angie murmured.

Then Brock was at her side with the woman who had been at his table.

"Miss, seriously, please, it's all right—this is a restaurant. We do have spills," the woman said.

"I know, but this one was my fault," Maura said.

She was startled when Brock took her arm. She looked up into his eyes and saw that she was overdoing her apology.

She was still looking at him, but she couldn't help herself.

"I am so, so sorry!" she said again.

"Maura, it's all right," he said quietly. And, looking back at him, she realized she was as attracted to the man he had become as she had been to the boy he had once been. And maybe, just maybe, she had been apologizing to him, and he had been telling her that it was all right.

But…

"You never tried to reach me," she blurted as the waiter and busboys—and whoever the woman with Brock was—all scrambled around, cleaning up.

His frown instantly assured her that something was wrong with that statement.

"I did try," he said. "Repeatedly. I called, and I wrote and… I guess it doesn't matter now. There's no way to change the past."

Angie cleared her throat, "Um, excuse me. I think that they want us to sit. Maybe get out of the way? Brock! Wow, weird coincidence. Nice to see you—want to join us? Maura, we really need to sit."

"Yes, of course," Maura said, wincing again—wishing more than ever that she could sink into the floor and disappear. Her mind was racing; she was stunned and felt as if she had been blindsided.

She had great parents. Loving parents. But had they decided that there was no proof that Brock had really been cleared—and that he shouldn't contact their precious daughter? What else would explain that he said he'd reached out but had never actually reached her?

She was still standing. And everyone was still looking at her.

She smiled weakly and took her chair, continuing to be somewhat stunned by Brock's words, wishing that they might not have been said under these circumstances. She supposed that was her fault. But she hadn't been able to stop herself.

"This is charming, absolutely charming," Angie said when they were seated, her eyes on Brock. "We had no idea that you'd be here—and even if we had, how convenient that we came to be in the same place! Have you had dinner? Will you join us for the meal?"

"I have not had dinner, though I did have a great lunch," he said.

"You were here investigating?" Angie asked.

"Yes."

"I know some of what's going on, of course," Angie said. "There's news everywhere these days—even on our phones. Hard to miss. I understand that the last girl who disappeared near the ranch had been living here in the city."

"Yes," Brock agreed. Angie frowned slightly; she'd obviously been expecting more info.

"Do you think there's any possibility of finding any of the missing women alive?" Maura asked him.

"There's always the possibility," Brock said.

"Ah," Angie said, studying him. "A politically correct answer."

"No," Brock said. "They haven't been found dead. That means there is a possibility that they will be found alive."

"Even after the woman's bones were found in sheets?" Angie asked.

"Even after that. It's still unknown if the cases are connected. That three young women have disappeared in a relatively short period of time does suggest serial kidnapping, but whether they were connected to the murder of Maureen Rodriguez is something that we still don't know. But," he added, "as I tried to say, I think it's a dangerous time right now for any woman from the ages of seventeen to thirty-five or perhaps on upward. Frankly, I'd be much happier if all those I knew were in Alaska right now—or Australia or New Zealand, perhaps."

He glanced over at Maura and she felt bizarrely as if her heart stopped beating for a minute.

She had been so angry for so long.

And now she realized that he hadn't been trying to get rid of her, per se—he was worried about everyone.

And maybe, because of the past, *especially* about her.

"But I do say it's a good thing that you stick together," he said, offering them a smile. "So, did you enjoy your day?" he asked politely.

Maura didn't have to worry about answering—Angie had no problem excitedly telling him about all that they had seen and done.

Their waiter—the same man who had collided with Maura—came and suggested that they have the snapper; the preparation of it, a combo of lemon and oil and garlic, was simple but exceptional. The three of them ordered. Maura and Brock were both driving, but Angie was at her leisure, so she indulged in the restaurant's signature drink—the Saint. It came out blue and bubbly, and she assured the waiter she didn't care much about what was in it. It was delicious.

"Have you all finished up here for the day?" Brock asked.

"Oh, yes, Maura is amazing. She knew where to go, what to get—we don't do full-length documentaries, you know. Just little bits. There have been all kinds of surveys about the modern attention span. You'll have tons of people look at something if it only takes them briefly out of their scanning. Unless it's something they really want to see, they pass right by when things become long. Two to three minutes tend to work really well for me. I was doing terribly, then I started working with Maura. She edits, although half the time we get just about perfect in one take."

He glanced over at Maura. "Are you in business together?" he asked.

"No," Maura said.

"Are you kidding? She's in megapopular demand!" Angie answered. "Artists, authors, performers—Maura knows how to make everyone really show off in that two to three minutes," Angie said.

"And I should definitely put in," Maura said quickly, "that Angie is truly a shooting star—her books on truth being stranger than fiction, weird places and so on do amazingly well."

"I have some pretty generous sponsors for my video channel. Whoever knew that being a nerdy and somewhat gruesome kid would pay so well, huh?" Angie asked.

"We never do know where life will take us, I guess," Brock said, turning his attention to Maura once again. "But sometimes you pop before the camera?"

"When Angie wears out," Maura said.

"No, she's great," Angie said. "The video-cam thing loves her—and she's so smooth. A grand storyteller. She'd have been perfect in the old Viking days or in Ireland when history was kept orally and people listened around the fire. Of course, I keep telling her that it can't be her life. We've worked together about three years now and I'm always amazed that she never says no. Work, work, work, I tell her. I put things off when I'm in the middle of a relationship. Maura won't take the time for a relationship."

Maura glared at Angie, amazed that her friend would say such a thing—especially when she'd been flirting with Brock in front of Maura and was unabashedly interested in men. If not forever, for a night—as she had often said.

Maura wanted to kick her. Hard. Beneath the table.

And she might have, except that Angie was a little bit too far away to accomplish the task.

But Brock looked at Maura, something strange in his eyes. "Some of us do make work into everything," he said.

Angie pounced on that. "So—you're not married. Or engaged. Or steadily sleeping with anyone?"

Once again, Maura wanted to kick Angie. She damned the size of the table.

Brock laughed. "No, not married, engaged or sleeping with someone steadily. I think you only want to wake up every morning looking at someone's face on the other pillow when that person is so special that they know the good and the bad of you and everything in between. When you know… Well, anyway…my work takes up a lot of time. And it takes a special person to endure life with someone who works—the way I do." He sat back. "I'd like to follow you back to the Frampton ranch. Being perpetually, ever so slightly paranoid is a job hazard. I know you're fine, but…humor me?"

He was looking at Maura.

She still loved his face. His eyes, the contours of his cheeks, the set of his mouth. He'd been so determined and steady when they'd been young, and she had been so swept into…loving him. For good reason, she thought. He'd grown into the man she'd imagined somewhere in the back of her mind.

The man whose face she had wanted to see on the pillow next to hers when she woke up every morning.

"Maura?" Angie asked.

"Um, yes, sure," Maura said.

Brock stood, heading to find the waiter and pay the check.

"He is so hot!" Angie said. "He's got a thing for you. But if you're going to waste it—"

"Angie, he's working down here."

"You must have been the cutest kids."

"Oh, yeah, we were just frigging adorable, Angie. It was twelve years ago. Come on, let's get the car and head back. I have a lot of editing to do."

"No, you don't. Almost every take was perfect. I should have gotten that check—I'm really making money. Unless, of course, he has a budget for dinners out. I'd hate to ruin his budget."

"Angie, it's all right—look, he's motioning to us. We're all set to go."

Brock wasn't parked far away; he walked them to their car and then asked that they wait for him to come around on Avenida Menendez so that he could follow them.

As Maura waited behind the wheel, she thought about the years that had gone by.

She'd been stunned at first that things had ended so completely with Brock, but slowly, she'd felt that she was more normal—that heartbreak was a part of life. There had been other men in her life. But anytime it had gotten to *we're either going somewhere with this, or...*

She had chosen the "or."

She hadn't planned on making that choice forever, she'd just never met anyone else she wanted on the pillow next to hers every morning.

She wondered what it meant that he'd never found that person, either.

Brock drove up slightly behind her, allowing her to move into traffic. She headed out of the historic district of the city with him behind her, easily following.

"I wonder if I should have ridden with him," Angie said. She glanced over at Maura. "I mean, if you're going to waste a perfectly good man…"

Maura was surprised that she could laugh. "Angie, I rather got the impression that you liked Nils Hartford or Mark Hartford. Maybe even Fred Bentley…"

"Bentley? No, no, no!" Angie said. "I like them tall and dark—or a little shorter but with that ability to smile and charm, something in their eyes, love of life, of who they are…not sure what. But Bentley? Nah. He's like a little tram coming at you—no, no. Although…" She turned in the passenger's seat to extend her seat belt, allowing her to look straight at Maura. "Now, I'd love to find out more about Donald Glass. Power and money! We all know that those are aphrodisiacs. Even when a man is sexually just about downright creepy. Somehow, enough money and power can change the tide, you know?"

"Uh, you know he's married," Maura reminded her.

"Ah, well, I heard that didn't always matter to him so much." Angie said. She laughed. "He even has a younger wife—younger than him. But that's the problem—there will always be younger, and younger will always be replaced with younger still."

"See, a warning philosophy," Maura said.

"But I know plenty of couples where there's an

age difference—both ways!—who are happily going strong. I mean, there are older men who stay in love, and even older women who stay in love with younger men who stay in love."

"Of course," Maura murmured. She wasn't really paying attention to Angie anymore—she was only aware of the car following her.

It seemed forever before they reached the Frampton Ranch and Resort.

Angie talked the whole way.

It was all right. All Maura had to do was murmur an agreement now and then.

At long last, she pulled into the great drive and out to the guest parking. Brock was still right behind her, turning into a parking space just a few down.

He headed over to them while Maura went into the back seat of her car to grab her camera bag.

"An escort all the way," Angie said, greeting Brock as he joined them.

"All the way to the lobby," he agreed.

As they walked, Maura realized that despite the fact that he had joined them for dinner, she had never asked him about the woman in the Saint shirt who had been his companion at his table before she and Angie arrived.

But oddly, she didn't want to ask him in front of Angie. She glanced his way as they neared the entrance to the lobby, once the great entry to the antebellum house. He glanced back at her and, for a moment, it was strangely as if no time had passed at all. She'd always been able to tell him with just a look if they needed to talk alone.

He seemed to read her expression. Or, at least, she thought that he gave her a slight nod.

They walked up the porch steps and then through the great double doors to the "ranch house."

That was rather a misnomer. When the house had been built, it had been based on the Southern plantation style.

The integrity of the plan had been maintained with the registration desk to the far side and the doors leading to the coffee shop and the restaurant on opposite sides—one having once been the formal parlor and one the family parlor. The floors were hardwood, polished to a breathtaking shine without being too slippery—a great accomplishment by maintenance and the cleaning crew. There were great suites in the main house on the second floor while the attic had been heightened and rooms added there. Two wings—once bunkhouses— had become smaller one-room rentals.

Angie had, naturally, taken one of the big suites on the second floor.

Maura just hadn't needed that much space; she'd been perfectly happy up in the attic, and though she enjoyed working with Angie, she liked her own room, her own downtime and her own quiet at times.

"Safely in," Brock murmured.

"Welcome back…did you all decide to hit the entertainments somewhere nearby together?" a voice asked.

Maura was surprised to see that Fred Bentley was behind the registration desk. There was someone on duty twenty-four hours, but it wasn't usually Bentley. He lived on the property, having something of an apartment at the far end of the left wing, and she'd never really figured out what he considered his hours to be, but he was usually moving about in different areas, overseeing tours, restaurants, housekeeping and everything else.

"Our night clerk didn't show," he said, apparently aware that they were all looking at him curiously. "Not appreciated," he added.

Maura didn't think that the night clerk would be on the payroll much longer.

"I ran into Maura and Angie in St. Augustine," Brock told him, answering Fred's earlier question. "It can be a surprisingly small world."

"That is a strange coincidence," Bentley said. "Well, as I said, welcome back. Oh, Angie, Mrs. Glass was hoping that you'd tour the place a bit with her tomorrow, get an idea of what you could do…more videos on the resort as a whole. The swimming pool and patio out back are really beautiful." He nodded toward Brock and Maura. "Those two used to love it—our summer employees have always been allowed use of the pool and gym during their off-hours."

"It was a great place to work," Brock said. "Well, it's been long day. I'm going to head up."

"I think we all are," Maura said. "Good night, Fred."

An elevator had been installed; Maura usually took the stairs, but Angie headed for them and she thought that maybe Brock was on the attic floor, as well. "Night, Angie," he said, heading for the elevator.

"Good night. But long day—I'll take the elevator, too!" she said, joining him and Maura, who pressed the call button.

"I'm in the Jackson Suite," Angie said. "Have you seen the suites?" she asked Brock cheerfully in the elevator. "You're welcome to come see my room."

"I've seen all the suites, and thank you, but tonight… I'm ready for bed," he told her.

Angie laughed softly and said, "Me, too."

Angie was always flirtatious—and she'd honestly stated what she wanted to Maura. Usually her easy way with come-ons didn't bother Maura in the least.

Tonight…

It wasn't the night. It was that she was coming on to Brock.

The elevator stopped on the second floor. Angie stepped out. "Well, lovely day, lovely dinner. Thank you both!"

"Thank you," Angie told her.

The elevator door closed.

"She's subtle, huh?" Brock murmured.

To her surprise, Maura smiled. "Very."

"So, what did you want to ask me?"

He could still read her glances. And in the small elevator, they were close. She wondered if it was possible for so much time to have gone by and there still be that something…

The elevator door opened. They stepped out into the hallway. Brock stood still, waiting for her to talk.

"None of my business really, but that was rather bizarre running into you. And you were with that woman at a table, and then just came on over with us so easily... I..."

"I went in search of Lydia Merkel," he said. "She had a coworker, Katie Simmons, who insists that Lydia didn't disappear on purpose. She'd gotten two gigs playing her guitar and singing, as well as working as a waitress. One of those gigs was at Saint."

"Oh! Well, yes, of course, you were working. And the woman you met... She hired Lydia Merkel?"

"Exactly. Lydia played there the Wednesday night of the week she disappeared. I was hoping to learn something more. But I pretty much gained the same information. The manager did have a few minutes to speak with Lydia. Katie said that she was the perfect entertainment for their night clientele—charming, speaking between songs, performing at just the right volume for diners. She asked her back for a few nights each week and Lydia was delighted. But she had a bit of a vacation planned. She was heading to the Frampton Ranch and Resort, and it was a long-held dream. The manager told her that was fine. Lydia could come in the next week and they'd discuss the future. Of course, as we all know, Lydia never went back."

He paused for a minute and said very softly, "I'm sorry. I never meant to come off the way that I did earlier. But a woman was murdered. Three young women are missing."

"I'm sorry, as well. I thought... Never mind. I don't know what I thought. But you seriously think that...there will be more kidnappings? And that the same person who murdered the poor woman whose remains were found at the laundry has taken these other women?"

He nodded grimly. "From what I've learned, there is no way Lydia Merkel just walked away from her life. I haven't had time for other interviews yet, but I imagine I will find that neither Lily Sylvester nor Amy Bonham just walked away, either. And—while other businesses had sheets and used the laundry and fall in place with other leads as well, the Frampton Ranch and Resort still comes out on top of every list. Maybe I am touchy as far as this place goes, but in truth, I was sent here because of my familiarity with not just my home state but with the Frampton Ranch and Resort. You... you need to be so careful, Maura."

"I will be—I always am. But I'll be very careful. And...thank you."

He nodded. He knew that she was thanking him for the warning—and for telling her just how hard he had tried to reach her years ago.

He still hadn't moved; neither had she.

There were five rooms in the attic. The space was small. The walls were old and solid, and they were speaking softly, but it had grown late.

There was nothing more to say.

And there were years and years of words that they might say.

And, still, neither of them moved.

"I, uh... I'm so sorry for the families and friends of those poor women. And it's truly horrible about that young woman who was murdered, but do you think that they're all related?"

"We don't know. But they did have this place in common. And there's the past."

Maura shook her head. "You mean Francine?"

"Yes."

"But…that was twelve years ago."

"Yes."

"Peter committed suicide," Maura said. "I remember reading about it, and I remember him fighting with Francine. But then again, I remember everyone fighting with Francine. Still, with what Peter did…killing himself. Peter was a bit of a strange man with intense religious beliefs. He also had a temper, which usually came out as a lot of screaming and boiled down to angry muttering. It wasn't hard to believe that he had gone into a rage and dragged her out to the History Tree—and then been horrified by what he had done and regretted his action. Committed suicide."

"That's what was assumed. Never proved," Brock told her. "He was stabbed in the gut, something someone else could have done. Wipe the knife…put it in his hand. Leave him in the freezer. Easy to believe he might have done it himself. Especially when there were no other solid suspects. Just as easy to believe he was stabbed—and that the scene was staged."

He took a slight step back—almost as if he needed a little space. "Well, I'm in room three. I guess we should call it a night. I…uh… Well, you look great. And congratulations. I understand that you're doing brilliantly with your career. But I guess we all knew that you would. You're a natural storyteller—easy to see how that extends to directing people, to making them look great on video."

"Thanks. And you're exactly what you wanted to be—an FBI agent." She paused and took a deep breath. "And… Brock, I never received any of your messages. I don't know if my parents thought they were protecting me… They're good people, but… I am so sorry. I really had it in for you for years—I thought you just walked away."

He shook his head. Shrugged.

"Well, where are you?"

"I'm the last down the hallway, in five," she said.

"I'll watch you through your door," he said with a half smile. "I mean, I'm here—might as well see it through to perfect safety."

"Okay, okay, I'm going. I… I assume I'll see you," she murmured.

"You will," he assured her.

She turned and headed down the short hallway to the end. There, she dug out her key, opened her door, waved and went in.

Finally alone and in the sanctuary of her room, she leaned against the door, shaking.

How could time be erased so easily? How could the truth hurt so badly…and mean so very much at the same time? What would have happened if she had received his messages? Would they have been together all these years with, perhaps, a little one now, or two little ones…

She could have turned to him, laughed, slipped her arms around him. She knew what it would feel like, knew how he held her, cupped her nape when he kissed her, knew the feel of his lips...

Time had gone by. She hadn't received his messages.

She hadn't known he'd tried to reach her; she should have. As soon as she was home, her parents had gotten her a new phone with a new, unlisted number. They'd insisted that she change her email and delete all her social media accounts—not referencing Brock specifically, so much as the situation and the danger that could possibly still come from it.

Maybe she should have tried harder to get in touch with him. But when she'd never heard from him, she'd given up. Tried to move on.

Now they were living different lives.

She pushed away from the door. It had been a long day. She was hot and tired and suddenly living in a land of confusion. A shower was in order.

Maybe a cold shower.

She doffed her clothing, letting it lie where it fell, and headed into the bathroom. And it was while the water was pouring over her that she felt a strange prickle of unease.

It was like a perfect storm.

She was here. Brock was here...

Nils and Mark Hartford were here. Donald and Marie Glass... Fred Bentley...

And then, today her and Angie in St. Augustine, Brock in St. Augustine.

In the same restaurant. At the same time.

She turned off the water, dried quickly and stepped back out to the bedroom. She knew that Brock was working—that they all needed to be concerned. One poor woman was beyond help. Three were still missing, and maybe, just maybe...

There was nothing that she could do except, of course, be smart, as Brock had warned. And suddenly she couldn't help herself. She was thinking like Angie.

A night, just a night.

As Angie had made sure they all knew at dinner, Brock wasn't sleeping with anyone now in his life. There was no reason that the two of them shouldn't relive the past, if only for a night, for a few hours, for...

Memory's sake. If Maura just revisited the past, she might realize that it hadn't been so perfect, so very wonderful, that Brock wasn't the only man in the world who was so perfect...for her.

She knew his room number. It was wild, but...

Yes. It was too wild. She forced herself to don a long cotton nightgown and slip into bed.

And lay there, wide-awake, staring at the ceiling, remembering the contours of his body.

Chapter Five

Brock closed and locked his door, set his gun on the nightstand, and his phone and wallet on the desk by his computer. He shrugged out of his jacket and sat at the desk, opened his computer, keyed in his password and went to his notes.

He quickly filled in what he had learned that afternoon.

The most interesting had not been his conversation with the manager at Saint.

It had been earlier, when he had visited the offices of SAMM.

The event Lydia Merkel had played had been a social for members of the society. It hadn't been a mere boat, but the yacht *Majestic*, and fifty-seven members of SAMM had been invited.

Donald Glass and his wife had been among them.

The contact at SAMM had known that Maureen Rodriguez—or her sad remains at any rate—had been discovered. Every hotel, motel, inn and bed-and-breakfast that used the laundry facility had been questioned upon that finding. But no evidence had led to any one property.

Donald Glass knew about the women who had disappeared. He had never mentioned that he had met any of them.

To be fair, he might not have known that he had met Lydia Merkel. She had been working under her performance moniker—Lyrical Lee.

And, of course, the proprietors of many of the properties that used the laundry service were among those who had been on the yacht.

It was still a sea of confusion.

Except that Frampton Ranch and Resort was the location where the missing girls had been—or been headed to.

Brock filled in his notes, then stood, cast aside the remainder of his clothing and got into his shower. He needed to shake some of the day off. His puzzle pieces were still there, but he was missing something that was incredibly important.

Hard evidence.

And back to the old question—what the hell could something that had happened twelve years ago have to do with the now?

And why, in the middle of trying to work all the angles of the crimes, concentrating on detail and logic, did he keep seeing Maura's face as she stood before him in the hallway?

He knew her so well. He smiled, thinking that she hadn't really changed at all.

She'd been polite, always caring, never wanting to hurt another person.

She'd been so stunned to see him in the restaurant and stopped short and then…

He smiled again, remembering her face. So mortified.

And then trying to clean up the mess herself because she'd caused it. When they had spoken…

She'd obviously been stricken, hearing that he had tried to reach her. He'd seen the pull of her emotions—she had to be angry with her parents, but they were good people and she did love them, and now, with the passage of time, she surely knew that they had thought they were doing what was best, as well.

He showered, thinking that washing away the day would help; sleep would be good, too, of course. He felt that learning about Lydia Merkel and her aspirations to be a full-time musician were another piece of the puzzle—not because she entertained, but because of who she had done entertaining for: the hospitality industry—including the Frampton Ranch and Resort.

Brock and Maura had once been part of that. And they had intended to work part-time through college. His future had been planned out—he'd known what he was going to do with his life. And he had done it.

But Maura had always been part of his vision for his life, and maybe the most important part, the part where human emotion created beauty in good times and sustained a man through the bad.

He wasn't sure he ever made the conscious decision to go to her. He threw on a pair of jeans and left his room, years of training causing him to take his weapon and lock the door as he departed.

Which made him look rather ridiculous as he knocked softly on her door. When she opened it—he hoped and assumed she'd looked through the peephole before doing so—she stared at him wide-eyed for a minute, a slight smile teasing her lips—and a look of abject confusion covering her features.

"Um—you came to shoot me?"

She backed into the room. He entered, shaking his head, also smiling.

"Can't leave a gun behind," he told her.

"I see," she said.

For a moment, they stood awkwardly, just looking at each other, maybe searching for the right words. But words weren't necessary.

He set his holster and Glock down, fumbling blindly to find the dresser beside the door. He wasn't sure if she stepped into his arms or if he drew her in. But she was there. And time and distance did nothing except heighten each sensation, make the taste of her lips sweeter than ever. Their kiss deepened into something incredible. He felt her hand on his face, her fingers a gentle touch, a feathery brush, something unique and arousing, incredible and just a beginning.

His hands slid beneath the soft cotton of her gown and their lips broke long enough for him to rid her of it. He felt her fingers, teasing now along the waistband of his jeans. A thunderous beat of longing seemed to pound between them; it was his own heart, his pulse, instinctive human need and so much more.

Her fingers found the buttons on his jeans.

He couldn't remember ever before stepping from denim so quickly or easily.

Nor did he remember needing the feel of flesh against flesh ever quite so urgently.

They kissed again, his hands sliding down her spine, hers curving from his shoulders and down to his buttocks. They kissed and fell to the bed, and as his lips found her throat and collarbone, she whispered, "I was on my way to you."

He found her mouth again. Tenderness mixed with urgency, a longing to hold the moment, desire to press ever further.

It had been so long. And it was incredibly beautiful just to touch her again, hear her voice, bask in the scent of her...

Love her.

Familiar but new.

Their hands and lips traveled each other. He loved the feel of her skin, the curves of her body, loved touching her, feeling her arch and writhe to his touch.

Feeling what her touch did to him, hands traveling over his shoulders and his back; hot, wet kisses falling here and there upon him; that touch, ever more intimate.

As his was upon her. The taste and feel of her breasts and the sleekness of her abdomen, the length and sweet grace of her limbs.

And finally moving into her, moving together, feeling the rush of sweet intimacy and the raw eroticism of spiraling ever upward together, instinct and emotion bursting upon them with something akin to violence in their power, and yet so sweetly beautiful even then.

They lay together in silence, and once again he heard the beat, the pulse, his heart and hers, as they lay entwined, savoring the aftermath.

At last, he kissed her forehead, smoothing hair from her face.

She smiled up at him. "Twelve years," she said. And her eyes had both a soft and a teasing cast. "Worth waiting for, I'd judge."

"How kind. May I say the same?"

"Indeed, you may," she said, curling tighter against him. "You may say all kinds of things. Good things, of course. My hair is glorious—okay, so it's a sodden, tangled mass right now. My eyes are magnificent... Well, they are open. And, of course, you've waited all your life for me."

"I have," he said gravely.

She grinned at that. "You joined the FBI monastery?"

"I didn't say that. And I'm doubting you joined the Directors Guild nunnery."

She smiled, but she was serious, looking up at him. "I—I knew some good people."

"I would expect no less," he said softly.

"None as good as you," she whispered.

"Now, that can be taken many ways."

"But you know what I mean."

"I do. And don't go putting me on a pedestal. I wasn't so good—I was...a bit lost. The best way I had to battle it was to plunge head-on into all the plans I had made. Most of the plans I had made," he added softly.

"I am so sorry."

"Neither of us can be sorry," he assured her.

She kissed him again. For a while, their touching was soft and tender and slow.

But it had been so many years.

Somewhere in the wee hours, they slept. And when morning came, he awoke, and he saw her face on the pillow next to his. Saw her eyes open and saw her smile, and he pulled her to him, just grateful to wake with her by his side.

"Perfect storm," she murmured. "And I'm so sorry for the cause of it. So grateful for…you."

"We can't change what happened then. Now it's all right to be glad that we've…connected."

She nodded thoughtfully. "I keep thinking…there's something in history, something in the books, something that has to give us a clue as to what is going on."

"You need to stay out of it all," he told her firmly.

She rolled on an elbow and stared at him. "How? How would I ever really stay out of it? I was here when Francine was killed. That in itself…it's most horrible that a woman was so cruelly murdered, but, Brock…it changed everything. Changed us. And you do believe that what is happening now is related."

"There is really no solid evidence to suggest that," he said. "In fact, as far as profiling and evidence go, there is little reason to suppose that a killer might have hanged Francine—and then stuck around for over a decade to murder one young woman and kidnap three more. Really, the best thing would be for you to head to Alaska—as quickly as possible."

She smiled. "I would love to see Alaska one day. I haven't been. I'd love to see it—with you."

He was certain that, physically possible or not, his heart and soul trembled. They had just come together—tonight. And, well, thanks to Angie, they were both aware that nothing else had ever really worked for either of them in the years that had been lost between them.

He had never found *her* again. And she had never found him.

He grinned, afraid to let the extent of his emotion show.

"I don't think I have vacation coming anytime soon. But how about Iceland? What an incredible place for you to do legends and stories."

She was next to him, the length of her body close, and she touched his forehead, moving back a lock of his hair. "I don't work for myself—well, I do, but I'm a vendor hiring out my services. We need to be realistic. This is your work and more than your work. And now I'm working here, too. And I can help. I'm not stupid, Brock, you know that. I lock doors. I stay where there are other people. Whoever is doing this—be it a new thing or a crime associated with the past—they're smart enough to work in the shadows. No one is going to be hurt in the resort. You're in room three, and I'm in room five, and I'm not worried at all about the nights. Brock, I'm all grown-up. Quite a bit older than the last time, remember."

"And around the same age—"

"The missing women weren't wary or suspicious. They were just leading normal lives, trying to work and survive and simply enjoy their lives. Brock, most people are wonderful. They will lend others a helping hand. They just want the same things. Maureen Rodriguez was probably a lovely person—simply expecting others to be like that, too. From the little I know, the three missing women were probably similar—expecting human beings to act as human beings, having no idea that a very sick person was out there. I know that there's a predator. I won't be led astray, into any darkness—or off alone anywhere with anyone."

"Okay," he said quietly. "But if we're apart, I'll be calling you on the hour. Oh, screw the hour. Every five minutes, maybe."

"That will be fine. But unlikely. I think most of your interviews and investigations will take more than five minutes. And you really don't need to worry about me today—we'll be videoing out at the pool, in the restaurants—and I'm sure Angie would like to show herself speaking with Marie Glass—maybe Donald, too."

He heard a buzzing from the floor and leaped up. Luckily—he hadn't thought about it when he had left his room with just pants and his Glock—his cell phone was in the pocket of his jeans.

He dug for his phone.

"Yeah, Mike," he answered, having seen the detective's name on his caller ID.

"I'd like you to come with me to the Gainesville County morgue," Flannery said.

Brock gritted his teeth; the morgue meant a body. A body meant that his actions thus far had failed to save anyone.

"One of the missing girls?"

"I don't think so—I believe—or the ME there has suggested—that the remains are much older. But… Well, I'll fill you in. How soon can you be ready?"

"Ten minutes," Brock said.

"Better than me. Meet you downstairs in fifteen. We can grab coffee and head out."

"I'll be there."

"First man to arrive orders the coffee. Never mind— Rachel will beat us both. She'll order it."

"I'll be down."

He hung up and slipped into his jeans, looking back at the bed. Maura was up, staring at him, her face knit into a worried frown.

"I have to go… Not sure when I'll be back. Keep in touch, please. And stick with Angie and Marie Glass— and don't go walking into any old spooky woods, huh, okay?" he asked.

She smiled. "I promise," she told him. "But—"

"Old bones—we have to see what they are. And no—not one of our three missing girls. You'll be here all day?"

She smiled back at him.

"I'll be here all day," she assured him.

He hurried out of her room, heading to his own, hoping he wouldn't run into anyone while he was clad in his jeans only—but not really caring.

He would shower, dress and be ready in ten minutes. He wasn't worried about that.

He did hate that he was leaving.

And hoped it was something he was going to have to get used to doing.

MAURA WAS HAPPY—and determined. No, she wasn't an agent. Or a cop of any kind. No—she wasn't even particularly equipped to defend herself should she need to do so.

But she was smart and wary and everything else that she had told Brock.

Like it or not, she had been at the ranch when Francine was killed. And she was here now, and she was a Floridian and these horrible things were happening in her state. Today she would be filming around the estate with Angie and Marie, and she'd be speaking with all those here as much as possible—especially Fred, Marie, maybe Donald and Nils and Mark.

Her reasoning might be way off. Just because they had all been here twelve years ago and were here now didn't mean a thing. The solution to Francine's murder and answers about the girls who were dead and missing now might be elusive. It was sad but true that an alarming percentage of murders went unsolved. She'd read the statistics one time—nearly 40 percent of all homicides in the US went unsolved each year.

Except on this, while it was in his power, she knew that Brock wouldn't let go.

So, in her small way, she would do her best. And maybe that meant going through the library again—

finding out everything she could about the Frampton Ranch and Resort—and the people who were here.

Maura showered, dressed and set out to edit some of her video from the day before. At nine she decided to go down to breakfast; Angie, she knew, would wake up when she was ready and come down seeking coffee.

Maura took her computer with her, curious to see what various search engines brought up on the ranch. As with most commercial properties, the results showed every travel site on the planet first. And the history of North Central Florida didn't provide any better results. She didn't find much that was particularly helpful—nothing she didn't know already.

Frustrated, she was about to click over into her email when she noticed a site with the less-than-austere title of Extremely Weird Shit That Might Have Happened.

Once there, she read about a strange organization that had sprung up in the area in the 1930s. Various local boarding schools and colleges had provided the members—usually rich young men with a proclivity for hedonistic lifestyles. They had created a secret society known as the Sons of Supreme Being, and considered themselves above others, apparently siding with the Nazi cause during World War II, dissolving after the war, but supposedly surfacing now and then in the decades that followed.

They had been suspected of the disappearance of a young woman in the 1950s, but it had been as difficult for police to prove their complicity as it had been to prove their existence. Members were sworn to secrecy unto death, and in the one case when a young man had admitted to the existence of the society and the possible guilt of the society in the disappearance of the girl, that young man had been found floating in the Saint Johns River.

"My dear Maura, but you are involved in your work!"

Startled, Maura looked up. Marie Glass had come to her table. She was standing slightly behind her.

Maura quickly closed her computer, wondering if Marie had seen what she'd been reading.

"I'm so sorry," she said. "Have you been waiting on me long?"

"No, dear, I just saw the fascination with which you were reading!" Marie said, sliding into the seat across from her. "Today is still a go, right? You and Angie will shoot some of the finer aspects of the resort?"

"Oh, yes, we're all set," Maura said. "Or we will be, once Angie is down."

"That's lovely. I thought we'd start with the pool and patio area, maybe scan the gym so that people can see just how much the resort offers? I know that Angie's forte lies in a different sort of content—as does yours—but she does have such an appeal online. She reaches a big audience. I can't help but think it'd be good exposure."

"Of course. Whatever you'd like."

"It's lovely that Angie Parsons will use her video channel for us."

"She couldn't wait to come here. She's fascinated with the resort."

"Well, her fascination was with the History Tree—"

She paused a bit abruptly, then smiled. "I've seen some of Angie's videos and heard her podcasts and I even saw her speak at a bookstore once. The tree does seem right up her alley. And, of course, since it does seem to draw much of our clientele, I do appreciate the tree. Or trees. But... Well, those of us who knew Francine can't help but take that all with a grain of salt. Anyway...when do you think we'll be able to get started?"

"I imagine Angie will be down anytime," Maura told her. "I don't want to see you held up, though. Do you want me to call you when she's had her coffee?"

"Well, dear, this is my plan for the day, but if you could... Oh, there she is now," Marie said with pleasure.

Maura turned toward the entry to the coffee shop. Angie was walking in with Nils Hartford. She was her smiling, bubbling, charming self, talking excitedly.

She saw Maura sitting with Marie and waved, excused herself to Nils and came over. "Good morning. Mrs. Glass, you are bright and early."

Marie slowly arched a silver brow. "If one can call ten in the morning early, Angie, yes, I am bright and early." Apparently in case her words had been too sharp, she added, "But I'm certainly grateful for your work and ready whenever you are."

"Right after one coffee," Angie said. "One giant coffee!"

"Wonderful. I'll just check on the patio area and make sure someone's darling little rug rat hasn't made a mess of the place."

Marie rose and smiled again, perhaps trying to take

the sting from her comment. "At your leisure," she said and sailed out of the coffee shop.

Angie made a face and sat. "If America had royalty, she'd be among it. If she hadn't been born into it, she would have married into it. Oy!"

"She is a bit…"

"Snooty?" Angie said.

Maura shrugged.

"Kind of strange, don't you think?"

"What's that?"

"Donald doesn't seem to be as…well, snooty. Best word I can come up with."

"To be honest, I don't know either of them that well. I mean, I worked for them before, but I was among the young staff—they hardly bothered with us. Fred was our main supervisor at the time."

"Along with Francine Renault?" Angie asked.

"Yep."

"And wasn't your beau kind of like the ranking student employee here?"

"Yes."

Angie smiled and leaned toward her. "And?"

"And what?"

"What about last night?"

"What about it?"

"Oh, you are no fun. Details. Ouch! You can feel the air when you two are close together. I'll admit—well, I don't need to admit anything, I frankly told you that I was deeply into him."

"Angie, you're deeply into a lot of people."

"True. So I've turned my attention to Nils. He is a

cutie, too. Maybe even more classically handsome. Not as ruggedly cool—not like fierce, grim law enforcement. But damned cute. And, hmm, we are here a few more days. I do intend to have some fun."

"Angie—"

"Yes, I mean get laid!" Angie laughed at Maura's reaction. "Too graphic and frank for you? Oh, come on, Maura, you know me."

"And I wish you luck in your pursuits. I'm sure you'll do fine."

"Ah, you see, I shall do as I choose, which is much better than fine." Angie frowned suddenly. "Where is your law-and-order man?"

"He's here working, Angie. He went off—to work."

"Well, I suppose we should work, too. Let me grab my coffee."

"Great. I'll run my computer up and grab the camera."

Angie didn't need to get up for her coffee; Nils arrived at their table with a large paper cup.

"Two sugars, a dash of cream, American coffee with a shot of espresso," he said, delivering the cup to Angie. Her fingers lingered over his as she accepted the drink.

"Thank you so much," Angie said, smiling at him brilliantly. "When we talk about the restaurants, you will be in the video with me, won't you?"

"My absolute pleasure," Nils assured her. He smiled over at Maura. "Morning. I saw you earlier, but you were so involved, I didn't want to interrupt."

"You can interrupt anytime," Maura told him. "I was really just web browsing."

"Anything in the news—or have Brock or that Detective Flannery made any progress on the missing girls? Or, wow, I keep forgetting—Rachel?"

"Not that I know about."

"Something is going on this morning. There was a discovery just south of the Devil's Millhopper," Nils said. "I saw it on the news. Human remains were found. A Scout troop discovered them during a campout."

"I—I probably should have started with the news," Maura said. "I didn't." She didn't tell him that she knew something had been found because Brock had taken off early with Detectives Flannery and Lawrence to investigate. "More human remains. How sad."

Angie didn't seem concerned. "The Devil's Millhopper?" she asked. "That's…a cool name. What the hell is it?"

"A sinkhole," Maura told her. "Devil's Millhopper Geological State Park—it's in Gainesville. It's a really beautiful place, a limestone sinkhole about 120 feet deep. The park has steps all the way down, a boardwalk—sometimes torn up by storms—and beautiful nature plants and trees and all that."

"We need to go there," Angie said. "How did I miss a sinkhole?"

"I don't think it's haunted. But, hey, who knows? Anything can be haunted, right?" Nils asked. "It's not all that far from here—a cool place. Hey, I'd love to take you. I have a day off coming up, if you want to go."

"I'd love it if you could go with me… We'll need Maura, of course, for the video," Angie said.

"I'd love to go with both of you," Nils said.

While Angie smiled back at him, Maura found herself remembering the Nils she had known before—the young man who had thrived on being so superior. She tried to remember if she had noted any of his interactions with Francine. Francine most probably wouldn't have reacted to any of his behavior.

Could Francine have angered Nils…and could he, at eighteen, have been capable of murder?

Ridiculous. He'd been the same age as Brock; they'd all just been kids.

"Seriously, I love the park, too," Nils said, looking at Angie and then flashing a quick smile at Maura. "It's really a pretty place."

"Isn't Florida at sea level? Doesn't it flood?" Angie asked.

Nils looked at Maura again and shrugged. For a moment, he just looked like a nice—and attractive—man. One with a sense of humility—something he had once been lacking.

"Hey, we even have hill country in this area. But honestly, I don't know. It's a sinkhole. It has something to do with the earth's limestone crust or whatever. Geology was never my forte. Hey, we really do have hills in the state—not just giant Mount Trashmores, as we call them. And we have incredible caverns and all kinds of things. Most tourists just want warm water and the beaches, but it's a peninsula with all kinds of cool stuff. I'll find a ghost there for you if you want!"

Angie laughed and even Maura smiled.

"Great—we'll set it up," Angie said.

Maura quickly stood. "Meet you by the pool," she told Angie.

She clutched her computer and ran up both flights of stairs to her room. Housekeeping had already been into her room, she saw.

It seemed so pristine now. Cold.

Maybe just because Brock was no longer there.

She shook her head, impatient with herself. And for a moment, she paused. Being with him again had been so easy, so wonderful, so…perfect.

And she was, perhaps, wrong to dwell so much on one night. Things had torn them apart before.

She was suddenly afraid that events might just tear them apart again.

"When remains are down to what we have here," Dr. Rita Morgan told them, "it's almost impossible to pinpoint death to months, much less days and weeks. The bones were found just south of the Devil's Millhopper, as you know, deep in a pine forest. The area was just outside a clearing where the Scouts set up often, but not in the clearing, and it was only because a boy went out in the middle of the night to avail himself of a tree—no facilities out there, camping is rugged—that he came across them. Of course, the kid screamed and went running back for his leader or one of the dads along on the trip, and the dad called the police and… Well, here we are. The bones were scattered and we're still missing a few. I believe that all kinds of creatures have been gnawing upon them, but…there are marks—here, there—" she pointed to her findings "—that were not made by teeth. This young woman—we did find the pelvis, so we can say she was female—was stabbed to death. Oh, these are rib bones I'm showing you with the knife marks. I guess you figured that."

Brock nodded, as did Michael Flannery and Rachel Lawrence.

They were all familiar with the human skeletal system.

"But you think that she was killed sometime in the last year?" Brock asked.

"The integrity of the bone suggests a year—and a few teeth were left in the skull," Dr. Morgan explained. "I'm going to say that she was killed sometime between six and twelve months ago. She was most probably buried in a very shallow grave in an area where the constant moisture and soil composition would have caused very quick decay of the soft tissue, and insects and the wildlife would have finished off the rest. We're still missing a femur and a few small bones. And I'm afraid so many teeth are missing I doubt we'll ever be able to make an identification. We can pull DNA from the bones and compare to missing persons, but as you know, that will take some time."

"She's not one of the three recently missing women, though, right? We are talking at least six months?" Brock asked.

"At least six months," Dr. Morgan agreed. She indicated the pile of bones that were all that was left of a young life, shaking her head sadly. "I wish I could tell you more. She was somewhere between the ages of eighteen and thirty, I'd say. Again—the pelvis is intact enough to know that. We'll keep trying—we'll do everything that we can forensically."

They thanked the doctor and left the morgue.

Outside, Michael Flannery spoke up. "I think that whoever killed Francine Renault twelve years ago got a taste for murder—and liked it. I think that whoever it is has been killing all these years. Maybe slowly at first, fewer victims. I'm not a profiler, but I've taken plenty of classes with the FBI—and I'm sure that you have, too. He's speeding up—for years, he was fine killing once a year. Now—or in the last year—he's felt the need becoming greater and greater."

"It is a possibility," Brock said. "Michael, it is possible, too, that whoever killed Francine did so because she was really unlikable and made someone crack—and that these two dead women we've found have nothing to do with Francine's death. And that the kidnappings aren't associated, either."

Rachel shook her head. "You're playing devil's advocate, Brock."

He was. Brock didn't know why—maybe just too much pointed to the Frampton Ranch and Resort, and he didn't really want it to be involved. Despite what had happened, he had a lot of good memories from his time there.

They now had the bones of two women killed within the past year. Three women were still missing. He'd barely had a chance to scratch the surface of what was going on.

"Come on, Brock. I've been chasing this for twelve years," Flannery said. "I did something I came to learn the hard way simply wasn't right—and now I'm chasing the results of my mistake."

"It wasn't your mistake. You weren't high enough on the food chain back then to insist that the case not just remain open, but that it continue to be investigated with intensity," Brock said. "But say your theory is right. If the killer is at large, then the killer hanged Francine and stabbed Peter Moore to death to make it appear like a suicide and provide a fall guy. That may have been where the killer decided stabbing afforded a greater satisfaction than watching someone strangle to death."

"Where they got a taste for blood," Flannery agreed.

"And you think it's someone who was or is still involved with the Frampton ranch," Brock said.

Rachel watched them both. "Honestly, Nils Hartford was a bona fide jerk—but I don't believe he was a killer," she said, though neither of them had accused Nils. "He… I mean, he and I were never going to make it, but we did become friends. When his family lost all their money, he admitted to me that he loved restaurants and he loved the ranch and that he believed Fred might give him a chance. And as to Mark… Mark was just a kid."

"Kids have been known to be lethal," Flannery reminded her.

"Fred Bentley?" Brock asked, looking at Rachel. "He wasn't a bad guy to work for—and I think he was well liked by the guests. He's still holding on to his position."

"And he'd oversee any laundry sent out by the hotel," Rachel said.

"If not Bentley...and you're right about the Hartford boys..."

"That leaves Donald Glass himself," Brock said.

Donald Glass—who was married. Who, it had been rumored, had been indulging in an affair with Francine Renault.

A man who had acquired quite a reputation for womanizing through the years.

But would a man brilliant enough to have doubled a significant family fortune have been foolish enough to commit murder on his own property—and leave clues that could lead back to him?

"Time to head back," Brock said. "I say we casually interview all of our suspects. Let them in a little on our fear that the three missing women are dead—and that there is, indeed, a serial killer on the loose."

"Can you get someone at your headquarters tracing the movements of our key possible suspects at the ranch?" Flannery asked Brock. "FDLE is good—but your people have the nation covered."

"Of course," Brock said. He hesitated. "I haven't spoken with Glass that much, but he expressed pleasure that we chose his place as a base. Of course, it's possible that such a man thinks of himself as invincible. Above the rest. But still, I'd say there's another major question that needs to be answered."

"What's that?" Flannery asked.

"Where are the missing women? There are no bodies. Of course, it's difficult for police when adults disappear—they have the right to do so, and often they have just gone off. But the woods were searched.

Bodies weren't found. If it's Glass committing these crimes—or someone else at the Frampton property or someone not involved there at all—he might be taking the women somewhere. Keeping them—until he kills them. If we can find that place…maybe we can still save a few lives."

"And maybe we're all barking up the wrong tree," Rachel said. "And if we concentrate too hard in the wrong direction…well, there go our careers."

"We have to put that thought on hold—big thing now is to find the truth and hope that we can find the missing women. Alive," Brock said. "Agreed?"

Rachel winced. "Right, right. Agreed."

"Agreed. Oh, hell, yeah, agreed," Flannery said.

Brock didn't like what he was coming to believe more and more as a certainty.

A killer was thriving at the Frampton Ranch and Resort.

And Maura was there.

A beautiful young woman who had a history with the ranch.

A perfect possible victim.

Ripe for the taking.

Except that he wouldn't allow it. God help him, he'd never allow it.

He had found her again; he would die before he lost her this time.

Chapter Six

Maura and Angie wrapped up at the pool. Out in the back of the main house and nestled by the two wing additions, the pool was surrounded by a redbrick patio. While the many umbrellas and lounge chairs placed about the pool were modern and offered comfort and convenience, the brick that had been set artfully around managed somehow to add a historic touch that made it an exceptional area.

Maura didn't have to appear on camera; she took several videos of the pool itself and then several with Angie and Marie Glass seated together, sipping cold cocktails, with Marie talking about the installation of the pool twenty years earlier and how carefully they had thought about the comfort of their guests.

A young couple had come out while Maura was filming the water with the palms and other foliage in the background. They'd been happy to sign waivers and be part of the video—laughing as they splashed each other in the water.

When Maura's cell rang, she was so absorbed in detail that she almost ignored it—then she remembered that she and Brock had made a pact and quickly excused herself to answer the phone, leaving Angie and Marie to sit together chatting—just enjoying the loveliness of the pool and one another's company. It was evident that Marie did admire Angie very much. The two women almost looked like a pair of sisters or cousins sitting there, chatting away about the adults around them.

Maura turned her back and gave her attention to the call.

Brock sounded tense—he reminded her to stay with Angie and in a group at all times.

"I won't be leaving here," she assured him. "I'm with Angie and Marie. We're going to go film the restaurants and then the library. We'll probably record in Angie's suite. Are you heading back?"

He was, he told her.

She smiled and set her phone down and looked at Angie and Marie, who were watching her, waiting politely for her to finish her call.

"Onward—to the restaurant," she said.

"Perfect. They won't open for lunch for another twenty minutes," Marie said. "We can show all the tables and will let Nils describe some of our special culinary achievements."

"Yes. Perfect," Maura said.

"Oh, yes, that will be wonderful—we'll have the daily specials, and Nils can serve them. First, Maura can take the restaurant empty, and then some of the food—it's going to be great!" Angie said, always enthusiastic.

Angie and Marie went ahead of Maura; she collected her bag and the camera and expressed her appreciation to the young couple again.

They thanked her—they couldn't wait to send their friends to Angie's web channel when the video was posted.

Maura hurried after Marie and Angie.

The restaurant was pristine when they went in—set for lunch with shimmering water glasses and wineglasses and snowy white tablecloths. The old mantel and fireplace and the large paned windows created a charming atmosphere along with all that glitter. Angie did a voice-over while she scanned the restaurant.

Nils stood just behind Maura; that made her uneasy, but she wasn't alone in the restaurant, she was with Marie and Angie, and a dozen cooks and waitstaff lingered just in the kitchen. She knew that she was fine.

She wondered if Nils made her nervous because she did suspect him of something, or…

If she was just nervous because she didn't like anyone at her back.

When Nils touched her on the shoulder, she almost jumped. "Sorry, sorry!" he said quickly. "I don't want to mess this up—if I do something wrong, you'll tell me, right? You'll give me a chance to do it over?"

"Nils, this is digital. We can do things as many times as you want, but I believe what we're trying for is very spontaneous, natural—just an easy appreciation for what the resort offers."

"Okay, okay—thank you, Maura," he said.

She smiled. "Sure."

Marie was going to sit with Angie. Before she could,

there was a tap on the still-locked door. "Let me just tell them we'll open in a few minutes, right at twelve," Nils said.

Angie and Marie took a seat at a circular table for two right by a side window.

But Nils didn't come back alone.

Donald Glass, elegantly dressed in one of his typical suits and tall and dignified—as always—arrived with him.

"I'd thought it would be good if I popped into one of these videos Marie thinks will be such a thing. If you don't mind. Darling," he told Marie, "would you mind? I think I speak about our wine list with the most enthusiasm."

"No, darling, of course, you must sit in," Marie said.

She rose, giving up her seat. "I'd have thought you might want to do the library," she said. "You do love the library so."

He grinned. "Yes, I'm proud of my libraries. But even then...good wine is a passion."

"Okay, dear."

Maura thought that Marie seemed hurt, but she really didn't show anything at all. She smiled graciously, telling Nils, "They'll need the menus and wine lists."

"Already there, Mrs. Glass, already there," Nils said.

"Okay, then," Maura said. "In five, four..." She finished the count silently with her fingers.

"Angie Parsons here, and I'm still at the Frampton Ranch and Resort. After a day at the oh-so-beautiful pool—and before a night at the incredible historic walk—there's nothing like a truly world-class dinner.

And I'm thrilled to be here with Donald Glass, owner of this property and many more, and—perhaps naturally—a magnificent wine connoisseur, as well."

"Thank you so much, Angie. Marie and I are delighted to have you here. I do love wine, and while we have Mr. Fred Bentley, one of finest hotel managers in the state, and Nils Hartford, an extraordinary restaurateur, manning the helm, no wine is purchased or served without my approval." He went on to produce the list, explaining his choices—and certainly saying more in a few words than Maura would ever know, or even understand, about wine.

But the video was perfect on the first take.

Nils came in as they discussed the menu. He spoke about the excellence of their broad range of menu choices. He suggested that Angie enjoy one of their fresh mahi-mahi preparations, and that Donald order the beef Wellington. That way they could indulge in bites of each other's food.

He might have been nervous, but he did perfectly.

"And now we really have to open the restaurant," he said.

Donald Glass smiled and nodded. "No special stops—we run a tight ship. But, of course, that will be fine, right, Maura?"

"That will be fine. I can avoid other tables, not to worry," she said.

But people were excited when they noted that something was going on.

Many had been at the campfire when she had filmed. They wanted to be involved.

As she spoke to other diners pouring in, Maura knew that Marie Glass was watching her. She turned to her.

"Is that okay?" she asked.

"Yes, yes, lovely," Marie said. She glanced back at Donald, chatting away still with Angie at the table.

They were laughing together. Angie was her ever-charming self—flirtatious. She basically couldn't help it. Glass was enamored of her.

Marie looked back at Maura, her eyes impassive. "Indeed, please, if others wish to sign your waivers, it will certainly add on. Hopefully the food will come out quickly for my husband and Miss Parsons, and we'll be moving on. I can lock down the library, though, of course, Donald will want to be on the video then, too, as I suggested earlier."

"Thank you," Maura told her.

Marie was at her side as she chose a table close by to chat with the guests and diners who arrived—wanting to be on video.

She was startled when she accepted the last waiver and Marie spoke.

But not to her…

Not per se.

She spoke out loud, but it was as if she believed that her words were in her mind.

"And I have always vouched for him. Always," she murmured.

"Pardon?" Maura said.

"What? Oh, I'm so sorry, dear. I must be thinking out loud."

She walked away; Maura went to work.

The head chef himself, a new man, but well respected and winner of a cable cook-off show, came out to explain his fusions of herbs and spices with fresh ingredients.

The videos were coming out exceptionally well, Maura thought.

But she couldn't help remembering the way Donald Glass had sat with Angie—and the way Marie reacted to her husband.

BROCK WAS PARKING the car when he received a message from his headquarters. He hadn't contacted Egan. He had gotten in touch with their technical assistance unit and had reported on the remains that had been found, but it was Egan who called.

Egan wanted to know about the body that they had seen that morning; Brock told him their working theory, thinking that Egan might warn them against it.

He didn't.

Then he put Marty Kim, the support analyst who had been doing extra research for Brock's case, on the phone.

"I did some deep dives this morning," Marty told him. "Before coming to the Frampton Ranch and Resort, Nils Hartford was working at a restaurant in Jacksonville, Hatter and Rabbit. Trendy place. He left there for the Frampton resort, but there was a gap between jobs. I found one of the managers willing to talk. Nils resigned—but if he hadn't, he would have been fired. There was a coworker who complained about sexual harassment. Hartford was managing. The young woman was a waitress. She told the owner that she was afraid of Nils Hartford."

"Interesting. And do we know if the waitress is still alive and well?"

"Checking that out now," Marty told him. "I can't find anything much on Mark Hartford. He went to a state university, majored in history and social sciences, came out and went straight to work for Donald Glass."

"Fred Bentley?"

"He's been with Glass for nearly twenty years—at the Frampton Ranch and Resort for fifteen of them. Before that, he was working at a big spread that Glass has in Colorado."

"Anything on Donald Glass himself?"

"Nothing—and volumes. If you believe all the gossip rags, some more reliable than others, Glass has had many affairs through the years. Some of the women kept silent, some of them did not. He has been married to Marie for twenty-five years, and if I were that woman—I'd divorce his ass." Marty was silent for a minute. Then he added quickly, "Sorry, that wasn't terribly professional."

"You're fine. So…he's still playing the dog, eh?"

"One suspected affair he enjoyed was reportedly with Francine Renault. That hit a few of the outlets that speculate on celebrities without using their names—avoiding legal consequences. Over the years, he did pay off several women. One accused him of sexual assault—except, when it came to it, she withdrew all charges. There was a settlement. But most of these are confidential legal matters, and without due process and warrants, I can only go so far."

"Thanks. He's been spending most of his time and effort down at his property in Florida, right?"

"Oh, he travels. London, New York, Colorado and LA. But yes, most of the time he is in Florida. His trips to other properties tend to be weekends, just twice a year or so."

"Does Marie go with him?"

"It seems he does those trips alone. But, of course, paper trails can only lead you so far," Marty reminded him. "I'll keep searching. I'll naturally get back to you if I find anything else that might be pertinent to your investigation."

He'd parked the car. Detectives Flannery and Lawrence had waited for him.

He reported what he'd just learned to them.

Flannery shook his head. "A man with all that Glass has… Could it be possible?"

"We have nothing as yet, so let's not go getting ourselves thrown out of the resort before we have something tangible, okay?" Brock said.

"Of course not," Flannery said, and he looked at Rachel, frowning. "You should try to get some talk time in with Donald Glass," he said.

"Are you pimping me out?" she asked him.

"Never," Flannery said. "But maybe he'll respond more easily to you on many levels."

"You mean that you doubt that he takes me seriously," Rachel said.

"Rachel, Rachel, you have a chip on your shoulder," he told her.

Brock groaned slightly.

Rachel looked at Brock and he shrugged. "You never know."

"Yes, Rachel, I'm pimping you out—whatever works," Flannery told her. "He might still think of you as the teenager who spent summers at the resort, instead of the whip-smart detective you are now. You might catch him off guard."

She grinned. "Okay, just so I know what I'm doing."

"Let's get lunch," Flannery said. "Oh, and feel free to flirt with your old beau, if need be. I'm sure you've got enough wiles to go around."

Rachel paused before they reached the house, looking at Brock. "Maybe Brock could get Maura on that one," she said.

"Maura is a civilian," he said, hoping he hadn't snapped out the words.

"Yes, but…" Rachel hesitated, glancing at Flannery, who nodded. "Everyone around here always had kind of a thing for Maura. I know that I'd be with Nils— and see him look after her longingly, even though she was a summer hire. And I'd see Glass looking at her, too, and I even think that Francine Renault was hard on her because the others seemed so crazy about her. If she could just draw Nils into conversation—with us around, of course, and see where that leads."

"We do remember that we are professionals, that we play by the book," Flannery said. "But come on, Brock, what led you to law enforcement was the knowledge that you had instincts along with drive. What made me follow your career as you moved on was…well, hell, like I said. You obviously have the instincts for it. Sometimes lines get a little blurred. I am not suggesting that we really use Maura—I'm just suggesting that she could help us chat some of these people up—with one of us right there."

Brock stared at the two of them. He didn't agree, and he didn't disagree. He was surprised by Rachel's words, but he'd been mostly oblivious to others back then. He shouldn't have been surprised by Michael Flannery's passion; he'd always known that Flannery was like a dog with a bone on this case.

Brock would never use Maura. Never.

But on the other hand she was in there interacting with all the persons of interest right now.

Twelve years ago, Maura had been with him; he had been with her. No room for doubt, and certainly, they had never thought to mistrust each other.

Now she had grown into an admirable professional—and a courteous and caring human being. And she was with him once again, although he reminded himself that they had been together just a night. There had been no promises. In the end, whether there was or wasn't a future for them didn't matter in the least. She was a civilian, and that was that.

He raised a finger in an unintentional scold. "She's never alone—never, ever, alone with any of them. With Fred Bentley, either of the Hartford brothers or Donald Glass."

"Right," Flannery said.

At his side, Rachel nodded grimly. He turned and they followed him.

"I'm starving," Rachel murmured as they entered the lobby and tempting aromas subtly made their way out and around them from the restaurant.

"Yeah, it's lunchtime," Flannery said.

"I'll join you soon," Brock told them. He headed to the desk; there was a clerk there he hadn't seen before.

"Good afternoon, sir. How can I help you?" he asked.

"You're new," Brock said.

"I am, sir."

"What happened to the young lady who was working?"

"I don't know, sir, and I don't know which young lady you might mean. Mr. Bentley gives us our schedules, sir. I'm doing split shifts, morning and night now, if I can be of assistance."

"Yes, I understand Angie Parsons is doing some filming here at the resort today. Can you direct me to where they're working now?"

"They're in the library, but they don't wish to be disturbed, sir. Sir!"

Brock turned and headed for the library.

"Sir! I shouldn't have told you. They don't want to be disturbed. Please, I have just been hired on—sir!"

Brock paused to turn back. "It's all right. I'm FBI," he said.

His being FBI didn't really mean a damned thing in this scenario. But he felt he had to say something reassuring to the clerk.

He went through the lobby and down the hallway that led to the library, in back of the café.

The door was closed.

There was a sign on it that clearly said Do Not Disturb.

Well, he was disturbed himself, so he was going to do some disturbing. He knocked on the door.

To his surprise, it opened immediately.

Marie Glass stood before him, bringing a finger to her lips. He nodded. She closed the door behind him.

Angie was holding the camera. He had arrived just before they were to begin a segment. While she loved being the director and videographer, Maura was also a natural before the camera. She smiled right into the lens and said that she was in her favorite area of the resort—the library. She was with Donald Glass, who kept the library stocked, not just here, but at all of his properties, and that he bought and developed places specifically because of unique or colorful histories.

"A true taste of life, the good, the bad and the evil," Maura said, smiling.

"Exactly, for such is life, indeed, and history can be nothing less," Glass said.

Maura knew what she was doing; Glass had been interviewed so many times in his rich life that he was apparently well aware of a good ending.

"Cut! Perfect!" Angie said. "Marie, what do you think?"

Marie smiled—her usual smile. One that maintained her dignity—and gave away nothing of her real thoughts. "Excellent. If we can just do an opening at the entry…perhaps have Fred giving the guests a welcome along with Angie." She turned and looked at Brock. "Oh, would you like to appear in a video, Brock? This was once a home away from home for you."

"No, thank you—though I would enjoy watching," he said. He looked at Maura, who was looking at him then, too. He couldn't read what she was thinking, but she had that look in her eyes that indicated there were things she had to say—but to him alone.

He glanced at Marie. "Not sure my bosses now would like it," he explained.

"Well, we can finish up then," Marie said. "Donald, dear, would you like to find Fred? He has been our general manager now for over fifteen years. He should be shown greeting Angie."

"Good thinking, my dear," Glass told his wife. "Meet you out front."

Donald left. Brock smiled, excused himself and hurried after Glass.

"Sir!"

Glass stopped and turned around with surprise. "Oh, Brock, yes, what can I do for you?" He frowned. "Have you learned anything? I caught a 'breaking news flash' about thirty minutes ago. More remains have been discovered, but those over south of Gainesville. It wasn't… Did they find one of the missing girls?"

He seemed truly concerned.

"No, sir. Whoever they found has been missing much longer. They don't have an ID yet."

"You never know if that's true, or if it's what the media was told to say."

"It's true. They have no identity on the remains yet. Indulge my concern for a moment—there was a young woman working at the front desk here. She might have been just on nights, and I may be a bit overly cautious, but I noticed you have a new hire on the desk."

"We do?"

He appeared genuinely surprised. "You'd have to ask Fred about that. I must admit, I don't concern myself much with the clerks. I worry more about the restaurants and our entertainment staff. But Fred will be able to tell you."

"Thank you."

"Have you seen Fred?"

"No, I haven't, but—"

"He's probably at lunch. I'll take a look in the restaurant. Excuse me."

Brock watched him as he went on by. The man was polite to him—always had been. But he couldn't imagine that dozens of reports were all false—the man evidently had an eye for women and an appetite for affairs.

Did he leave for tours of his other properties because he just needed to work alone, or because he needed space for casual affairs?

Or maybe he didn't really leave every time he said that he was doing so, or go exactly when and where he said that he was going.

Power and money.

Maybe Glass lured young women with those assets.

Brock hurried out front.

Maura wasn't alone. She was with Marie Glass and Angie, and they were standing in broad daylight.

He was still anxious to be with her.

More anxious to hear what it was she might have to say to him alone.

IT WASN'T THAT her work was hard, but Maura was weary—ready to be done.

Most of the videos had gone very smoothly.

Angie spoke spontaneously, and they had needed no more than three takes on any one scene that day. Maura had known what she'd wanted to say—she truly loved any library, especially one as focused and unique as the library at the Frampton Ranch and Resort.

And still, she was tired.

The idea made her smile. She was happy to be tired—because she was happy that she hadn't spent much of the previous night sleeping.

She didn't want to be overly tired that night, though!

Brock appeared on the steps of the porch before Donald Glass got there. He had an easy smile as he joined them and waited for Donald to appear with Fred Bentley.

"The Devil's Millhopper! Sounds like a place I have to see!" Angie said, smiling and looking at Brock.

He shrugged. "It's geographically fascinating—and has great displays on how our earth is always changing, how the elements and organic matter often combine to make things like sinkholes and other phenomena work. Sure—I love it out there." He laughed. "I love our mermaids, too. Weeki Wachee Springs and

Weeki Wachee State Park. Absolutely beautiful—crystal clear water."

"Mermaids, eh?"

"Mermaids," he agreed politely and turned away; Glass was coming down the steps with Bentley. The stocky manager was beaming.

"I get to be in a video!" he announced.

"You do," Angie said.

"With the famous Angie Parsons," Fred said. He paused, frowning. "Or with our beautiful Maura—which is fine, too. Love our beautiful Maura."

Maura smiled. "No, sir—thank you for the compliment. You get to be with our famous and beautiful Angie."

"What do I say?" Fred asked.

Maura already knew exactly where she wanted them to stand for the afternoon light—and how she wanted them walking up the steps to the porch and the entry for the finale of the little segment.

"If you could give a welcome to the Frampton Ranch and Resort—and tell us how you've been here for fifteen years," Maura said. "Naturally, in your own words, and you can add in any bit of history you like."

She probably should have expected that something would go badly.

First, Fred froze and mumbled.

Maura smiled and coaxed him.

Then he went blank.

Then he forgot to follow Angie up the stairs at the end.

He apologized and said that he should be fired—from the video, not the property. He tried to laugh.

Maura encouraged him one more time, and they were able to get a decent video.

Brock stood nearby through the whole painful process, as did Donald and Marie. The owners—the married pair—did not stand next to each other.

Nor did they speak with each other.

And when they were done, Marie thanked Angie and Maura, bade the others good-afternoon and said that she was heading out for some shopping.

Donald thanked everyone and said that he'd be in his office.

Fred thanked Angie—then Maura.

"I was horrible. You fixed me. I guess that's what a good director does. Anyway, back to work for me. See you."

He lifted a hand and started up the steps.

"Fred," Brock said, calling him back.

"Yeah?"

"I noticed you have a new hire on the front desk."

"I do," Fred Bentley told him. "Remember when I was night clerk—well, I don't like being night clerk. Heidi didn't show up at all—and didn't call with an excuse. That's grounds for dismissal, and everyone knows it, so I left a message telling her not to come back."

"You never spoke with her?" Brock asked.

Bentley frowned. "No, I got her voice mail. She must have heard it. She never came back in."

"What's Heidi's last name and where does she live?"

"Heidi Juniper. She lives between here and Gainesville," Bentley told him. His frown deepened. "You don't think that—"

"I'll need her address and contact information," Brock said. "We'll just make sure that Heidi is irresponsible—and not among the missing."

"Of course, of course, I'll get it for you right away," Bentley told him.

When Fred was gone, Angie turned to Brock, repeating Bentley's concern. "You don't really think—"

"I don't know. I think we'll just check on her, that's all," Brock said. He looked at the two of them. "Lunch?"

"Are they still serving lunch?" Maura asked. "They do close for an hour, I think, between lunch and dinner."

"I bet they'll serve us," Angie said. She smiled broadly. "Oh, I do love it when people feel that they owe you."

She started up the steps. Maura was glad; she wanted a few minutes with Brock alone.

She believed that she'd have all night, but she needed a moment now.

But Angie stopped, looked back and sighed impatiently. "Come on! Let's not push our luck too hard, okay? I want them to keep owing me."

She was waiting.

No chance to talk.

Maura started up the stairs to the porch, grateful, at least, that Brock was with her.

Grateful, in fact, that he was simply in the world—and in her part of the world once again.

Chapter Seven

Brock saw that Michael Flannery and Rachel Lawrence were still in the restaurant when he arrived—they had taken a four top, expecting him to join them.

They hadn't expected Maura and Angie, but Michael quickly grabbed another chair and beckoned them all on over.

Angie was happy to greet them both, offering to film some of the campfire fun again with them in it. She hadn't quite figured out that law enforcement officers didn't often want their faces on video that went around to the masses—especially when they worked in plain clothes.

Both politely turned her down.

"I feel like a terrible person," Angie said. "I mean, I'd seen the news. I knew that women had been kidnapped and one had been found dead...or her remains had been found. I just didn't associate it with worrying about the central and northern areas of Florida. And the state has a huge population... Not that having a huge population makes terrible things any better, but statistically, they are bound to happen. I had no idea that the FBI and the FDLE would be staked out at the resort. But I can't tell you how glad I am. Though we did finish here today. And we went to St. Augustine yesterday. I want to see this Devil's Millhopper—the big sinkhole. But I'm not sure if Nils can go right away, and he did say that he wanted to."

Nils must have been close; as if summoned, he was suddenly behind Angie's chair. "While you're waiting to go to the Devil's Millhopper, there's some other cool stuff for Maura's cameras not far from here. Cassadaga—it's a spiritualist community, and the hotel there and a few other areas are said to be haunted. There's a tavern in Rockledge that's haunted, a theater in Tampa... It goes on and on. We can find you all manner of places."

"You need permits for some of them, advance arrangements and all," Maura reminded him.

Nils grinned. "Well, there's more here, too. Hey, I know what we have—and near here! Caves. Yes, believe it or not, bunches of caves in Florida. Up in Marianna, but closer to us—not really far at all—Dames Cave. It's in Withlacoochee State Park, but...outside the state park, on the city edge, there's an area that's not part of any park system. Not sure who owns the land but you can trek through that area and find all kinds of caves."

Maura glanced at Brock; he knew from that look that she definitely didn't want to go off exploring caves alone with Angie.

"Caves! Cool—haunted caves? Weird caves?" Angie asked.

"Oh, yes, there's an area called Satan's Playground. Not in a state park, and not official in any way. I know that Maura and Brock know it—they used to love to go off exploring when they were working here and they had a day off," Nils said. He smiled at Angie. "I'd truly love to explore the Devil's Millhopper with you, if you don't mind waiting."

Angie leaned toward him, smiling. "I don't mind at all. We'd intended to spend several days here."

Nils nodded, apparently smitten; they might have been a match made in heaven.

"Well, hey, Nils, can we still get lunch?" Maura asked.

"No," he said. "But yes, for you. Order quickly, if you don't mind. Chef saw you come in and he said that you're going to help make him more famous, so he'll wait. But he did have a few hours off before dinner, so…"

"I ate," Angie said, smiling. "Two of Chef's lunches would be great, but I just don't think I could manage to eat a second. I suggest the mahi-mahi."

Brock looked at Nils and then Maura. "Two hamburgers?" he asked.

Rachel cast Nils a weary gaze. "Mike and I had the hamburger plate. Chef makes a great hamburger."

"Yes, hamburgers sound good," Maura said.

"Done deal," Nils told them.

When he had walked away, Flannery leaned toward Angie. "I know how important your books and your videos are to you, but for the time being, please don't go off to lonely places on your own."

"I would never go on my own," Angie said.

"Good," Rachel murmured.

"I wouldn't be alone. Maura would be with me," Angie said. She turned to watch Nils. The chef had come out of the kitchen and they were speaking.

"Good-looking man," she murmured.

"So he is. Many women think so," Rachel said, studying something on her hand. "Anyway, the point is…"

"Don't go off anywhere alone as just two young women," Flannery said.

Angie smiled at him. "Detective Flannery, did you want to come along with us? Brock? It could be fun."

"Actually, if you want to see the caves, sure," Brock said.

Maura stared at him, surprised. She quickly looked away.

She knew that if he wanted to head out to the caves, there had to be a reason. And yes, he did have a reason.

Remains had been found not far from the caves.

And there were areas where more remains might be found, or where, with any piece of luck, the living just might be found, as well.

"Nice!" Angie said. "Great—it will be a date. Well, a weird threesome date," she added, giggling. "Unless, of course, Detective Flannery, Detective Lawrence, you two could make it?"

"We're working," Rachel reminded her sharply.

"Yes, of course," Angie said.

"And," Rachel added, "we don't want to be picking up your remains, you know."

Angie stared back at her, smiling sweetly. "Not to worry on my account. Brock will be with us, and when we go to the Devil's Millhopper, we'll be with Nils. Anyway! If you all will excuse me, I just popped in for a few minutes of the great company. We did such a good job with the video this morning that I'm dying to get into the pool."

She stood, motioning that Brock and Flannery didn't need to stand to see her go. "If you take work breaks other than food, join me when you're done."

Angie left them. When she was gone, Rachel stared at Maura.

"You *like* working with her?" Rachel asked.

"She's usually just optimistic about everything," Maura said. "And I guess she has that same feeling that most of us do, most of the time—it can't happen to me."

"Until it does," Brock murmured.

Maura glanced at Brock uncertainly. She had things to say that she hadn't been about to say in front of Angie.

"What is it?" Brock asked her. "We're working a joint investigation here—Rachel and Mike and I are on the same team."

"You want to go to the caves—really?" she asked.

She hoped he would just tell her the truth. "I want to go out to the area south of the Devil's Millhopper we talked about before. The remains today were found between the Millhopper and the caves. I think it might be a good thing to explore around there some more, though it could so easily be a futile effort," Brock told her. "People tend to think of Florida with the lights and fantasy of the beaches—people everywhere. There are really vast wildernesses up here. Remains could be… anywhere."

"It's so frustrating. Nothing makes sense, and maybe we're just creating a theory that we want to be true because we don't want more dead women, and we're all a little broken by Francine's murder. Maybe these cases are all different," Rachel said, looking over at Flannery. "One set of remains in a laundry, another in a forest where a Scout had to trip over them trying to pee. The one suggests a killer who wants to hide his victims. The other suggests a killer who likes attention and wanted to create a display. I mean, it's the saddest thing in the world, the way these last remains were discovered, by a kid…out on his night toilet rounds. Oh, sorry—you guys didn't get your food yet."

Brock waved a hand in the air and Maura smiled, looking down. She hadn't been offended.

But their hamburgers had arrived. And it wasn't how the remains had been discovered that was so disturbing—it was simply that now a second set had been found.

Rachel was looking at Brock with curiosity. "Do you think that the killer could be hiding kidnap victims in a cave or a cavern? Wouldn't that be too dangerous?"

"The better-known tourist caverns?" Brock asked. "Yes. The lesser-known caverns that are just kind of randomly outside the scope of the parks? Maybe. I don't know. He'd keeping them somewhere for days, maybe even weeks. Then there are also hundreds of thousands of warehouses, abandoned factories, paper mills…" He broke off. "I just know that there are three missing women somewhere, and I'd sure as hell like to find them while they're still just missing."

"And not dead," Flannery said grimly. He turned slightly, looking at Maura. "Do you remember anything, anything at all, from back then that might suggest anyone as being…guilty? Of killing Francine Renault."

Maura shook her head, then hesitated, glancing at Brock. He nodded slightly, and she said, "I was stunned—completely shocked—when we came upon Francine's body. When the news came out that Peter Moore had killed himself, I was already far away, and we were young and… I didn't know what else to believe. I—I was exploring on the internet today, though, and came across something that might—or might not—have bearing on this. It's a bit strange, so stick with me. There was a society in this area, decades ago, called the Sons of Supreme Being. They were suspected of the disappearance and possible death of a woman in the 1950s. That's why it struck me as maybe relevant. One of their members was supposed to testify in court—he died before he could. Now, I got this information from a random site—I haven't verified it in any way, but…"

Brock looked over at Flannery. "Have you ever heard anything about this group—this Sons of Supreme Being society or club or whatever?"

Flannery shook his head and then frowned. "Maybe, yes, years ago. I'm not sure I remember the name… When I joined the force, some of the old-timers were wondering during a murder investigation if the group might have raised its head again—a girl had been found in a creek off the Saint Johns River. She was in sad shape, as if she'd been used and tossed about like trash. But her murderer was caught—and eventually executed. Talk of rich kids picking up the throwaways died down. But as far as I know, nothing like that has been going on."

Maura was still looking at Brock.

"You have something else," he said.

She nodded and lowered her voice. "I don't think that Marie Glass realized that she was standing by me or that she was speaking aloud, but...she was watching her husband with Angie. And she said something to the effect that she shouldn't...cover for him. And she acted as if she hadn't said anything at all when she caught me looking at her. But in all fairness... Glass has always been decent to the people who worked for him, even if..."

"He's paid off a number of women through the years," Rachel said. "He was always decent to me. But there were rumors about him and Francine."

Glancing over at Maura, Brock said, "I want to find out if a young lady named Heidi Juniper is all right."

"Heidi Juniper?" Flannery asked him.

"She was working here. She didn't show up and Bentley left her a message that she was fired. He's supposed to be getting me contact information for her. Under the circumstances, I think it's important to know why Heidi didn't show up for work."

They had all finished eating. Flannery stood first. "Rachel and I will get to work finding out about Heidi

Juniper. I was thinking you might want to talk to your old friends Donald and Marie Glass."

"Hardly my old friends," Brock said.

"I'm going to go to the library," Maura said. She paused, looking at them all. "It really wouldn't make sense. Donald Glass may be a philandering jerk, since he is a married man. But he is so complete with his libraries, with his campfire stories…he included Francine's murder in the collection. Would he be so open if he was hiding something?"

"Being so open may be the best way of hiding things," Flannery said. He hesitated, glancing from Brock to Maura.

"Young lady, you are a civilian. You be careful."

"Not many people think that reading in a library is living on the edge," she said, smiling. "Brock will be near, and reading is what a civilian might do to help."

"We thank you," Flannery said. "Rachel…"

She rose and the two of them headed out.

"I'm going to the library with you," Brock told Maura.

"But I thought you wanted to speak with Marie and Donald," she said.

"What do you want to bet that they both show up while we're there—separately, but…"

"You're on," she said softly, standing.

MAURA KNEW WHAT she was looking for—anything that mentioned the Sons of Supreme Being. She delved into the scrapbooks that held newspaper clippings through the decades, aiming for the 1950s. Brock was across the room, seated in one of the big easy chairs, reading a book on the different Native American tribes who had inhabited the area. It was oddly comfortable to be there with him, even though she did find her mind wandering now and then, wishing that they could forget it all—and go far from here, someplace with warm ocean breezes and hours upon hours to lie together, doing nothing but breathing in salt air and each other.

Gritting her teeth, she concentrated on her research.

After going through two of the scrapbooks that went through the 1950s, she came upon what she was seeking.

The first article was on the disappearance.

In 1953, Chrissie Barnhart, a college freshman, had disappeared. She had last been seen leaving the school library. Friends had expected her to meet up with them at the college coffee shop to attend a musical event.

She had not returned to her room.

There was a picture of Chrissie; she had been light haired and bright eyed with soft bangs and feathery tresses that surrounded her face.

The next article picked up ten days later.

In a college dorm, a young man had awakened to hear his roommate tossing and turning and mumbling aloud, apparently in the grips of a nightmare. Before he had wakened his friend, he had heard him saying, "I didn't know we were going to kill her. I didn't know we were going to kill her."

The event was reported to the police and an officer brought the student who had the nightmare in for questioning; his name had been Alfred Mansfield. At first,

Mansfield had denied doing anything wrong. He'd had a nightmare, nothing more. But the police had put the fear of God into him, and in exchange for immunity, he had told them about a society called the Sons of Supreme Being. Their fathers had been supportive of Hitler's rise to power in Germany. After the war, they had made their existence a very dark secret. Only the truly elite were asked to join—elite, apparently, being the very rich.

Alfred Mansfield hadn't known who he had been with, but he was certain he could help bring those who had killed Chrissie to justice. He had simply accepted a flattering invitation, donned the garments sent to him late one night and joined with a small group, also clad in Klan-like masks, in the clearing.

All were anonymous—but he thought that their leader might have been Martin Smith, the son of a wealthy industrialist.

They hadn't killed Chrissie on the day she had been taken; Alfred didn't know where she had been kept. He only knew that he was in the clearing with the double tree when she had been dragged out, naked and screaming, and that the leader had spoken to the group about their need to make America great with the honor of those who rose above the others; to that end, they sacrificed.

Alfred had tried not to weep as he watched what was done to her and how she died. He didn't want to be supreme in any way. He wanted to forget what had happened.

He wanted the nightmares to stop.

He would serve as an informant for the police.

He was released, both he and the police believing that they had taken him in for questioning quietly and that he was safe out in the world. He'd done the right thing by letting the police know, and they would take it from there.

Alfred's body had been dragged out of the Saint Johns River twenty-four hours after his release. He had been repeatedly stabbed before being thrown into the water to drown.

The body of Chrissie Barnhart had never been found.

Maura turned a page to see an artist's rendering of Alfred's description of the murder of the young woman.

She gasped aloud.

It was a sketch created by a police artist. But it might have been the clearing by the History Tree, looking almost exactly as it did today.

Minus the masked men.

And the naked, screaming woman, appropriately hidden behind the sweeping cloaks of the men.

"Brock… Brock…"

Maura said his name, beckoning to him, only to hear him clear his throat.

She spun around. As they had both expected to happen, a Glass had come into the room.

Marie. Brock had risen and was blocking the path between Maura and Marie.

"Mrs. Glass," Maura said, rising. She felt guilty for some reason—and she must have looked guilty. Of something. She quickly smiled and made her voice anxious as she asked, "Did we miss something? I know that Angie will be more than happy to start up again with anything else you'd like."

"Oh, no, dear, I think we did a great job today. I just heard that someone was in the library—I should have known that it was you two! My bookworms. Still, in my memory, the best young people we ever hired for our summer program," Marie said.

"Thank you," Maura said.

Marie was looking at Brock. "Such a shame," she said. "And I'm so sorry. What happened… Well, the mistake cost all of us, I'm afraid."

She did appear as if the memory caused her a great deal of pain.

"Marie, it's long over, in the past—and as far as things went, my life hardly had a ripple," Brock told her. Maura looked at him; he was so much taller than Marie that she could clearly see his face. His look might as well have been words.

She'd been much more than a ripple; losing her had been everything.

She lowered her head quickly, not wanting Marie to see her smile.

"It wasn't your fault," Maura assured her.

Marie was silent for a minute, and then said, "Maybe, maybe I could have… Um, I'm sorry. I didn't mean to disturb you. Get back to it—I have to…have to…do something. Excuse me."

She fled from the library.

"See?" Maura whispered to Brock. "See? There's something bothering her. She has, I think, been telling law enforcement that Donald was with her—*when he wasn't*. Brock, you have to come read this. Donald Glass didn't go to school here, but…if there was ever a candidate for the Sons of Supreme Being, he is one! Do you think that he could be resurrecting some old ideal? And look—look at the police sketch. Well, you have to read!"

Brock sat down where she had been. She set a hand on his shoulder, waiting while he went quickly through the clippings.

He was silent as he studied the pictures.

He turned back to her, rising, and as he did so, his phone began to ring. He pulled it from his pocket, glanced at the ID and answered. "Flannery. What did you find?"

His face seemed to grow dark as he listened. Then he hung up and looked at her.

"What is it?" she asked.

"I think we have another missing woman. Which frightens me. I just don't know how many this killer of ours keeps alive at one time."

"I'LL BE FINE. I'll stay right next to Angie—and the group. We saw Mark Hartford in the hallway—he said that he had twenty people signed up for tonight. Oh, yeah—and Detectives Flannery and Lawrence are staying behind," Maura told Brock.

"I wish you'd just lock yourself in this room until I got back," he said, smoothing his fingers through her hair.

They hadn't slept; they weren't waking up. But they

were in bed, and he was still in love with her face on the pillow next to his.

They'd left the library, making plans. But while talking, they'd headed across the lobby, to the elevator, up to her room.

And then talking had stopped, and they were kissing madly, tearing at each other's clothing, falling onto the bed, kissing each other's bodies frantically—very much like a pair of teenagers again, exploring their searing infatuation.

"Reminds me of staff bunk, Wing Room 11," she had told him breathlessly, her eyes on his as they came together at last, as he thrust into her, feeling again as he had then, as if he had found the greatest high in the world, as if nothing would ever again be as it was being with her, in her, feeling her touch and looking into her eyes.

And it never had been.

"I wonder if Mr. and Mrs. Glass ever knew how much the staff appreciated the staff room?" he'd asked later when, damp, cooling and breathing normally again, they had lain together, just touching.

Their current conversation had started with, "We have to get up. You have to go and see Heidi's family, and I'm taking my camera out for the campfire and ghost walk again."

"No. You're locking yourself in this room."

"No, that would be ridiculous. I'll be with about two dozen witnesses. No one would try anything."

The argument had been done; she did have logic in

her favor. And so they dressed, reluctant to part, knowing that they must.

The evening had been decided.

Brock hesitated. "Do you think that Angie knows we're together again?"

"Probably, but…"

"But?"

"I'm not so sure she'd care. Angie is—Angie. Unabashed. Men are dogs—adorable dogs, and she loves them. But one of her great sayings is that if men are dogs, women definitely get to be bitches."

He frowned, thinking about Angie's behavior at lunch. "Does she know anything about Rachel and Nils having once been hot and heavy?"

"I don't think so. Why would she? She wasn't around way back then. Angie does like Nils. She likes you better, but…"

"I'm spoken for?"

"She might actually think that you're more interested in me—and that wouldn't sit well with her ego. She did tell me that if I wasn't interested, she'd move in."

He laughed. "Well, honesty is a beautiful thing."

"It can be—it can be awkward, too," Maura assured him. "So, are you leaving?"

"Not until I see you gathered with a large group of guests and Angie to head out to the campfire."

"Okay, then, we should go down."

He opened the door for her. They headed for the lobby. It was busy—people were gathering. One was a family, including a mom and a dad and three children:

older boys and a girl of about five. The couple from the pool was going to be at the campfire that night; they greeted Maura warmly. A few people seemed to be alone. There were two more families, one with a little girl, one with twin boys who appeared to be about fourteen.

Angie was there already, chatting with Mark.

"Hey—are you coming out tonight?" Mark asked Brock. He seemed pleased with the prospect.

"No, duty calls," Brock said. "But hopefully I'll catch up by the end."

"You have to go?" Angie asked.

"I do."

"You can't send that other cop?"

"No—because Mike Flannery and Rachel Lawrence are coming here tonight. Rachel knows all about the campfire and the walk and the stories, but Mike has never had a chance to go. And there are things I like to do myself," Brock said.

"Ah, yeah, every guy thinks he's got to do everything himself," Angie said.

"Just on this. Mike and Rachel have really been taking on the brunt of the load. My turn for an initial investigation," he said pleasantly.

He saw that Mike and Rachel had arrived.

"I'll just have a word with Mike—maybe I'll see you later."

He walked over to join Flannery and Rachel, aware that they'd be heading to the campfire any minute.

"Thanks for doing the interview tonight," Flannery

said. "Really. I know you don't want to leave. I swear, we'll watch her like a pair of parental lions."

"I think male lions just lie around," Rachel said.

"I'll be a good male lion," Flannery said. "I feel that I do need to do this. Everyone really knows the stories and the tree—or trees—but me."

Brock didn't want to admit that he really wanted to interview Heidi's parents himself; there were often little things that could be said but lost in retelling. It was always better to have several interviews with family, witnesses and more. And he did owe this one to Mike.

"I'll be back as soon as possible," Brock told them.

"And really, we don't know that you need to be worried."

"I don't know. Glass is looking like a more viable suspect all the time," Brock said.

"Glass won't be out here. No need to fear," Rachel said. "And I may be small, but trust me—I am one fierce lioness."

Brock smiled. "I know," he told her.

He turned. Mark Hartford was deep in conversation with Maura. She wasn't looking Brock's way—she was listening.

He turned and headed out to the parking lot and his car. He knew he couldn't be ridiculous—he'd never keep his job that way.

It was a twenty-minute drive east to Heidi's home in a quiet neighborhood just south of St. Augustine. He noted that the girl lived in a gated estate.

The houses were about twenty years old and reflected an upper-working-class and family atmosphere.

Heidi's parents were eagerly waiting for him. Her mother, Eileen, a slim woman with curly gray hair and dark, tearstained eyes—was frantic. Heidi's father, Carl, bald and equally slim, kept trying to calm her.

"The police didn't even want to start a report until today—they said that she hadn't really been missing. I know my daughter—when she says she's coming home, she's coming home!" Eileen said and started to cry.

"When was the last time you spoke with her?" Brock asked gently.

"She was at work. She said she was leaving soon. It was right at the end of her shift—for that day. Shifts could change, and she didn't care at all. She sometimes worked double shifts, but she said that she wasn't going to work double that day. She was tired. She was coming home. But she never arrived. I waited up. I woke Carl. We drove all up and down the highway. I mean, nothing happened to her here—our community is very secure."

"Did you call her work—talk to anyone there?"

"Some man answered the phone—he just sounded irate. He said that they weren't a babysitting service and she wasn't even with the summer program. That she probably ran off with some friends!"

"You don't know the man's name?"

"He just answered the phone, 'Front desk, how can I help you?'" Eileen said.

"Rude. If I'd known how rude… You'll investigate, right? The detective who called us—Flannery—he was the first one who seemed concerned," Carl said.

Brock nodded. "We'll take this very seriously, I swear," he assured them, taking Eileen's folded hands.

"This is important. Did she say anything else? Had she been having any trouble with anyone there? Had any of the other employees or guests been ugly to her—or come on to her inappropriately?"

"She loved her job," Carl said. "Loved it." He looked at his wife. "She said that Mr. Glass was nice, but she hardly saw him. Or Mrs. Glass. Fred Bentley was her supervisor, and he seemed to be fine. She said he was a stickler for time and the rules, but she was always on time, and she never broke the rules, so they got on fine. Oh, she loved the guy who was like a social director—and she was welcome to use the pool and the gym and go on the walks—as long as she wasn't disturbing or taking anything away from the guests. There wasn't anything she told you that she wouldn't have told me, right?" Carl asked his wife. "As far as I know, she simply loved her job."

"Yes, she did," Eileen agreed. "But…"

She frowned and broke off.

"Please, tell me what you're thinking," Brock said. "Even if it seems unimportant."

Eileen's frown deepened as she exhaled a long sigh before speaking. "Something odd… She was muttering beneath her breath. She said…"

"Yes?"

"Well, I think… I'm not even sure I heard her right. The last time I talked to her on the phone—before she left work and disappeared—she said something like… 'Supreme Being, my ass!' Yes, that was what she was muttering. I didn't pay that much attention—I thought she was talking about a guest—someone acting all superior. I didn't think much of it—people can act that way, when they think they're superior to those who are working. And my daughter would deal with it—and mutter beneath her breath. Yes. I'm almost positive, and honestly, I'm not sure what it can mean, if anything, but… Yes. She murmured, 'Supreme Being, my ass.'"

Chapter Eight

"The beautiful Gyselle," Mark Hartford said, "is sometimes seen in the woods near the History Tree. Running from it. A ghost forced to live where she saw the end of her life. Or, as a spirit, does she remember better times? Is she running to the tree—where she would meet her lover and dream of the things that might have been in life?"

He told the tales well, Maura thought. And even after they had finished at the campfire, he spoke as they moved along the trails into the woods, and finally, to the History Tree.

Mark had asked her to speak twice and she'd obliged; she'd had the camera rolling again, too—she might as well since they were out there. Angie could decide later which night's footage she liked best.

Maura noted with a bit of humor that Mike and Rachel were being true to whatever promises they had certainly given Brock—they hadn't been ten full feet away from her all night.

But at the tree, she found that she wanted it on video

from every angle. She kept picturing the police artist's rendering she had seen that day.

Creepy figures surrounding the tree, unidentifiable. The victim from the 1950s, Chrissie, caught in the arms of one of her attackers.

Were the current victims being held—as she had been held? And if so, how in the hell were they being hidden so well…until their remains were left to rot in the elements?

"You are getting carried away," Angie whispered to her.

"Just a little," Maura agreed.

"Questions—anything else?" Mark asked his group pleasantly.

Maura wondered if she should or shouldn't speak, but her mouth opened before her mind really worked through the thought.

"Yes, hey, Mark, have you ever heard of a group called the Sons of Supreme Being?" she asked.

He looked at her, a brow arching slowly.

His entire tour group had gone silent, all curious at her question.

"Yeah," he said. "I—yeah. I thought it was kind of a rumored thing." He lifted a hand. "No facts here, folks, just stuff I heard at college. They say they existed once. They were a pack of snobs—thought they were better than anyone else. They were never sanctioned by any of the state schools—in fact, I heard you got your butt kicked out if you were suspected of being one of them. They were like an early Nazi-supporter group—seemed they watched what Hitler was doing in the 1930s. But, hey, nothing like that exists now, trust me!" He grinned at his crowd. "I'm a people person. Someone would have told me. Where did you hear about them?"

"Oh, I read something," Maura said. "I was just curious if it had been real or not."

"I can't guarantee it, but I heard that they did exist. No one I know has anything on who the members might have been or anything like that," Mark told her. "Although I did hear that while the rumors of the group started in the 1930s, it really went further back—like way, way back. It was the rich elite even in the 1850s—dudes who came to Florida from the north and all, and built plantations and homes and ranches after Florida became a territory and then a state. They considered themselves to be above everyone else—everyone! If you ask me—a theory I've never spoken aloud before—I have a feeling that Gyselle's death might have been helped along by members—even way back then. Those dudes would have thought that this tree was a sacred spot. And Julie Frampton could have easily whispered into someone's ear. Gotten them to do the deed."

"There is an idea for you," Maura murmured. "Thanks, Mark."

She felt Detective Flannery take a step closer to her.

"Okay, time to head on back, folks. No stragglers—no stragglers. We don't know what's up, but we're asking people to stay close." Mark pointed to the way out.

His group obediently headed back along the trail.

As they came out of the woods, she saw that Brock

was walking from the parking lot toward them. "Brock!" Angie called. "You missed new stuff—the beautiful Gyselle might have been killed by a secret society. Wild, huh?"

Brock frowned and glanced past her at Maura, Mike and Rachel.

"I asked Mark if he'd ever heard of the group," Maura said.

"Oh," he said. "Well, you got something new and fresh on a tour. Great."

He wasn't going to talk, not there, not then—not with others around them. She thought, too, that he seemed tense.

Maybe even with her.

Because, perhaps, she shouldn't have spoken.

But the day was done at last; she wanted nothing more than to get back and close out the world—except for Brock.

She knew that he'd meet first with Mike and Rachel. And, she knew, he'd probably had a rough last few hours—talking to the parents of another girl who had disappeared.

She yawned. "Long, long day—I'm going up to bed," she said. "Angie, we can head out to those caverns tomorrow—at least, I think we can. Brock, can you take the time?"

"Yes. In fact, I think that maybe Detectives Flannery and Lawrence can join us."

Flannery might have been taken by surprise; if so, he didn't show it.

"Yes, we'll all go. Search those woods—close to where the last remains were discovered. You okay with that, Angie?"

"You bet—that will be perfect. Oh, I do hope we find something!" she said enthusiastically. "Oh, lord, that sounded terrible. Terrible. I mean, I didn't mean it that way. Except, of course, it would be cool to find a lair, a hideout—save someone!"

"That would be something exceptional," Maura said, looking at Brock. He still seemed disturbed. "So," she added, "Angie, an excursion tomorrow means you have to wake up fairly early."

"Oh, I will, I will. Meet in the coffee shop at 8:30 a.m.?" she asked.

"Sounds good," Brock said.

"Adventure day—nice break," Rachel murmured.

"You're really going to be there at eight thirty?" Maura asked skeptically.

"Ah, and I even have plans tonight! But yes, I'll be there," Angie said.

"You have plans tonight?" Brock asked her.

"Not to worry—I'm not leaving the property. I'm just meeting up with a new friend in the coffee shop— or not the actual coffee shop, you know, the little kiosk part that stays open 24/7. We'll be fine."

Maura wanted to get away from everyone.

"Okay," Maura said. "I am for bed." She didn't wait for more; she hurried past them and straight for the resort, anxious to get to her room.

And more anxious for Brock to join her.

BROCK REMAINED OUTSIDE, just at the base of the porch steps, with Mike and Rachel—waving as Angie at last left them, smiling and hurrying on up the steps to meet her date.

He quickly filled them in on what Heidi's parents had told him.

Flannery shook his head. "It just gets more mired in some kind of muck all the time. I can see a serial kidnapper and killer, but... You think that there's some idiot Nazi society that has been going on for years— oh, wait, even before there were Nazis?"

"I know, I never heard of it before today—and then that's all that I've heard about. So there is a cult—or someone wants us all to believe that there is," Brock said.

"That could mean all kinds of people are involved," Rachel mused. She frowned. "I never heard what Mark was saying tonight before—that a really narcissistic group being 'supreme' might have existed as far back as the end of the Seminole Wars. Seriously, come on, think about it—and let's all be honest about humanity. At that time, males were superior, no hint of color was acceptable and no one had to say they were or weren't supreme. Society and laws dictated who was what."

"Okay, historically, we know that Gyselle was dragged out of the house to the hanging tree and basically executed there. History never told us just who did the dragging," Brock said. "I do believe that Heidi was taken by the same people who took the other girls—and I don't believe that she's dead yet, and we can only really pray—and get our asses moving—to find them."

"Brock, we have had officers going into any abandoned shack or shed, getting warrants for anything that was suspicious in the least. The state has been moving, but yeah, we need to get going on the whole instinct thing. You think that the caverns might yield something?"

"I think that remains were found very close to them," Brock said. "Anyway, I'm going up for the night. I'll see you in the morning."

"Yep. We'll say good-night and see you in the morning," Flannery said.

By then, the group from the campfire tales and walk had apparently retired for the night. The lobby was quiet as Brock walked across it.

The young man he'd met the night before was on the desk. Brock waved and headed for the elevator, but then noted that he didn't see Angie or the date she was meeting.

He headed to the desk.

"Yes, sir, how may I help you?" the young clerk asked.

"Miss Parsons was down here, I believe. I think she was meeting up with someone in that little twenty-four-hour nook by the entrance to the coffee shop. I don't see her."

"She was down here… I guess she went up."

"Was she alone?"

"I… I said hello, and then I was going through the reservations for tomorrow and okaying a few late departures. I didn't really notice."

Angie's room was on his way to the attic floor. Brock could knock on her door and check on her.

According to what he had seen and learned from Maura, Angie might well have cut to the chase with whomever she had met.

She might be in her room—occupied.

Well, hell, too bad. He was going to have to check on her—whether he interrupted something intimate or not.

MAURA WASN'T SURE what was taking Brock so long, except that he'd be filling Mike and Rachel in on whatever had gone on with Heidi's parents.

She paced her room for a few minutes, then paused as her phone rang.

She answered quickly, thinking it was Brock.

It was not.

It was Angie.

"Maura," Angie said. "You've got to come out—find Tall, Dark and Very Studly, and come on out here."

"Come on out here? Angie, where are you?"

Angie giggled. "Almost getting lucky!" she said in a whisper. "You need to come out here—first. I've found something. Or rather, my own Studly found something for me. Come on, quickly, just grab Brock and get out here."

"Out here where?"

"The History Tree. I have something for you!"

Maura heard a strange little yelping sound—excitement or a scream? She dropped the phone and hurried out into the hallway, just in time to see Brock coming up the stairs at the end.

"Brock, come on. We have to go." Maura said.

"I tried to check on Angie because I didn't see her in the lobby, but she's not answering her door," he told her.

"She isn't there. She's out at the History Tree. Brock—she said that she's found something. She was excited, but then, it was strange—come on!"

She didn't wait for the elevator—she headed straight for the stairs. He followed behind her, calling her name.

"You shouldn't go. I should go alone. Maura!"

He didn't catch up with her until they were out on the lawn, halfway out to the campfire and the trail. He caught her by the arm. "Let me go—you get back in the resort, up in your room—locked in."

"I don't think there's anything wrong," Maura said. "She wanted me to see something. Brock, you're armed and she said to bring you. She just wanted us both to come."

He shook his head, staring at her, determined.

"It could be a trap."

"Angie sounded like Angie. What kind of a trap would that be? Come on."

"No! You don't know—go back into the resort, into your room and lock the door."

She stared back at him.

"Please, Maura, if we're to go on…"

"But, Brock, I just talked to her. This is silly. I'm with you, and… Please, let's just hurry!"

She broke away from him, but he overtook her quickly. "Maura!"

"What?"

"You can't put yourself in danger," he told her. "Let me do my job."

"Oh, all right!"

"Go!"

She did. And since she knew that he'd wait until he saw her heading back into the resort, she turned and headed for the steps.

Something was bugging her about Angie's call. There had been that strange little noise. And then Angie hadn't spoken again. The line had gone dead.

Irritated but resolved, she hurried back into the resort. She waved to the night clerk and headed to the elevator—too tired and antsy for the stairs.

She walked down the hallway, feeling for her phone to try calling Angie again. She remembered that she'd dropped her phone on her bed.

That was all right; she was almost there.

She walked down the hallway to her room and pushed open the door.

The room was dark.

She hadn't left the lights out.

And neither had she thought to lock the door.

She had no idea what hit her; something came over her head, smothering any cry for help she might have made, and then she hit the floor.

And darkness was complete.

Brock walked carefully through the woods, swiftly following the trail to the History Tree but hugging the foliage and staying in the shadows.

Long before he reached the tree, he heard the cries

for help and the sobs. He quickened his pace, but continued to move stealthily.

When he reached the clearing, he saw that Angie was tied to the tree.

She hadn't been hanged as the long-ago Gyselle had been; she was bound to the massive trunk of the conjoined trees, sobbing, crying out.

Brock didn't rush straight to her; he surveilled the clearing and the surrounding areas the best he could in the darkness. The moon was only half-full, offering little help.

There seemed to be no one near Angie. Still, he didn't trust the scene. It made no sense. Girls disappeared. Months later, remains were found.

None had been tied to the History Tree.

He pulled his phone out and called Flannery. "History Tree—backup," he said quietly.

And then, with his Glock at the ready, he made his way forward, still waiting for a surprise ambush from the bushes.

"Brock, Brock! Be careful, he knows you're coming... He knows... He could be here, here somewhere..."

"I'm watching, Angie," he said, reaching her. He found his pocketknife to start sawing on the ropes that bound her to the tree.

When she was free, she threw herself into his arms. "You saved me. Thank God I called Maura. He might have come back. He might have... He would have killed me. Oh, Brock, thank you, thank you."

Mike and Rachel came bursting into the clearing.

Angie jerked back, frightened by their arrival.

"It's all right, Angie. It's all right—who brought you here? Who the hell brought you here?" Brock demanded.

She began to shake. "I don't believe it! I still don't believe it!" she said, and she began to sob.

MAURA AWOKE TO DARKNESS. For a moment, the darkness confused her.

At first she had no recollection of what had happened. When she did start to remember—it wasn't much. Someone had attacked her when she'd walked into her room.

She touched her head. No blood, but she had one hell of a headache.

Brock had been right. The call had been a trap.

Angie had called...and there had been that little yelp, and then the phone had gone dead. But Brock hadn't allowed her to go with him.

Whoever had done this knew how Brock would react. Knew that he would never allow Maura to chance her own life.

She didn't know who it was. Mark or Nils Hartford? Bentley?

Donald Glass himself?

She tried to move and was surprised that she could. She struggled her way out of the covering that all but encased her. It was a comforter—the comforter from her bed at the resort.

She struggled to sit up and realized the earth around her was cold—as if she were in the ground. Struggling, she sat up—but she couldn't stand. The space was too tight. She could see nothing at all.

On her hands and knees, she began to crawl, blinking, trying to adjust to the absolute darkness. Where was Angie—had they taken her, too? Had Brock raced out to the clearing—to find nothing?

If so...

He'd wake the very dead to get every cop in the state out to start looking.

Maura began to shake, terrified. Then, wincing at the pain in her head, she moved forward again.

Brock would search for her, she knew.

She also needed to do her damned best to save herself.

She paused for a minute, listening. Nothing—but it was night. Late at night. She breathed in.

Earth. Earth and...

She paused, and suddenly she knew where she was—well, not where she was, but what she was in. There was earth, but she'd also touched something hard, a bit porous.

And native to a nearby area. Coquina. A sedimentary rock made of fossilized coquina shells that had been used in the building of the great fort in St. Augustine, that still graced walkways and garden paths and all manner of other projects. But to the best of her knowledge, there hadn't been any at the Frampton Ranch and Resort, unless it had been long, long ago.

Maybe she was no longer near the resort. She didn't know how long she had been unconscious.

She kept crawling, not even afraid of what night

creatures might be sharing this strange underground space with her.

And then, suddenly, she touched flesh.

"Who, Angie? Who did this to you?" Brock demanded, his arm around her still-shaking body as they headed back toward the resort. Flannery and Rachel had searched the area, a call had been put out for a forensic team and cops would soon be flooding the place.

"It was—it was Donald Glass!" she said, still sounding incredulous. "He was so polite, so gracious, and he said that he wanted me to see something very special. It was him!"

Flannery, right behind them, pushed forward. "Let's see if the old bastard is at the house. Supreme Being. I'll bet he sure as hell thinks that he's one. What the hell was he going to do? Did he think that Angie would die by herself by morning? Or was he coming back to finish the deed—right where he probably murdered Francine years ago?"

As they neared the house, Brock called to Rachel. "Stay with Angie, will you? I've got to go and bring Maura down."

"Don't leave me!" Angie begged, grabbing his arm.

He freed himself. "I have to get Maura."

Rachel had gotten strong; she managed to help Brock disengage a terrified Angie.

Brock raced up the stairs to Maura's room. He could tell the door to her room was open from halfway down the hall. He sprinted into it.

Empty.

The comforter was gone from the bed; her phone lay on the floor.

The breath seemed to be sucked out of him. His heart missed a beat, and for a split second, he froze.

It had been a trap. And he'd been such an ass, he hadn't seen it.

By the time he raced downstairs, the terrified desk clerk was hovering against the wall and Flannery had Donald Glass—in a smoking jacket—in handcuffs.

"No, no, this is wrong—I've been in my room. Ask my wife! Angie! Why the hell would you say these things, accuse me? I did nothing to you. I opened my resort to you. I… Why?"

Angie was shaking and crying, but Donald Glass was agitated, too. He appeared wild-eyed and confused.

"You meant to kill me!" Angie cried.

"I've been in my room all night!" Glass bellowed. "Ask my wife!"

Marie Glass was coming down the stairs, her appearance that of a woman who was stunned and stricken. Her hands shook on the newel post of the grand stairway as she reached the landing.

"Marie, tell them!" Glass bellowed.

Marie began to stutter. Tears stung her eyes. "I—I can't lie for you anymore, Donald."

"What?" he roared.

Brock strode up to him, face-to-face, his voice harsh, his tension more than apparent. "Where's Maura?" he demanded.

"Maura?" Glass asked, puzzled. Then he cried out, "Sleeping with you, most probably!"

"She's gone—she was taken. Where the hell is she?"

Donald Glass began to sob. He shook his white head, far less than dignified then. "I didn't take Maura. I didn't hurt Angie. I swear, I was in my room. I was in my room. I was in my room—"

"Get every cop you can. We have to search everywhere. Maura is with those other girls, I'm certain, and they're near here," Brock said.

A siren sounded, and then a cacophony of sirens filled the night.

"We'll get him to jail—you can join the hunt," Flannery told Brock.

"I'll get out to the car with him. By God, he's going to talk." Brock said. He set a hand hard on Donald Glass's shoulder, following him and Flannery out to the police cruiser.

A uniformed officer jumped out of the driver's seat and opened the back door for them.

"He's not going to talk, Brock, get on the search—" Flannery began. "Or don't," he said as Brock shoved Glass into the rear of the car and then crawled into the seat next to him.

"I don't have her. I don't have her. I don't have her!" Donald Glass screamed. "Don't kill me. Please, don't kill me!"

"I'm not going to kill you," Brock said. "What I need to know from you is anything I don't. Where around here could someone hide women?"

"But I swear, I didn't—"

"You—or anyone else. Dammit, man, I'm trying to believe you! Talk to me."

"WATER…PLEASE… Don't kill me… Water…"

The flesh Maura had encountered spoke.

"I don't have water. I'm not going to kill you," Maura assured the voice she heard. "I'm Maura Antrim. Who are you?"

"Maura!"

The person struggled in the darkness. Maura felt hands grab for her. "I know you… I know you… I'm Heidi… I'm so scared! I stopped because a car had flashing lights and… I went out to help and there was no one to help, and someone hit me, and… I'm dying, I'm sure. I'm going to die down here. I'm so scared. It's so dark. I don't know… Did they take you, too?"

"Yes, they hit me over the head in my hotel room. You don't have any idea of who did this to you?"

Maura felt the girl shake her head.

"We're not far from the resort—I know that. Not far at all."

"But where…?"

"I think we're in a bit of a sinkhole—covered up years and years ago—but someone used it as something. They shored up the sides with coquina. But they got us in here—there has to be a way out. Can you still move?"

"Barely."

"Okay, so stay still. I'm going to try to find a way to escape."

"No! Don't leave me!" Heidi begged, clinging to her.

"Then you have to come with me," Maura said firmly.

She began to crawl again, and she felt the earth grow wetter.

They were in a drainage culvert. They were probably right off the main highway, and if she could just find the grating...

Her mind was numb, and it was also racing a hundred miles an hour. Angie had called her because she had been meeting someone. That someone had lured Angie out and let her lure Brock out and, of course...

That someone had known Brock. Yes, she'd thought that right away. Known that he would make her go back, that he'd consider himself trained, ready to meet danger.

Brock would want Maura safe.

Whoever it had been walked easily and freely through the resort, knew where to go—how to avoid the eyes of the desk clerk and the cameras that kept watch on the lobby.

Thoughts began to tumble in her mind. One stuck.

It couldn't be. And, of course, it was just one someone...

It wasn't a society or an organization—but rather someone who had known about it.

She suddenly found herself thinking about the long-lost Gyselle, the beautiful woman running from her pursuers, those who would hang her from the History Tree until dead.

Maybe they had been part of a society. Maybe they hadn't. Maybe they had just...

She saw a light! A tiny, tiny piece of light...

THE NIGHT WAS ALIVE. Police were searching everywhere.

Dogs were out, each having been given a whiff of Maura's scent. But while they searched the woods and the house and the gardens and the pool, Brock headed off toward the road.

Donald Glass had spilled everything he knew. No, there had never been a basement; there were foundations, of course, but barely wide enough for one maintenance man. There had been a well, yes, filled in years and years ago.

Outbuildings had been torn down. The wings on the resort were new. There were no hidden houses; the one little nearby cemetery had no mausoleums or vaults...

Where to hide someone?

Warehouses aplenty on the highway. And the drainage tank off the road, ready to absorb excess water when hurricanes came tearing through.

A perfect place for a body to deteriorate quickly.

Donald Glass had been taken off to jail.

That didn't matter to Brock right now. Nothing mattered.

Except that he find Maura.

He reached the road and raced alongside the highway, seeking any entrance to the sunken areas along the pavement.

He ran and ran, and then ran back again, and then noted an area where foliage had been tossed over the drain.

He raced for it.

And as he neared, he heard her. Crying out, thundering against the metal grate.

"Maura!"

He cried her name, surged to the grate and fell to his knees. His pocketknife made easy work of the metal joints. He pulled her out and into his arms, and for a long moment, she clung to him.

And then he heard another cry.

"Heidi—she says there are other women down there... Dead or alive, I don't know."

He pulled Heidi from the drain. She crushed him so hard in a hug that he fell back, and several long seconds passed in which it seemed they were all laughing and crying.

Then, in the distance, he heard the baying of a dog. He shouted, "Over here!" Soon, there were many officers there, many dogs, and he was free to take Maura into his arms and hold her and not let go.

Epilogue

"You know," Maura said, probably confusing everyone gathered in the lobby of the Frampton Ranch and Resort by being the one to speak first. "Sometimes, really, I can still see her—or imagine her—the beautiful Gyselle, running in the moonlight, desperate to live. Legends are hard to shake. And I'm telling you this, and starting the explanation because, in one way, it's my story. And because Gyselle's life has meaning, and legends have meaning, and sometimes we don't see the truth because what we see is the legend."

She saw interest on the faces before her. The employees knew by now that Donald Glass had been taken away. They knew that horrible things had happened the night before, that Angie had been attacked by her host and that Maura had been attacked—but found, and found along with Heidi and the other three missing girls. Heidi was already fine and home with her parents. The other girls were still hospitalized. For Lily Sylvester it would be a long haul. She'd been in the dark, barely fed and given dirty water for months—and it had taken a toll on her internal organs. Lydia

Merkel would most probably be allowed to go home that afternoon, and for Amy Bonham the hospital stay would be about a week.

There was hope for all of them. They'd lived.

The resort guests had all gone. They had been asked to vacate by the police and Marie Glass until the tragedy had been appropriately handled.

The resort was empty except for the staff, Detectives Flannery and Lawrence, and Angie and Maura.

Donald Glass remained gone—biding his time in jail before arraignment. But if things tonight went the way Maura thought they would, that arraignment would never come.

"Thinking about Gyselle brings to mind—to many of us—what happened to Francine Renault. Well, I don't really see her in a long gown running through the forest, but she, too, met her demise on this ranch. And through the years, we suspect, so did many other young women. They didn't all come to the tree. After Francine they were stabbed. Yes, by the same killer. Brutally stabbed to death. As Peter Moore, a cook here back then, was stabbed. It doesn't sound as if it should all relate. One killer, two killers, working independently—or together? All compelled by just one driving motive—revenge."

Blank faces still greeted her. She wasn't a cop or FBI. They were curious, but confused.

"I thought they were random kidnappings," someone murmured.

"Yes and no," Maura said.

Brock stepped forward. "We discovered a longtime

association or society. It was called Sons of Supreme Being. They don't—we believe—really exist anymore. So legend gave way to what might be revamped—and imitated."

"I thought the police were going to explain what really went on here," Nils Hartford said.

"I guess Donald Glass did consider himself a supreme being," his brother added sadly.

"Well, he might have," Maura said. "But…there you go. I'm back to beautiful Gyselle, running through the forest. Her sin being that of a love affair with the owner of the plantation."

"I'm letting Maura do the explaining," Brock said. "She's always been a great storyteller."

Maura turned and looked at Marie Glass. "Donald didn't kill Francine, Marie. You did."

"What?" Marie stared at her indignantly. "I did not kill Francine. My husband killed Francine."

"No, no, he didn't. He didn't kill Francine. Nor did he kill Maureen Rodriguez or the other woman whose remains have been found. Donald loved history—and kept it alive. He loved women. You found your way to take revenge on those who led him astray—and, of course, on Donald himself. Oh, and you killed Peter Moore—that's when you discovered just how much you enjoyed wielding a knife."

"This is insane! How do you think that I—" Marie gestured to herself, demonstrating that she was indeed a tiny woman "—could manage such acts? Oh, you ungrateful little whore!"

"No need to be rude," Brock said. "Marie, you were good—but we have you on camera."

"Really? How did I tie up Angie and get back and…"

"Oh, you didn't tie up Angie."

"Of course not!"

"Angie tied herself up," Brock said calmly.

Angie sprang to her feet. "No! I wasn't even around when Francine Renault was killed. Or the cook. Why on earth do you think that I could be involved?"

"I still don't know why you were involved, Angie," Brock said. "But you were. There was no one else in the woods. We've found sound alibis for everyone else here. Oh, both Mark and Nils Hartford were sleeping with guests that night—a no-no. But you weren't one of those guests. And there's video—the security camera picked it up—of Fred Bentley talking to the night clerk right when it was all going on. What? Did you two think that we were getting close? That we'd figure it out—that Marie's hints about her husband were a little too well planted? Then, of course, there was you—wanting to see where the bones had been discovered. Strange, right? But I'm thinking that the bones washed out in the drainage system somehow—and Marie panicked and wrapped them in hotel sheets, thinking she could dispose of the remains with the laundry. And maybe you were hoping that you hadn't messed up somehow. Maybe you didn't know. But for whatever reason, you and Marie have been kidnapping and killing people. Marie getting her rage out—certain she could frame her husband if it came to it. But you…"

"That's absurd!" Angie cried.

"No, no, it's not. We checked your phone records—you talked to Marie over and over again during the last year. Long conversations. She chose the victims. You helped bring them down."

The hotel staff had all frozen, watching—as if they were caught in a strange tableau.

"You're being ridiculous!" Angie raged. She looked like a chicken, jumping up, arms waving at her sides in fury. "No, it was Marie! I didn't—"

"Oh, shut up!" Marie cried. "I'm not going down alone. I can tell you why—she wanted to hurt Donald as badly as I did. We were willing to wait and watch and eventually find a way to create proof that made the system certain that it was Donald. And those women… Whores! They deserved to suffer. We could have seen that Donald rotted for years before he got the death penalty. There's no record of it—her mother was one of my husband's whores. He paid her off very nicely to have an abortion. The woman took the money—she didn't abort." She looked at Angie. "You should have been an abortion!"

"Oh, Marie, you lie, you horrible bitch!"

Angie tore toward her in a fury.

Rachel stepped up, catching her smoothly and easily, swinging an arm across her shoulders.

She then snapped cuffs on Angie.

And Marie—dignified Marie—was taken by Mike.

She spit at him. She called him every vile name Maura had ever heard.

And then some.

They were taken out. The employees stood in silence, gaping.

Then, suddenly, everyone burst into conversation, some expressing disbelief, some arguing that they were surprised.

"No," Fred Bentley said simply, staring after them. "No."

"Yes. You saw," Brock told him.

"So, what do we do now?" Mark asked.

"Well, Donald Glass is being released. Right now he's sick and horrified at what has happened. He believed that he caused Marie to be cruel. He never knew he had an illegitimate child, and now he's left with the fact that his child…became a killer. He needs time. He's the one who has to make the decisions," Brock said. "For now, he has said to let you know that you don't need to worry while he regroups—everyone will be paid for the next month, no matter what."

There was a murmur of approval, and then slowly the group began to break up.

Fred stared at Brock and Maura for a long time. "Well," he said. "I will be here. I will keep the place in order. Until I know what Donald wants. I'll see that the staff maintain it. I'll be here for—for anything anyone may need." He started to walk away, and then he came back. "I'm… I can't believe it. Imagine, that cute little Angie. Who could figure…? But thank you, Brock. Yeah, thank you so much."

He turned and left, heading behind the restaurant toward the office.

Brock and Maura stood alone in the center of the lobby.

"Shall we go?" he asked her.

"We shall, but…"

"But where, you ask?" Brock teased. "An island. Somewhere with a beautiful beach. Somewhere we can lie on the sand and make up for lost time, hurt for those who died and be grateful for those who lived. You are packed and ready to leave?"

"I am," she told him.

They drove away.

MAURA COULD FEEL the deliciousness of the sea breeze. It swept over her flesh, filtering through the soft gauze curtains that surrounded the bungalow. She could hear the lap of the waves, so close that she could easily run out on the sand and wade into the water.

It was beautiful. Brock had found the perfect place in the Bahamas. It was a private piece of heaven, and no one came near them unless they summoned food or drink with the push of a button. The next bungalow was down the beach, and they were separated by palms and sea grapes and other oceanfront foliage.

It was divine.

Though nothing was more divine than sleeping beside Brock so easily, flesh touching, sometimes just lying together and talking about the years gone by, and sometimes, starting with just the slightest brush against each other, making love.

There would be four days of this particular heaven, but…

"You did talk to your parents, right?" Brock asked Maura.

"Of course! If news about what happened had reached them and they hadn't heard from me…they would have been a bit crazy," Maura assured him. She inched closer to him. "I almost feel bad for my mother—she's so horrified, and she admitted all the messages she'd gotten from you and kept from me… poor thing. And then, I have myself to blame, too. I was hurt that I didn't hear from you—and so I never tried to contact you myself. I thought I was part of your past—a past you wanted closed."

"Never. Never you," he said with a husky voice. Then he smiled again. "But your mom… She is coming to the wedding."

Maura laughed. "Oh, yes. She didn't even try telling me that we were rushing things when I said we were in the Bahamas but coming home to a small wedding in New York at an Irish pub called Finnegan's. And my dad… Well, he thinks that's great. Why wait after all this time? Now or never, in his mind. It's nice, by the way, for your friend to arrange a wedding and reception in one at his place—his place? Her place?"

"Kieran and Craig have been together a long time. Craig is a great coworker and friend. Kieran owns Finnegan's with her brothers—they're thrilled to provide for a small wedding and reception. And you…you don't mind living in New York? For now? Maybe one day, we'll be snowbirds, heading south for the winter. And maybe, when we're old and gray, we'll come home for good. Or, hell, maybe I'll get a transfer. But for now…"

She leaned over and kissed him. "I lost you for twelve years. I'm going to say those vows and move to New York without blinking," she promised. "Besides… Hmm. I'm going to be looking for some new clients— New York seems like a good place to find them."

He smiled, and then he rolled more tightly to her, his face close as he said, "It's amazing. I knew I loved you then. And I never stopped loving you—and I swear, I will love you all the rest of my years, as well. With or without you, I knew I loved you."

"That's beautiful," she whispered. "I love you, too. Always have, always will." She smoothed back his hair.

He caught her hand and kissed it.

Then the kissing continued.

And the ocean breeze continued to caress them both as the sun rose higher in the sky.

Later, much later, Maura knew that the ocean breeze wouldn't be there every morning. They wouldn't be sleeping in an oceanfront bungalow with the sea and sand just beyond them.

And it wouldn't matter in the least.

Because his face would be on the pillow next to hers, every morning, forever after.

* * * * *

COMING SOON!

We really hope you enjoyed reading this book.
If you're looking for more romance
be sure to head to the shops when
new books are available on

Thursday 26th February

To see which titles are coming soon, please visit
millsandboon.co.uk/nextmonth

MILLS & BOON

MILLS & BOON
Love Always

Celebrate true love with tender stories of heartfelt romance, from the rush of falling in love to the joy a new baby can bring, and a focus on the emotional heart of a relationship.

OUT NOW!

3 BOOKS IN ONE

In the
Spotlight

★★★ WRITTEN IN PASSION ★★★

B.J.
DANIELS

ROSANNA
BATTIGELLI

MAUREEN
CHILD

Available at
millsandboon.co.uk

MILLS & BOON

THE HEART OF ROMANCE

A ROMANCE FOR EVERY READER

MODERN

Prepare to be swept off your feet by sophisticated, sexy and seductive heroes, in some of the world's most glamourous and romantic locations, where power and passion collide.

HISTORICAL

Escape with historical heroes from time gone by. Whether your passion is for wicked Regency Rakes, muscled Vikings or rugged Highlanders, awaken the romance of the past.

MEDICAL

Set your pulse racing with dedicated, delectable doctors in the high-pressure world of medicine, where emotions run high and passion, comfort and love are the best medicine.

Love Always

Celebrate true love with tender stories of heartfelt romance, from the rush of falling in love to the joy a new baby can bring, and a focus on the emotional heart of a relationship.

HEROES

The excitement of a gripping thriller, with intense romance at its heart. Resourceful, true-to-life women and strong, fearless men face danger and desire - a killer combination!

From showing up to glowing up, these characters are on the path to leading their best lives and finding romance along the way – with plenty of sizzling spice!

To see which titles are coming soon, please visit

millsandboon.co.uk/nextmonth

MILLS & BOON
MODERN
Power and Passion

Prepare to be swept off your feet by sophisticated, sexy and seductive heroes, in some of the world's most glamorous and romantic locations, where power and passion collide.

MILLS & BOON
Love Always

Celebrate true love with tender stories of heartfelt romance, from the rush of falling in love to the joy a new baby can bring, and a focus on the emotional heart of a relationship.

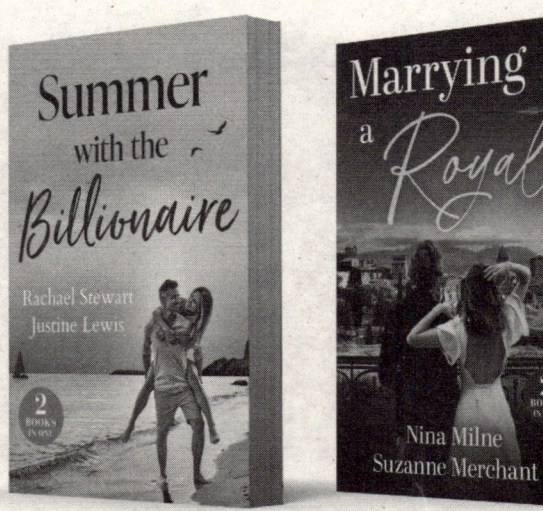

MILLS & BOON

HEROES

At Your Service

Experience all the excitement of a gripping thriller, with an intense romance at its heart that will keep you on the edge of your seat. Resourceful, true-to-life women and strong, fearless men face danger and desire – a killer combination!

Eight Heroes stories published every month, find them all at:

millsandboon.co.uk

MILLS & BOON
MEDICAL
Pulse-Racing Passion

Set your pulse racing with delectable doctors, hot-shot surgeons and fearless first resonders. Escape to a world where life and love play out against a high-pressured medical backdrop, where emotions and passion run high.

afterglow BOOKS

Afterglow Books is a trend-led, trope-filled list of books with diverse, authentic and relatable characters, a wide array of voices and representations, plus real world trials and tribulations. Featuring all the tropes you could possibly want (think small-town settings, fake relationships, grumpy vs sunshine, enemies to lovers) and all with a generous dose of spice in every story.

♪ @millsandboonuk
📷 @millsandboonuk
afterglowbooks.co.uk

#AfterglowBooks

For all the latest book news, exclusive content and giveaways scan the QR code below to sign up to the Afterglow newsletter:

SCAN ME